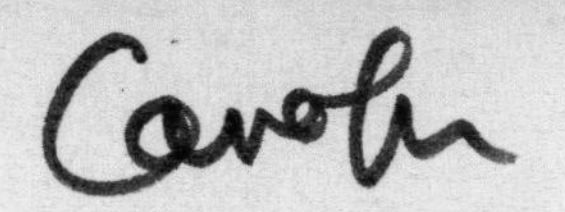

HOUND MUSIC

Rosalind Belben's fiction has been consistently admired. Her previous novels include *Choosing Spectacles*, *Is Beauty Good* and *Dreaming of Dead People*. She is a Fellow of the Royal Society of Literature.

ALSO BY ROSALIND BELBEN

Bogies
Reuben, little hero
The Limit
Dreaming of Dead People
Is Beauty Good
Choosing Spectacles

Rosalind Belben

Hound Music

VINTAGE

Published by Vintage 2002

2 4 6 8 10 9 7 5 3 1

Hound Music contains half a dozen phrases that resemble phrases to be found in a volume of hunting reminiscences, to which it is indebted, *With Hound and Terrier in the Field* by Alys F. Serrell (William Blackwood and Sons, 1904)

First published in Great Britain by
Chatto & Windus 2001

Vintage
Random House, 20 Vauxhall Bridge Road,
London SW1V 2SA

Random House Australia (Pty) Limited
20 Alfred Street, Milsons Point, Sydney
New South Wales 2061, Australia

Random House New Zealand Limited
18 Poland Road, Glenfield,
Auckland 10, New Zealand

Random House (Pty) Limited
Endulini, 5A Jubilee Road, Parktown 2193,
South Africa

The Random House Group Limited Reg. No. 954009
www.randomhouse.co.uk

A CIP catalogue record for this book
is available from the British Library

ISBN 0 099 42954 3

Papers used by Random House are natural, recyclable products made from wood grown in sustainable forests. The manufacturing processes conform to the environmental regulations of the country of origin

Printed and bound in Great Britain by
Cox & Wyman Limited, Reading, Berkshire

Contents

Acknowledgements

Whilst the responsibility for any howler or infelicity lies with me, I offer affectionate tribute to ANTHONY SHEIL – for his guidance, his unflagging energy and patience, his perspicacity. Few novels can owe so much to someone other than the author.

To Paddy Kitchen, a particular word of thanks. I am grateful to all friends who etymologized, read or were of comfort; and to my niece, Nicky Belben.

R.B.

I IN PURSUIT

1 The faithful

George dreamt this perhaps six or seven times in each year. Whilst he was still asleep he half knew it was familiar, yet half of him dreamt it with amazement, utter amazement. He'd wake never sure that it had been a dream.

For several minutes, then, he racked his brains, staring, with puzzled eyes, not seeing the room; rather, he was casting his mind over the ground, most of which he knew very well, and drawing through his memory, as though it were a covert, to discover whether it could possibly be true; that he had left an animal there, in the paddock behind the cottages, on a south-facing slope, and forgotten all about it.

He thought there was a donkey with it; or that once there had been. The faithful, waiting for him, shut into a smallish paddock, bored, even if sun poured onto that in the winter afternoons, ready to turn its head at his approach, *who* was this faithful, which of them; for however many had passed through his hands! He thought he knew. Had the animal been fed, and by whom? By a fellow long ago dead. And the donkey? He strained to remember.

What shall I find if I go to look, he wondered. George felt a damnable pain, a chill ran down his spine. He woke properly, and was himself again.

He hadn't the faintest notion what it meant. Ah, it wasn't real; but it was altogether too close. While he was shaving he didn't hum, though he didn't notice; for his mind was darting ahead.

He regarded himself shyly: a big, bluff man with strong, thrown-back shoulders, a face brown and high-coloured which went out in all weathers, fair hair and thoroughly blue eyes. He shot from the dressing-room without a second glance, because he was hungry.

He had porridge at six and joined the others for kedgeree, kipper or bacon at a little past eight.

Dorothy's eyes, at the breakfast table, were shrewd and sweet.

She never dwelt on the occasion of their nuptials when he'd gritted his teeth and said quite kindly, "Don't move, darling, not you." She hadn't attempted to move since that night, though she'd been puzzled; and they were so happy.

There were no other contradictions in George.

When he was a child, his father, for a birthday, his fourth, she thought, or fifth, had ordered a dead fox to be put from a bag up in a cedar on the lawn. Hounds had bayed Reynard, curdling George's blood (he'd been told the fox was quick) and delighting all present. Among them had been Rhymer, famed for his cry. The fox had been poked or dragged down; and broken up. It was a treat. George nowadays said such spectacles were archaic, if innocent.

The reflection caused Dorothy's nostrils to be pinched.

Her daughter Ida, with hair enough to sit upon, could have informed Dorothy that Papa didn't by any means, as some masters did, often dig out; a modern propensity he deplored. He'd use the terrier to bolt a fox from drains and sundry holes; he'd leave the man to dig should the terrier have got stuck. But to pursue with a spade, no.

Either, in Papa's view, the earth-stopper had done his job or the hunted fox went to ground and that was that. However, he listened to his farmers, and made sure of accounting for any fox that had made a nuisance of itself. For their part, hardly a man shot foxes or would poison a vixen with cubs; and they were noble in the way they put up with hedge-gaps unmended until spring. They'd been staunch throughout the decade of agricultural depression.

George nursed his country, paying out liberally for damage to fence or crop; and from the poultry fund.

He was a great preserver of the fellow and – according Reynard *fair play* – a great destroyer of him.

Papa hunted hounds himself, which was less usual than it

would have been a century before; and prevailed upon the field master to be rude to people, if that proved necessary. There were some encroaching sorts.

He loathed bagged foxes.

It was the universal consensus: he hunted hounds most beautifully; and it was a joy to hear his horn. Papa, accorded Dorothy with her whimsical smile, was much loved.

Her gaze alighted on Esmond, whose birthday arrived with the holly and tinsel, and passed on to Griselda (talking with her mouth full), hers was in high summer and was already a ritual, they took a picnic-hamper to the blue pool, year in, year out; and to the little head-in-air, Bevis, he'd been a February baby, feet first while the older children had been eating their boiled eggs at dusk, after a soggy day (had said George) with poor scent; and rose lastly to Ida again. In October they were cubbing. Ida's presents were rarely opened on her bed.

To ma'am another delicious event soon, thought Nurse upstairs.

To Nurse one could mention Roland; and from her have an answer. George talked to her about Roland. Griselda and Ida, separately and alone with her, spoke about Roland. Dorothy felt able to broach the subject, provided no other was within earshot. It hadn't occurred to Nurse that there was silence about Roland; that the family was constrained.

Esmond and Bevis remained in some ignorance, because even Nurse didn't bring Roland up.

Roland had died of raging diphtheria, when he was eleven. Although long faces weren't something one went around with, it had been awfully sad.

No other children the children knew had breakfast downstairs. Master was an engaging father, said the hunting folk. Lupus? What a "strange, excellent man", said the county; and, Dolly Lupus, they said, what a dance he led her!

Griselda had inherited Grandam's looks and pressed prayers into her pillow lest she inherit more.

When Dorothy and the elder children went to stay with Grandam, they never set eyes on the latter; no one ever did, except the butler, and he had to get up in the night to do so, which is why *two* under-butlers were employed. Dorothy's mother, in widowhood, rose when everyone else was asleep; in order to drive a pony in a trap down a tunnel no one else had ever seen to a summer-house no one was allowed to stray near; where she occupied herself, having luncheon, tea and dinner; to drive back to go to bed, before anyone else appeared.

Dorothy much preferred her own house. "M'mother would be wounded if we failed," she invariably said.

Ida took after George. Esmond was the picture of Grampy Lupus, without dispensing with a jot of a boy's spirits. To Dorothy, "Grampy" was an offence: what George had called his grandpapa she'd been obliged to support...

Bevis resembled nobody anyone could recollect.

Nurse, who had soft, furrowed skin and smelt all her life of zinc and castor oil, took after no one too, she said; though when Nurse's sister Miss Tyler came for a visit, it was plain that they were as alike as the peerless, match Cleveland Bays.

Between his porridge and the breakfast with his children, George had managed to visit Kennels; resolving to take a gun out after business.

Hounds adored him.

They'd lifted their voices, sterns gay, the clamour would have carried all across the park. He'd spoken to them, and let some of the ladies fawn on him.

The puppies that had been out at walk had well forgotten (back since April) those easy quarters and had adopted the demeanour of their seniors; but many of the trees were green, if faded; and the swallows, darting past so prettily, hadn't yet left. The big horse-chestnut was orange, although the sweet chestnuts of the covert were still lush. The iron railings at the Kennels were cool.

The gypsies had appeared in the lane. He'd waved cheerily to them. A lurcher had lunged towards him with a pointed nose and swerved into the shadow of a van.

George refused to see where the gypsies went to poach; not from him, that was all he needed to know; the hunt servants' fowls flourished, and the Indian Runners at the farm.

He was glad to provide gypsies with mistletoe, with spindle

and chestnut for clothes-pegs. The grandma came up to the laundry to darn. He was a genial host to their hobbled coloured ponies, though he execrated coloured cobs in the hunting-field and had bullied the parson cruelly until at the Rectory a black fed at the piebald's manger; as dignified as the long-tailed mare and her other stable companions; whereupon George asked for what reason had Goblin not been perfect for clerical duty!

Trios of hunt horses had overtaken him in a string.

Then the entire pack, fifty-nine couple; with Fontley, decently mounted (for the summer, when the kennel-huntsman went on foot or a pony, was by), and both whippers-in; hounds had swirled round the Master's tall figure magical there with his boots deep in dew.

Nobody cursed him in private, for he was no spy.

Each man had put a finger to the brim of a bowler; the lad Colin, so serious, had inclined a peaked cap to his whip; and Master, whose scrutiny ranged from the raggedy, the bumptious, to the dear favourites round his knees, had nodded.

That *he* had favourites he allowed none to sense: they, they chose him. Fontley, superior in this respect, no doubt held every hound equal in his regard as a matter of principle, knowing that otherwise it didn't do.

There were seven and a half couple of youthful bitches entered and three of dog, a good proportion of them the pick of their litters and puppy-show prize-winners.

After their return from walk and the peril of distemper was by, the young entry had gone out in couples until nine weeks before cubbing. Exercise would have been extended by degrees until they kept up with a horse at half pace for three miles.

Strolling back through the park deep in thought, George had met Esmond, who was to have a .410 this next birthday, out with a catapult. On Esmond's belt a moorhen had hung. The boy was too old to play, and George too sage to ask why a bird with dull, decaying plumage, from whose innards the maggots were practically visible, was a trophy.

Instead, he'd enquired, "Duck in?"

Until she was too big to be a child, Ida would join the beaters at the decoy pond: it was assumed that, wrapped in a cloth shawl to keep her from prickles, she wished for this honour.

She'd bang her stick on trees, she heard the sudden flap and splash with tingles of excitement, she liked eating duck, her nose absorbed the tweedy, tobacco smell of the guns and the tanned necks and resiny hands of beaters, with all of whom she was acquainted; but, when it came to shouting, she was a faint-heart.

It was to Ida that the parson's granddaughter, the pert Morwenna, had said no wonder that brother had died, Lupus was the name of a disease; and Ida had repeated it to Griselda, Griselda to her mother, Ma had repeated it; and George had roared.

Papa did occasionally roar, to their pride.

The summer had brought Ida, tall for her age, her quality hunter, Old Haunts; a sixteen-hand nutmeg grey, on whom she would look (had said Slade) "a positive young lady".

She couldn't yet be permitted a veil.

And Miss Griselda, thought Frank Fontley (riding at the head of hounds), as to she, Griselda will have had her side-saddle for six seasons, the trim picture there was credit due to Slade up at the Grange.

Slade had made them start bareback at two and a half.

Papa hunted the country four days a week.

When they had swallowed their last morsels, Esmond, Griselda and Ida bolted to the school-room; and Bevis vanished. Soon he slid into the gypsy camp and, bashfully sure he was welcome, squatted down by the fire.

Esmond at much the same age had been sent to Meavy. Bevis had been granted a little longer. No one knew how, except that Papa believed in licence. Papa as a boy had enjoyed a lot of it himself; and considered that from it scholarship took no harm.

Bevis, eager to make claim to it, was to remain with the gypsy children until past twelve o'clock; though he possessed scant idea of time.

2 Cub-hunting

Esmond was up before dawn on cubbing days.

He scrambled into his breeches and jacket, he buttoned his gaiters with stiff fingers and drank his milk; then with his soft collar studded at the back (when the season proper began Nurse tied a stock for him) but at the throat bobbing he ran to the stables where the lanterns were still alight. Somebody would finish him off.

Little John, hoofs oiled and his docked tail banged, was led out by Clarence. Esmond mounted with his gloves in his teeth.

"Now then, Master Esmond!" said Slade; and set off at a brisk jog.

They met at Lower Slaughter. The farmer's wife nipped out and pressed on him a slice of treacle tart in a fold of cotton. He grinned. She was an old friend. He moved it to an inside pocket, though; because Papa did think poorly of bulges. Sandwiches and cake belonged in the case and drink in the flask and both had to be strapped to the saddle.

George forgot Esmond. A small boy, even his, was not his affair.

With six couple of trusty hounds and all the new entry, George moved off to draw Farmer Holkham's plantation: he entered it from the open stubble.

The terrier ran with them.

George took care to rattle through his coverts regularly. There was natural furze; then copse, the hazel wands lissom after the hurdler had been in two years before. The floor, unadorned brown when the stools had stood tall, had been intruded upon by all manner of growth; and was inviting. Beyond that was the oak, beech and chestnut.

The few followers, neat and nondescript in rat-catchers, bunched by the double hedge: George didn't favour their spreading out or their being able, by slapping their crops against their saddle-flaps, to turn the fox. He reckoned the cub at six to seven months to be fair in cunning yet none too strong; and he had no desire to account for all.

His boy had hoped to be sent to the point, but wasted no sentiment over it. He tucked himself in until his pony's quarters stove in the twigs, and trained his eyes on a short view of greenery. Little John tossed his bit. Esmond sat impassive, grave, with his heart a-thump, his crop still as a hare.

The Master had dismounted and was walking through; his horse, led by Percy, kept pace with him on the outside. Hounds leapt on their hind feet, with smirking faces, to spot where they were and where George was: their bodies crashed through the surface of the leaf. His musical, huntsman's voice carried his cry to them.

The farmer twisted his hands together. He'd seen what he'd seen, and darn it if they now drew a blank.

Roguish spoke to an old scent, there was a whimper, they went mute, feathered a different line. A face poked through the edge, and stared about in a puzzlement; put a nose down, lifted it, thought, retreated and was hidden.

They were on: Esmond, listening, shivered. The pack was split, and both halves in glorious tongue. Under the tweed cap his hair rose.

One lady had a deep voice of quite unearthly beauty. George knew them all, but to this he smiled. He cried, "Hark to Harebell, hark to Harebell!"

The fox (not a strong 'un, thought Esmond) twisted back; and hounds chopped him quickly inside.

George had heard the holloa, with exasperation; the choler irrigated the veins in his cheeks. But Colin Payne had sent the young hounds back.

In due course, George took his horse and swung into the saddle.

The earth splattered clots up onto the face of the youth who had caterwauled with relish and who now, as hounds hit off the second line and George hopped the ditch, re-knotted the cord in his braces.

Esmond glowed from the joy of the canter to catch up.

A slight wind rose.

Bevis regarded Gypsy Jem's dinner, which Jem said was squirrel, though it was cony, and resolved to return for it.

They ran to Withy Bottom, where a fresh one got up. Led by Dauntless, Burnish, Harebell, they hunted on steadily nonetheless. The quarry was sitting up in a hedge watching them. He ran on toward the barrow: hounds rolled over their fox on clear ground.

He was perceived to have had a weak leg.

The Master went to Shute Common.

In Shute he drew a blank. The sun, weakened and pale, radiated some warmth. He clattered over the metal laid where old Max Draycott, beaming, held the gate open for him; slid the horn between two buttonholes of his coat; and rode Carrickfern, who at the trot creaked, the half-mile to the great oak.

It had seen Monmouth in its day; and under its boughs he, George, would pass from downwind into Cranmer Wood, his horse's hoofs muffled on moss and crushed bracken, a smell in his nostrils of delectable decay.

He was busy in there all the morning, while the field sat and listened outside; until at a quarter to twelve he went home.

3 George's ghosts

To the amusement of many, George could see ghosts. He took it very calmly. He'd never come across an antagonistic ghost. He saw them in other people's houses, in his own, outdoors in the countryside, in cottages, in the stables. He saw them when others couldn't. He'd say to Dippy, "Look, do look!" Oh so quietly. He'd wake her; because she'd wanted to be woken. He'd touch her arm. When Dorothy followed his gaze there was nobody there. George had remained alert, watching one of his ghosts.

He was faintly proud of this gift, which had been his from

childhood. He expected one of his offspring to inherit it. None had so far.

Once, to his delight, he'd found a ghost in the act of ploughing, arms outstretched; neither plough nor horse visible.

His head groom and Mrs Slade had a tragedy behind them. George never said a word and indeed didn't dream of broaching the subject. He regarded with a kind of sublime tenderness the damsel that flitted past Mrs Slade and about her heels.

Not all the dogs could see ghosts. Yet the hen clucked to sweep her brood of ducklings from under the swift feet of Mrs Slade's gal, though it might have been coincidence. George looked at that hen, a stately Plymouth Rock, with respect.

The spaniel Mop was so attuned to his mind that she saw, he believed, all he saw and probably more.

One of the hunt terriers hackled and shook and was thoroughly a coward. In normal circumstances she did her job, was rare to go; wasn't required to bolt ghosts, so it was no matter.

For a long time, George had expected to find Roland. A wistful yearning seemed to creep across his chest whenever he trod over the threshold of the pineapple-house: he brought Roland more vividly to mind in the pinery than anywhere else on earth.

Without being maudlin he thought what a pity it was that infectious and contagious illnesses meant you had to snuff it in your distant bedroom, scarce be bid *farewell.*

The Master felt under no obligation to show good sport during the cubbing. Those who came out gained a businesslike intimacy with the hounds and hound-work.

He met at half past five at the beginning of September, and at six when the sun rose more lazily; and at seven o'clock by the end of October. The pack sallied forth from Kennels in the dark; or travelled to Nyland the night before, if the meet was to be on the other side of the country.

He went upstairs.

George was the sort of man who became larger the moment

he set foot on the stairs during the hours of daylight. His tread seemed suddenly loud, even clumsy, and he filled – he who could go as soft as any prey, any predator – any upstairs room into which he chose to step.

"Nursie?" he said, brushing the door panel.

She thrust her mending down the cushion of her button-back chair; from where it cascaded to the floor.

Her pleasure in his arrival spread across her face and over her whole, starched form; so he grinned, and pulled his moustache.

"If it's madam, you've no need to fret."

He eased himself onto a small wicker seat.

4 The company of women

George was fond of the company of women. His mother's dying when he was no older than Bevis had affected him. It amused him to talk to them. It might have been this which had explained his pain when Bevis and Griselda painted red – fresh and sticky – the mahogany adornment over the blue dragons in the china bowl upon which various females of the household went to be enthroned.

No good for them to protest they hadn't meant to catch Inkpen, because they hadn't been able to say whom they had meant to catch, let alone why. Miss Inkspindle, Dorothy thought, had always been a favourite with them, so it was unkind; for the poor woman had suffered embarrassment. She'd had to ask for turpentine.

Inkpen would swallow hard at the very memory. She taught water-colour.

Such ingenuity had deserved a blighting punishment: George wrapped himself in his aura of Master and went off to a pow-wow with Fontley.

In the summer the children could earn a florin for every

adder killed and no one who sent his children out on adder-hunts could himself sanction whatever was to be meted out.

He'd been less of a skirter when it had come to the affair of the lodge-keeper's wife. The unsuitable creature Foyle had wedded had made the most of that spell Foyle had spent on his back to make hay with a fancy-man. Mrs Foyle's fancy had alighted on Arthur Morder.

Mrs Foyle was as good-natured as she was lascivious, and simple; for she would undo her faggots on Bevis's say-so and let Gypsy Jem scuffle the contents all across the drive, be cursed for a witch, or sent in tighter and tighter circles in their circus ring, screeching at every crack (pretend) of the whip.

5 The beloved

Not the Rector, not Nurse, or anyone who had been acquainted for many years with George, such as Slade and Frank Fontley, would have guessed that when he was hurt, or had reason to want to throw up a palisade around himself, or was wrestling with a conundrum, he gazed not at the world but at a beloved foxhound whose name he didn't know. Beloved after the passing of time, she had at first been as if clay, unbreathing, insensate.

The more often he summoned her, the more he looked, intent, in his uncomplicated fashion, at her, the more real she became. It was as though one day she breathed. It was as though one day he felt warmth emanate. Skin and coat were quick. He saw her ears twitch, when she flexed that tiny muscle nearest the brow. He saw her smiling, and her whiskers stir. He saw her muzzle wrinkle slightly, and her lips, as light as butterflies, sucked in and blown to release them. She was like a living hound poised on her toes; so beside herself with excitement that this charged stillness alone conveyed the message which blazed from her eyes.

When he conjured her forth (because that was what it was)

she faced him; mute but speaking; a tan and white lady not, he thought, of his breeding; he wanted to lift his hand and dared not; he couldn't see beyond her shoulder; there in the ether; there she faded.

She was his beloved hound.

When he tried to say her name it dried in his mouth.

6 Civilities

On Sunday after Matins, George found himself in patient conversation with Cornforth's daughter Charlotte Beynon, who had "descended upon Papa" at the Rectory for a fortnight. Of course she had to ask after everybody.

"Archie, oh, I don't know, Chatty," said George, "I believe he's pretty fit. Doesn't choose to accompany us, the rascal, though."

George had none of the melancholy which all saw hovered about his brother Archie after the latter was back from the wars and defeat at Spion Kop; or any of the insouciance of Rupert. Oliver, a keen Arabist, was, said George, *exploring in the desert.*

"Nesta, and John Chieveley, they're in the Near East. Their boy you remember, Gerald, a cherished visitor to our lot at Quarr," said George.

Laura had followed a husband to Ceylon. Martin in India was the utter drain.

"M'brother remains in India," said George, courteously. He recollected that Chatty's bosom had once palpitated for Martin. How an Indian Army officer, not terribly distinguished, could or had the scope to carry on as the dear fellow did baffled George, whose blue eyes glinted then.

"Tell me of your people?"

His wife noticed and swept to his rescue.

When would she have to relinquish church?

Arthur Morder, Mrs Foyle's fancy-man, who now sauntered into view, had first turned up, furnished with yark and crook, to give the shepherd a hand at lambing. That was from the autumn on, for they kept Dorset Horned.

George raised his hat to Chatty again, and offered Dorothy his arm.

Hers displayed a tasteful confection of silk cherries and their stems; because he wouldn't let her have her hats dressed with plumage from Brazil or the East Indies.

George was full of restless go. After luncheon, he went out; Mop, ears flattened, pious at his heels.

Mrs Slade, with whom he passed the time of day, was arrayed in her Sunday best.

Frank Fontley had taken off his suit and was back in his breeches and long buff coat; with his feeder, Maurice, well on at the pudding; the boiled flesh already in the coolers. Master and kennel-huntsman were almost agreed on which were to be drafted. Fontley ruminated sorely, since he'd tried hard with Dragoman.

Ruffler and Dragoman were of an irrepressible disposition to riot; big, coltish dog-hounds with plenty of bone. Dusky ran mute, lone; would slip out on a line only to speak to it when she'd gone half a mile; an exceeding tiresome thing that was.

The Belvoir Muffin, a dark, heavy hound, rich tan with a lot of black, exchanged in '99 for their Streaker, he was a thoroughly sound one. Ardent and Amulet would do; and Elegy.

George didn't shoot on Sundays.

They went to Evensong.

Dorothy's voice supplied George with pleasure too. She sang when sleep and doses of fresh air rendered his mind into a state of hammock-like passivity. They'd dine in solitary content; although often the house would hum with comings and goings of guests and Porlock, in his element, enjoyed himself more.

Their choice of book, for books consoled each of them at any moment of the day, was illuminating. George galloped through sporting memoirs and treatises on the chase and stories of adventure and derring-do but as a cultivated man he read also Swift and John Donne and Horace and that work of Virgil he regarded as peculiarly his own; whereas Dorothy's poets were Tennyson and Shelley and Swinburne; and, whilst there were many novels in the drawing-room, she was *devoted* to Guy de Maupassant and Mr Thomas Hardy.

The next morning, Esmond couldn't avoid the disaster of school. He was dispatched with his trunk. He wouldn't see Little John again until the exeat. Papa tipped him handsomely and he went off meek as a cat.

Bevis, left behind, lay on the tiger-skin, his arms clasped about its head, and thought.

George was not a man who went up to town to his club much. He conducted himself discreetly, never seduced housemaids.

He would have called folly the slap-and-tickle behind haystacks Rupert pursued. Rupert was not a cow-hand.

His taste wasn't so different from Rupert's after all. There was a succession; and these moved. The current paramour to enflame him was quite volcanic.

Ida had witnessed, with Roland, when they were little, the covering of a mare and George had been outraged. These were events gentlewomen simply never saw, even as infants; and he'd castigated himself as a vile papa.

He'd bought ten new horses for this season, having replaced the seven of the hunt horses sent to Tattersalls, and added three more in the Grange stables.

7 The camera

'Tis like Mrs Lupus d'pick brimbleberries for jelly and all they others for fool, reckoned Mrs Slade.

Dorothy, as a child, had meant to be a colonial wife, like Nesta or Laura (though less humble), and rise above hardships. She'd despised the bucolic. The political hadn't appealed. The services might have done; so long as he'd become C.-in-C. India.

She was remarkable in that she had, at the age of fifteen, when dry plates became obtainable commercially, purchased a photographic apparatus.

Her subjects were even more unusual.

Interested in herself, she'd transmuted her feelings into scenes of beauty, her turmoil into serenity.

She'd acquired a habit of capturing the spirit of a woodland dell; or of a great stand of oak-trees, a clump of elms; or of sunset.

On her marriage, the pioneer in Dorothy had been forgotten. Then Roland and rolls of film had arrived together. An invigorated camera shutter was turned on toys. She'd make Jumbo, Golly, pig-tailed Wang and blue-eyed china Katie, liberty horses and clowns, Jasmine Bear and Dhobi-wallah with his bucket, Mr Crosby (monkey), Peter Bobby, stuffed Owl and Weasel sit in a row on one of the steps of the Grange, to be taken.

This drew admiration.

People would, though, quibble over her bluebell dells. They didn't say as much, yet she was conscious that what she, Dorothy, saw when she looked at the photograph was not totally revealed to eyes that hadn't seen the dell on the day she had.

They provoked her.

Of course, the one whose praise put her in a glow was George.

8 Science

Truly he was lost to the world when he was hunting hounds, he thought of nothing else. The comic pageant which presented itself at all other times in that head of his was wiped away. He often recollected his bemusement at the discovery, when a boy, of our ambivalent sight of reality; of a dual method of progression which let us dance through images and follow lines of private thought whilst chatting, or shooting, or paying attention to the conversation of others, and reading too.

Palpably a man of action, he knew himself for an inveterate dreamer.

Hunting took all of him, from his first sweet note on the horn until he called it a day and was jog-jog-jogging home with hounds; on his weary second horse.

He'd remember then, slowly, the face of an under-groom from Coker Hall, riven by tear-drops, at the job of leading a broken-down favourite towards Kennels, his own uttering of the word of acknowledgement. On the frozen decoy, Dippy, in another winter; her skating with a chair for the sake of Bevis and Griselda. Or closer again at hand, the terrier man, digging, he'd heard, under the stars for Rags, who'd not come out. They'd found her.

It was his life, to be soaked to the skin, so soaked that rain worked inside his top-boots and his body clacked and slithered in the saddle. To be so cold in the wind his teeth ought to have chattered; toes to have been dead. To ache, strong though he was. To feel such *joy*, confident in his science.

He provided followers with pleasures to the extent that they worshipped him. To that notion (impossible to be oblivious of it) he accorded a little smile.

And Fontley, happy that the hours of road work back in the summer had hardened pads and forged a hound fit and stout enough to go all day; Fontley, alert to every transgression, who never, ever, chastised unless a hound knew and understood the why and wherefore; who had a kind tongue to praise them; who called them to the trough by name (it was a picture, how they waited) and by name sent them back; oh yes, Fontley took from it immense pleasure. Frank Fontley was a bachelor man; married to his vocation.

Only thrice, during the cub-hunting, had the young hounds attempted to go away after a hare, and as many times after deer. A humble, cheerful Dragoman was still at the Kennels; hadn't been banished.

Though it might rhyme with war, Quarr, George didn't want to kill too many foxes. Cubbing brought a delicate judgement to bear on the equation, which an intimacy with the country made as much instinct as calculation.

Instinct also meant listening to what folk told him.

Many of the vixens he knew by sight; and one or two dog-foxes were famously alive. If he was familiar with them it stood to reason that their offspring would offer some glorious runs later in the season.

He had to reduce numbers, pacify the farmers and cull the weak, without making for scarcity; thus instruct both the young fox and the young hound.

George, at this particular minute, viewed Josh Coachman and the bays – en route for the stables. Dorothy had driven out to pay a morning visit. The people, who had taken recently the place known as Orchard House, had been said (by Runner Ramsey) to be "nice".

They doted on animals, and boasted specimens of a rare breed of . . . but of what George couldn't recall.

His land agent, Major Ramsey, had drawn up the lease. No member of the family, or none with a yen to occupy Orchard House, had been at a loose end. The hitch to letting was that inhabitants commanded a glimpse into the park!

Soon Dorothy would withdraw from these duties.

So George said, "And were they pleasant? Do they hunt?"

Dorothy laughed.

"Well, darling?" he said, surprised. "Don't they?"

"Were you allowed in to observe the remarkable specimens?" asked Griselda.

"Were they in horrid cages?"

Ma had spotted no cages.

"You might have gone round to the back!"

Mrs Barge's husband, of Orchard House, had been in the Rifle Brigade; and had been passed over. Being passed over could damage a man's esteem of himself; a cause for his deportment to go awry. "He smothers his chagrin," said Ida. Ida hadn't laid eyes on either Barge.

Dorothy frowned her down.

"Do keep that dog of yours in order," said George.

That was a soppy bull-terrier (now busy sliding in the hall) who'd inherited the characteristic of his breed which his peers would have been glad to have seen left out of him; for a small snarl or two would result in his sinking his teeth into somebody's ear and his jaws would lock, the victim screeched, or howled, blood poured onto the rugs, disappeared through the boards or stained the carriage-sweep a horrible pink; and the household had to be dissuaded, Papa had decreed, from bursting from pantry and kitchen with pails of water and Ida shown how to put a foot on the muscled white rear and tug hard on the tail. The somebody would have to be comforted, the other beaten, though he'd already look terribly conscious, poor Rabbit.

Forbidden the house, he was always able to squirm back in. He was very charming.

"Curious the dogs," George said, "don't appear to bear your rascal any resentment."

With such lack of formality, the Lupuses, motto *touch me not*, in high spirits, lived.

When George was introduced, by and by, to Captain Barge, he ignored the signals from which he deduced Barge (she'd ushered him, "my husband Evelyn", to the fore after church) to be an apron wallah.

Army, thought George, bound to hunt. His blue eyes flickered quizzically.

He'd looked over a mare in the week, an eight-year-old; admired good shoulders, deep-barrelled chest; felt the shortish legs; run a hand over back and croup; examined feet, teeth and sight; sent Clarence to gallop her for her wind, put his ear to her heart; had her trotted up several times again; and finally shook his head. She'd had a kind eye. He wondered whether he wouldn't pay his guineas for her yet. The sort he liked for the banks and ditches of the Wednesday country.

In the dying days of October he had her on trial. It wasn't his practice to buy horses late; the horses were got into condition from July. She was bold; and in temperament, he thought, honest.

With the dog pack tight around him he went to cast over the headland of the fallow by Gramer's Wood, its earth leafed in this twelvemonth or more, where his wit told him he'd pick up the drag of a fox still on the way home with a belly full of forage to lie up below Hengstbury Clump.

In the early weeks of cubbing he'd found in a like manner (though you could lose your quarry) daybreak after daybreak, using his lore, all over his country, until the new entry understood its work and the pack hunted steady and true.

Now songbirds took to flight. No other birds were there.

He walked the brown mare quietly and sent hounds forward. Walked on, and halted.

Prosper lifted his head to stare at George.

Walked on.

The worn gap of a badger track over the ditch, through toppled grasses, was visible.

Walked her on, and halted. He regarded them so acutely he was aware they'd found in that instant before Nimbus and Reaper spoke.

Then silence, a mew; and they were on; in full cry.

Their voices echoed among the trunks of the big trees, beech, silver birch and oak. The fox had passed straight through the covert; and gone out to Hengstbury opposite. Permanent pasture raked downwards to a lane (there, rose-hips hung on the briers) and climbed in lynchets. Scent was high. Hounds ran over-swift. Their music shut off as a cock its water. They checked; leading couples (Argot, Striver, Vandal, Bowman) turned back. By themselves they cast round and were on again to him.

On the far hill George saw a streak of red. A different fox. Restless bullocks. On the brow the sun lit the furze from behind, and irradiated the pine branches and wisps of cloud.

His earth stopped, Reynard, whom George loved for his beauty and cunning, had pressed on east, deep into the heath; where in the end, after a point of some six miles, they lost him.

George wasn't dissatisfied; much though he preferred them to have their reward.

9 The lawn meet at Coker

The Opening Meet was too glittering an occasion for Bevis, and an arduous hack. He turned out on Tanga on the Saturday, for a meet at Coker, on the other side of the village; with the uneasy suspicion that he, the rebellious, the stoic, the self-reliant, felt not all that happy; and, further, that his pony was more excited than he.

His mouth seemed to hunger to suck his glove; and Clarence, mounted on the blue roan cob, was a fellow of few words.

It made little difference that Tanga was in no sort of fuss. Bevis looked at the pricked ears and at the tremble that twitched the skin of her shoulder and could see himself cannoning into several gentlemen (even though he and Clarence weren't at all in the thick of it), neatly to tip the cherry brandy down their coats.

Bevis glanced toward his sisters, statues in dark habits with the hair netted in the napes of their necks beneath their bowlers; frightfully rarefied, side by side; fiery Grenadier, clipped out and silken, silhouetted against Old Haunts. They hadn't a thought for him. Their noses in twin profile seemed averted.

Bevis watched people ride up to Major Collingfleet. Children and servants weren't capped. With the Quarr, cap-money was no longer taken for the huntsman upon the death of the fox; but now and for all the hunt servants.

Major Collingfleet manoeuvred his horse amongst the field, without ever allowing a soul to have the impression he was approaching; to say "good morning" and raise his top-hat. Small silver was passed over and slid into his pouch.

When Major Collingfleet greeted a stranger he was exceedingly courteous.

Ida proffered her coin.

When Major Collingfleet's mare Gwendolen stepped slowly by Bevis, Major Collingfleet said, "Ha!" Bevis removed his cap and squashed it on the pommel.

During the season proper the Master was driven to meets, far and near alike; a-clip-clopping behind a nag in the brougham; or (unspeakable of him) in Quick-As-Can-Be; with, lest she expire, a led nag behind them.

When, today, he'd arrived in the barouche with Dorothy and Dorothy's spinster cousin Cecily, a frequent guest of theirs, he'd *noticed* various sorts and responded to many a bashful "good morning, Master"; and brought fire to the cheek of Miss Haunchley, hahnchly as in venison or launch.

Blois had blared to Crashwood, "Y'know, he'll go to Pie, eh, Crashwood!" To that, George had lent a deaf ear.

Miss Haunchley sported an old-fashioned habit. The skirt trailed below the girth. She had been a gal in a more robust era; and, the flush notwithstanding, rode in a very slapping style.

She seized the chance to chaff Parson Cornforth on his having sold his famous Goblin after the battle with George Lupus in respect of that animal's common colour.

The Rector claimed he was a man of peace.

The Coker servants had already begun to relieve people of their glasses: the footmen carried trays and trod up on the near side of both horses and traps. The field numbered at least ninety, since Coker, the second big house of the neighbourhood, was a popular meet, with the chance of a gallop over the grand old turf; and two dozen or so folk drove after hounds, round the lanes. All warmed their insides with port or cherry brandy, which had been brought out to everybody regardless.

It was a joyous thing about hunting (thought Miss Haunchley), all classes met on the hunting-field conjoined in a love of the sport.

About the Master and Fontley, hounds bunched in a mood of expectation; that is, they grinned with open mouths and their tongues lolled, though they were not hot.

In a generous half-circle about them, the foot-followers had a purposeful appearance; mostly ancient, leaning on ash-plants, or youthful and ragged.

And on the carriage-drive were drawn up in array the gigs, governess cars, bicycles and discreetly by the stable-yard the terrier man's dogcart (and those of numerous gentlemen who had rejoined their mounts to ride the last mile). Rags and Tiny had run to the meet with the pack. Now they were coupled and Brian stood with them shyly under the mulberry-tree. The Master wasn't in favour of a terrier's being carried all day across the saddle by a whip and arriving cramped at the first drain.

The grand-dam of Rags had come up from Devon, from the parson Jack Russell.

At that moment George, on his pure grey Pasha, stared straight through Bevis.

It was George's conceit to mount his hunt servants generally also on greys; and Frank Fontley, whipping in this day himself although often he bided at the Kennels to see all well, had out The Duchess. Beer was up on Dorcas, and fifteen-year-old Colin had Marauder.

The second horses would come out a little later; quietly along the lanes. Hard-goers among the members, too, had second-horsemen adroit at keeping in touch.

Most of the gentlemen were in scarlet; most contented themselves with buff tops, not white, to their boots. Some of more venerable age wore blue coats with squashy top-hats. Several persons in bowlers were in black coats. Others were tidy in pepper-and-salt and so on. Their jockey caps marked out, as well as hunt servants and Master, the farmers: the more notable of these (as to tops, dark brown) Messrs Hayter, Maber, Donkin, Dyce, Wareham, Box and Rood.

The ladies liked dark blue or black; except for one, whose habit and, front-laced in the crook of the ankle, hidden boots were brown.

Roy Dyce, all apple cheeks and sooty lashes, scion of Farmer Dyce, was astride a pony long ago bought (as Tanga had been) out of the Forest. An infant came in a basket on a Dartmoor with a lady on foot; and two tots on the leading-rein with grooms.

Morwenna was late.

The butcher's boy, on the butcher's cob, which took more kindly to the shafts than a saddle, would appear in the afternoon. The butcher's cob, in his knee action, danced on hot bricks. The butcher's boy was a familiar sight, bumping at a rapid trot to find hounds. George, always so stuffy about how the gentry and yeomen turned themselves out, had a tolerant glimmer of a smile for Hubert.

Those of the ladies who'd been leaning over the carriage party to chat now straightened, and collected their reins. Dorothy's lips were perhaps a trifle martyred; but she preserved all the appearance of complaisance.

Against the cold she was well wrapped up. Hunting, though, was purgatory.

The field master, Mr Sawbridge-Walter (his mare had cost his wife over three hundred guineas), fastened his gimlet eye on a stranger he understood to be the tenant of Orchard House. Barge was unprepossessing. His hat was too far back on his head, he rode slumped and round-shouldered, his curb-chain was done up too tight, his hands appeared to have much to be desired. His hideous ewe-necked gelding had a red ribbon and a lather up.

This Captain Barge, though his regiment was acceptable, hadn't even introduced himself.

It was a cool day, at a quarter past eleven, with a slight, bright wind; and a pale sun shone out of a cumulous sky.

10 Moving off

It dawned on Bevis that there was no cosy country lane to hem in the field, blocking the boys and girls to the rear (and Clarence), but open parkland; and that Papa would go quite swiftly to covert; that the rest, led by Mr Sawbridge-Walter's bay, would spread out and some stretch their horses' legs in a canter. Bevis had to hope she'd stay, his Tanga, with the roan.

Lady Persephone Sawbridge-Walter bore down on him with her pilot, Mr Urnhurst, and Bevis snatched at Tanga's mouth. She flung up her head. His string gloves were slippery. Clarence didn't have Slade's gift of foresight in these matters of etiquette. Slade would have waited. Bevis gasped. Clarence hadn't waited long enough.

Mr Urnhurst would have travelled with his horses by train and hacked from the Halt.

Lady Sephie rode at fourteen stone ten and had hunters well up to her weight.

Tanga did her best to be the reliable first pony she was. She knew Bevis was fluttery; but she paid no attention to nerves.

She was small for a Forest pony, 12.2 hands.

By a stroke of luck Bevis fetched up behind Mr Armour. Mr Armour had a tin leg that was a source of fascination to children. He pulled a top-boot over it (or had, Esmond said, a leg the boot was made on) and though it stuck out at an odd angle when the foot was home in the stirrup-iron he managed with some aplomb to ride. He didn't jump more than could be hopped over but Bevis and Tanga *went round* rather, too. When Mr Armour wanted to shake up his horses he brought his crop down on the tin.

Dorothy had lingered, to amuse her cousin.

Gervase Sturt, secretly attached to Mrs Egmont, eased a path to a station not far from her at the covert-side. Both wore the hunt button; that is, had been invited by George to do so.

To all intents and purposes Sturt was their host, though the old man was still alive. Sir Hereward spent hours in the mausoleum he'd built for himself: it was warmer than the house. It had elaborate heating-pipes and these cushioned his last days. He and his dogs enjoyed themselves very much in the mausoleum and he had, it was rumoured, arranged for the boiler to be stoked even after his death. The pipes would remain piping in perpetuity. He'd brought the Gainsborough, the Landseer and the Mrs Evangeline Burrell water-colour, all of which he valued equally, to the mausoleum but coming from a more Spartan age the Gainsborough didn't appreciate the warmth.

As hounds passed, Sir Hereward emerged. He waved, quite with his old gusto. The mausoleum stood on a mound, so to George he looked like a squat god Bes against an ornate rotunda of brick.

11 Drawing the covert

The foot-followers had barely started to trail across the turf when George entered the covert. The fringes of it were dense with wild rhododendrons.

Beer had slipped quiet to the far side and Mr Rhodes was at the point by the Pheasantry.

George felt the hush of Home Wood and the shadows fell across him. He sent Pasha slowly forward, calling, "Loo in, loo in!" A small note on the horn (rarely) advertised his progress. Presently there was a thin, distant holloa.

Hounds lifted their heads but George wasn't going to leave covert with the first fox and by his voice alone kept them at their business. He heard the crack of Colin's whip: Wistful and Melody came back to him. The hollerer, in the belief that she went unheard, for it was the keeper's daughter, must have put her hands to mouth and repeated her wail.

The covert went back to medieval times, with boundary banks to divide the plantation and a hefty ditch to surround it. There was ancient oak, pine, beech, twisting sweet chestnut and silver birch, with glades of brimble and bracken.

He heard the snap of twigs and a whirr when some pheasant got up and the scream of a jay.

Outside, desultory conversation irritated those who kept their ears cocked and their eyes peeled. One horse chucked his head; but otherwise there was a general decorum. The horses too, after all, liked to listen.

A groom, brown gaiters and dun bowler, had held a green 'un to a walk and approached in a calm manner.

Old Haunts and Grenadier were still side by side.

One of the strangers, mounted by Sturt from the Hall stables, stood in his stirrups while his horse staled. Sturt would give a groom a wigging: no sound man sent an animal out for a day's hunting on a bladderful. Ida and Griselda had often watched Slade or Corbin or Clarence at the whistling which would tell a horse to stale. Nurse and the month-nurse would do similarly with the new baby, have it potty-trained at two weeks. The visitor's horse splashed the ground; and a musty and ammoniac scent rose, not unpleasantly, to the nostrils.

The lie of the land muffled and concealed everything.

Afar off the whipper-in had disappeared. Sawbridge-Walter, who that very minute had meant, by raising his topper, to invite the field to go farther down the covert-side, held his crop up. The hard-of-hearing stared at their neighbours' faces. Hounds had found; George had sounded his urgent two notes: he was gone out and blowing "gone away".

Bevis with Clarence followed those who plunged into the wood; towards the Pheasantry with its track to a gate onto the road. The procession of turn-outs bowled along the back drive; way behind, three second-horsemen contented themselves with a jog. And behind those was the woman with the infant in a basket seat; faint yet game.

The Misses Lupus were with the majority, who set off for a brisk gallop in the park and a pop over the tumbled place in the wall.

12 A short burst

Hounds were in glorious voice and, it seemed, running fast.

The only visible sign of them was in the person of Beer: as she rose in the distance over a straggly hedge the grey mare Dorcas had been spotted by the first to reach the lane.

The boldest crossed it at once. A ditch with rails took them into a broad pasture. Here they were offered the bliss of a country which opened up in front of them, half a dozen queuing briefly to jump the stile in the far corner, for that was the shorter line, and many more taking the two farm gates before others came up and there were fellows gallant enough to open them, leaning from the saddle, for those who liked to save their horses.

Lady Persephone never ventured out without a pilot. "Let us make for the drove road," she said to Francis Urnhurst.

He concurred.

There was a cut-and-laid onto a bank and a drop into an unrutted track up which Lady Sephie could thunder.

Her mother had worn a little pill-box in the hunting-field; she herself believed a high-crowned silk to be right in the shires. Lady Sephie had glanced into the plough and noted that one such duchessy hat, tweaked off by a branch, had danced on the shoulder-blades of the Cosgrove creature *for an indecent length of time.*

Several, less familiar with the Coker estate than he, joined Urnhurst.

Those who'd chosen the stile had skipped the plough by finding some stiff timber into the spinney and had threaded through that onto firm ground which now presented them with a succession of grand, galloping fences.

Shorthorn heifers, noses poked forward in curiosity, stumbled at a half-trot across an enclosure on ahead. So there was no doubt in people's hearts as to where hounds were, and they rode as straight as was possible.

They weren't running any longer, though.

Parson Cornforth reined back to a walk in the drove so as to listen. They were baying to an earth or a drain. Then hounds' voices subsided and all went quiet. He trotted on, smartly yet composed.

13 Cecily intrudes

"Dolly, I did enjoy going to the meet!" said Cecily.

No other soul was permitted the intimacy of calling her Dippy, and George only because she hadn't been able to stop his doing so: she was aware that once, in her girlhood, she'd been lumbered with the sobriquet of "Stables Despair" (she'd driven a decent animal in a phaeton until she'd taken too many corners).

At Quarr, Cecily had descended from the carriage; posterior foremost, although the footman had been there to hand her down.

Cecily said, "D'you know, Dorothy, I heard that old Lady Sturt once suffered a broken leg when following hounds; a heavy gate swung on her; and she rode a score of miles to Coker without a word of complaint; with a stop at the doctor's house in Lackham Magna to desire him to attend. Most redoubtable!

"So long as that fate doesn't await the intrepid Ida!" uttered Cecily.

"Don't be absurd," said Dorothy, although it had been the truth about Lady Sturt; and Cecily blanched.

"Oh, and I've been retailing that to Agnes! I *consider*," Cecily said with the sycophancy (thought Dorothy) of a maiden cousin, "you're to be admired, for you have never, so far as I am aware, poured cold water on this passion for the chase!"

She even put up with "Ma". What she chose to be called was "Mother".

It was indeed her earnest fear that Ida, no doubt bespattered by now and repulsively happy, might grow up to be *tedious*. It was a fear upon which she often dwelt. To Cecily she said in a tranquil tone, "Nonsense!"

Dorothy could remember having said: "George, would you mind if I were not to hunt?"

That was all. No breath of censure or reproach. He hadn't felt it. Could his eyes have betrayed faint relief?

She was proud of her current bay hack; and, whilst it was ineligible at the moment, sent her orders to the stables with a most genuine anticipation. He wasn't an easy horse, for he possessed a difficult mouth.

The black, Sable, had also had a difficult mouth.

"You wish George would look after his birds," said Cecily; "more than he does."

"Why?" said Dorothy, as though inviting no answer.

Cecily recollected how Dolly had fought to marry him. He still caused her a flutter, Cecily was positive of *that*.

"You relish shooting parties," she said.

"My dear Cecily!" said Dorothy, with a whimsical glance that was hard to fathom.

"Your keeper isn't permitted to rear pheasant," ventured Cecily, "in any plenitude."

Dorothy tweaked at the fingers of her gloves. She contemplated the airless tips.

"Agnes has a notion of what a fine shot George is," said Cecily.

"You must be glad of her company," said Dorothy judiciously. Cecily resolved to take a hint.

Agnes, run to earth in the library, inclined her head towards Cecily.

"My cousin Dorothy is a poor horsewoman," murmured Cecily, "hence the antipathy to you-know-what!"

"How odd," said Agnes. "A donkey has me defeated, and I don't abhor it!"

"Dolly all over," observed Cecily.

14 Bolting the fox

When he came up with them, Cornforth saw that it was indeed a culvert.

George had dismounted. Hounds had been drawn off. Colin was collecting one or two couple which had got separated; the old man could hear, behind him somewhere, Colin's whistle and the crack of his whip. Beer was absent, making for the metal that had swung round in a great loop from the Coker back lodge; to fetch the terrier.

Parson Cornforth eased his weight. His long-tailed mare was well within herself.

There was some snorting and sneezing. No one had done very much.

Lather had so soaked the neck, shoulder, flanks and rump of that new fellow's gelding that it dripped in gobbets. Instead of being walked the latter had been made to stand; he'd get chilled in the wind. People tried to address cheery remarks to Barge, but the red ribbon rather spoke and they kept a distance. Barge munched his teeth, as in sleep.

Certain enthusiasts, of both the sexes, simply burned; being near to the Master. Others continued the communion of the covert-side. Sturt in particular, an arm through his reins, could be seen at Mrs Egmont's knee. His horse pressed its browband, to relieve an itch, into the hollow between his shoulder-blades. Sturt side-stepped, hardly aware of this.

The preponderance of gentlemen was large but Miss Haunchley was there; Lady Sephie, Mrs Egmont, Mrs Foster and more; and Mrs Cosgrove, whose hat had been plucked up by a thoughtless tendril of old man's beard, retreated to poke at the net in her nape.

Beer met the terrier man a few hundred yards from the road. Brian was hot-foot with a spade. Diana when left never stirred. It was essential, for Brian often had to abandon the dogcart and leg it over field or furrow.

Back at the drain, Blois had Pasha's rein as well as his own. It was a courtesy to the Master; not a necessity. The hunt horse didn't exist that wouldn't stand; and Diana knew, when Brian had hitched up her reins, she was in charge of both trap and its other canine passenger.

Brian uncoupled Tiny, and Beer gathered her under his arm in such a way that her forepaws rode on his pommel and her hindquarters perched on his thigh. She might have run but like so a panting terrier didn't have to be restrained before being put in.

Fontley with Colin took hounds out of sight. The field yielded ground.

Master remounted.

Tiny nipped in and very close on that the fox shot out the other end; a red vixen with a ragged ear; George knew her; had known her earth; seen her, with four cubs of her own, adopt two orphans.

They'd hunted her twice the previous season (she'd given

them respectable runs), and hounds were whipped off her in February; he thought this and in the same breath called hounds up.

They streamed towards him, Roguish, Rakish, Harebell and Hebe; Burnish, Bunty, Ruthless, Fearless, Rhapsody, Snowmaid, Vivid and Topaz, Melody, Elegy, Amulet, Ardent and Hurry, Decorous and Diligent, Dido, Hero, Tumult and Flinty; Silken, Sippet, Attica and Ringlet, Siren, Precious and Wistful; followed by Fontley.

As Tiny scrabbled through the mouth, a callused hand fell on her scruff; to her chagrin. Colin had remained to restore her to Brian, who hadn't arrived in time to see the fun.

The ladies were swifter than the dog pack. The fox could run more swiftly than either.

Lionel Sawbridge-Walter, with the field right on top of them, would be exercised to keep any merry soul from committing a solecism.

The horses too had their blood up, fidgets in their legs, and there was a plunge or two; Farmer Box had a devil of a job to hold Irish whose mouth was of iron; and young Bleadham went bucketing off along the hedgerow to circle round before coming up with the rest; at least, thought everybody, he had that much sense, when out on a thoroughly unschooled animal.

Sawbridge-Walter, among the first, didn't see that Bleadham's horse, yawing away from that hedge and getting its head down and then up, was about to bolt towards a rasper; and, rapping its knees badly, give its rider a nasty toss.

If Sawbridge-Walter had witnessed the mishap his fierce eyebrows would have rocketed.

The hunted fox turned to make for refuge in Pie Wood, no more than a mile and a bit due westward, but was headed: ignoramuses were peering, noisy, from the bank above the deep lane. She sent them into a frenzy of hollering and hat-waving.

They shouted "yere Master", and "Master, garn thataway".

By and by, when the daughters were in earshot the blacksmith's wife shrieked, "'Morning Miss Ida, Miss Grisella." It was but a few minutes to one o'clock and soon people would wish they'd eaten pieces of their chocolate if they weren't to have their sandwiches for some time.

15 The hunted fox

Out of the drain she ran for her life, with her second wind. When she'd recovered from the fright of having hounds quite hard behind her and been headed at the lane she started to summon her cunning. She still wanted to cross and would do so farther down. She sped over the pasture with the breeze for once on her ear, and dived into a double hedge of hazel. Within, she popped along it, momentarily slowed, until she could go through the dairy herd. Without hesitation she went as close to their cloven feet as she could and they, agog, trampled where she'd been and whisked themselves ponderously around. On the far side she made a zigzag through a deserted yard and the edge of a pond. She followed a strip where roots had been got up and soil balled a little in her pads but she didn't muddy her brush; she slipped out beneath the eyes of a team of heavy horses and a man bent over a harrow. He stared at her speculatively. He nodded, bringing his chin up: it was how countrymen greeted other folk. He returned to his work.

Hound music still filled her ears.

She slunk into the lane; nipped between the broken lower bars of a gate; and made for the river; the Friggle Brook. When she was near it she eased through a tangle of withy and alder and went on to the low bank. Here she stooped to lap; to gollop, though not overly. She listened. She stepped calmly into the water and struck out.

She half swam, half plodded, then swam, for it narrowed and was of a sudden much deeper, downstream, under the reeds, for a good quarter-mile. She let herself ashore again on a bend of poached mud where cattle drank; shook herself, sprang from the shallows to the bank and set off at a trot. A long, long hedgerow brought her at last to the Pie Wood. She found the earth stopped with clods.

Sounds had diminished and all had fallen quiet. There was a strong smell. She moved on to a former badger sett where a dog-fox sometimes lay up. It was stopped too. She walked out of the smell and hesitated, listening. Red and yellow leaves floated from the trees. She swung through a corner of Pie Wood. When Snowmaid threw her tongue, and they were on again, Silken, Roguish, Hurry, Harebell, the vixen heard them. She left the covert.

Weary, she went away to Iddesleigh; on to Winbarrow Wood; and on to Duncterbury Beacon. She didn't skirt it, she was up and over and down towards the Brook; the same big Brook, swollen by tributary springs and looping towards the sea. Yet after Pie Wood she'd run straight. She quickened her pace. They seemed strangely close. The vixen drew breath with pain. She sank into the water, and the water met over her. She surfaced, swimming rapidly, and staggered over the steep lip opposite.

The meadows were flat and marshy.

She didn't hear the splashes when the foremost hounds sprang into the river. They were hooking their strong forelegs over the lip, before she was half-way to the sandy ground where the furze grew. They had her in view and were lifting their heads. Her turn of speed couldn't serve her, had been long spent. But she heard the throttled clamour from their throats; an unaccountable din; and the thump-beat of hoofs. She was sobbing.

16 In full cry

George thought, blasted idiots!

After she'd been bolted, he'd imagined some thruster in the jostle had galloped up but it was a loose horse which endangered his hounds: Bleadham's, with mud in its hog mane from the somersault and a leg through the reins. Beer rode at it and got it above the bit.

Ahead of George, hounds had been pouring exuberantly through the timber fence at the end of the second pasture; some between the rails, some under; some had gone over the top; according to temperament. He glanced round.

Bleadham's kind would fly it, hands up, shoulders back, toes forward, on flattened equine backs as in a steeplechase. At a good canter, Pasha measured his stride.

Then four fences on George realized that the spectators in the lane hadn't the sense or manners to stand there silent. They would head the fox; and he thought, damnation.

He pursued her with his eye when she veered, and lost her. Here hounds worked slowly, yet without a check. Burnish and Diligent and some others did try upwind; were swift to hark to Harebell. George never meddled. In and out they flowed and round and out and on, like a molten substance. Harebell and Siren and Fearless and Rhapsody within and the pack cleverly without, they ran along the double hedge. It was a blind seven foot tall. George trotted; waited. Once they were out to the other side he spurred on, over-faced, to find his way.

Clarence had caught up to the ten-acre, more or less where those folk had headed the fox; and he elected to shepherd his charge into the lane (Tanga's passenger was thankful). It was so sunken they couldn't see much.

Clarence's idea of keeping up was a smart clatter to the village and round by the roads ("Downwind and they d'fetch up to 'ee!"). They watched the field come streaming down the hill; and, blessed with fortune, they saw the fox.

The cows had their heads up and when hounds faltered among them Daisy and Primrose gave exaggerated starts and tossed their horns, and Buttercup lowered hers, and some of the herd swayed off to stop and stare.

The pace picked up.

Melody with Harebell and Snowmaid led the pack towards a deserted yard where a thatched barn was black-green with age and sprouted grass. Several couple gulped at the pond but, puffing their chops, let the water slurp and splash.

They ran mute when they got to the end of a strip where roots had been taken up; and puzzled around the clamp there. George stood in his stirrups and saw, in the next field beyond the row of three straw-ricks, a man with a team of Clydesdales and a harrow.

The man touched his cap.

"'Morning," said George.

"Ah," said the man.

"Seen the fox, my good man?" asked George.

"Baint bin yere, sir," said the man.

George had instantly glanced at the farm horses when he'd ridden up but had learned nothing from them.

Hounds spoke, and ran on.

"Cheerio then," said the man, "sir."

Yonder, across the valley, the Pie Wood massed on the horizon. George could swear she was making for that.

People hastened to open gates and hold up old Mr Holkham senior and the pretty mare he had between the shafts. The vixen had gone towards an orchard – full of geese – near to Plash, yet slipped into the bottom of the ditch, hopped out soon and darted by the spinney in the damp lee of its fringes to the Friggle Brook.

When hounds checked there, almost all the foot-followers, whose cottages called them, went home; the ponies and traps were reduced in number; the baby in a basket and the Dartmoor, into the long, dark mane of which the mother had entwined her fingers with the thrill, turned back; the feebler, the faint-hearted, and the green 'un out for a look all broke off.

George, after a quick, careful cast, lifted hounds and galloped downstream for a half-mile. He'd observed how the rooks, feeding on a field on the slope up to Pie had risen into the air and flapped down again or flown over something which must have been moving and which they still marked.

She didn't cross the Brook, he thought. She's off to the Pie Wood.

With the uncanny skill that made him beloved of all, he reckoned it precisely: there by the bend where cattle drank.

He threw hounds forward, encouraging them with his

voice. Ringlet hit off the line and spoke with such confidence that they sped to her. They ran uphill.

One blithe spirit had sent his horse Sir Roger at the legendary Friggle anyway, and had been obliged to wade ashore wet through: his boots oozed and weed trailed on his spurs and his mount still stood belly-deep in the middle, blown.

By blandishments and a patted pocket Sir Roger was unmoved, and gazed at his master with, or so it occurred to Lady Sephie, dumb insolence. "Ha ha!" she barked.

The chap waited, humble, for young Simkins to ride in and fish Sir Roger out.

Crashwood, with a half-dozen more crass than bold who hadn't reached the river, and Rhodes, whose gallantry had persuaded him to go to the aid of a novice, now had the chance, by cutting a corner, to get on terms.

The earth-stopper had been with his lantern in the night through Pie Wood. George "saw" already the land it hid from his view.

They ran right-handed.

Although the music was audible, some of the field became lost inside, crashed back and forth along the same sticky ride until, on jumping out over trappy timber, they discovered themselves left behind, with no clue as to where hounds were. They set off pell-mell in the wrong direction and that finished their day. Barge was among them.

Jackdaws chuckled in the caw-cawing overhead.

Hounds went away to Iddesleigh. A big hare leapt up and scudded off but they took no notice of Puss. In the rabbit warren by Iddesleigh there was alarm too.

Miss Haunchley drew rein and walked her horse (a breather for both).

George believed the vixen must have been distressed after Iddesleigh.

Before Winbarrow she'd stopped to roll in muck (they were spreading night-soil); and scent went very cold. Hunting with difficulty, hounds pressed slow but sure on towards the Beacon.

Between Iddesleigh and Winbarrow Wood there were big doubles, ditch-and-rails onto a bank and out over a hedge and drop, or similar, and some of the field came to grief. A hurdle had to be fetched for Sturt's visitor. He hadn't broken his neck. He'd lamed the horse, though. Changing legs on the bank, Farmer Box's steed had been interfered with (Box had dreadful hands); had skewed, hesitated, gone on bravely; and had pecked heavily. Box had pitched over and his cap, falling off and then being banged back in his face, had made his nose bleed. Box remounted. It was plain the stuffing had been knocked out of him.

Before the Beacon a shout of "*'ware wire*" went up.

In a thin hawthorn hedge a single strand, treacherously unflagged: the first wire had appeared in the past decade.

George had a glimpse of a hat which was waving attached to a hand. But he wouldn't lift hounds, ever, while they were on, no matter how laboriously. The hat vanished, and, as it happened, without trace.

After consigning Sturt's guest to the hurdle and telling him there was little amiss with him the doctor, Mahon, was to ride very hard indeed, but to small avail; for his fellow managed to over-reach. Mahon had found himself binding a nasty gash; and an eight-mile trudge ahead of him.

He thought morosely (not in the right spirit), Sturt was least in sight, when his friend had the tumble. Lupus's man Clarence had been asked to lead the horse to the Coker stables.

The fallow-deer, disturbed on the Beacon, had, unlike Puss, who sat so tight, drifted off ages ago.

Alice Plummer waved her knuckles at the Master.

"Might I thread through your kitchen garden, Mrs Plummer?" he called. He put Pasha at the wicket: it was tied with twine. The track was barred at the other end by a pole-ladder.

In the country before him, he saw a fleeing shadow of burnished red.

Clarence said, "Right, Master Bee. Us d'take the Coker horrse on."

Bevis was contrary, and wished to stay with hounds.

"They be miles, bin um," said Clarence.

Miss Haunchley called, "Come with me, little boy, if you care to." This was what Bevis did, much to the perturbation of Clarence and his own surprise.

Down the Roman road cantered Miss Haunchley and Tanga until they were arrested by the sight of Bleadham off his horse and two unknown gentlemen, all of them splattered in mud, who were gazing at a couple of hounds. Bleadham had visited the bushes. He was saying, "It's Romany, I'd recognize her anywhere!" He liked to be a knowing one. "Romany, here, Romany," he called.

Bevis hissed to Miss Haunchley, who seemed to be benign, "It's not *Romany*! Amulet and Ardent."

"What?" said Miss Haunchley.

"Master's little boy," enunciated Miss Haunchley, "tells me these are Amulet and Ardent. Romany's daughters, I understand." The gentlemen opened their mouths. "By Argot. Well, we must collect them."

She fixed her bulgy orbs on Bevis.

"Come along," commanded Miss Haunchley, whether to the hounds or to him he wasn't sure.

Bevis rode forward. He pursed his lips. Agonized hiatus. He whistled. He cracked his whip; but the lash snaked feebly. He couldn't make it crack. "Ardent, Amulet," he piped. They obeyed, rather slavery and grateful. He held his crop out so the thong hung down; and trotted on; twisting, as Frank Fontley did, as Beer did, in the saddle; and calling in a sweet voice.

Miss Haunchley brought up the rear. The gentlemen jumped into the field and careered over that!

Miss Haunchley was sporting mad. Bevis had heard Papa say that with her pack of terriers, entered to otter throughout the eighties and nineties, she'd killed the last otter in the Fawern River, to Papa's utter dismay; and the very last polecat in the county; as though she hadn't known any better.

Papa said one should never kill the last of anything. Also, quite as killing in its way, that she possessed the most immortal view-halloo of his acquaintance. So with the killer-of-the-last-otter-in-the-Fawern-River (and the last pole-cat) behind him, Bevis took Ardent and Amulet to find the pack.

All hint of them had died away.

Bevis stood in his stirrups and listened.

There was a sliver of grey and sleeve of scarlet at the Beacon: Colin. Colin emerged onto the Roman road and started towards Bevis.

"Ah," said Colin, when Bevis was up. "Ye be of a mind to help I." He grinned. He touched his cap to the lady.

From the Beacon they could look down on the country below. They perceived that hounds had crossed the railway. "They have caught their fox," said Miss Haunchley. But Collie Payne rubbed his chin.

"What do we do at the Brook?" said Bevis (without a quaver, it was mere curiosity).

After Duncterbury Beacon, hounds ran swiftly. George, as he swept down the hill, groped for his watch. An expression of anxiety on Fontley's face told Beer all he needed to know. "Ride for the ford!" bellowed Fontley to Beer.

"Goo arn!" And Beer, broad in his speech, thought: mun larnch theirselves a' thik ther Friggle.

Pasha's nostrils were distended and the veins in them shot with blood. A sour, reedy odour assailed them.

Pasha had already done quite a lot.

He felt George's legs get him up together. Splosh splosh, went Rhapsody and Rakish, and splosh went the pack, and they were swimming over; and splosh went Decorous; and the vixen toiled ahead with a film over her eyes. George galloped at the Brook. Pasha lengthened and saw water before him and the far bank and leapt, flying it with not a tuft to spare.

The Duchess was trembling. She knew Fontley wanted some prodigious exertion of her. Fontley had spotted the puff of smoke over Lackham Parva tunnel.

The meadows ran rank and marshy to the rise where the furze grew; and the vixen's ears drummed, deafening her. There was thunder beneath her feet. Her mouth was stretched open. She went up and over. On the other side there'd been a fire and a loose grey ash covered the ground. She turned and, still on ash, dragged herself along until the ash ended. Here she mounted the singed slope and straightaway entered a clump of near-bare brambles. In the centre there was an old log, a fallen tree-trunk, and, beneath this, a hollow. She crept into the hollow and lay, with bitten tongue, in easy earshot of the hoo-ha that ensued.

The train whistled when it spotted them.

George, his horn to his lips, and Fontley, they both had anguish in their guts. They uttered frightful oaths. Decorous faltered. Siren too. Master spurred to cry 'em back from the rails. They stopped hounds; whilst passengers crowded the windows, hung out.

The event shook everybody.

When presently they crossed and found that fire from a spark had made such a sugaring of ash, George tried in the gorse and all around without success. Roguish and Harebell cast with their heads up and scented the air almost to the brimbles; but were disappointed.

Then he took swigs from his flask and looked for his second horse.

Those with fine hunters, and one or two without, had jumped the Brook; and created mayhem, since Messrs Rood and Maber and a stranger got a ducking. Gervase Sturt and Mrs Egmont triumphed, in style.

Lesser mortals forded it.

In the lull, the men mostly dismounted to take their weight off; and their animals stood and blew. There weren't so very many, and of these several, with a considerable hack home, thought now was about the right moment to break off.

Though the vixen was lost she'd given them indeed a jolly run.

Mr Shapgut, at the age of eighty-four, was so skin and bone and light that he remained in the saddle. He thrust his legs forward in the stirrups, against stiffness.

When Bevis with Colin, Miss Haunchley, Amulet and Ardent came up, George was distinctly surprised; though he vouchsafed not a word.

17 Breaking off and the poultry-fund certifier

The boon of a side-saddle was that it was very difficult to fall off. You were so secure. You sat straight, kept your left heel down in the stirrup, your left leg tucked under one pommel (to hold you in "lepping"), and your right leg hooked over the other, your stick acted in lieu of your right leg; and in my Grenadier, Griselda thought, I have an exciting ride. Grenadier, a bright chestnut, could boil up (when he hadn't understood what was required of him); not that she minded. Clipped, he was pale gingery.

Ida's grey, Old Haunts, had grand paces and perfect manners. After a day with hounds he'd bring her home at the most sensible jog!

Between Iddesleigh and Winbarrow Wood, there was apparently some grief and a gentleman was carried off on a hurdle; with his mount perceived to be dead lame. Farmer Box's Irish had dislodged his rider and had gone on over at least two big ditches. Mr Rhodes saw to the Coker horse and Mr Urnhurst caught the runaway but Box had a fearful scramble to regain him, since no one could jump a led horse back over those fences. Mahon, the doctor, was held up in the affair but Ida and Griselda, taking a different line, had escaped all this.

Grenadier, 14.1 hands high, shown the way by Old Haunts, was indeed a brilliant little horse, and her sister Grizel capable; but Ida, with a certain responsibility to Ma, tried for caution.

So it was that they went over eight gates (three hurdles and five gates), two of them smashed by Rodham's Tommy, who despite a martingale and the curb of the double bridle carried his head so high he didn't look properly.

Mr Rodham, a solicitor, was a much mocked man. He liked to hunt; he had but the one Tommy, whom he brought out for more days than was decent, or humane, often twice in a week. Tommy deposited him in the drink, muddied his coat for him, and cost the Hunt sums in compensation. Tommy, up to weight, slow, nicknamed the Siege-Machine, appeared to be indestructible.

Rodham was despised as well as mocked, because he learnt no manners in the hunting-field; and he didn't have the lingo either.

How Mr Rodham could be in front was a mystery better unsolved.

Their instructions were: go where other people go, never take your own line. So Ida was conscious of the unwisdom of disobedience when they bustled past a hayrick to come upon Mr Rodham in difficulties.

There was the Siege-Machine, blown. His stumpy forelegs had leapt a cut-and-laid and his hind legs hadn't. On the other hand, the hind legs had got across the ditch and were searching for firm ground in bouncy blackthorn. This was all that prevented his sitting on a stake, which pointed, pale and shiny, up at his belly.

"My sister will give you a lead," called Ida.

Grenadier failed to entice poor Tommy.

He'd discovered some means whereby the blackthorn bore his weight and he intended to stand like that until he'd recovered his wind. The Siege-Machine stared at his helpers with his cool, indifferent eyes.

"Should I dismount?" said Mr Rodham, humbled.

"Sit still, Mr Rodham," said Ida, "or you'll send him onto a stake."

Griselda looked all around. She could hear hounds. But the countryside had emptied of any movement.

"Sit still," repeated Ida. Rodham licked his lips. He tried to put on a smile.

"Ride up behind and give the brute a thwack," he said.

"Wait," said Ida; with good sense.

When the Siege-Machine was ready to extricate himself, he heaved forward on his shoulders instead of slipping back into the ditch, lifted his quarters, twisted and somehow hoicked himself over, setting off at a determined canter on the other side. Determined, that is, to set his own pace.

"Whew!" said Ida, and came at it again.

They'd felt the strangeness of the man. The air sang on their cheeks.

They thought they would go by Cold Harbour below Winbarrow. Here they were hallooed by the farmer's wife.

"Hallo, Mrs Crumpler, have you seen hounds?" they called.

"Miss Ida, well, and Miss Grisella, ah, I yeard as how they'm garn Lackham way. The fowls yere be got by th'fox, step on in directly, Miss Ida, Crumpler have tried for to send to th'certificater, er baint bin and it d'grieve I to let um lie wher they was took."

Ida said, "Oh dear, how very unfortunate. I don't know that I can."

Mrs Crumpler said, "'Taint no mor'n a five-minute."

Griselda said to Ida, "But hounds are *running*!"

Ida said desperately, "I'm not the proper person."

Mrs Crumpler said, "We'm not partikler. Do irk your Pa sommat rotten when 'tis claimed *after*. Er doan go much on argifying! Er doan, do er! Horrses can bide yere, in th'yard."

Ida slid from the saddle, and gave her reins to Griselda.

"Doan 'ee fancy a peek, then, missie?" said Mrs Crumpler.

Griselda was in a fever of impatience but ghoulish curiosity got the better of her. They hitched Old Haunts and Grenadier to the wain.

"We mustn't be long," said Ida.

"Bring they in! Whyever not!" said Mrs Crumpler. "I got cake, see, I got milk. Out th'wind."

"Ida!" said Griselda, in an agony.

There were two fowl-houses on small iron wheels, and arks with runs among the apple-trees. One house was shut up, the pegs home in the latches. Two dead white corpses, Sussex, missing their heads, lay on the grass. Mrs Crumpler ushered Ida to the big door. She didn't clean out her fowls all that often: the reek knocked them backwards. Red mite plastered the faded creosote.

"How did it happen?" said Ida, who ought, she thought, to be making notes for the Hunt Secretary. "How on earth did a fox break in? Were the hens shut up early enough at night?

"Did the dogs not bark?" Ida said.

"A twenty-four did stop yere," said Mrs Crumpler.

Strewn beneath the perches and about, there were seventeen; some a sticky mess, mauled badly; some with and some without heads; one head. Some positively serene; but the heads of those were engorged with blood. Mouthfuls of feathers seemed to have been gaily tossed.

Ida handed crop and gloves to Griselda.

She ducked and, clutching her habit, went in. She picked up an intact hen by its legs and with her fingers felt the neck. Had it not been wrung? She looked at the farmer's wife wonderingly.

There was a place in the floor where the boards had been rotten. A piece of tin over it hadn't been tacked down well. The "fox" had gnawed the hole bigger.

"I suppose it *was* a fox?" said Ida. "Do you keep ferrets?" But she didn't have the experience to judge. Puppies, could it have been? She wished they'd never been drawn in on this affair.

"Right daft, they foxes!" the farmer's wife said. "Mental like. Murders the lot. They always does, doan um!

"'Twas a girt fellow."

"You saw the fox?" asked Ida.

"Afore, ah. Us d'reckon 'tis th'identic animal," said Mrs Crumpler.

Ida glimpsed in one nesting-box a *brown* egg.

"They were all Sussex, were they?"

"Ah," said Mrs Crumpler. "They poor beggars bi thik yere fowl-house was lily-white."

Somehow they had to accept milk and cake, though they did try to make their excuses. The Crumpler son, Stan, was fighting the war in South Africa. Old Haunts and Grenadier would be chilled, said Griselda, *should* have been *walked*. Mrs Crumpler had sold butter at the Friday market and part had gone for the War Fund.

"I think," said Ida, "it would be as well to wait for the proper certifier. Isn't it Mr Armour?"

"No call for that," said Mrs Crumpler. She beamed. "Whyfor pester he? Peg-legged an' all."

When they'd mounted from the trough, and ridden away,

Ida said, "Now what! I suppose we meant only to stay out half the day."

"Go home while they're still running?" said Griselda.

"Whoa," said Ida. "Listen!" They listened.

"Oh come on," said Ida. They turned back towards the Pie Wood.

Their faces bowed, they didn't even see the geese that flew over; or hear them. They overtook Gypsy Jem, bareback, elbows out, on a skewbald cob with large feet and a lot of feather. He'd a-spotted hounds beyond the Friggle Brook, he said, no-o, he didn't reckon as how they'd killed. He were in the Lackham lane when the engine did go into thik ther tunnel.

They trotted on.

They cheered up in time to greet old Father Blackmore who was driving a pig down the street in Plash. And then, walking towards them in a large-brimmed hat, was Mrs Barge; all of a quiver.

"It's Ida, I believe," she said, "and Griselda."

They smiled politely; and, when they were by, they shrugged.

"*Come* on, Jem," shouted Griselda, "keep up with us, do." Though Bevis's friend, he was twelve.

With a sheepish twinkle for them, he caught up.

18 In at the death

Tanga had plenty of stamina. A New Forest pony could go all day.

She was enjoying herself, her winter coat in whorls of sweat on chest and belly. Bevis was solemnly handed a large, shapeless, peppermint cream by the killer-of-the-last-otter; made, she said, by her Betsy.

The sun was gone in. The wind had chivvied off the fair-weather clouds; veered, and dropped. Bevis was radiant; tired, though. On his small pony he was polite, so behind everybody: he was close enough to see the tiny swallowtails of the ribbon on his papa's velvet cap.

The grass was cropped very short between the gorse bushes, and was covered in rabbit droppings.

They narrowed to single file. For Bevis there were prickles. It was like being tickled through your breeches. Everybody threaded at a sedate walk along hardly more than a deer track and by some birches halted.

Bevis craned; only to grasp that the track vanished into the abyss of the Roman road below and that Tanga was required to slide on her hocks down a big steep place.

For an uncomfortable minute, he thought he'd rather dismount. "Go on," he said.

He let out his rein and, as Slade had taught him, leant right back. She made nothing of it. He gave her a pat. With no eyes on him, he dropped his reins and embraced her.

George, riding Rajah in the midst of his hounds, went quietly on; and everybody behind him. They halted again.

There were thickets of birch and stunted fir, high in heather, draped on the face of an old gravel working. A fresh fox was found at once.

Merrily they went away and a brisk run on the heath favoured sure-footed Tanga. While the lithe fox bounded over that ground, full of twists and turns and dips and terrible ruts and concealed tracks and traps and bogs and furze and no flying fences, she could keep up with people's long-striding hunters rather well.

There was a rail to jump and Miss Haunchley said, "Lead the way, little boy," and Tanga unfussily nipped over it, and they seemed to be quite up with hounds and as they came out at the top of the sand-pits, with a view, Bevis saw Papa and Fontley fling themselves out of the saddle. Frank Fontley waded in and they fought him for the fox and then he was, over the baying heads, holding Reynard up by the scruff of the back: mask and brush hung dead to either side.

George blew for the kill. He looked around.

"Come here, Bevis!"

Bevis jumped off and led Tanga towards the throng.

George had the brush in his hand. Bevis's blazing eyes were suddenly solemn. George touched first one of his boy's cheeks, then the other; and said, "How old are you, sir?"

Bevis felt a wet wateriness on his cheeks and said, "Seven and three-quarters, Papa." His face was hot. Miss Haunchley cried, "Well done, well done!"; and so did pretty Mrs Egmont, and Mr Gervase Sturt came and held out a hand to be shaken.

Hounds had broken up their fox.

It began to rain.

Dorothy, passing through the hall at the Grange, tapped the glass of the barometer. "You're too close, you'll roast," she said to the spaniel; "you'll spoil your nose."

They got on their horses and George thought, the child ought to start for home. But there was no one in whose company he could go. All in the party now were to stay until the end.

There was that warm sense of a "shared thing".

George drew the scrub towards the sea and the banks of the withy bed behind the Crown Inn. However, hounds did no more; and he did in due course call it a day.

"Good night, Master."

"Good night," they said to each other.

The boy, his brush borne on his saddle proudly and his cheeks glorious for all to see, jogged in a dream the miles home with them. Also with Parson Cornforth and Gervase Sturt; Mr Shapgut until Lackham Cross; Mrs Egmont to the fork at Folly Ash.

The kind protectress had said "good night" and turned off near Duncterbury.

He was beat. Somehow he sat up. He'd heard a wren, scolding in a brimble bush, later he heard the caw-caw in the rookery and watched the rooks flapping off the trees, alighting and squabbling.

The rain fell steadily; it stained the bark, dripped from branches, made lank the faded last leaves; and he was chilled.

When they'd passed the terrier man, Brian had prodded the seat; Tanga could be tied on behind the dogcart, or Colin'd lead him; but Bevis had summoned a grin.

When they met Clarence at last, then Bevis couldn't contain himself. Clarence clattered towards them on the roan cob, Mother Goose; duty bound to retrieve Bevis from, had thought the groom, wherever er were to.

"Clarence," he shrieked.

"I say, Clarence, I've been b. . .blooded!"

II IN THE VALLEY BELOW

19 A fellow is terribly fortunate

"A fellow is terribly fortunate," said George, "to live in a place he loves."

Ida leant forward.

"Darling," said George, "you'll have to leave it, won't you, and all that, marry away, grow attached elsewhere, you'll never quite forget, you know."

"I know," said Ida.

One is, thought George often, or one was, brought up here, one buried one's nose in it when released each term from banishment to school ... jolly old Esmond ... and it sits, somehow, in one's heart, always, breathed deep ...

"Esmond," said George to Ida.

"Sent for."

"They're fetching him home, then!" said George. "Good heavens."

"Yes," said Ida.

Every moment at Quarr, palpable pleasure.

Stuff gets taller, thought George, or withers, or falls, or is felled; and by the time one's grown up the place is transformed; yet it isn't; it is and it isn't. For it's been festooned with memories.

He cogitated over the word "festooned".

"Terribly fortunate, to love deeply one's place."

"I know," said Ida.

"You do?" asked George.

"Did you nod, Ida," he said.

She bowed her head.

"I don't want to be maudlin," he said, "but I do like your hair when it falls forward.

"Esmond," he said again; then, "Eclipse. Is somebody seeing to Eclipse?"

"I think so," said Ida.

"What d'you mean, you think so."

"Yes," said Ida miserably.

George pressed his cheek into the pillow and she saw his intent look.

"Get Slade to come up and tell me, will you. I'm not sure I remember exactly," he said. "The mare got on her legs?"

"Eclipse wasn't hurt," said Ida, "only winded."

"That's splendid," said George.

"Well then," he said.

Ida stared at the wall.

"Spit it out."

Ida hadn't intended to say a word.

"Ma had her destroyed," she uttered.

There was a long, stunned silence. To Ida's dismay George's lower lids swelled with tears.

"*What!*" he exclaimed.

"What on earth for," he said.

She saw his moustache twitch as though he were chewing. When he'd digested the implications and got that instant of grief battened down, he said, "That was rather extreme of your mother."

Poor Fontley knew the Master wouldn't have countenanced it. Not a soul could speak to Dorothy. Somebody ought to have spoken to her. A perfectly sound mare, the brown mare christened Eclipse after a steeplechaser the Master had once ridden, they all knew it was a rotten idea, to re-name a horse, it brought ill luck, yet if an animal arrived in the stables and you didn't care for what it'd been called it seemed an act of love when, after grave contemplation, you supplied it with a name of your choice.

They'd been aghast, at the Kennels; aghast.

"You've gone off in a dream, Ida," he said presently; "aren't you supposed to be entertaining the invalid!

"How many days have gone by?" he said. "Frank Fontley's hunting hounds, I trust."

"Three," she said. "Tomorrow will be a Wednesday."

"It will?

"I didn't realize," he said.

"I haven't the foggiest what's the matter with me," he said. "Have you?

"Altogether too precipitate of her," he pronounced in a very chagrined tone.

He dropped off to sleep and they drove Ida from the room.

When he woke Nurse was sitting there. "Hallo, Nursie," he remarked.

Thoughts revolved in his head. The cold snap which had followed Christmas was over. The snow heavy; had filled the lanes to the tops of the hedges; set in for weeks; bound to, that heavy.

Hard frost. No hunting. No hunting. Sudden thaw. Pools of wet. Lot of drip-dripping.

"Shush," said Nurse, "Mr George dear."

What is wrong with me, he wondered. Weak as a cat.

"Cats weak, grigs happy," he said. "Curious, that. Horses sick."

A full minute later he said, "Don't blame Ida."

20 The universal unease

No one tried harder to reach George than Mop. To each person who came through the hall she directed a stare, harsh and interrogative.

Her assaults – worn short her claws made the slightest tap – sounded like the twittering of birds, accompanied by the patter of her pads. Far away in an upper corridor somebody might scold her, a different somebody speak to her in tolerant sympathy. This ended in her being repulsed.

The other dogs took their mood from her, so there was a constant canine swirl that made Porlock mutter under his breath.

Mop was the daughter of the liver and white Tuffet who

was by Mr Egmont's fine dog Charles; and a half-sister to the keeper's Sylvan, known as Syl and, to the children, Silly; Hanham's having asked for one of Tuffet's by the young dog Swimmer. Mop had got her colouring from her sire: she'd passed on, in her first litter, the liver and white to three of six puppies.

Mr Egmont, of Rivers House at Nyland, was the spouse of Mrs. She was secretly attached to Sturt, although of this all were aware.

George liked the black and white in his springers. Tuffet was no more. He'd been quite as attached to her. The children when small had left dandelions on the dogs' graves but Bevis at four and five had laid fossils. These didn't droop and dry up. George hadn't commented. He rarely had cause to visit the graves. Ammonites and a shark's tooth by Tuffet's fresh headstone had met with his approval. He could recollect having been sentimental as a child himself.

A full sister of Mop, called Lupin, had gone at seven months to Cecily and adorned that female household; she even slept indoors; in the scullery, it was to be believed. Lupin had turned out to be gun-shy. Springers were unruly without any work but Cecily walked stoutly; and Agnes too.

Mop's piety, thought Dorothy, who wanted to ponder, strolling alone beyond the shrubbery, was all the more preposterous because it was belied by her exuberance once she and George were out of sight. No flat-coated retriever, no pointer she. It was a show, all that walking to heel and model comportment. Yet no dog could serve him better whether he went down the hedgerows or round the brimble bushes with a gun and she flushed out the bunnies or there was a grand shoot and duck to be swum after or pheasant to be retrieved. Dorothy recalled some of Mop's naughtier exploits and managed to laugh.

Dorothy had a wish to ride; as in all situations which told on the nerves. Baby had put a brake on that. Her delight in horses was not, she believed, of the order of George's: hers was more moderate, yet spoke volumes. And it was as though people doubted it!

Hers had been a glad spirit. The unusual whites and pale colours throughout the house demonstrated it.

She thought of the mystified sentinel in the hall more agreeably occupied, nose to ground, following the tracery of scent over the white frosted lawn where a cock pheasant had stalked, its line crossed by a fox which had come up close to the house at dawn, and wood pigeon, and then the cats . . . Mop left long, silvery streaks in the dew of summer. Or of Mop, in need of George, putting her nose down to find him; how, engrossed, she'd run by the very man she was after, until she fetched up on his scent in front of him, with a paw on his boot.

Game and only game riveted her; with fox, badger, treated to convulsive sniffs; squirrel or cat of but idle interest.

Unheard of though it might be for George to accompany them to the stables before luncheon on Sunday, how very peculiar it was, thought Dorothy, for the children to be handing out carrots, lump sugar and stale bread to the horses while Papa, back at the house, ailed.

The corners of her mouth drooped; and were scooped up by muscles in her cheeks and pinned to the molars within. It was an expression that on some faces seemed peevish and on hers was glum. This made her look girlish. Nobody was there to mark it, however.

They were congregating at Quarr and Mrs Cockerell wished to consult the mistress and the mistress couldn't be found; not in the drawing-room, not nursing Baby, not with the master; and Mr Rupert, there since last night, had elected himself to potter in Quick-As-Can-Be to the railway station for Esmond, so neither Corbin, occasional chauffeur when spared, nor Clarence in his blue coat should be sent. Esmond, alighting later from the 3.09 p.m. at Holtworthy Halt, was to be alarmed; for Rupert's eyes, usually so merry, were grave, his hand awkward.

The whole countryside was under a pall.

There wasn't a soul when they crunched through the village who didn't fall silent, and not an indulgent grin which wasn't smothered. In Plash the affairs of the Grange were felt keenly. In the village they weren't awkward. Far from it. Mishaps and loss, thought Dorothy, in a dazed, resentful way, are bread and butter to these folk. Esmond saw only friends, concern written over their faces, to reassure him, with the simple country nod.

Uncle Rupert didn't smile at anyone, even mechanically. It was left to Esmond.

Of an evening, at the Tom Thumb, in the oak-wainscoted tap, front room of a thatched cottage, Frank Fontley, Oswald Beer, Collie Payne, Clarence, Corbin, the keeper Dick Hanham with his favourite Syl, Coker head groom Brown and his cousin Brian the terrier man, these met and mulled it over; while Shepherd Grace and his crony, old man Blackmore's second son Bill, sat mute and the cobwebs in their cider revolved in their tankards. Bill Blackmore had seen his sixty-eighth birthday backalong; so the old fellow, Tom Blackmore, he of the white beard and whiskers, must have been a good age.

Dorothy, before Esmond arrived, and standing on the threshold, looked across at George.

He managed to lift his head from the pillow. A puzzled frown decorated his beloved face; somewhat quizzical. There was strain in his eyes.

A distant creak sounded: feet on the back stairs.

She moved closer. Between them – Titball had risen on her opening the door – they raised his shoulders and she puffed up his pillows.

"I'll stay with the master, you may have a break."

To George, she said, "It's Dorothy."

"For pity's sake," said George. "I recognize you."

She laughed.

"Gloom at the Kennels, I dare say.

"Have you been down to the Kennels, Dippy? I'd like to see Fontley. Send a message, will you.

"Don't be foolish," he said, "will you, and fend off people I should be seeing. In fact . . ."

"What!" she asked.

"He could bring dear old Rhapsody, I'd like that; and Argot and Striver. I bet they'll make a fuss of me," he said.

"Tell Fontley," he said.

She smoothed a wisp of hair away from her brow and sleeked it with her ring finger to a hair-pin, a light poke tucked it beneath other strands.

On receiving this command the kennel-huntsman was to feel, as though its implications were of the most dire, for a second quite stricken.

Frank Fontley wasn't at his wits' end, he wasn't het up; he'd a lot on his mind. He didn't have much patience with they that made worrits for theirselves; but in the Tom Thumb he didn't stop and he didn't saunter in the lane neither. He passed the time of day with folk, courteous. That was all.

Fontley disremembered a day when hounds hadn't been able to sense some ill come to the Master. He wanted to disabuse them of any such idea, but honesty forbade it. It was funny, for Master didn't live on top of them, he lived up at the Grange; he might go up to town in the summer; during the season he might have other business on hand; nor did he visit Kennels on hunting days the other side of the country. Hounds knew him for the man who treated them to exquisite delight, who found foxes for them; they were his, and in their hound-ish brains and hound-ish hearts they carried each and every one a torch for him.

21 Strange communion

Titball couldn't relieve his feelings because he'd taken the pledge. That was the consensus of opinion. But he was a likeable fellow, very devoted; and he was popular in the servants' hall. Fond of the children, he unbent towards them in an almost frivolous manner, though it was no part of his duty to be bothered at all.

Esmond, rather shattered by his first sight of Papa in a bed, had been told to make Titball go for a walk.

Swallowing, Esmond had said, "How can I do that?"

George didn't say "don't ask how, but do it". His fingers twitched.

They sounded thunderous on the linen sheet.

"Master Esmond," said Titball, "be so kind as to say to the master that Titball will go outside for a minute or two."

"Don't return for an hour," said Papa. "Tow him along, Esmond."

"It'll be dark, Papa," said Esmond.

George stared at him, without a blink. "Need that stop you?" George said in a gentle voice that brooked no argument.

Titball went to find Nurse – the Infant entrusted to the nursemaid – to take his place; and to his quarters for his hat and coat. There he decided to be more suitable for the park, and changed into trousers of thick twill; and added a muffler to his Harris tweed, a cap and natty calf gloves.

Master Esmond, in the back premises to collect the poor man, had full measure of the sepulchral silence.

Together they passed the end of the yew hedge and, of one mind, heading for the bridge which carried them over the ha-ha, right through the home meadow and onto the track downhill to the decoy pond.

Titball took out his cigarette case. The moon had risen. They rounded the bend.

"They fetched you from school, then," remarked Titball.

"Were you up all last night?" asked Esmond.

"I was," said Titball, and sighed; "mostly, you might say."

"Ida thinks . . ." said Esmond, "Ida thinks . . ."

"We all think," said Titball.

"I see," said Esmond.

Titball tripped forward blindly. On any other occasion he would have said, "I hope you can see, Master E., where we're going." Instead he drew hard on his exotic cigarette. The stables and garden favoured a pipe, Porlock appreciated a nice cigar and Pinkie bought packets of Players. Titball, Somerset-born so a foreigner, had a silver and mother-of-pearl case, and in his case were the Turkish cigarettes of a gentleman. Titball had style.

He would have died rather than smoke in the street; but

unobserved on a private estate he permitted himself this lapse in his conduct.

Titball and Esmond had been walking for some while. The gloom, where the larch-trees were tall, had outgrown their might and were crashing one or two every winter to lie cocked up on each other, perilous until sawn into lengths and taken away, that was behind; and the ruts, sullen with the cold, knocked Esmond's boots and made Titball teeter.

There was no scent now from the bog myrtle, which in hot months enticed you over the rough ground, all rust-coloured channels and tufts, reedy and heathery. Although it was only six o'clock, the night air slapped them around the face and night cries could be heard. They stumped on. The track rose to meet them; somebody had done some filling in and the rubble was bruisingly bumpy. Titball took out his watch. He tried to divine what it said.

As one in a dream, he saw himself reach the little jetty, climb into the boat and be rowed by the boy out onto the decoy pond, he saw himself helped by Esmond to clamber into the hide right out in the middle of the water, he saw himself all of a shiver; and the two of them, sitting in the hide, didn't, he saw, speak. He'd listened to the creak of the oars. He'd obeyed the boatman's orders. Helpless, he'd done what he was told, though perfectly capable. Infantile paralysis might have afflicted him, for all he'd lifted a hand in the matter. And he saw they sat, cramped in the hide, with their legs and feet well below the water level, uncannily dry, and their fingers shut between their knees for warmth; and how they peered forth, at the opaque sheen.

They must have done that once, for how else could Titball, the master's man, know what the hide was like?

Instead, they were already legging it up the rise and back towards the house; their eyes strained to pierce the shadow, their breath came quick and chilled.

"You run on then, Esmond," said Titball, "Mr Porlock's opened the front door to someone come."

22 A clouded spirit

Gregory, with the surname of Pink, was known as Pinkie: the master, the mistress, the family, the household, all, even his lady-love, called him Pinkie.

He and Mr Porlock were on the go, because people were staying; and others visited throughout the day, the doctor twice for instance; most of them to leave cards. There was soon an Acting-Master to be appointed, no doubt. Joint Acting-Masters probably, Mr Gervase Sturt and A.N. Other Esq. Mr Rupert Lupus, Mr Porlock thought. Mr Rupert had a place in the Quarr country, Enmoor, over by Fawernbridge.

Pinkie had been in service since the age of fifteen and made a splendid footman, he was six foot one and decorative in a very manly way. But he could and did blush, to his mortification, and he was chaffed no end; few hid their amusement.

For once Pinkie was having a rest from his rôle as a butt. None looked at him much.

In truth, the appointment of an Acting-Master or of Acting-Masters hadn't even been mooted. It was a rumour that had flown around. Frank Fontley had readied himself to meet at Okecombe on that Wednesday, but the frost, which had let up so briefly, so disastrously, now forbade it.

Mr Rupert was joined by gay, pretty Mrs Rupert, who'd been in Perthshire. Mr Martin in Lahore had been telegraphed; and, with less hope of success though this was prejudice, Mr Oliver in Mesopotamia. Mrs Martin could be presumed to be passing, in a cabin on the port side, through the Red Sea; she might be caught at Aden but a duplicate message went on ahead to Kurrachee. Mr Oliver was unwed. Mrs Chieveley, Miss Nesta that was, hers had been sent to Alexandria for, soon after Omdurman, Chieveley had been seconded from the Colonial Service to administer the Sudan in Khartoum; and Mrs Chootham's (Miss Laura, married four years ago), to Trincomalee. Young Master Chieveley, well, it had so far not been thought imperative to summon him from Rugby.

Mr Archie, the Colonel, had been at home. He couldn't hunt, though maybe he hadn't the heart to any more, for his gammy leg put paid to all but the gentlest hack around the estate. He'd had a spent spear – or something – in his guts, too; lucky it hadn't penetrated much. A woman's sweetness might have brought him out of hisself, but Mr Archie had a clouded spirit. He'd been a proud, upstanding man. They said he had a wound which never would heal; that it was worse than having your leg blown off. They said that Archie as a boy had never been one to let an ache or a pain get the upper hand; and that, seasoned campaigner and a Lieutenant-Colonel in our brave regiment, he'd witnessed dreadful scenes.

Since the Colonel had been fighting the Boers, and the Boers didn't go in for spears, Pinkie had got it a trifle garbled: Mrs Cockerell slapped her palm on the table in derision when he repeated for the umpteenth time that about the spear in the innards, a daft girt dumpling he were. Pinkie went scarlet.

Dorothy knew it was to Rupert she must turn. Archie proved a broken reed if you were foolish enough to depend on him. He issued promises and offers of help, generously, out of instinct, without any inner resource. Archie cut a sad figure.

George, however, refused to see it. George thought Archie convalescent. They were the nearest in age. Of the children, Griselda alone held solemn chats with the latter. He avoided all children. He couldn't stand Morwenna. The arrival of cousins sent him to the gun-room or to his den. As for Inkpen, she felt he was positively morose. Nurse kept her own counsel.

Archie was foul to Gypsy Jem; and that was inexcusable.

He had an idiosyncrasy, which might have been thought to make him irresistible: despite his not speaking to people he could be heard talking to himself. Whisper, whisper, whisper, went Archie. And if you listened, it proved awfully funny. Yet no one did. If you heard the whisper-whisper, mutter-mutter, approach you along the path from the stables or in the garden or between the trees, you turned aside.

The Rector had prayed for Archie in church when Archie was in South Africa; and had, or so Bevis assumed, given up a lost cause.

23 Misty, a pastoral visit

Bevis was the easiest visitor the invalid had. "'Morning, Bee," said George, feebly. "'Morning, Papa," said Bevis, tipped his soldiers out on the floor and became absorbed in a skirmish. When he was grown up he was going into the Regiment. They hit the rug with lead thumps and raps but thereafter were treated to tenderness. No anomaly in this occurred to Bevis.

The most difficult was Cornforth. He didn't seem to know whether he'd come to talk of sport or of Our Lord.

Encountering Mrs Lupus in the hall he'd clasp her slender fingers in all of his.

Cornforth was with George when there came an unholy noise on the oaken, back stairs, a mewing, throaty, scrabbling noise, and somebody's boots, the boots of somebody who was self-conscious at finding himself in the house at all. Titball, who'd withdrawn, reappeared, his eyes pregnant, a tremulous smile on his lips.

Then Cornforth said, unaccountably for a clergyman, "Upon my soul, by *Jove*," for he was to see a sight he would remember until the end of his days.

Fontley, having already fetched up that famous sire of Quarr hounds, Argot, together with Striver, who stationed himself always to trot home at night by the Master's near stirrup, and the good bitch Rhapsody, had had orders to return on the morrow.

Cornforth heard a little, sweet peep of the horn; and half rose to his feet. He stretched a hand, far from white, over the counterpane which was folded with the sheet beneath the

Master's chin; stretched out as though to protect George from the onslaught he, Cornforth, feared.

Titball opened the door, ushering in not a duchess but a foxhound. Her stern waving, a look of delight on her face, Roguish led them, nose up, bright gaze fixed on the figure in bed. "George, my dear fellow!" uttered old man Cornforth. "Titball, your master cannot . . ." his voice tailed away, he perceived that he must yield to . . . however many couple? Yield to the pack. Fontley and so many old favourites.

He thought they would overwhelm Master.

"Good morning, Frank!" the Master said.

Fontley's watered-down hair and, beneath the long kennel-coat, exhilarated demeanour were of the mere moment for he was sorely grieved. A hand, closed over the brim of the dun bowler he'd forgot to leave below-stairs, shook.

In they milled, and poured even across and over the bed, stood on hind legs and stared at George, drooled and mewed, an adoring, vibrant throng; those in their prime, Harpist, Arcady and Adamant, Harebell, Rufus, Velvet and Tragic, Snowmaid – "Snowmaid," said George, whereupon she pressed closer – and puppy-show prize-winner Ardent; Rakish; dowagers Echo, Romany, Rarity and Tireless, the renowned Trojan; Prussian, Rasper, Hostile; and, not the least of them, Satirist. Ten and a half couple and Misty, aged, half blind, pensioned off and collected from her cushions by Mrs Slade's range. "Misty," said George, "Misty."

It could only have been a second or two; though for Cornforth it was an eternity. He'd caught his breath and his old chest didn't seem big enough and he choked.

A word now from Fontley and they'd stilled theirselves, quieted; sat on their haunches, a good few, tongues a-lolling; looking about, expectant.

Only Snowmaid was jumped up with her tan hind-pads on the Isfahan rug and her elbows creasing the sheet, her face but three inches from George's. He held her there, transfixed, held her with his mind alone; there and no farther.

Don't you slaver over me! his mind said; and Snowmaid knew.

George was so frail.

Cornforth felt a tear from his rheumy eye trickle along a furrow of his cheek and arrive in his whiskers.

He'd seen something amazing.

24 His normal state

Mop's jealousy was poignant to observe. She knew that a great injustice had been served on her. If she could have realized that George hadn't even whispered her name, she'd have suffered enormous chagrin.

Since hounds had stormed the breach it didn't seem worth anybody's while to stop her so George, waking from a doze, discovered a cold nose on the back of his fingers and a faithful head. Mop was no exuberant foxhound. She at once understood she was in the presence of an invalid. She had to be quiet. She had to be stealthy. She had to watch her master, whom she'd come on asleep, and wait for a sign. She had not to slip or slide on the rugs. She had to make herself indispensable: it was her turn to issue comfort, not be importunate. She squeezed her chest as close to the bed as she could, but no over-bold paw sullied the whiteness of the counterpane. And if the slow, waking hand flexed, if the fingers were to reach out and stroke that faithful head, she would tremble, stertorous, but not stir. Her stump of tail wagged, with furious passion. That was all.

She was polite to Titball, conspiratorial you might say; humble with Dorothy and Nurse; and gracious in general.

So they didn't have the heart to exclude her again.

When it appeared plain for a day or two that George's phenomenal strength might pull him through and that Esmond could return to school, summoned too precipitately, several more individuals set their sights on an ascent of the main staircase at the Grange; and some, either because it was a soul who knew his place or for the sake of concealment, on a flitter up the way that Fontley went with the pack. Most wanted to shake his hand, pick up crumbs from the floor, store away in the memory the glimmer of a smile; and a very few to make their peace with him. Fewer still had a message to impart rather than receive.

George had to endure a succession of visits.

George, dreaming, had to be amiable when he felt only feeble.

He wasn't used such an existence. To while the time, and to force his mind to concentrate, he walked or rode in the park, then ranged over the whole estate and finally managed to take hounds to draw his favourite coverts. The ground shook under him, or squelched, or, out on the heath, bounded. The odd smell sprang suddenly to his nostrils; a rare delight, that; and one on which no imprecations had any effect; for it arrived when little anticipated.

He rode more briskly. Soon he would gain the open, galloping country. He felt better. As in life, his life, he was in a strange fashion ahead: there were close companions, there were followers, but he carried his head alone into whatever was to be met, the air around it was palpable, and he propelled with a ferocious detachment the outer rings of this air forward in gentle prods and shoves.

He was so very accustomed; and felt a gladness at recognizing his normal state.

George lay there and the fire danced and his eyes rested on that.

Griselda was considered too old to have broken into wild boo-hoos and until she could control herself was kept from alarming him afresh. Inkpen set her problems in the school-room at the blotched table. A person with a fluttery heart was of no use in a sick-room. She had to learn to be staunch. Inkpen found her a book, the heroine of which rose above the most lowering of circumstances and was rewarded by the retrieval of a lost, lone parent.

One should never give way to sentiment, sorrow, grief, anxiety or adversity. Never. No matter what.

It might be hard, but it was a lesson advisedly absorbed in childhood. Early childhood. It would stand one in good stead all one's life long.

"Don't keep on at me, Inkpen dear," said Griselda.

For life was without mercy to those who proved spineless.

"Yes," said Griselda.

"You're old enough, at eleven, to understand. Your papa will draw strength from his visitors provided they come to him full of fortitude."

"Please don't scold me," said Griselda.

"Otherwise you distress him."

"I do see," said Griselda.

"He will know how sorry you are to discover him like that."

"Oh," said Griselda. A small frown gathered.

"Naturally," said Miss Inkspindle, whose own heart indeed bled. "Unnecessary to tell him. Unspoken words are best."

"He speaks to Mop," said Griselda. "I heard him."

"Mop is a dog," said Inkpen. "Now ..."

Later Inkpen said, "You children should go out for a nice ride."

Slade had thought Esmond would have been all of an itch to get his leg across Little John, but Esmond stumped about by himself and had to be coaxed into exercising his own pony. A bit of shooting was more what Esmond was inclined towards. Or he'd hang around indoors.

A fall of snow (without a hard frost) on the Thursday bestowed upon Ida and Griselda the gift of a larky (an improvident) sort of canter, which would do much to restore them and put colour into their cheeks. Grenadier and Old Haunts, their hoofs greased against balling, swept down the Ladderback. At Orchard House, Mrs Barge spotted them in the distance; and put her hand to her mouth.

In the wastes of the east drive Mahon, oblivious, black bag on the seat beside him, sent on his dun cob Nobby at a reckless trot. But Nobby's shoes had been provided with caulk. Since it wasn't that icy, the doctor had forgotten the pangs of a desire for a motor.

Keeper Hanham, in the lee of Quarr Wood, where he had a grisly larder, saw them. He stood among his carcasses, those skeletons of empty eye sockets and feathers without sheen, magpies and stoats and buzzards, and made several hum-hum noises, for he was given to much clearing of the throat; and, if truth be told, his heart bled too.

25 Through the snow

"Good Lord, your ticker's easier!" the doctor had said.

"Tell me, Mahon," had said George, "what in the world happened to me?"

"Nobody knew!" was the reply. "Your brown mare fell. Maybe you'd felt it and hadn't held her up after she'd rapped that damn timber, which we know she made a muck at; wasn't clever, let's say, there; or you were stricken after she came to grief, in consequence; or by sheer coincidence. A strange thing, what! Bolt from the blue. Or you'd got it before and you *brought* her down somehow.

"Not like you not to sit tight."

"Horse not to blame," said George.

"Horse not to blame," said the doctor, "no, not really."

He forbore to add, You were borne in (to Ellsworth's scullery!) on a hurdle, black ribbon for your Queen half torn from your sleeve.

Remarking Lupus's baffled expression, Mahon had said, "In short, a *coronary*."

George was left to ruminate. Titball hovered; but his master wasn't aware of his presence.

He fancied four of his children stood there, hand in hand, and stared at him rather mournfully; and that Dorothy was that statue with the fingers of its right hand on the top bar of the tapestry-seated chair which was in fact the commode Titball had provided. A commode as yet ungained.

"Baby," he said aloud, "should have brought Baby with her."

"Sir," responded Titball, "you try to sleep. Sleep," said Titball, "is restorative."

"I dare say," said George. He moved steadily along the ride. It was covered by snow. He looked down at the slot of deer and a shower of black droppings. A scuffled smear of earth dirtied the pristine floor of the wood. Cusps of snowflakes hung from the twigs and fell with little plops. The tenderer twigs were dipped by the weight. A dim pool now shone through the tangle of alder. Birds and animals had marked its surface with an array of prints. He heard a blackbird. And then he heard a woodcock. Then he understood that he'd come out alone for some reason, no hounds, no, nor a rush of spaniel fervour, no Hanham, no Rupert with a gun on his arm. No footsteps. No cracking noises in the ice. Hoofs. The sound of a horse. The tiny kick the snow made before shod feet. Saracen, it was his old Roman-nosed Saracen. The pricked ears twitched and flickered.

He whistled.

He felt for his horn between the buttons of his coat; and at his saddle for the horn-case. No horn. Afar off, a dead branch snapped, as though trodden upon. George thought a body was hurtling in his direction. He whistled again, hopefully.

Saracen put a foot in what must have been a rut and stumbled. Hold up, said George.

Presently, Saracen shied: he snorted. George cast in that moment a keen eye to the thicket.

His spaniel Mop burst out; and on her heels, Rabbit; with Archie's sad dog Pantagruel, the black and tan terrier from the lodge, two of his brother Rupert's setters, and Sylvan, four dachshunds and an unknown brindle lurcher. Of this excited gaggle, the spaniels, the English setters and the bloodhound stormed his horse to fawn.

By the lower gate George saw Hanham's predecessor, Grampy's head keeper, a fellow by the name of Orange, a corruption, it was assumed, of Horrings, or Horringe, who now touched his cap and beamed a bashful, toothless smile.

Good morning, Herbie, said George, are you keeping well?

Ah, said Orange.

And Mrs Orange too, I trust!

The missus be, ah.

George said, I'm jolly glad to hear that.

Obliged to 'ee, sir, said Orange. And grey Saracen jiggled along at a jog.

"You dogs!" interjected Titball in an indulgent tone of voice.

George thought, I ought to be getting out of bed. "I'll sit out in m'dressing-gown, Titball," he said.

I ought to be fitter soon, George thought, or said. I'll do better. Not so much of this dreamy . . . this dreaminess. I'll walk, or ride, carry a gun, hunt, I'll take a peek over at the farm, visit all our favourite corners; not like *that*, suddenly awake to the fact that Saracen, old Saracen, dead, is in my mind, bears me down the ride to the lower gate, through *snow*, hoofs muffled in the snow, the white snow, he thought, or whitish, stained by all the birds and animals of my life . . .

And I must speak to the children, to each of them. I must say to them words they may remember all their days, don't you know. "Titball!"

"I know, sir," said Titball.

Dorothy, alone in her bedroom, placed thumb and forefinger to her lips, pressed them together; and pitched onto the silk of the eiderdown.

26 The philanderer

Dorothy sped Titball on his way to lie down for a couple of hours while she sat with the master. She was even brought Baby and from the nursery the nursing chair. So she turned her back to George, loosened her blouse and nursed the infant.

Pinkie could have told his mistress a thing or two.

To the distraction of his mother and tut-tuts of his well-wishers he was, it was well known, not walking out with a sweetheart. On his monthly day off the sparkle, it was fancied, danced in the eye of his lady-love for he walked instead to Fawernbridge, all of three and a half hour.

To be flaunted abroad, under the nose of her neighbours, by a grasswidow was the kind of gig Pinkie did relish. Edwina was the wife of a sergeant, Claudie May, in the 7th Lancers; at present fighting the Boer in South Africa. Pinkie was young for his age and dispensed with qualms.

About his business on a rare and blissful afternoon, in other words slipping round to Edwina's, Pinkie had been pulled up short by the sight of the master.

Edwina lived in a street of quite genteel folk. Four houses down was inhabited by Mrs Whatley, who worked at the drapers' by the Cornmarket. Mrs Whatley's eldest son Wilfred had been apprenticed to a joiner and now had a nice line of his own in pews; the second son was in Penang; the third son, Alan, was a clerk at Studman, Saunders and Nash; the fourth son, Digby, was on the flat a jockey of some renown; the fifth son was on for Farmer Dyce over Lackham way, not far from Quarr. That left Gertie.

Mrs Whatley, a forceful woman, had had to provide for her brood since Art Whatley had perished in the mill machinery. So six days out of the seven she wasn't in.

George wasn't a man to stroll. Pinkie marked how George had fair *idled* on the pavement, an impish smile on his lips and his cane drawn up under his arm; an' if it hadn't 'a bin, thought Pinkie, 'twould 'a bin twirling. George passed Edwina's house; and went on as to the town bridge. Pinkie might have thought no more of it. But out of the Whatley back door and round the side had skidded Gert, in a pretty hat, hurrying a little; and then, when caught up to a few paces behind the master, she'd followed him. And both had looked altogether too guileless to be true.

Pinkie's blush hotted his face. Unobserved, he'd stared, until he'd recollected himself. Not so as to spy, but he set off after. By and by he'd be ashamed of that. He'd been too agog to notice where his feet led him. He saw George, most debonair, stop, lean on the coping-stones and, as Miss Whatley drew level, offer his arm. You couldn't bargain on its not being a public spot. Many would step forward to greet Mr Lupus no matter where he went. Pinkie pursed his lips, did an about turn and hopped back to his Edwina's. In the servants' hall at dinner-time the next day he'd thought it right to keep his gob shut. He weren't, said Pinkie to hisself, one to give Mr George Lupus MFH away. Nor sweet-sixteen neither.

Gert had double the bulk of the fourteen-year-old Ida, if such a comparison wasn't invidious. She was a verdant armful, but not brazen. She wriggled and kicked; and was very free. George was in fact the first with whom she'd gone the whole hog. But she'd gone so far with the others it made little odds. She reminded him of a heifer calf, all thrusting lips and nudges.

The town bridge wasn't the usual rendezvous.

Twenty yards on beyond the north bank, off a corn-chandler's yard, Farmer Dyce rented some stabling and store-rooms. Over the warren of stalls a loft had been boarded, floor and rafters; but housed nobody. When there were horses – and often there were not – the carter slept at his ma's. The trap, up through which wooden stairs led, could be bolted from above. A stove below could be stoked to supplement their ardours. At the gable end a window gave onto an alley and that a hand would fling it open from time to time was not a thing to provoke remark.

His pursuit of Miss Gertie had provided Lupus with a degree of fun.

The brothers George and Rupert weren't half as legendary as old Mr Holkham or the elder Blackmore boy, Bill's son Albie, barely out of his prime.

In the know was Farmer Dyce; and had undertaken to be blind to it. Farmer Dyce had a pride in having Master's trust. Farmer Dyce's carter, Grev Whatley, was in ignorance; reckoned his sister still a maid. Gert didn't want to fall pregnant, otherwise she was aflame.

This had all fitted George's notions of discretion.

He was more than twice her age, of course; but ever so handsome, and he was manly. She'd served a twelvemonth of her apprenticeship to the two milliners of East Street, Mrs Bourne and Miss Bude, and begged to be released from it, thrown it in: who could say she couldn't concoct agreeable hats on her ownsome, she nourished dreams of patronage, that of his daughters, and suchlike. For his missus she had a jealous fury; and, because she was childish, disdain.

When the dire, dire news had reached Fawernbridge, that he was stricken, she'd come over dreadful.

Gert was shaping all her young life to be a calamity.

She'd wondered whether she could accost Gregory Pink, who was footman at the Grange, and fancy-man of that Edwina four doors on; supplicate he to get her in and up the stairs to see her old boy.

27 Dorothy tries to comfort Esmond

"Don't let her lick your face, darling," he said in a tone of some censure. "Think where a dog's tongue goes."

He tried to pull his hand back and it occurred to him that his hand was being held by a man's hand and that behind that hand, on the far end of its arm, was Archie, eyebrows and whiskers a-twitch, for Archie was as apprehensive as a rabbit and hadn't since the previous August let himself be shaved. George shut his eyes more tightly. Soon the other hand went.

He became aware of a face with hot breath and rolling eyes. "Why don't you go and find Esmond?" he said kindly. "Esmond," he pronounced. Mop went to the door, it was opened for her. "Very knowing dog, that," observed Titball. Mop descended to the hall, but a doubt got hold of her and she faltered. She looked around with a frown. Not minutes after, a scratch and a low whine saw the handle turn, and she'd had to be let in again.

Esmond was at that precise moment caught by Dorothy in the pinery. It wasn't that he wasn't allowed into the pinery: it was that he, at ten years old, ten last birthday and owner of his first gun, was being torn by sobs.

Ma's methods were meant to brace you, needless to say. First, she laughed. To Esmond's ears it was not a nice laugh.

Then she said acidly, "Oh dear, what is the matter! This," she said, "isn't what we expect. Is it!"

There was almost a silence.

"If I am not weeping," stated Dorothy, "why should you?"

Esmond's misery was replaced by a sense of impotence. He fumed.

Dorothy straightened her back.

"You don't want to grow up to be like Uncle Archie," she said. She left another swollen silence. "You'll have to be careful, won't you, otherwise you'll grow to be exactly like him."

The wet on Esmond's cheek dried and the skin shrank as though his tears had been glue.

He cast a resentful glance at his mother from beneath his brows. He didn't speak.

She stood there.

Seldom adroit at handling children, Dorothy sighed. "You do resemble Archie so," she said. And laughed that hateful laugh.

He went stiff as a fox and waited. He wasn't going to run to Nursie or Slade or Inkpen. He knew suddenly she was at a loss and that she couldn't touch him. He felt cold towards her.

"Really, Esmond!" she said.

Her footsteps took her out of the pinery and were lost.

All the same, a pity Mop had forgotten the boy in the hall; had he but known.

To George, Griselda, Nurse and Mrs Cockerell, it was folly to despise the Colonel. "He was brave once," pronounced Nurse. "Nobody comes to be a Colonel for nothing," bristled Mrs Cockerell. "He was decorated, damn it," said George.

"Are our horses starving in South Africa?" said Griselda.

"I fear so," said Archie.

"Being maltreated?" said Griselda.

"Yes."

"Maltreated as well as starved?"

"Probably."

"South African horses?"

"British horses too."

"Don't our fellows care?"

"Makes them very sick," said Archie.

"Tell me about enteric fever," said Griselda.

"I don't suppose there's much to tell. You feel ill. Rotten."

"Do you die?"

"You do die; and if you don't you do if not taken care of, and sent home."

"I expect you break out in boils. And carbuncles."

"No carbuncles," said Archie. "High temperature."

"Worse than influenza?"

"Yes, worse. You have the skitters. Grow weak."

"You must feel vile then."

"You do.

"Don't know much about it, though," he added.

"And why not?"

"Altogether too seedy."

Griselda said, "You have to enlighten me because I'm to be a doctor."

"How can you become a doctor!"

"You'll see," said Griselda.

"You won't require a profession," said Archie, "and in any case I don't think our family . . ."

"Doctor Mahon will take me on his rounds when I'm twelve, I've arranged it with him."

"You could make a start with your . . ." And Archie recollected himself.

Griselda said humbly, "I get distressed at the sight of him."

"Oh dear," said Archie; but it was a nice "oh dear".

"I too," he said.

"Mm," replied Griselda.

"I must be off."

"Very well," she said.

He slunk towards his den. She ran after him.

"Do people always have to be there when other people die?"

"D'you mind, Grizel," he said, "if I say that's enough."

"I shan't mind," she said.

28 Nurse distracted

News of our defeats in Black Week had come before Christmas in 1899. Archie, who had gone out with General Sir Redvers Buller in October to be wounded at Spion Kop, January 24th 1900, had fought on with the Tugela Ferryman (Buller) to relieve Ladysmith.

When, invalided home, he'd reached Quarr soon after Mafeking Day, broken, thin and appalled (that Plash men should have taken the horse out of the shafts and drawn him), the view had been marred by an upstart: Quick-As-Can-Be, standing on the carriage-sweep.

It could have accounted for his lack of enthusiasm for her.

When she'd first arrived there'd been some discussion as to whether you were accompanied by a groom or a footman. The groom could act as chauffeur or sit arms folded *next to you*; whilst a footman presented an odd appearance. She was, after all, to be "seen to" by the stables, in the coach-house! So long as no member of the family was to be conveyed, the footman could go on the seat behind. *However* ... To Pinkie's chagrin, for he loved to be asked to crank her and to be driven juddering down the country lanes, a liveried groom, in the event Corbin, won.

Quick-As-Can-Be was deficient as to springs and temperament: those captivated were matched by those that scoffed; and a multitude abominated her. Animals steady with steam engines had bolted or reared.

Every whip prayed he might be spared the joy of meeting her.

Quick-As-Can-Be was admired by the Quarr children and their cousins; and sometimes Gypsy Jem rode in her with Bevis. In June, on the afternoon of the church do, Corbin had driven the whole village, big and small, back and forth at a farthing apiece, in the Rectory Field.

Soon the Egmonts, always abreast, had exhibited theirs, attempting to induce mufflers to flutter and her veil to balloon, before the noses of the envious. Sawbridge-Walter couldn't abide the notion of new-fangled noises and stinks. Urnhurst alone hankered sorely. Archie hadn't vouchsafed an opinion. He was troubled by his system, his nerves, his unhealing wound.

Then at Coker they too were in possession of a *crack* specimen, with four cylinders, that outdid the rest.

When he strode through Plash now, in an unusual, sombre mood, to go to Fawernbridge, Pinkie was beset at that hour by enquiries, by commiserations, how was Master, on the mend, please God not ailing, not overly weak, how was Mr Lupus, how was Mr George going on; so he, Pinkie, doubted whether he should have taken his day off. Whether it was fitting.

Mr Porlock would be worn by the pulls on the bell at the door, the cards to be received on a salver, the morning visitors with whom only Mr Porlock had the experience to deal. Mr Porlock knew at a stroke which the mistress would want let in, which turned away, which permitted up the stairs. And those were but they at the front. Round the back, also, it was constant.

Pinkie was on the frozen path across from Plash to Lackham Parva when Griselda was telling Nurse, "You know, Nursie, you have to refrain from drinking the water unboiled."

"Why's that, my poppet?"

"Not you. One does have to."

"Which water would that be?"

"Water people have, well, done big in."

"I should hope so indeed."

"D'you have things on your mind, Nursie?"

"I do."

"A poor thirsty innocent swallows it, you see, and he goes down with it. The fever's in it."

"Why don't the Boer swallow it?" asked Bevis. "The Boer commando is a brave soldier, Uncle Archie does say!"

"It's the war that is miserable," Griselda explained to Nurse.

"Uncle Archie swallowed water with big in it," said Bevis: he waggled Baby's nose.

"The Boers are kinder to our horses than we are! Can you imagine!" said Griselda.

"Bevis, will you hush!" said Nurse.

"They let us water them at their supply!"

"They carry him off to isolation, if he's British. Or he'll go back to the water, and . . ."

"You watch your lip," said Flo, "Master Bee dear."

"Griselda, Bevis, out of my nursery, and will you take that Rabbit," said Nursie, "with you. Out!"

29 Only ignorance

Clarence, of a mind to divert them, said to Griselda, "I d'year as how Poacher Toady have got a fox bi thik wagon. Er doan treat un fair, or not according."

"I expect it's only ignorance," said Griselda. "We shall have to go and see!"

"Who be that?"

"You and I."

"My horrses to do," said Clarence.

"I'd rather not visit Toady Trenchard's on my own."

"Wher be Miss Ida to?"

"I shall deal with it," said Griselda, "I myself."

"Shall 'ee!" said Clarence. "You'm shapin' to be a right badgerer, Missie."

"You don't expect to tell me such a morsel of news and for me to say 'oh thank you Clarence is that so'!" said Griselda.

Clarence, some old how, kept his eyes solemn.

"I'll ask Slade if we may harness up David, we'll be glad of the dogcart; we don't have to drive, we can walk at his head."

"Whyfor the dogcart?" said Clarence.

"You believe I should take the goat and her carriage?" asked Griselda.

"Gawd," said Clarence. "Mean to bring un away, do 'ee!"

"What else?"

The upshot of this was that Griselda burst in on Papa with a request for a guinea.

The dogcart had returned empty, for Toady, who had the fox on a chain in a filthy condition beneath the axle (until, had said Toady, the "fur be fit to sell"), had mercenary ambitions. Toady Trenchard lived over on the Coker side of Plash in a gypsy wagon with lovely red and yellow paint and steps that went up to a sack for a door. Toady wanted a guinea for him.

Dorothy had hustled Griselda off and called for Nurse or Miss Inkspindle.

"Will you not wave your arms about!" Ma had said.

"I think it's a young fox, a last year's whelp," breathed Griselda. "I think he's weak and has to be looked after for a while. I think I should ask Slade for a loose box. I think . . . One can't leave him in Toady's hands.

"You don't *understand*. He'll be very unkind and then kill him for fur."

"Certainly I understand," said Dorothy icily. "You are unable to control yourself. I advised you to keep away from your father."

"Nobody has tipped me lately," wailed Griselda, "I have no more than half a crown."

"The place for a caught fox is on a chain," said Dorothy; "whether in the village or at Quarr."

"Papa has never kept a fox on a chain."

"One puts a fox on a chain. So he cannot chew through it!"

"You must recall," uttered Griselda, "Papa had that sandy vixen to set her broken leg, and tempted her back to health in the loose box next to Rajah's, whereupon she leapt the grille, hid from Slade and slipped away. Very clever it was."

"No," stated Dorothy. "Nor am I listening. Run along, please. I don't like children who argue."

"Can't you give her five shillings?" George presently said. "A crown suffices. Or tell Brian to rescue the fellow!"

Griselda, though, had borrowed two and six from Porlock, fourteen shillings from Mrs Cockerell and a florin from Esmond. With her own half-crown, it was a fortune. Toady Trenchard, though, had no more than a slight, crushed dent in the blown snow beneath his wagon and no chain in sight: Toady had scented trouble.

It was quite cruel.

30 Titball is faultless

George woke in the night to the sounds of a thaw. In the firelight he could see a figure was slumped in a chair. Titball. He could hear the rustle of drops and drips. The droplets collected themselves together to fall, pulsing and swelling until they could hang on no more. There was even the odd hiss from the grate: he wouldn't have credited it had his own ears not told him ice had crystallized high above on the rim of the chimney-pot.

Titball slept quietly, only his breath rose and fell. Nor did he slump in an extravagant fashion which might have caused irritation. Titball was faultless.

The fire needed to be made up rather. That didn't fret George. He'd been detached from such considerations all his life.

Nobody could be as meticulous as he in the details of hound and horse manage.

The temperature was going to go below for the night; and, though hoarfrost lingered in the hollows, the sky was a dry blue. The sun shone with chill austerity, and there was a frisk in the air. It was a sparkling day for scent. He shook up Eclipse and trotted on; her hoofs went thump-thud up the ancient grassy track sunken between ditches. He had in mind to draw the yew grove over by Cowfold; on Canmell Down; high above the hamlet of Trench. The turf had a drum-skin thrust to it. He loved the chalkland, full of barrows and iron-age camps: he bore its profusely gated roads with a grace. He saw a far glitter on the sea. He heard the creak and slather of leather, then the ring of shoe on stones.

He remembered and stopped. Not Eclipse.

Another with a mealy muzzle and a star.

After that hiccup he carried on, but less comfortably. Not Eclipse: The Tartar. It didn't bother him that she was in foal again, safe and warm rugged up in her stall, and had been retired unsound some years ago, was a successful brood mare, dam of the promising 1900 colt foal Modder River by the Coker stallion Martial.

Hounds, with sterns very gay, poured onto the open ground. The blackbird sang his winter song. Soppy flakes of snow wobbled out of the sky to brush the horseman's nose. Ah no . . . birds were muted in snow. If not, the blackbird chucks and flies off.

He discovered he couldn't keep his concentration from wavering. He was back at Quarr. Sweet-oil, he murmured, to that hurt. He heard the response: ah, I d'reckon.

It was Sirius. The hound, whom many called Serious, had . . . mm, he knew . . . limped out of Bagber Copse on three legs towards Brian; his skin ripped and mangled. Sprung by thik there Miss Haunchley from a poacher's gin, got off of her horrse, seed he were frantic bi the agony like, a-snapping at two gents, the lady d'gie un sommat 'tween the teeth quick, an' stept on the darn contraption. A mercy the bone baint broken. Right in a trice.

The sweet-oil we always employ.

How does a fellow, said George helplessly, reason with a time, his time on this earth, devoted to this single passion.

Not fighting for the Empire. Not in politics: no ambition there (odd for a Wykehamist!). As it happened, he'd been for Gladstone; and he detested Salisbury. Tepid vis-à-vis the Bench. Philanthropy paltry.

Pretty wizard offspring.

He felt his smile go awry; and then take heart, like the Cowfold sunshine, on the chalk, in the Friday country.

"It was what I had to do," he said aloud; and Titball jerked himself awake.

"Sir, what is it, sir?" he said.

George repeated with more care that it was what he'd had to do. But he was unconvinced.

Titball's timid fingers touched his cheek.

31 Sour milk

Before the Friday was by, nine persons not related and with no essential business such as Mahon's or Cornforth's had gone upstairs.

The successful had included Mr Gervase Sturt, old Lady Sturt, for Coker and Quarr had been close, also George's land agent Major Ramsey, known as Runner Ramsey, the bailiff Draycott, also Frank Fontley, also Slade; and excluded, nicely but firmly, Miss Haunchley with fiery mottled face, also the wife of the Lord Lieutenant, also, with disbelief, Mrs Barge, and not once but twice, which had caused remark.

George was not disconcerted that Jacky Draycott wept.

"Fortitude, Jack," he'd said. "Fortitude! I shall pull through, don't y'know."

Meanwhile Gert could hardly contain herself. She was so het up she had palpitations. She thought her bosom would burst. Unable to utter, for her mother had to be shut out of her confidence, she clapped eyes on gallant Gregory Pink with relief.

"'Morning," she said, when he appeared in the street.

Pinkie grinned broadly. He would whatever maid were to accost him.

"'Morning," he replied, and gave her a nod.

"Over from Quarr?" she asked.

"Ah," he said.

"Icy underfoot."

"Nought to hinder I," he said in the dialect he'd learnt to drop at will for proper speech.

"They d'have trouble, do um."

"Ah."

"Be in a pickle."

"Hm."

Gert smoothed her hair. Pinkie's gaze wandered to it and was brought back to her features which, it so struck him, were portentous with unspoken questions.

In town there'd been talk, his own love had telled him. He

stared at Gertie with perturbation. He made to dodge into Edwina's.

Too quick, Gert was. "Hang on," she said, "hang on." A choke.

"I mun *akst* 'ee sommat."

"Oh ah," he said doubtfully.

"Mr Lupus," she said, "be er bad?"

"Ah."

"Mortal bad?"

"Seemingly," he said.

"Thas terr'ble," she said.

"Ah."

"I disremember when I di' feel more of a tremble."

Pinkie frowned and twitched his lips from side to side, in a not unpleasant sort of way.

"On account of what! Acquainted wi my master, be 'ee?" he enquired.

"I be acquainted wi George Lupus, ah."

Pinkie reckoned that forward and he took on a stolid look. Gertie was stumped.

She drew a painful breath.

"See yere, Pinkie, they d'call 'ee Pinkie, doan um . . . *Wher be er to?* Up or down."

Pinkie responded, "Upstair. Laid down."

"Reckon I can skip up they stairs at Quarr, then?"

Pinkie was dumbfounded.

"Eh?" he said.

"What I d'say."

He shook his head blindly.

She clasped her fingers over his sleeve.

He went on shaking his head.

"Help I, will 'ee," she pleaded.

"Thas daft," he said.

"'Tis really daft."

"No 'tisn."

"Let go of I," said Pinkie, "*you.*"

Back at the house George was to sit out in a chair while Titball straightened the bed. He was making progress.

Gertie could talk prim and proper as well as Pinkie could;

but she'd perceived the country speech as friendly. It hadn't worked. She wrung her little hands.

Almost at once she hit on another idea. She'd visit her brother Greville who was on for Farmer Dyce over at Higher Slaughter, a mere couple of mile from Plash village near to Quarr.

She dropped the shovel and the besom and abandoned the dirty snow.

Instead of the warmth of labour a chill had crept upon Gert. She spent a few minutes by the range. She rubbed at her boots; and her fancy, which was lurid, galloped her through a fresh escapade, a betterment on the last.

George was in bed again before Cecily arrived with Agnes. They'd brought lapdog Lupin. Which was the greater penance, nobody was sure. Lapdog Lupin was too big for the liberties she was allowed. It saddened people when a gun dog became a fool. Agnes had taught her tricks; and that was common. The animal was fat; she waddled. She was fed on biscuit, sour milk and poultry-meat; and expected to gollop scraps out of hands lowered from the table. Dorothy was forced to draw Cecily aside and say, "I think your girl will have to be shut out when we're eating, dear."

32 The felicity of choice

Dorothy knew intuitively that George would like to be read to, that the man of action and the man of intellect faced some kind of internal collapse when confined to a sick-room. The choice of reading matter was a delicate one. The invalid mustn't be convulsed by laughter; yet he should be amused. The book couldn't be too abstruse, since he might lose the thread. For a person who dozed off from sentence to sentence a stirring yarn might be the answer. But she didn't want him to be dragged awake. Perhaps in the circumstances, for poor George had come close to death and, although there was hope now, his life hung in the balance, a Christian direction to his thoughts wouldn't have been inappropriate. Nurse had reported that Mrs Rupert, the frivolous Lydie, who was popular with George, had turned the pages of *Punch* and held up the cartoons under his nose. Nurse had seen it as charming and nonsensical. George, she'd said, had smiled anyhow. Dorothy had fingered a volume of Donne, rejected Dante in Italian, fallen on George Herbert and finally alighted on William Cowper, which was inspired of her.

Cowper went down well, it seemed. Porlock offered to step upstairs and read to the master items from *The Times* and, since Porlock had no duties in the master's room and adored him, Dorothy had the sense to let him. Porlock had agreeable tones and George signified appreciation. When the nursemaid, far too presumptuous, had penetrated, in Nurse's wake no doubt, this sanctum and, perceiving a lack, said she could bring her Bible, Dorothy had forestalled this. Dorothy couldn't imagine that anyone ever could want to listen to a perfectly uneducated voice.

Thinking about books soothed Dorothy. She didn't acknowledge the need. She was, and had to remain, in control; of herself, of the household, of this hoo-ha.

Cornforth said prayers to comfort and to point George's thoughts onto the right path; and all too soon got diverted onto the equally eternal subject of sport. That was not George's fault but Cornforth's. However, Dorothy saw that for neither of the two men was there any clear distinction. George Lupus had simple faith.

And, or so Mrs Lupus believed, Quintus Cornforth's was simpler.

With relief, she felt a smile stretch her cheeks.

She was displeased that her son Esmond, requested to enhance the sick-room with some violin music, should appear so aghast. Unaccompanied Bach, she'd proposed.

His father's love was for the pure and sublime, rather than the romantic admired by other Victorian gentlemen.

33 Aunt Lydie's race

Sometimes Aunt Lydie's frivolity led to grief. Because she was pretty and gay she got away with it, carried off the quite outrageous; not so her fellow pranksters.

Lydie saw the wan Quarr cheeks and heavy Quarr eyes and deemed them too tragic.

The thaw had made the going soft to squelchy when she persuaded Rupert, who chuckled, that he could race Quick-As-Can-Be against Esmond on Little John. Esmond was her particular favourite and, though his heart wasn't in it to begin with, he found it hard to resist such a sporting suggestion.

She invested it with the seriousness that underpinned all her fun. She organized a book; and herself took bets.

Titball was bold enough to place a bet. He backed Esmond to win. The other servants felt – for what would the mistress say – caution was the better part of valour and forbore to lay any money on at all. Mrs Lupus didn't know; but she would.

The odds shortened until you couldn't get better than six to four on, while poor Quick-As-Can-Be went out to three to one. "Lunatic," said Rupert, "sentiment. Once the motor's cruising what will a mere pony do against her! You put your thruppence on me, Bee, and trust Uncle Rupert."

Quick-As-Can-Be had doubtful form. She could stall. She was liable to put wheels in troughs; puncture her tires. It was true she did spin along when asked.

There was to be no handicapping! The course would hamper the pony here, the motor there; with delicious elements of the incalculable. Rupert and Esmond together agreed it; though Lydie and, respectfully, Slade entered observations. Reckoned to be two miles and three-quarters, with several tight turns, several stretches of straight, and permitting Quick-As-Can-Be the metal while Little John could gallop on the grass, it was about as fair as it could be.

Quick-As-Can-Be could have her engine running, and Esmond be mounted. Or Corbin would spring to work whilst Slade saddled and bridled Little John.

Esmond might hare off bareback, even neck-rein with a halter-rope, Rupert thought.

Quick-As-Can-Be could be in gear with Uncle Rupert but to engage it, Little John lined up beside her; snorting, sidling, since John tended to take exception to the motor.

Little John was spanking fresh.

Titball watched from the upstairs window. Slade stood, arms folded, out of sight of the house. Clarence openly grinned.

"Miss Ida, sir," stated Titball, "is the starter. Miss Ida holds the flag high. Now Corbin climbs into Quick-As-Can-Be and seats himself beside Mr Rupert. Little John is very full of himself, sir. Master Esmond sits beautifully still."

It was unforeseen but perhaps lucky that Parson Cornforth should have ridden up at that crucial moment and set up a cheer.

Ida called for a delay.

Titball stared down at him: Esmond, pale and unsmiling, didn't look up.

"There's a bit of conflab with the parson," said Titball. "I believe they're fending the old gentleman off from the line.

"Well I never, he must be desirous of ... now this is masterly of Miss Ida, sir, *he's* to be the starter, he has the flag in his fist, and ... *well!* this must mean a hitch, he has his timepiece out, you might say there's an argy ... he's pointing to the motor ...

"If you could *see* their faces, sir ... oh d...dear! ..."

"A snag?" enquired George.

"Master Esmond nods. He nods! Reins back. Bless me! The flag has fallen! Mr Rupert's away ... cock-a-hoop, if you'll pardon me ... struggles with Quick-As-Can-Be somewhat ... she's running smoothly, has opened up a lead of *yards* ... goodness, sir ... the off for Little John at last ... and Parson waves his hat in the air ... a great clamour, can you hear, sir, they're all a-cheering and our noisy dogs.

"Mr Esmond's in pursuit. May Mr Cornforth not have put a stick in our spokes! They're to head out ... via the park road ... out into the country. Oh my, the motor-carriage has hit a hazard, a rut or hole, ha ha! Mr Esmond leans low over the withers and slips beneath the branches of the Pooley Oak, he's gaining on Mr Rupert, the latter's still up at the corner, a sharp turn, that pony of Mr Esmond's can dance on a button, can he not, Mr Rupert near to tipping Corbin out, lost ground there, again has a fight with his levers and knobs, now Mr Rupert has the better going and Master Esmond not yet licketty-split, good boy, oh good boy, he won't take too much out of his John, it's wonderful to see, sir . . ."

George's eyes had lit up and a smile lingered.

"Mrs Foyle has put her best foot forward, I take it, she's all of a gasp, and that's her pinny she's waving!" said Titball.

The race had swerved to the left. There were bumps for Quick-As-Can-Be. Esmond rode as though he were out with hounds and had licence to clatter over flints and stones at an unconscious pace. He didn't hesitate. For Titball he was lost to view. Wild whoops and hollering announced his reappearance. Those below could hear in the distance Uncle Rupert's horn. Rupert had honked his horn not to scare off hens and ducks but to cause Little John to shy and bolt, bolt straight onto the greensward of the disused Griffin Gate drove where the course dictated a bend round three hayricks and a dodge into the Middle Go. Esmond looked over his shoulder. Poop, went Rupert then, so Corbin made his own gloved finger wet in his teeth. Esmond tickled John up with the stick and the pony, hitherto well within himself, found a new pace and galloped for home.

The motor had nothing in hand.

Titball's voice acquired the glow of hot coals, which entertained George rather.

Parson Cornforth stood in his stirrups. "Esmond!" went up the cry. "Esmond, Esmond!"

"Past the post, sir," sighed Titball. "Master Esmond's won! By lengths and lengths and lengths."

"Stout fellow," said George.

"I knew he'd do it," said Titball. "I have to call that a true thrill!"

George asked, "Is Mrs Lupus about?"

Titball caught the bland tone and plumped to earth; with the abrupt recollection of how Eclipse had been, *through Mrs*

Lupus, destroyed. He shook his head. "Ma'am has lain down, or so I understand, on the morning-room sofa," he said, "sir."

Surely the children could liven themselves, fitting or not with Papa so ill?

Corbin unblinkingly regarded the splattered mud on Quick-As-Can-Be's body. Little John's nostrils flared red, and his flanks heaved.

Esmond slid out of the saddle with, on his burnished, out-of-breath face, a cold and dreamy smile.

34 Gert storms the Grange

Although Gert had got her boots mired she fetched up at Higher Slaughter and did the pretty with Ma Dyce to such an effect that she found herself lodged for a pair of nights at the farm cottage where Grev had been took in, at the cowman's and his auntie Winnie Cox's.

Carl Cox and his aunt Winnie hadn't a five-year between them and, so as to help Ma Dyce out with putting up the men, made do with the one bed. Winnie said they turned their backs to sleep. They lived in a one up, one down; and Greville had the landing room; so Gert was made comfy on the settee in the kitchen, Winnie's not liking to mess up the front.

Winnie Cox opened her eyes wide and Gert thought she was simple.

It never so much as crossed Mrs Dyce's mind that she need speak to Dyce. They there were often in a bustle and she saw no call to mention the descent upon them of a gal to stop (before the article in question set off back to Fawernbridge) a night or two.

Farmer Dyce was brought up short by the spectacle of Master's dandle-dolly a-leaning of her arms on his cowman's wicket gate. If she'd come for to milk he wouldn't be agreeable, he thought; cruel though the want of workfolk nagged him.

Then more alarming a notion began to spread through his grey matter.

In his yard he had a couple of Quarr youngsters, for he was of the faithful number of puppy-walkers. He went to fondle them, crumpled their unrounded ears in his hoary palm; and was sarcastic with their boisterousness. No painful operation awaited them. The Master didn't go much on rounding ears. Quarr ears bided natural.

Gertie said to Winnie Cox that she had an errand.

Blissfully, the folk at Quarr Grange were pocketing their winnings. Griselda had put sixpence on Esmond when Aunt Lydie had (deluded) made Quick-as-Can-Be the early favourite and you could still get three to one against! Ida had got only evens. Rupert, it was learnt with much mirth, had backed himself in the motor and hedged his bets, with half a crown on Esmond as well. He ended tenpence down. Bevis, with the same idea and a penny on Esmond, twopence on Rupert, didn't recoup either. The book, though, had failed to make a killing! Then Dorothy emerged.

No one had foreseen quite how badly the story of the race would go down. So everybody was upset.

Ma Dyce had spotted Gertie's missing innocence. But the errand sounded true enough. Besides, Ma Dyce was busy. Mrs Bourne and Miss Bude might send their smart boxes out through Fawernbridge behind Horace and the cob and arrange more genteel travel to the farther afield: that they would pop in Gert's basket some mere trimming for Mrs Cockerell at Quarr and a pin of quivery cherries to old Mother Holkham at Lower Slaughter stood to reason.

To start for Quarr after dinner would have been folly.

So Gert leant on the wicket gate and wondered at her brother, who was, she mused, "that countrified". On Farmer Dyce was bestowed a nice nod.

She was fair dancing with haste and it dawned a damp sort of day. Mother Holkham thrust her on a chair and telled Lorna to fry an egg. Gert wasn't ungrateful. At Lower Slaughter they kept two indoor servants.

From Lower Slaughter to Plash she rode on the tail of Reg Slinger's cart; on a dry sack.

Since she'd not set foot hereabouts and was enamoured of a native inhabitant she drank in the lie of the land and the look of the village. An idle remark of Reg Slinger's gave her to think: was she Miss Whatley, fit to trip, with some presumption, along the avenue of chestnut-trees, or Gert, sent by Mrs Bourne and Miss Bude to see Mrs Cockerell, who should seek the lower drive. In her state of cocky palpitation she felt herself for the front.

Reg Slinger left her by the ford.

Reg Slinger was addled and his directions had led her wrong when, in what he'd said was Loose Lane, she rounded the bend and her eyes fell on a motor. A gentleman stood beside a wheel that had (she surmised) shuddered itself half off. "Blast!" the gentleman was saying, "blast"; but his voice stayed indulgent. The motor made a gobbling noise.

Gert didn't hold with motors.

Back at the Grange, Titball had painted his throat and was in an agony of dread lest he be afflicted by a cold while his master most needed him. It would slay him, to be deemed an unsuitable sick-nurse.

When the gentleman turned, Gert let out a gasp; for he bore the features of her beloved, watered down.

The eyes, after a moment, narrowed.

Gert, who'd come stock still, opened her mouth.

On the seats two dapply dogs reclined with straight forelegs and their chins propped on the side-upholstery.

"'Morning," said the gentleman.

Coyly she responded.

"Forgive me," drawled the gentleman, "if I mistake the matter, but could you be heading for Quarr, Miss!"

Gert was struck dumb.

"I believe you're Gertie? Fawernbridge Gertie."

She didn't understand.

"Gert Whatley?" said the gentleman.

He d'know I, flashed through her mind. "You know me," said Gert. She didn't "sir" him.

"I wouldn't do that if I were you," said the gentleman, stern-ish. "They're in trouble there. M'brother lies very ill."

There was silence. They stared at each other.

"Things in my basket for Mrs Cockerell," stammered Gert.

"Aha!" he said.

"How do you get to these parts?" he said.

"Visiting my brother Greville, I am," said Gert, "who's on for Farmer Dyce."

"I see," he said. He smiled charmingly.

"Don't think me unsympathetic," he said, and barked a short laugh, "but I suggest you get me to take the whatsits for Mrs Cockerell."

"I promised Mrs Bourne and Miss Bude," she said.

"Mrs Cockerell's an old friend of mine," he said.

"How is . . . how is . . . Mr . . . your brother," she said, "if I may ask, so to speak?"

Her child-like hand, he saw, clenched on her wicker handle.

"In bad shape, I regret."

Heartless! she thought.

"Colossal strength there, though."

Uhf-ha! she thought.

"Tremendous."

He cleared his throat. He gazed at her frankly. "M'brother wouldn't want you to go and make a to-do." He spoke in a softer manner: it was the voice he'd used to the motor.

"If there is more news by . . . well," he said, "you go home now, and I'll see you . . . hm, hear it."

She reminded him of a plump farmyard duck, beak up, anxious for a sop.

"You'd like me to deliver what to Mrs Cockerell?" He sounded to her ears too resolute. How to withstand him she had no notion.

Her hand, all of its ownsome, fetched out of her basket the parcel. Dully, she trusted Mrs Cockerell wouldn't thank Mrs Bourne or Miss Bude for it. Then she didn't much care.

The gentleman said, "There's a good gal. A shame Quick-As-Can-Be can't carry you to Higher Slaughter."

Gert bobbed an ironic curtsy and turned on her heel.

When he couldn't see her face, she began to pout; she drew lungfuls of breath; she stamped her boots into the road; she swung her basket over and over so the contents never dropped out. She'd refuse to be defeated, or so she did reckon.

When she was out of sight, she stopped for thought.

35 George says goodbye to Esmond

Titball whisked himself from the room when Esmond came midway through the morning. Since George knew Titball and Esmond to be the best of friends and Esmond's arrival not usually to precipitate such punctiliousness, he smiled a little.

"Not out then!" said George.

"No," said Esmond.

"Where were they meeting?"

"At the True Lovers' Knot."

George eyed the dark clothes and Eton collar.

"Fontley hunting hounds, is he?"

"Yes."

"Not much scent! Sisters out?"

Esmond said, "No, Papa."

"Too far to hack?"

"No, I don't think so," said Esmond.

"Better not to squander this middling weather."

"No, probably not," said Esmond.

"I hope not out of sentiment over the invalid?"

"Ma says," said Esmond dispassionately, "not all that suitable."

"Good Lord," said George.

Esmond rushed the next fence. "I return to school, sir," he said. "Being put on the two ten."

"Old chap," said George, "you can't hang around."

"I suppose not." Esmond added, "You knew."

"I did not," said George.

"Would you have liked me to have remained?"

"Quick-As-Can-Be?" asked George. "Or Josh Coachman?"

"Gig," replied Esmond, "and, I expect, Clarence."

"Can't always have what we want. Selfish," said George.

Esmond sighed.

"Quick-As-Can-Be isn't to be relied upon to get me to the train. 'She's a toy'!"

There was a painful silence.

"Esmond," said George. "If anything happens to me, look after your mama. Your sisters and brothers. Be brave and honourable! Love your country! Enjoy good sport."

"I will," said Esmond.

"Made Titball richer yesterday."

"He did say."

"Since Roland died, you've been the eldest boy."

"Yes."

"Shield Uncle Archie from uncharitable souls. And work for your Common Entrance, won't you."

"Yes," said Esmond, "but Doctor Mahon says *you're* remarkable and so I consider you'll be hunting hounds next season."

George's face was illuminated by a curious expression.

Esmond said, "Grizel's at the lodge to see Doctor Mahon reduce Norrie Foyle's goitre."

George started to laugh weakly.

"Doctor Mahon says he'll make an exception with patients on the estate, Papa. Otherwise she's too young." Esmond flushed.

"Don't keep too many secrets from your mother," George said.

Esmond shook his hand.

The flush died and a slow grin came.

"Goodbye then," said the invalid. He dragged air from his lungs.

Esmond's light step retreated.

When Titball was there George said to him, "Don't you say a word, but . . . pity, pity, eh. *Beastly* race. May never . . ." and Titball strained ". . . Esmond again . . .

"Collected your winnings, I hope?"

Titball wrestled with himself. It wasn't in any case his place to respond.

It wasn't until George had been helped from the chair back into bed and was lying there that his failure to speak to Esmond from the heart struck the invalid as quite dismal.

36 Lydie in disgrace

In this condition, George hadn't devoted a single minute to thoughts of Gertie. He'd forgotten her entirely.

Her boots were stout but Loose Lane was the image of its name; and nasty underfoot. She tugged her shawl round her and wriggled her cold toes. She would hoof it to the village and buy a bun. There she might become acquainted with a native.

George's next visitors were Cecily and Lupin, neither of whom he greeted with any fervour. Cecily droned and her dog was a nuisance.

"Do send her out," said George. "Can't she be company for the consort?"

"George, you're so droll," said Cecily.

"It's Agnes who is my companion," said Cecily, "not I hers."

"Indeed. Yet I stand corrected."

"You don't stand at all," said Cecily, "you are in no position to chaff me."

In the dressing-room Titball lipped at a pastille.

"I went through the Births, Deaths and Marriages before it was sent up to you and . . . nothing today, George. Nobody we know."

"What else of interest?"

"I don't believe . . . I make a point of . . ."

Titball eased the eucalyptus-soaked sugar, grain by grain, from the body of jelly.

"You could read me the Law Reports."

"Willingly," said Cecily.

Gert tripped down the village street, to which Strange's

shop lay gable-end on. The stone step was warped from the sharpening of knives. Gert bought a pie and a tiddly cottage loaf and was invited to rest her legs in a corner of the bakery. She let herself be led into the warm, passing a huge bloated dough in a cast-iron bath. She sat on some flour sacks. Her nostrils widened with pleasure.

Clement Strange was dusted in white from top to toe and his apron was still white as white although he'd been wrapped in it since four in the morning and was onto the afternoon batch. Ruth bawled at him, "The gal be weary." "Oh ah," he said. Ruth said plainly, "Father don't hear."

George's release from Cecily appeared in the form of Lydie.

"Hallo darling," said Lydie.

"Dear Lydie!" said George.

Cecily didn't rise.

They both turned their heads to look at her.

"I see what it is," said Cecily, "you'd like to me continue after luncheon."

George and Lydie exchanged tight little smiles.

When the door had closed Lydie said, "D'you know, ducky, there's something at Enmoor which begs my attention, will you keep yourself safe until I get back?"

"You're not going!" said George.

"I'll try not to be long."

"Rupert too?"

"No, Rupert is to stay at Quarr."

George's eyes quizzed her. "Why so sudden?" he said.

"You shouldn't have to fuss over my . . ."

"Your what?"

"Well, I'm not sure, I've been summoned back by Wirral. Silly boy, I dare say."

"Retire him," said George flippantly.

"He'd die of misery!"

She didn't speak. At last she said, "George, you have oodles of people dancing attendance, and you won't miss me."

"Oh but I shall," he said.

"Esmond," he said, "now you."

"Don't," she said, "make it difficult for me."

"Very well," he said.

"Fontley will be wounded if you don't have some days with hounds," he said.

She lowered a lavender-scented cheek to his face.

Gertie had perked up and decided to shift to the shop in order to engage Ruth Strange in carefully angled chat.

The upshot was that she was taken in tow by Ruth's cousin, Angela, who was the under-parlourmaid at Orchard House. It was but a step from there to Quarr. She, Gertie, was to assure Mrs Cockerell that though the parcel was lost another supply of hat bits would be forthcoming. Angela would point her right. You could make out the Grange from Captain Barge's place.

So Gertie trod up Loose Lane for a second time and caused Ruth's cousin Angela to forget herself and guffaw. And then Angela (far be it for her to betray another's confidence) muttered to her lady, when the figure of Gertie had waned small on the bottom Quarr drive, that there was a love-child of Mr Lupus's in the district, all of seventeen year of age, a rare bloom to her cheek, hot to cast her eyes on Father at the very last.

At which Mrs Barge, lady or not, goggled.

37 Gert storms the Grange

George found himself straining his ears for sounds of Esmond's departure. He was unrewarded. Lydie too, it seemed, went like a mouse. No egg-shell whisper of wheels on the carriage-sweep, no horses, no motor.

Ida and Griselda, doing French with Inkpen, tried not to feel crushed. Ida said in studied French to Inkpen, "To whom do our animals belong?"

"Dear me, is that a moral question?" asked Inkpen.

"Practical," said Ida.

Griselda stared, as if to fathom her drift.

"Is Old Haunts mine, truly mine, for instance?"

"What a queer notion!" said Inkpen.

"Is it?" said Ida.

"Your animals belong to your father," said Inkpen, "I should say."

"To Papa."

"Well, yes."

"Rabbit isn't Ida's . . ."

"He is!"

". . . but Papa's?"

Miss Inkspindle considered the matter more profoundly.

"While one might claim that your dogs are the property of you children, your equine dears are in the gift of your father, have been purchased by him, and are his to sell at will."

"Is that fair?" said Griselda.

Ida put out a hand.

"He feeds them, houses them, his people exercise them when you cannot. He mounts you, Ida, when you hunt more than three days in a fortnight."

"He feeds the dogs too," said Griselda.

"That is a quibble," said Inkpen.

Ida's hand on the table twitched.

"And Little John," said Ida, "does he not belong to Esmond?"

"To your father," said Inkpen.

"To m'father," said Ida, "and to nobody else!"

"To your father," said Inkpen.

"To nobody else," Ida said.

"I think we may say that with some confidence," said the governess.

By now Gert was ploughing along merrily and what should she spy on the crown of the track but a perambulator and a slender figure in starched uniform and cap, a nursemaid, a youthful one; and, although the vulcanite spat up a spray of wet, country-born.

Gert waved. She made out a smile on the nursemaid's face.

They approached one another with gestures of amiability, ready to pass the time of day.

Buried in the pram's finery was an infant so tiny Gert would have kept it indoors. She forbore to say so.

Mrs Barge bumped into her husband in the narrow hall of their abode and he perceived her to be bursting. "Evelyn!" she said. "The most extraordinary thing. Come into the drawing-room a moment."

"I suppose I must," he replied.

He squashed flat any idea that it was his duty to pursue "the love-child". "What should I do with the gal!" he said caustically.

"I'm sure Quarr would thank us if we were to shield them from a scene at this juncture," said Norah.

He only snorted.

"Seventeen years old! And when did he marry?"

He said to himself, Good God, women!

As Gertie accompanied this Flo and the perambulator back to the house she pumped her avidly. Her hunger for news of her old fellow had made her rash. However, Flo, for whom life could always be more diverting, drew a deep, gratified breath.

A wind got up from the south-west.

Ida and Griselda went down to the stables. Bevis followed them, a few paces to the rear. Clarence hailed them cheerily. "That ther drat dog a your'n, Miss Ida!" he said.

Little John stood in fresh wheat-straw in his stall. He turned his head, pricked his ears and whickered.

Ida and Griselda stared at him in perturbation; pursed their lips.

"What is it?" said Bevis.

"We're thinking," said Griselda. "Or Ida is."

"Swear, Bee."

"I swear," he said. "Cross my heart."

Griselda pulled his ear towards her gently. She whispered. At length.

Bevis almost leapt on the spot, remembered not to startle the horses, opened his mouth instead.

"How!" he said.

"Precisely," said Ida.

"Slade," said Griselda.

"Better not," said Ida. "Put yourself in his place and imagine the consequences."

"There absolutely has to be no hoo-ha," said Ida; "but who can say Slade won't kick up if *not* in the know. It's a conundrum."

"What's a conundrum?" said Bevis.

"This is."

They filed silently over the russet bricks within and out into the open air. "Don't look sombre," said Ida.

"Why not," said Griselda, "we were before!"

38 "Mrs Lupus was thunderstruck"

Mop sat by his chair and leant her shoulder against the eiderdown over his knees.

Gert wouldn't have been human if she hadn't let her mind run over what was to happen, how it would be when they were face to face, she and he, she in his presence; and in his house. She perched on the oak settle where she'd been put to wait, in a corridor with the faint smells, she thought, of soda and isinglass. So these were "nether regions"! She hadn't for a start imagined Georgie's house like this. She had it more lavish; polished and fragrant, not scrubbed and, well, puritan. She comforted herself. It would never have done for her to have come in the front. She was on a romantic errand. Discretion, they said, were the better part of valour.

George had demanded to be placed so he could see out of the window. Fontley would have taken his second horse. The February light across the park was sullen.

It occurred to Ida, returning from the stables, that there was no time to lose. Little John had to be spirited from Quarr under the noses of Slade and his cohorts. Very vigilant, those noses.

"Gypsy Jem knows how to paint 'em a different colour," observed Bevis.

"But where is Gypsy Jem when we need him!" said Griselda.

"Away to Gloucester," said Bevis.

"And a message will take too long," said Griselda.

For an impulsive soul, time might even have hung heavy. Gert went off into a dream.

"Should we not hide him tonight whilst we debate?" said Griselda.

"Where?" asked Bevis.

"The egg-house."

"Foyle's shed."

Foyle's shed was the reputed trysting-place for Mrs Foyle and Arthur Morder, so Bevis started to snigger and infected Griselda.

It was as though Ida hadn't heard.

"Succession houses."

Griselda and Bevis laughed out loud.

Gertie, two floors below George (though not directly), was bolt upright: already she had crept "behind a faithful servant" up the stairs . . .

The servant was agog. The boards creaked. When Gertie Whatley entered his room his head was turned on the pillow; the pale image of the sun looked through the clouds. She hesitated on the threshold, not wishing to break his trance. Perhaps his poor organ wouldn't stand the joy. The servant bowed to her, said, Now then, miss, you won't excite the master overly, I'm sure. Gertie vouchsafed a gracious nod; and the servant was vanished.

Old Nurse was a firm believer in carnal pleasures. When Flo relayed the story, poured out to her on the lower drive, Nurse was taken aback but inclined to take an indulgent view. Had ma'am been the witness ma'am would have been fair pole-axed. Mr George (uxorious or not) had a roving eye, which was proper, if we mortals were to derive our due dollops of fun in this world. That a fancy piece should roll up at the Grange was another matter.

Flo had brought her the Infant enveloped in a quilt from the perambulator. Until he was pottied and Mrs Lupus had visited the nursery and he was burped and put down serene, Nurse was busy. Flo must go and ask the advice of Mr Titball.

"I can't never," said Flo.

Nurse told her not to be foolish.

Gertie Whatley uttered his name. As he bent his gaze upon her a great glow illumined her beloved's features. Dear gal, her Georgie murmured. So you've come to me! She swept towards the high bed, with its starchy bleach-white linen, and unpinned her hat, setting it on a velvet ottoman.

Titball, summoned by the nursemaid's signal, stood a few paces beyond the door; flabbergasted.

"I will speak with Nurse," said Titball.

"You can't that!" exclaimed Flo.

He blinked.

"The mistress'll be in the nursery."

"Are you certain?" he said.

"Think, Mr Titball!" said Flo.

Titball felt his throat.

He whisked himself into the room.

Flo thought, this is the best ever!

When Titball reappeared he said, "I will see the young person."

Gertie, all unconscious and full of the wonderful endearments she'd received from the sick man, heard the rattle of the door knob, the heavy ceramic door knob, in a corner of her wits; but she didn't raise her eyes. So the sight which met Mrs Lupus's was perfectly astounding. Mrs Lupus's husband, beatific of expression, sunk on his pillows, and at the side of him, arms buried in the bed, a strange lady, very pretty, very youthful, who had taken her hat off. With great presence of mind this little lady said, Changing his stone, mum! The hot-water-bottle poked up the bedclothes suggestive.

The little lady withdrew her arms. Too dazed was Mrs Lupus to perceive that a body who had arrived with a fresh stone must have a chilly one to take down! You'll feel more comfy, sir, the little lady said, and permitted herself a warm smile.

Closing her fingers over her the mulberry brim of her hat the lady slid with ease born of elegance to the door. Mrs Lupus stood aside to let her go. Mrs Lupus didn't know what she'd seen. That stricken look was as much puzzlement as grief, had concluded Gert.

Titball descended, followed by Flo.

The person was still in the passage and in conversation with Constance Cockerell. Mrs Cockerell, who had taken possession of the parcel from Mr Rupert two hours previous, was charmed. "My," she said, "my! You'll be glad of a sip of tea and a dainty, I reckon. But you oughtn't have. Mr Lupus give it me."

Titball was swift to pick up on that. "Miss Whatley, I understand?" he said in a constricted tone.

Mrs Cockerell's nose was sharp.

Flo directed hers to the quarry tiles.

"It wasn't necessary for you to have come, Miss. Since you have, we shall convey you to wherever you desire."

Mrs Cockerell gaped at him.

"Mrs Cockerell is most grateful!" said Titball.

"Well, Mr Titball," began Mrs Cockerell.

"Good," said Titball. "I shall myself accompany you to the stable-yard."

As for Gert, she cast one anguished glance at the nursemaid and let herself be thrust from the house.

"And who might you be?" said Gert.

Titball knew he'd have to change his shoes.

"The master asked me to say to you that he is cognizant of your visit. He appreciates your concern. He denies himself the pleasure," said Titball, "of meeting you."

"I be darned!" exclaimed Gert.

She was considerably stung.

They trod in silence.

"Clarence," said Titball, "this here is Miss Whatley what has to be got somewhere."

"Farmer Dyce's," said Gert in a truculent voice. She was unappreciative of her fortune. She could only quiver with chagrin.

Titball said, "I can't dally, Clar, while you harness up."

"Ah," said Clarence. His tongue tipped the straw from his mouth.

Titball turned on his heel. Enough stir, enough said. The whole household would be a-buzz.

Soon after George had wondered whether Fontley had called it a day and Titball was helping him back between the sheets, the latter broached the subject.

George looked up at him with his sweet smile. "Heaven preserve us, Titball, she hasn't been at Quarr!" he asked.

"Get rid of the gal," said George, "will you?"

Titball sighed with relief.

Dorothy in a minute or two would be there to have tea with George and read to him. She dropped the puff in the drawer and sent her powder flying.

Ida frowned into the school-room fire.

Clarence would light the lamps on the trap by Higher Slaughter.

George leant his cheek on the pillow. The rooks came and filled the sky on their way to bed.

39 Sanctuary

Bold was the word for it. Ida had reviewed umpteen accomplices and ruled them out. Maybe high-handed was the word too. She and her sister often rode before breakfast; or after breakfast and before lessons. Within the boundaries of the park they were at liberty to go alone; otherwise it was tacitly accepted that they be accompanied. Ida's strategy was so bold, so high-handed, that she felt no need to dispense with the conventions.

"Clarence," said Ida, "we're riding into the village. Why don't we lead out Little John?" Clarence considered it a fine notion.

"Steady like," he said.

Ida merely smiled.

So Clarence never suspicioned what was to. He discarded his apron in the harness-room and made hisself neat.

Ida stood on the mounting-block and waited for her grey. Griselda led out Grenadier herself, for she was that sort of child. Clarence saw them into the saddle. The elder Foyle boy, Ginge, held Little John and the roan in the yard. Ida leant over for Little John's reins. Clarence had a leg-up from Ginger. Grenadier chose to dance about a bit and cannoned into Mother Goose. "Now then, Miss Griselda!" said Clarence. "Thank 'ee," he said when he took Little John from Ida.

Ida and Griselda jogged ahead.

Clarence on the cob with Little John on his near side followed.

A milky sun shone and the air was pleasantly crisper. There was no hint of the untoward. Thus was Esmond's pony extracted from the stables.

A biblical sea of Mrs Slade's poultry parted in front of them.

Young horses turned out in the home paddock stared coolly, until the two-year-old Cranford, out of Dorothy's old mare Sable by Rustic Cott, gave a loud snort and sent them all cavorting.

They met and passed six of their hunters: Slade first, and Ivor Hutchins. All greys.

When he greeted them, Slade grinned.

As they came to the lodge they spotted Brian in the lane with Diana and half a dozen chestnut piles loaded up. He went smartly by, his whip bobbing.

A foxy-faced fellow scurried along with a fistful of what his gaffer said were "Bedlingtons". "'Morning, Foxy," they called. "'Morning, Miss Ida, 'morning Miss Grisella," he replied, finger to a greasy bowler, and hooked his chin at Clarence. His garments bore a dust of flour. The terriers' blue-woolly skin flickered.

Foxy was employed by Hopkins at the Mill.

Then they met some hunt horses: more cheery words, though all knew their hearts were dull.

From across the park the sound travelled of the Kennels; and, as though someone was calling stock somewhere, the cry of "com'arn, com'arn"; over and over again.

Where the lane fell down towards the village they walked. On the banks the snowdrops drooped and the celandines were half shut.

The first cottages drew nearer and there were goats tethered on the verge. Hubert on his butcher's bicycle (brand new) pedalled away up the crown of the street. Old Thomas Blackmore, who would stick a chair outside and smoke his pipe under the icicles from his thatch, was, they could see, stumping around his wintry garden in the half-thaw. From the bend they saw the row of back porches and the cabbages, the sties and hen runs and the privies built over the ditch.

Outside the forge, a hunter from Coker dozed, a blanket over his quarters; while the companion within had a foot through Drake's legs and the boy blew up the fire.

They trotted past the chapel, the bakery, the school and Mr Hallett's; and Griselda undid the gate to the Rectory Field, held it for the party and brought it to again. There wasn't an animal in George's stables that wouldn't open a gate. The street went on to the fork by the church and right round. There was a hard track across the meadow, and big chestnut-trees; and, from one chestnut branch, a swing. The two Jersey house-cows looked up indignantly. In an enclosure over the hedge the pigs were rootling in an acre of mud, never a blade of grass left on it.

"Fetchin' in yere!" asked Clarence at last.

At the far gate he jumped off and instead of riding up to the front door they squeezed between the wall of the kitchen garden and the dairy and crossed to the yard. Clarence had a stable crony.

Ida said, "Mr Cornforth not gone out, is he!"

"That er baint," said Derrick, "Miss Ida." He was broad in his speech.

"Splendid," said Ida.

"Haiming for to see Parson hisself, be um," said Derrick.

"Seemingly," said Clarence.

This wasn't at all difficult, since the old gentleman was still in his book-room and fond of children. The Master's brood was always welcomed. Milk and lemonade appeared and a plate of biscuits: riding made everybody hungry.

Mr Cornforth took Griselda on his knee and beamed at them. He pinched her cheek. With his other arm he gave her a hug.

"Tell me how your father goes on?" he said.

Morwenna and her mama weren't at Plash. (He could swear they knew that?) It would be Easter before he was descended upon again. But Ida and Griselda weren't to imagine he didn't adore the filial company.

Griselda watched his whiskers. When they trembled she wanted to laugh. At Christmas she made him spills for his pipe.

Young Esmond had ridden a perfect race.

His eyebrows too were ferocious.

"I bet your papa was proud! Uncle Rupert drove to beat him, no quarter there! Made prime entertainment. I was no end pleased I came up in time. Could spot half a mile away some sort of high jinks or other was in the offing. So I spoke to the black and said 'hup' and in a twinkle he was up with you, was he not!

"I didn't shake his hand, didn't have the chance, do so today," said Cornforth.

Griselda said quietly, "Oh but he's gone back to Meavy."

"Good gracious!" exclaimed Mr Cornforth. He clasped Griselda's hand kindly and said, "Hmm, well, he couldn't idle for ever, I dare say. Hmm."

Ida said, "Were you out yesterday? Frank Fontley was able to show decent sport, we gather."

He hadn't been but some reminiscing followed. Ida always had light hands.

Before the race had gone from his head, though, Ida, who had decided to be direct, said, "Dear Mr Cornforth, will you have Esmond's John to visit for . . . you know, a while . . . ?"

Griselda, on his knee, could sense his surprise. There was a check in his breath and a puzzled frown betrayed that he was disagreeably taken aback.

He'd forgotten the child he held. He looked at Ida, the skirt of whose habit fell to the carpet where she'd chosen to perch on his library steps. These were low when folded.

"Until the holidays are on us," she said and closed her lips. Hers was no bland expression. Her intelligent face was, he thought, full of unspoken messages. He tried to decipher them.

"Now, what is all this!" he said.

There was silence. He eased Griselda from his knee and rose to his feet. Parson Cornforth was a powerful old fellow, tall, his black heavyweight cob and the long-tailed mare carried seventeen stone; he gave off a strong scent of tobacco and horses.

That race was not popular! he thought.

He cleared his throat.

"You are conspiring," he observed.

"I believe I should pretend to misunderstand you," he said. "What in the world do you suppose ... you deem it necessary, do you ... ?

"Does this request come from Esmond?"

Ida said, "I shall write to Esmond after luncheon."

"Where is the animal now?" he said. "At Quarr, I suppose."

"Rectory stables," said Ida, "we led him. Clarence is with us."

Griselda said, "Papa is too ill."

He squinted at her and, rather sorrowfully, at the early crocus visible from the book-room window.

"Yes, but ...

"You should have brought Slade," he said.

"Slade is devoted to us," said Ida.

"Do you consent, then?" asked Griselda.

"Dreadful," he muttered.

"Esmond is a good chap," he said.

"Yes," said Ida.

He ground his teeth in a most unclerical manner. "Not your place to go pushing your stick into grown-up business," he said.

Ida was on her feet. "Would it be vile of us," she said, "if we were to implore you!"

"Not *vile* of you. You ask an impropriety of me.

"I should send you off with a wig in the ear."

They gazed at him with dumb hope.

At last he asked rather fiercely, "Is the pony lame, or has he cast a shoe!"

"If you'd prefer," said Ida; "I did wonder. But a shoe won't answer. We'd have left him and Clarence at the forge and he'd have been home in an hour."

"You terrible children," he said.

"But we're not," said Ida.

He digested that.

He stroked his nose.

"I've been acquainted with your papa for many a year."

Ida smiled at him and though he felt unutterably cross he melted.

"I'm a foolish old dodderer," he whispered.

In the garden he drew Ida's fingers through his arm and took Griselda's in his other paw; stumped with them to the stable-yard.

Ida said, "Clarence, Little John is to stay. Ben Sawyer and Derrick will take charge of him."

Clarence gaped. He pushed his cap off his forehead like a yokel, so far back his front curls showed.

Parson Cornforth said in a sermon voice, "That's settled, my man."

Clarence had had no idea what was afoot. His brain seethed. 'Twouldn't hardly, he reckoned, be on account of Miss Morwenna.

"I'll speak to Slade," said Ida. She was trying to reassure him, that much was plain.

He saw no particular reason why a Quarr pony shouldn't stop at the Rectory if that was what had been fixed. But why no mention previous, why no orders? Clarence surrendered; and was troubled sore.

They went at a smart trot, late for Inkpen. The sun spilt through and Griselda's spirits, churning before, lifted.

Slade however, who was a wise bird, signalled compliance, when told: the head groom only gave a wry smile, touched his cap to Ida and turned away.

40 A lull

Gertie got to Fawernbridge to discover her mother in a pucker. Not for a twenty-four hour did it dawn that she might well have been fobbed off with a fib. Her boy might never have known she was there. No sooner sworn to try afresh than she went straight off to Higher Slaughter. She was greeted even at Winnie Cox's by broad grins. News had gone about. In fact they'd all been cackling over her.

She had to put up with some vexation from her brother Greville.

Ida and Griselda waited to be found out.

George was carried downstairs and he sat in the warmth and light of the pinery in a wicker chair which had a wicker stretcher for the legs and thick arms and beside the arms deep wicker pockets for newspapers, and *Punch* and *The Field*, and a wicker table for a sherry decanter, glasses, tumblers and jug of barley water.

Little John's absence went unnoticed.

On Sunday after church the ritual inspection of the stables and the giving out of sugar lumps and bread was the greatest test of the imprudence committed. Dorothy's mind was elsewhere. Oddly enough, they found Tanga in John's stall and David in Tanga's. Since Dorothy drove David in the tub sometimes, she took no fewer than two lumps for him from the bag; and, though his titbits lay in her gloved palm and he arched his neck and his lips touched her hand, she didn't perceive that he wasn't where he usually was. And, since Slade did move animals into different stalls and boxes (every hunter had a loose box after a day's hunting and some their very own) and there were thirty-six horses at the Grange and all were to be visited and patted and whispered to, well . . . Little John, clipped out for the season, would have had to have been in, but . . . well, on this Sunday at least Dorothy apparently wasn't alert. She didn't see Bevis's round eyes or Griselda's rigid glaze. Ida was calm and assured.

For Ida the prime concern was not that Dorothy might

wonder where Esmond's pony was. The worry was that Esmond's mother would recollect Little John; and discover therein an affront.

Ida hadn't had to murmur to Cornforth the name of Eclipse. He'd *known*; he'd provided sanctuary; he'd made no fuss.

Gertie had seen she needed a messenger.

Mrs Slade brought Misty up to the house herself and left her to lie on a rug near the master. But the devotion of a decrepit animal, no matter how cherished once, with her wheeze, didn't cheer him; and Mrs Slade had tactfully to be fended off.

George in his chair had shrunk. He was thinner. He was smaller. His voice was quiet. Not unmusical, not without the timbre which was peculiarly his, it no longer rang out; in the house or anywhere.

He fretted. To have to lie down, or at best sit, interminably, that did irk him. The wealth of his responsibilities at Quarr called him. Fontley had been biting on his usual confidences. They all treated him to a consideration he didn't much relish.

He woke in the night and lay awake for what seemed many protracted hours: despair attacked him.

He asked for the curtains to be drawn back so the stars could look in at him. He'd sent Titball to sleep in his own bed, like a Christian, and Nurse; wherever Titball's bed was; for, now he thought of it, he wasn't certain. Nurse had always been in the night nursery.

He heard the tawny owl; and the wind when it came and started to sing through the trees.

41 The low land

Titball had fought off a cold. But he too felt weak. In his bones, he reflected, he longed for summer. The draughts and chills of the Grange were arctic when you had continually to trip through doors and corridors, and warmth was suddenly withdrawn from you.

Gert did the four mile from Higher Slaughter to Plash and back twice in the day. She went to the bakery to lie in wait for Angela Strange: Angela Strange never came. Gert spoke to all and sundry. She acquired a knowledge of them that saw Georgie; but the list was so far unpromising. She couldn't accost Mr Gervase Sturt, or Major Ramsey. She aimed for a man. A man would be the more sympathetic to George's desire, as she thought, to lay eyes on her. The servants and that, what went to the Tom Thumb, would be all like Titball and Pinkie. Then she heard tell that Frank Fontley, the huntsman, was frequent up to the Grange and half the pack with him. Hunt servants weren't servants at all, were a cut above. Frank Fontley was a bachelor man and if he didn't do there was Oswald Beer, what had Mrs Beer and childer. The head groom at the Quarr Kennels was a queer, touchy fellow, she'd do as well to avoid Gus Hutchins. His nephew Ivor, who worked under Mr Slade and was courting Ellen Drake, sounded more approachable. But Ivor wouldn't serve the purpose, since no one could reckon he got beyond the servants' hall. And why were Missie an-asking of all they questions?

Had Gert but been aware of it, Mrs Barge, who had swallowed the fib, might have been an ideal missionary.

By now the countryside was agog.

George strode over his low land by the decoy pond with his keen eye on the spaniels sent out to flush the snipe.

They'd brought loaders, he and his chums Sturt and Donkey Lorimer, for Ginger Foyle stood at his elbow. The other two guns had fanned out a little to the right. He saw his keeper Dick Hanham, behind a little, in the distance, a twelve-bore broken on his arm; and, drawn up by the tumbledown, the brake which had brought all of them together, the dogs and the provisions.

The grasses and rushes had withered a glorious autumn yellow and pocks of wet winked between the tufts.

When the spaniels were almost on them the snipe got up with their rapid, zigzag flight, he heard himself shoot; had the kick of the stock, both barrels, in the crook of his shoulder, and a smell of spent cartridge.

Then, suddenly, as he was closing his strong teeth on a piece of raised game pie, his appetite vanished and it was summer. The scent of bog myrtle filled the air.

There was a thing about bog myrtle which was unbearably poignant.

42 Tally-ho

Gertie perceived that salvation was on the doorstep at Higher Slaughter in the form of Farmer Dyce and prepared to waylay him; Mop rolled in caca (fox) and was taken by the stable-boy to be made better smelling; Rupert went to Enmoor; whereupon George suffered another go in the pinery.

George was back in bed and had to fight for breath and tears were trickling down Titball's face and old Nurse trembled.

The parson was sent for; and Mahon, bidden rush from Lackham Magna, had driven over already.

It seemed there was a woebegone procession of persons who must arrive.

"Frank," said George. But it was thought not appropriate. As Fontley waited miserably, the hounds caught his mood, shifted about and whined. He'd put a clean kennel-coat by. It dangled there and when it caught his glance he felt a humble pain.

Griselda was pushed in. Titball went to the door, took her hand and drew her forward.

"Hallo, Grizel!" mouthed George in a cheery manner. He was unnaturally still.

"Can't talk a lot until stronger," said Papa. She gripped an edge of the linen. He said, "What was it you wanted to be!"

Griselda said, "A doctor, d'you mean?"

"That was it," he said.

There was a long silence. He'd smiled at her and looked away.

It was very affecting.

Titball, who'd turned on his heel, presently came and propelled her gently until some invisible individual beyond the threshold retrieved her.

Her little brother Bevis's legs held up under him. He was made of different stuff.

His voice a thread, George asked, "Have you a special fossil for me, Bee!" Bevis didn't pretend not to understand. He was too young to dissemble. Quick as a flash he said, "A sea-horse, *and* a thunderstone."

"Really, Bevis," interjected Dorothy.

"*And* a thunderstone," said George. "Good boy!"

Once, yes once, on a famous occasion, never forgotten, never forgiven, Bee had observed disastrously, "You can't bear it that we love Papa more."

Ida had a single, anguished thought: she wished to be with Papa alone. It was not to be granted.

"Darling daughter," said George, as though it were a moment during charades, or up-jenkins, or sardines.

She might have frowned.

George, as a rule so sensitive, let his face droop; and she imagined that he, too, was unnerved.

"Ida," he said.

She leant over him. Her hair fell towards him.

"Listen," he whispered.

There was a hiss from the fire when Titball made it up and a click when Titball left the room.

Ida felt eyes in her back but they were directed, vacantly, quite otherwise. Dorothy stood and stared down at the terrace.

We must remember Baby, thought Dorothy. Those fingers will tickle the cheek of our recent addition; and in time we shall be able to tell the child that his father loved him, every inch, as much as the rest of us. Dorothy saw herself with black ink writing this in the vellum-bound book she'd kept for each of them. She read on as if in a dream and found she'd inscribed tomorrow's date and the bleak fact that he didn't have a papa to coo over him any more.

Tomorrow, she thought. How curious.

Fontley remained with the hounds and the lanterns were alight for hours after it was dark.

Mrs Cockerell the cook-housekeeper had sent crumpets up for the children to toast.

In due course, Dorothy went to change and dined downstairs. Archie, Cecily and Agnes were her only companions; but Rupert and Lydie blew in soon. That is, they arrived rather soberly: the cold wind rushed in when Porlock opened the door.

George's last words to Ida had released his mind somewhat.

There was a waxing quarter-moon. Nobody could drive with ease.

Quintus Cornforth, who'd come in the afternoon with the Host and led George with distinct tenderness through the words of the General Confession, examined his own conscience and found it wry, now paid a third visit.

" 'Wash it, we pray thee'," George heard, " 'in the blood of that immaculate Lamb, that was slain to take away the sins of the world; that whatsoever defilements it may have contracted in the midst of this miserable and naughty world, through the lusts of the flesh, or the wiles of Satan, being purged and done away, it may be presented pure and without spot before thee . . .' "

George spoke of his brothers Oliver and Martin, his sisters Nesta and Laura.

To Dorothy, George said, "Don't take on, darling. Been awfully happy."

He was aware of the need to keep a tight rein.

He was in a bit of a lather. "Fontley," he said, "where is the blessed fellow!"

Dorothy noticed that the blue of his irises had fogged.

"Like to see my favourites," he said in such a wistful tone that she wavered. "Fontley will have gone off," she said. "Should I send to the Tom Thumb, then?"

He nodded.

He hoped to save his breath.

Mop had endured a difficult day.

Ginger had been set to wash the stinky portion of her coat. She'd been told to roll in the straw and through some misunderstanding been shut up. A docile, well-behaved animal, she'd lain and licked for a while; even dozed. Her tummy had prompted a protest and she was indeed fetched to polish her bowl. She'd had to help the terriers with a rat in the harness-room and dislodged some hames which belonged at the farm: they should have been hung on a rack and not in that corner so certain hasty tempers were roused. Not a dog to bide where she wasn't wanted, she'd escaped. In the house various persons had appeared to suppose she ought not to go upstairs. She'd been obliged to lurk with the guile of a canine philanderer until she could penetrate to the hall, and from the hall she'd mounted to her master's door. Titball hadn't hesitated to let her in.

She lifted her nose to the bed, lowered herself to the floor and made herself unobtrusive.

Rupert came and sat with George.

Rupert had voted in favour of Frank Fontley.

Cecily came: Agnes mercifully did not. Archie was hunched in his den.

Lydie on tiptoes came.

Dorothy's mind strayed to recollections of other demises.

Griselda, with a mouthful of wet pillow, had been dwelling on tales of people in the village who, as they expired, had displayed superhuman vigour and leapt up to screech, to the dismay of their relations. Mother Blackmore had jumped at the opportunity to throttle Father Blackmore.

Ida in her night-gown came.

Nurse came, and took her away.

Titball had to raise his master if required and perform all that was necessary. He'd made the effort to go and swallow his supper. He had a lump in his throat. Outwardly he was calm.

There was not much for Dorothy to do.

George had a faint smile on his face.

He laboured.

Cornforth had gone and Mahon returned for the last time.

George said, "Speaking true, Mahon, to a line, are you, has he slipped from covert, or . . . tell me . . . have you . . . lifted your head . . . hunting by sight . . . you see Reynard, eh."

Doctor Mahon said, "Heavens above." But he twinkled, rather.

Dorothy cast back involuntarily to an earlier conversation in which George had said, "I must say this is a rattling thing."

She looked at Mahon.

He pursed his lips and crushed the bones of one hand in his other.

Dorothy, earlier, had reached out to George and, as Baby's did, his fingers had wrapped themselves around her two.

In the terrible, thunderous silence, with the loud tick-tock of the clock, Mahon said, "I'll be downstairs."

"Titball," said Dorothy, "be so kind as to ask Porlock to bring Doctor Mahon the brandy; also, would he make up the fire in the smoking-room."

She didn't allow herself to think how shaken she was. She selected a volume from the Pembroke table.

But would George want to listen to the poem about Tiny? Cowper was replaced. Somehow her decorum lost its bridle, for she picked up *Punch* and said, "There's a very jolly cartoon here, George. A lady in a railway-carriage has a pug on her lap. The pug seems to be in a rage. Another lady . . . oh the carriage is crowded . . . has her knees covered by a rug. She has raised the fringe and is saying 'I believe your dog must have discovered mine'."

Into another appalled hush, that of the Tom Thumb, Pinkie burst. "Frank Fontley," he blurted, "wher be er to!"

"Baint along of we," said Wes Brown, slowly. "Er baint bin by."

"Nor Oswald neither," Shepherd Grace said.

Pinkie's chest heaved; and he was well spattered.

"Er be wanted!"

"Oh ah," said Colin.

Pinkie turned about.

The Hunt Cottages lay a fair old hop, leastways a mile and three-quarter, from the Tom Thumb.

By five and twenty to eleven, Rupert was insistent that Ida be woken. Ida hadn't been to sleep.

"Draw the curtains," said George, "will you."

Dorothy went to the windows herself. "Look, Orion has swung up into the sky," she said, "with Sirius."

George and she had for ever enjoyed the stars.

"Here is Ida," she said.

Ida, very pale, had great hollows in her face.

George's eyes rested, not on Ida, not on the window panes, but on some presence at his feet.

"What is it!" asked Dorothy, with an odd laugh.

It was his beloved hound; and he saw beyond the shoulder. He tried to say her name.

Over the night air from the Kennels came the sound of singing and howling: all heard it, for it carried.

III QUARR FORGOTTEN

43 Fortitude does not suffice

Cynthia Stokes had notions that made distaste at her station heave in her bosom, for she didn't hold with service and Mrs Lupus often made her boil. (Dorothy, looking at a woodenly beaming face which hovered in the glass, thought Stokes a funny little woman.) And that Mr Oliver should call her Cynthia, in front of Mrs Lupus, without his having any designs on her person either, without condensation, struck Miss Stokes as spanking. Pride in a handle was for housekeepers. Nor did her heart flutter for him. Nor was she chaste.

The only sentiment Mrs Lupus and she had in common was that they were too hot in their stays, and that it must be worse in the summer.

Uncle Oliver is proposing to strand me (I shall have Stokes) on an island, Dorothy wrote to the children after Christmas . . .

She tried to sound game. She crossed out "strand" and put "maroon", since "maroon" was more romantic, and in "strand" lay a hint of resentment. *That is, while he goes on alone to a wilder place where there are, as yet, no European ladies.*

Your mother was to have seen troglodytes, reputed to have houses in holes, in the far South; and to have visited a French captain, Thevenet, an amateur of geology. I should have had to have ridden for two days across the desert. Uncle Noll has judged it unwise. I bow to his experience. It might have been intriguing.

Oliver proposed to abandon her because their tour had *not* restored her to health and composure.

It was a mortification. At moments she felt crushed by the disappointment; for she'd already succumbed to ailments of a tiresome nature in Morocco and become unnerved further by civilized Algiers.

The Grand Hôtel de France might have been in Vichy or Baden-Baden with its marble fireplaces and brass taps: Dorothy couldn't say that their mother, from a long line of doughty females, had, in Tunis, proved to be "not up to it" any more. The excursion (several weeks) to sketch and photograph the ruins of a Roman city said to be overpowering enough to startle the traveller was postponed.

Life at Quarr hadn't equipped her. The producing of six infants, draughts and the bracing cold, no preparation. Her inside had let her down. Seven separate doctors had had to attend since October. She didn't envy Oliver; at least not precisely, for his inside was wrapped in dry leather.

She couldn't concede (on her black-edged writing-paper) that she was too recently widowed to be racketing about and that somewhat arduously. ("Him not nine months in his grave," Stokes had told that English-speaking doctor that attended in Algiers.)

Noll was too vague to be an ideal escort for a sole female; and she hadn't discovered this until already abroad.

He had bachelor habits.

Dorothy, accustomed to persons with languors and megrims and the most boring of conversation whom she might not have chosen to entertain, had a different kind of resilience. His wilted once an expedition could no longer be contemplated.

She considered Oliver selfish. Viz. *his* choice of their destination, to suit *his* passion for stones, *his* Arabic.

The irony of it was that one became tired of Stokes, who was omnipresent and an encumbrance in the transport since she had to sit with them.

Perpetual difficulty as to where Stokes ate her meals.

Oliver was rather casual and called Stokes "Cynthia": Dorothy had noted that Stokes seemed to greet this with aplomb. "I warned you at the outset that you'd do better to cope with your own hair and local laundering," he'd said.

At least Stokes, enjoying herself, was no dismal figure that had to be dragged about.

None of that was proper in a letter. Instead, she described how Uncle Noll (so comic!) had ordained that their baggage be pared of photographic paraphernalia for the crossing to the islands. She was reduced to four rolls of film. Fearing she had to settle for a duller period, Dorothy signed herself their "affectionate mother, D. P. Lupus".

In a postscript the words, naturally crucial to Ida, Esmond, Griselda and Bevis: *Uncle Noll will be coming back for me!*

Oliver had been quite positive: his sister-in-law now would profit from a period of sybaritic repose. Her perturbation, loath though she might be to be "stranded", he knew would subside.

The trip had been for Dolly's benefit.

She would be all right. Her French was less stiff now (Dorothy was not stupid). His good acquaintances, Gaston and Ernestine Boissy, would coddle her. She would, he said, recover and be full of vim.

44 Voyage to the islands

With half a dozen horse brasses added to the luggage, of quaint and novel design, five-pointed star, crescent moon and the hand of Fatima, and a dear little chameleon resisted, they sat on the public quay.

The chameleon had been balancing, as though transfixed, on two legs on the rim of a box in which a great number of small tortoises spoiled a bed of green leaf. A foreleg and dainty, perfect foot, with the diametrically opposite hind limb, mimed, it seemed, the grilling sand; and a string was fastened to one ankle, to tether the creature.

"They must eat tortoises!" she'd remarked.

"Children's pets," had said Oliver.

The chameleon stared unblinking at nobody and nothing. "Our children would love him!"

"England might be too cold, don't y'know. Imagine how melancholy Bee would find a chameleon death. Besides, not kind, and indeed he's a *gecko*!"

"I dare say you're correct," had said Dorothy. She'd at once decided to attempt it, transporting a chameleon to the warmth of the pinery at home. (Not that chameleon, on that occasion. Before they left these exotic souks behind them!)

The Sfax quay-side was far from dull, for a packet-boat was being filled with mules and two dromedaries; crates, floppy baskets; and an astonishing number of passengers. "I thought you said the inhabitants were few," said Dorothy. She shaded her eyes with her hand.

"The islands are not so near, then." In an arch manner, to hide her dismay, she said, "It's bare, the horizon!" Noll said, "Yes, it's a mystery."

Cynthia Stokes noticed how nice people were, all these folk in their dashing rig, not to stare at strangers. Men, they were. She thought their eyes were neither cheeky nor sly either. It was tact, that was what it was. She approved. Her bosom swelled happily. A friendly curiosity wasn't irksome.

They didn't have to watch the ferry depart. Oliver, who hadn't wished to take his party on board the packet although he now saw a pair of French officials were content in her, had, in a spirit of adventure, negotiated for a private passage.

She was named, Oliver said, *Sea Blessing*. Cynthia, if asked, would have called her *Minnow*. Orange, blue and red stripes, the orange broader than the rest, ran from tallish prow to tallish stern, and she was built of palm-wood, mast and all.

Dorothy was thirsty, she'd rationed her liquids. She felt cross and irrational. So weary of constant change! Her body, though she didn't care to dwell on the word, had grown heavy.

She settled herself in the bottom with foreboding; tied down her hat with a veil.

Her skirts began to be wet at the hem and act like a rag. *Sea Blessing* had a sort of housing to her mast, no deck; other than bilge boards. Around her ribs some planking did for seats; and to run around on to work her.

The creak and slip-slop failed to absorb Dorothy's thoughts.

No ocean swell of course but rocky waves.

Oliver's sparkle, his whole attitude, told her that he at least was enjoying himself.

After enduring an age of this, an age, she realized there was a thin line between sea and sky, and that frills stuck out in long processions from it. On the thin line at last she could make out palm-trees, and the frills were of palm too; traps for red mullet, of palm fronds planted in the sea. By now the sun, which had been cool, was hot; was searingly hot; bored through her gloves to discover her delicate skin.

"Your islands are flat," she said.

Oliver smiled, maddeningly.

The palm-trees, she observed, were tattered.

Still well out, they passed to starboard of the shore. Their lugsail emptied and filled. She wouldn't have been astonished if they'd hove to. Fishermen did things in the sea, a mere English lady would surely not obstruct them. Mrs Lupus's tartness will be pricked soon, thought Cynthia in her wisdom.

Dorothy couldn't imagine what beauty she was supposed to see in such a meagre landscape.

The sun had slithered somewhat in the sky, and the sea was slacker. The waves, which before had fractured in a display of prismatic disorder, now fell into a rippling, stroked all in one direction.

Edges of terra firma, indented by bays, each more monotonous than the other, and these palm-frond fences which marched out into the shallow sea for miles, and the *preposterous* voyage, for how was she to contemplate the return crossing with anything but dread, caused her to look at Noll through her scorched eyes with incredulity. In the packet she would have been obliged to "wait" too.

With her poisoned constitution the ordeal was not to be repeated. She concluded she would never see children or home again. Expiry her fate, twenty-seven nautical miles, or so she understood, off Africa, in the company of a French lady and gentleman she hadn't met.

Her brother-in-law and Stokes, meanwhile, had sucked at some scalding tea, sweet as honey, had shared a little glass, the glass the fisherman had drunk from, its rim perfunctorily wiped by his two sons; who seemed not a lot older than Bevis. Stokes had been intrigued by the clay kanoun on which the tea, in a blue teapot decorated with roses, had been boiled. In the kanoun lay a nest of glowing charcoal.

Stokes faced the sun and her eyelids drooped. Noll was awake and alert.

They were both quite abominable.

45 The dust doesn't settle beneath Oliver's feet

On a promontory a monolith of crocks for octopus caught his attention. He pointed: Dorothy swished her lips about.

Sea Blessing had been sailing with the wind on her quarter. Closer into the wind, she shouldered her way past rocks and across the shallow, shallow sea until on the high tide she took ground beam on.

Oliver stripped himself of shoes, spats, socks and sock-suspenders, leapt over the gunwale and lent a hand with the easing of the boat in until the bottom boards on the starboard side and the keel stuck hard and she could be made fast, not three yards from a shelf of creamy, reddish sandstone. A white-domed koubba, built over the tomb of a holy man, or was it a small mosque, stood on the shore.

Dorothy had averted her gaze from the sock-suspenders.

In Arabia he'd been known to burden himself with none of these items.

Stiff, Dorothy allowed the boys to haul her to the gunwale, from which Noll was to pluck her. She smiled at them; for it had dawned on her that this, and only this, was the beginning of a prolonged nightmare; and panic rose in her gullet.

A surprise, therefore, to find a few days later that she could meet Noll's departure with equanimity.

They hadn't stood painfully by *Sea Blessing* and the gear, at the back of beyond; they hadn't endured further hours of wind and sun. The child Mohamed had belted off for their hosts . . . and a bumpy Bath-chair! In no time she'd been patting her face with supple linen and sipping mint tea in a civilized abode. A surprise, too, to find Ernestine Boissy and the husband, well, agreeable people!

In Madame Boissy, had thought Dorothy soon, I have someone who considers me delightful.

Noll had strode hither and thither in a very Gallic manner with the husband; ridden; and, on terms of intimacy, with Ernestine as well as with Gaston, done a great deal of shrieking.

46 Circe's island

Oasis, desert and troglodytes: as Dorothy began to be less shattered she began also to remember the stimulation she'd foregone.

In the Boissy conversation, Oliver cropped up with regularity. How clever he was, how gay, how he amused them when he recounted his exploits, how profoundly knowledgeable, how sympathique!

She had to murmur, "Mm, mm."

Nor could she warm to inadvertent mention of her deficiencies. "You didn't notice the fish during your sail to Grande Kerkennah?" asked Gaston Boissy. But she hadn't. The teeming fish. The rich fish in the shallow sea.

These were the only rubs.

They were more of Rupert's age, she believed, and younger than she. It behoved her to be tolerant.

She didn't think she'd ever weary of the fish on the table; and dishes of squid, soups of octopus pulp. She was eating better. She feared the water might be funny.

That table was to be exchanged. Gaston Boissy meant to *root* himself; on two impossible hectares, in the country! "Ernestine and I, we have taken you to our hearts," said Boissy. "We must take you to *our place*."

Dorothy stared vaguely about; since Ramlah was rural enough. Its dwellings could be counted in dozens. Twelve dozen, perhaps.

"An official residence? Ah!"

You're not tempted to purchase a boat! Dorothy wanted to say.

Instead she said, "We witnessed an hilarious to-do on the quay in Sfax. They were loading animals by sling. There was a cow. How the dromedaries groaned! And the discomfort for them on the voyage is unenviable. I imagine that when the hobbles are undone, which tie the foreleg, you know, above the knee to the cannon-bone and the foot, the dromedary is so stiff it has a job to stand up!"

Gaston Boissy said, "A cow, now that is rare, you may have noticed we depend on goats' milk, there isn't the fodder for cattle."

"When you are recovered, madame ..." said Ernestine Boissy.

Boissy rode his horse, el Khalifa. Ernestine and Dorothy were mounted on donkeys. It was necessary that each lady be picked up by the waist by Mansour and deposited on top to ride pillion-fashion; or otherwise be agile.

Dorothy was handed a switch of leafy olive and the halter-rope. The saddle, stuffed with straw, was high and wobbled frantically.

The mules drew the baggage, the baskets of food; and a pile of Djerba blankets made a seat for Stokes. Carts had straight shafts; and a "flat" bed. The animals went in a breast-collar; with the shafts cocked up by virtue of a colossal, motley pad, so the load didn't bear on the wither. Stokes felt herself more than likely to slide off behind.

The lane left Ramlah by the blind walls of houses.

Here and there a palm-wood door was open onto a tranquil courtyard. More often a trick of architecture hid the inner core. Some houses crooked themselves round a handkerchief garden in which hens pecked and a fruit tree might grow. The blind walls merged into unmortared stone.

In the orchards were pomegranate and fig, and small patches of green wheat, inches high, as one might in England have cabbages. Dogs barked or eyed the strangers silently. The lane was heavy with sand.

The view widened. Without climbing, they had emerged onto a plateau. There was no wind. Wild thyme was one among plants so parched as barely to cling on to a life that you had to divine from their skeletons. Olive groves embraced by banks and walls had fallen into a poor state. But the soil was redder.

The stones were so diminutive that making the boundaries must have entailed a great deal of patience.

Inside these boundaries the earth was lower and formed a pan.

The lanes threaded in a medieval style over the bleak land, and bulged to enclose the heads of cisterns, whilst stone conduits and slabs over small arches in the walls showed how these resources were deployed. At a certain point Stokes and the mules were obliged to separate from the party.

A lime-washed mosque could be seen, quite isolated in the country; and another; and, in the distance, the ruin of a Byzantine sort of fort.

This, Dorothy remarked to herself, is cultivation on a Lilliputian scale.

The Boissy house stood in the midst of its hectares, within shouting reach of its neighbour.

Its outer walls were higher and less thick and it faced its figs, pomegranate and almonds through four handsome windows and a front door complete with carved lintel. There were windows to the side and only at the back a courtyard.

Set into the wall of the house itself was a cramped po-hole, a flag with a hole and inconceivably minimal space in which to shut yourself. Dorothy thought this amazing and was gratified to see a commodious chamber under her bed. The

Mohammedans, she was convinced, would never be so dirty, but position their arrangements far from where they were to sleep and eat.

Boissy had "a miracle beyond compare": a well. The miracle was shaded by a gnarled olive. Gaston Boissy must have built on top of an older construction.

A chimney stuck its head up and this did imitate its neighbours, having a pointed hat and dove-cot neck, very endearing. The lintel motif had been of pineapples. On second thoughts, said Dorothy to herself, perhaps palm-crowns.

The interior was cool and the floor was tiled (marron and indigo) throughout. Light and air flooded in and a flight of steps led to a cellar, a natural cave. It was obvious they lived simply.

For wasn't it an island of sun, stars, wind and light? Yes, she thought, yes.

The fig-trees were silvery and almost naked. The first leaf showed not yet on all. Underfoot, there was white shell; and on the prickly pear, savage protrusions.

47 The immense sheen

The spot where Boissy and Ernestine lived "en colon" lay on the backbone, supposing the terrain to be a flatfish, and a walk to the western shore was by no means out of the way. Nor was it farther to the eastern shore, it was only that there was . . . a village.

The liberty was at once felt.

In late afternoon they put a best foot forward to witness the setting of the sun, swollen and red, over the sea; that sun which had risen on Ramlah and seemed eternal. Gaston stopped every now and then and his chest could be observed to swell too; and in deep satisfaction he let his breath go. Otherwise he monopolized the conversation. But Dorothy didn't mind. She was glad to get her bearings; for the first time, she was able to forget she was alone with strangers and marooned. She thought him quite pleasant. It was natural that he should want to hold forth.

She was, she reflected, a fresh audience. She contrived to look attentive.

There was not the vestige of a breeze. Some folk still sat in their little fields in the shade of an old olive-tree where a fire boiled the tea.

Boissy moved unerringly along a footpath littered in the white shell.

"You notice where you are, madame," said Boissy.

"My children," she said, "would be for ever turning round to fix in their heads the way back." Gaston's shoulders seemed to register a smile. Dorothy was vaguely curious as to why they were childless. He must like children, she'd concluded.

The ground began to dip off the plateau, to sink slightly: she saw that land, sea and sky were one.

With, or so Boissy thought, two or more inner courtyards, a solitary house announced itself; its beasts in thatched pens and hens in dust-baths. The walls seemed too stout for defence from mere wind and storm. A tiny window spied on the world outside: Dorothy could imagine without difficulty an arrow shot from such a slit. A seat of stone, a plinth, bore a handful of preoccupied, elderly men; who didn't omit to return Boissy's wave.

They'd been walking for perhaps half an hour.

At last they came to the sands. An immense sheen was spread in front of them, in a curving bay bound by rocky promontories. "Low water," said Gaston happily. Dorothy thought the tide couldn't go out much farther. At some distance a flat bank was uncovered and a string of jagged rocks. There were baskets rigged in the shallows. "Those disappear," said Gaston.

In the sea a fellow, his culotte drawn above his thighs, held a trident in one hand and a bag in the other. Quite frequently he struck, held his catch well from him while it spewed ink, then eased it into his bag.

Dorothy was entranced by this.

And all the time the sun hung above this scene, illuminating the water with a rod of crimson. As the sun sank the crimson spread and the sea shone back at the sky with a flush almost of blood. Dorothy touched her cheek to see whether it too was burning.

"How riveting," she said.

48 When I lost my husband

On another occasion there was an old man who was going for fish with a net. Dorothy and Ernestine had come on their own before luncheon, a feature of this superb freedom with which "Les Grenadiers" endowed them.

The old man, ankle-deep in the shallows of an ebbing tide, directed his candid smile of complicity towards them. He tweaked the folds of his net into place so that all the little pebbles stitched into its hem hung in order. He waded gently through ripples until, it seemed, he could see fish bigger than those that swam in infant shoals close to the hollows of shell and weed and darted all about. With one hand he threw a heavier stone, whereupon the other hand flung the net over the water thus stunned. The net was drawn out and from it he dug silvery bodies of a size Dorothy wouldn't have contemplated as food.

These he slid into a pouch slung from his middle.

"Couscous," he said, "couscous moi et ma femme." It was so plain they'd been observing this operation, Dorothy and Ernestine couldn't help but smile at him. Besides, he was quite aged. He had few teeth and his weather-beaten face was as corrugated as Old Man Blackmore's at home.

He was full of good will, for he stopped, his fishing complete, to make a crude seat out of a washed-up plank balanced at one end on a fallen palm and the other end wedged into the sandstone.

"Do you enjoy paddling, dear?" said Ernestine.

"My children do," said Dorothy.

"If we were to come without our stockings on," said Ernestine, "we could launch ourselves into the wonderful sea. There are so many shells to collect and once a young swordfish nosed my very skin."

"Ough," said Dorothy; but she knew herself to be a hypocrite, for she longed, longed, to plunge at least her feet in.

"You would prefer the presence of Gaston?" asked Ernestine.

Dorothy was hard put to it to know how to respond.

"When I lost my husband," she said, after a moment, "when I lost my husband George . . ."

"Please do tell me," said Ernestine, who felt it her duty.

"Yes," said Dorothy, "my beloved husband."

"I understand, it's too recent," said Ernestine.

"Not yet a year," said Dorothy. "You may think I shouldn't be abroad, that these travels have exceeded the bounds of taste."

"Not at all," said Ernestine.

"I never consider what other people may condemn," Dorothy said, aware that wasn't strictly true.

"It was a shock," said Ernestine.

"It was a cruel shock," said Dorothy.

Dorothy had a habit of resting the whole weight of her head on a single bony finger dug into her cheek while the index penetrated mere air beneath her chin. Consequently the view tilted, the skyline cocked up. Many females did this: she was alone in achieving the pose without a prop for the elbow.

She raised her head and said, "I was frightfully young to be widowed. And with a babe in arms! It was a felicity that I could be with him at the end.

"George was such fun."

"Is Oliver like his brother?" said Ernestine.

"Oh, in looks a little. But dear Noll has bachelor ways, you see. George was more dependable. George was . . . grander. Approachable yet somehow splendid."

She stroked the words, plus magnifique, plus beau.

"Of course he hadn't spent years in the desert. He belonged to Quarr. It to him. Very empty, Quarr, without its master."

She thought she was sounding sententious. "Oliver keeps himself hidden. Archie, the wounded brother, is of that character too. My husband was as open as a lark.

L'alouette."

Ernestine puzzled over this.

"All of us, we all thought George an utter joy," said Dorothy.

She didn't offer any more, and presently they strolled back, glad of the shade from their hats.

49 My son Esmond

Dorothy had been surprised to discover that Ernestine put her hand to quite a lot in the house; and, noticing that her hostess wished to polish glasses, the guest, keen to adapt, amused herself with a duster. Stokes saved that one up to take home.

While the ladies were having an hour of repose the first puffs of a wind arrived.

By the time el Khalifa brought Boissy over the plateau it was tearing at the fronds of the palm-trees. Then Dorothy understood why the islands looked quite so overwhelmed by wind and why their general appearance, in stillness, was so uncanny. It had struck her as curious that the little terrace at Les Grenadiers should face east, when it was so lovely to sit at sunset before that eloquent globe. The prevailing westerly is boisterous, she'd thought, of course. Now she saw it savaged the low fragments of land.

It didn't prevent Boissy from sallying straight out again in his shirt-sleeves to prune.

I fancy, scribbled Dorothy to Ida, *the tresses fall around the olive-trees much as the Plash hair drops to the ground outside our cottages when the scissors snip round the pudding-basins.*

The less whippy wood goes for charcoal. Up the lane, charcoal-burners have built a round pyre in which the lengths fit first aslant one way then another. The stones in the walls are positioned similarly, by the by. A portion of Monsieur Boissy's will be returned to him in charcoal. Olive groves are not so numerous that the yield of the entire district is able, I gather, to satisfy more than two pyres.

Boissy, who was minus a hat, continued to work while the leaves streamed around his bare forearms. He had rolled up his sleeves.

Dorothy disregarded the fond smile on Ernestine's lips and remarked, "After George died much changed. We were all affected but I fear my children made a frightful fuss.

"I never encourage the children to create."

Ernestine strove to follow.

"However," said Dorothy judiciously, "Nurse and Miss Inkspindle both made allowances, since the circumstances were so special."

"Poor Dorothée, these are sad thoughts you have."

"My son Esmond has always been sensitive. That doesn't do, does it, in later life; attractive though it may be in a boy. He has had to learn some hard lessons. George used to consider him rather clever.

"Esmond is a favourite with his Uncle Rupert and Aunt Lydie. And his good looks endear him to many. It's said he's the picture of George at that age. People have the advantage of me in that respect. I didn't know my husband until I came out."

Ernestine blinked. "You were eighteen, perhaps."

Dorothy inclined her head.

"Gaston," said Ernestine, "was seven when he first set eyes on me. Our mothers were enceintes and had taken us and our brothers and sisters to Evian. I myself was four. It was in August."

"Mm," said Dorothy politely.

"I should mention that Esmond plays the violin."

50 My daughter Ida

Boissy also broke off pieces of fig and stuck them each in a hollow he made in the soil where he could give them a drink. They would strike, he said. When he rode to Ramlah he took such cuttings from distant trees. Sometimes Dorothy spotted an invasion: the women-folk from a neighbouring place nipped over the walls to snap off silvery, skeletal bits from Boissy's. "It's customary," said Gaston.

The fig-trees behaved quite arbitrarily. Dorothy noticed that half a dozen would show leaf when others stayed wintry. She couldn't account for it. It seemed not a question of shelter, nor one of irrigation.

She liked to watch the hoopoes that visited the Boissy hectares. Her letter to Ida went on to the subject of birds.

"My daughter Ida will be a young woman of character," she commented to Ernestine.

Their crests flickered and their long beaks poked at the soil ploughed into stony furrows by the mule. *They remind me of snipe*, she'd written.

"When my husband died we were assaulted by the most absurd quarrel between Mrs Foyle from our lodge at Quarr and Mrs Brain from the village over which should lay George out. Mrs Brain's privilege it should have been, since she has laid out every soul for decades and her grandmother before her. Mrs Foyle claimed that the master had promised her she might. As if one would! Do you mention to your people that you would like to be laid out by one of them! It doesn't occur. But Mrs Foyle, in spite of being a giddy sort, was known to have had the master's ear. She came bolting up to the house, telling Mrs Cockerell, our cook-housekeeper, that the master had seen her laying him out in a dream. The impertinence of it! We all knew George dreamt dreams that nobody else would dream of dreaming."

Dorothy gasped, and clamped her fingers together.

"D'you see, we didn't think of enquiring just how large Mrs Foyle's know-how was. Mrs Brain had hot-footed it to the kitchen door, no sooner had she had wind she was needed. Downstairs they were obliged to prevaricate. Mrs Brain was incensed, for Mrs Foyle, with a start, the lodge's being a mere half-mile from the Grange, had stormed in with her, you know, sponges and cotton wool, and poured out this story of my husband and his dream. Mrs Brain is the senior of the two. Mrs Cockerell was reduced to tears. I dare say she was weeping anyhow."

Ernestine Boissy gaped at Dorothy.

"Into the mêlée went Ida. I was so shattered. It was, I might add, still the middle of the night."

"No!" cried Ernestine.

"It disgusted me that the news should have travelled so swiftly. Ida coped with Mrs Brain and Mrs Foyle. Stopped their coming to blows, I believe. And with darling Papa's expiring only the shortest while before! Not I, not Uncle Rupert, not the Colonel uncle, not our butler. A child, a mere gal.

"Now that," said Dorothy, "is illustrative of my daughter Ida."

51 My tomboy Griselda

"I'm afraid Mrs Foyle's schooling proved not to have been large, the creature didn't adequately tie up my husband's jaw," Dorothy added in a dry voice. "All rather awkward."

The hours of darkness (although they sharpened the pangs of losing George) Dorothy relished, because she wasn't obliged to take part in civil conversation. At Ramlah dogs had barked all night, left to watch over groves and enclosures: here in the quiet there were also dogs; fewer dogs, fewer alarms.

Instead, birds cried.

Embedded in the darkness were stars, so many that they filled what she told herself was the velvet dome of the sky, more stars than she could ever remember having observed. Her old favourites were particularly brilliant, the constellation of Orion, with Sirius and Regulus nearby, the Arabian stars Betelgeuse in Orion and Aldebaran in Taurus.

The sky at night she knew to be a comfort to her.

She said to Ernestine, "My daughter Griselda is the dark one." She meant only the colour of the child's hair.

They strolled towards the sea through wild mimosa which Dorothy thought ravishing. Presently they found themselves on a small rocky point where a seam of limestone shook off the encumbrance of land. Whilst the cove on one side shone with grit and shell, the bay on the other began with a slough of sand. Dorothy and Ernestine sat down on the rock and peered into the clear, clear water. Gaston Boissy decided to run along the beach. Dorothy thought this most comic: he pumped his arms and blew. He went barefoot. She couldn't imagine that any of the Quarr men would have lolloped in the sand; not, at least, in front of her; not even Oliver or Rupert. Good gracious! she thought.

"Griselda was a handful for Nurse," stated Dorothy.

"Then she developed a passion for the circus! She and her brothers performed tricks with their ponies for our entertainment. Until their daring became, shall we say, truly *out* of hand and my husband pronounced it too dangerous. There was a cob in the stables that George had bought from the gypsies, a spotted mare, and George let them practise standing on her at the trot and canter, which was splendid for them. Roland, my lost boy, you know, could vault cleanly on and somersault off. Griselda is, in consequence, tomboyish. I fear she will never be cured."

"Oh dear," said Ernestine, with a smile of sympathy for the absent Griselda.

Dorothy knew she'd been too strained in *Sea Blessing* to examine the bed of the sea. Perched like a cormorant in her charcoal attire on these low rocks, around about which the sea nosed smoothly, for there was no more than a breeze that day, she saw that the ribbed sand below the water was littered richly with shells. The pearly apricot shells of molluscs; flutes and horns and spirals of gratifying size. She had a twinge of excitement.

"We go into the water," said Ernestine, "Gaston and I, to pick them up sometimes."

"You too!" asked Dorothy.

"Or we drift in a small boat," said Gaston, dreamily; for he had returned, not all that out of breath.

"No one can spy on us," said Ernestine. "There is nobody."

"Besides," Boissy said, "the people are discreet. They don't speed to see if we disport ourselves. They withdraw, and wouldn't linger in the bushes either.

"Come, you can't do it from the rocks. Take my arm along the beach. The going is heavy."

Dorothy found the troughs of dry sand were indeed heavy and that the sand treated her boots ill. That didn't inspire her to leap about on the wet, though. Ernestine evidently couldn't contain herself.

Dorothy's hostess had nipped into the mimosa thickets and removed her stockings, was tiptoeing on her pretty feet into the sea, bending a little to clutch at her skirts.

"It's not warm," cried Ernestine, "the wind has chilled it. But often in the winter the sun makes it delicious."

Dorothy pinned a smile to her face which said that she regarded them indulgently. It also ruled herself out.

Since the sea was so shallow the two of them were soon at some distance from her and she felt alone. She couldn't catch their conversation. She saw that Ernestine was hampered and that neither could help but splash their clothes. How thankful I am I'm not impulsive, she thought.

Her fingers had gone to the place where she could feel a suspender through her skirt, petticoat and bloomers; the back suspender on the bulge of her upper leg. It wasn't difficult to undo suspenders like that; though front suspenders could be elusive. But she brought her hand away.

What insanity, she thought, and stepped in, boots and all.

Her skirt at once clung to her, soaked at the bottom; and wrapped itself between her legs in an indecent manner;

seemed likely to trip her and drag her down. She bowed her head and the brim of her hat shielded her from view.

When she had taken a stride or two she stood still.

She heard Ernestine shriek with pleasure; and so Dorothy waved gamely.

When she moved again she startled some creature which got from the tip of her toe and tore the sand in a waggling rush, creating a cloud.

Her boots were full of water.

She was better off than Ernestine because her hands were free and she didn't tend to topple over when she leant down. She collected those shells that attracted her eye. Her sleeves were sopping to the elbow.

Her hat had become somewhat dislodged. She tried with one hand to adjust the pin.

In her hand she held an exquisite razor-fish shell with dark lines at one end and a conch which had inky enamel stripes within; to take home, she thought, for Bevis.

Ernestine called out that she'd encountered a sole.

Dorothy knew herself to be quivering, for tiny fish were swimming under her skirts, she could feel them on her flesh.

They went back to Les Grenadiers in high spirits; and with gales of laughter from Boissy.

52 My scamp Bee

"I was a little foolish," said Dorothy to Stokes, and a smile hovered at her lips. Cynthia Stokes could have been knocked down with a feather.

"We brought but two pair of walking-boots, marm," she said; "and one already much worn."

"I fear you must manage," said Dorothy.

The upshot was that Ernestine and Boissy regarded her with a provoking gleam which wasn't ungratifying, was in fact more gratifying than had been the haste with which they'd got on Christian-name terms. That had ruffled her, since it had been for her, the senior, to make the first move: in retrospect, she chose to be charmed by it.

Dorothy often wore a hat indoors; if in and out. Ernestine seemed never to do so. Nor did Rupert's wife; although it was, Dorothy thought, increasingly hard to cast her mind back to Quarr.

"Bevis is an original child," she said. "He has plenty of imagination. I feel I needn't worry, he may be a young savage now, some day he'll go far. I believe he has several pretend friends. George used to allow the servants to lay an extra place for luncheon on Sunday."

"Not any more?" put in Ernestine.

Dorothy puzzled over that. "I cannot recall ever having forbidden it," she said.

"Naturally my children were stricken by the death of my husband. I still tremble to think of it.

"I too, I find widowhood strange," she said. "You do not want to hear about me."

"On the contrary," said Ernestine.

Dorothy was touched.

"But are you ready," said Ernestine, "to start! Look, Khalifa has his ears pricked."

Boissy came from the rear of the establishment.

"Bevis is a naughty boy," said Dorothy, with a measure of approval. "Robust."

When the expedition was assembled it consisted of the master and his Barbary horse; a mule-cart for the provisions; the black donkey, Bachnine, and the brown, Hanane, upon which Dorothy and Ernestine would be at liberty to ride according to whim, for they were to be gone all day; the servants, in red fez (known as a chéchiyyah) and white turban, Mansour and Kamel.

It was blustery out.

Whilst she was tying down her hat and slipping from the cool of the house, it occurred to Dorothy to wonder whether somebody had remembered in January to pack Bevis off to his preparatory school, for which he'd been down for ages.

He ought to have gone in the previous September. If not the September before that, when George had been alive!

Insufferable widowhood, she thought.

"I feel impelled to add, I was so thankful George was able to meet the last of my 'tinies'," she said. "It was my husband who named him."

"Yes," said Ernestine, "yes. How thankful you must have been. And now we shall ride to a spot we cherish, Gaston and I, where the sea is exquisite, which I think you will like."

Dorothy detected a note of glee.

"Guy Caspar Terence," she stated, with her sweet look.

53 Sidi Fankral

Off they went; lazily. Dorothy elected to walk for a while and Ernestine kept her company. From under the Caliph's hoofs the partridges rose, parting before him. Or so she fancied.

Through Boissy's vineyard they proceeded to gain a path that headed neither for Ramlah nor for the mimosa and the sea.

They wound across the plateau in the vague direction of the tubby fort.

The copper and green of the pomegranate leaf retreated behind them; alyssum was underfoot, and scylla, rock-rose; the skeletons of a strong oily lavender and orchids with spotted orange tongues bordered this enchanting path; whilst lizards with emerald gills briefly adorned the walls and tall yellow flowers sprouted out of clumps of smallish pink agave-like plants in the crevices. These forced the stone to accommodate them.

Nature began to load the scales in the clash between man and herself: the soil was less fertile. The bedouin who greeted Boissy were, they said, collecting fodder: "l'herbe", or in Dorothy's language bone-dry weed.

"Why don't you mount before the walling gives out?" called Gaston.

"He knows we come to more," said Ernestine.

"I am lost!" said Dorothy. "What leagues we must have marched!"

"Where shall we have second breakfast?" said Ernestine. "Are you thirsty, Dorothée?"

There was, Dorothy discovered, to be no diversion to explore the fort. Their vigour would be tapped too soon, the day over-prolonged.

Bachnine was not a slug. She stumbled along at a pace that was half jog-trot, half walk, and which made Dorothy feel very charitable towards her. Ernestine's donkey followed suit. The provisions lagged to the rear.

"We steer for the sea," said Boissy.

In a brief respite, Dorothy, reclining on a rug spread over tufts of esparto, had let memories of Quarr fill her thoughts. Gaston, who put as much of his vitality into being sleepy as he did into being alert, had nodded off; and Ernestine was listening to the curlews. Our Quarr ... thought its absent mistress.

The children would never forgive her, an excellent mama, if she were to omit to send home costumes for the dressing-up box.

"For what do you hunt?" asked Boissy all of a sudden.

"Scorpions," said Dorothy.

"There aren't scorpions in the winter."

A pleasant vista, most picturesque, of olive groves, in one of which a man laboured with a camel to plough between the trees a red-earthed, stony furrow, had debouched only to be forsaken. But as Dorothy rode on she perceived the reward. They came to a place where the bottom of the sky was quite close; and then to a low cliff; a rocky cove.

The mule-cart hadn't remained with them. A rough foreshore and a treacherous sea-bed, full of reefs, curled away in a long elbow. From its crook the palm-trees were evidently dense and covered the promontory; since the scatter of boats pulled up on the sand of a far-away beach was all there was to see.

What a lonely spot. So she remarked, "What a lonely spot." And Ernestine responded, "We knew you would like it."

54 A fatal hiatus

Boissy lit the fire there. A handful of fibre from a rotting frond blazed up at once. He trotted to and fro with flotsam. It was easy, little was too damp to burn well. Dorothy could find no fault in his skill in the construction of the wherewithal to grill. The ladies sat on the rugs decanted by the cart until the promised fish should arrive; wrapped, Ernestine said, in a basket of green palm in Kamel's arms.

A fresh breeze cooled Dorothy's cheeks, although she wondered whether her face-cream was truly up to the climate, and buffeted the brim of her hat; which was more disagreeable.

Languor, she thought, has claimed me; yes, claimed me; and in a departure from conventional behaviour she sprawled, or so she believed; leant back, in a girlish fashion, against her hostess's shoulder.

Gaston knelt beside her, took her hand and said, "Dorothée, we are so thrilled your brother entrusted you to us."

Dorothy raised her eyelids.

Ernestine twisted . . . so agile . . . and held Dorothy lest the latter topple. There was no other word for it, Ernestine had given her a hug. Well, what, oh had squeezed her indeed.

Dorothy widened her eyes.

It occurred to her that the two of them were regarding her oddly.

Ernestine pressed fondly against her, making her flesh creep. Boissy still clasped her hand.

She looked down at her glove. An eternity went by.

His thumb stroked it.

"Shall we," said Ernestine, "paddle?"

"Or shall we," said Gaston, in a practical, matter-of-fact tone, "move the rugs back beneath the palm-trees' shade!"

Dorothy was impelled to stagger up. This with some awkwardness, since all breath had departed from her chest.

"Where are you going?" Ernestine said. And, presently, calling, "Can you *manage*!"

Monsieur and Madame Boissy waited serenely on the sands.

55 Her flight

Dorothy knew herself to be a person of strong passions. The churning which now assailed her was dreadful.

As she bolted she lived again the moment: Boissy had moved his thumb, engrained by the flotsam, to and fro and she had looked up, and been unnerved. And it wasn't that she would have been so very shocked had some small, timid sign come from her hostess. Or even from her host. It was that they'd been in tandem, done it together. Far from timidly. Or had she been mistaken! Of course she'd been mistaken. And they would have understood that.

She nearly died from embarrassment.

Then she lived again the moment when Ernestine had embraced her; whereupon Boissy had moved his thumb and she'd raised her eyes, which had assumed the weight of cannon balls, and there'd been a sort of amused ardour in his.

. . . With the upshot that she'd paid no attention to the scenery; and hadn't the remotest notion where she was. She wasn't on any piste; and there surely must have been a crude one. Kamel and cart had rejoined them via it.

Knuckles that shook touched her flaming cheek. The sea now was nowhere. She believed it lay behind her.

The enormity of her action began to come home to her.

Flustered, she kept saying to herself, the two of them, how could they, do such desires exist; and, George would have deemed me fanciful; and, what on earth will Madame Boissy think of me! I can't go back to Les Grenadiers.

When she'd recovered some of her self-possession she saw she stood in the midst of desolation.

She swivelled her top half.

Her footsteps pursued her across an expanse of salt mud, a sebkha; or, as the French said it, "sebkra". The surface was crisp and crystalline.

For the first time, it dawned upon her that Boissy would follow; must follow and retrieve her if his duty as host and protector meant an iota to him.

With a laugh, that which cracks from one when there is little to entertain one ("demented", she thought to herself), she preferred to press on.

No plants could survive on this terrain. The fear that she might tread on treacherous sand and be sucked in did occur to her. She was not familiar with the nature of these phenomena. No birds flew over it or sang.

Her day-dreaming filled her mind again, bringing an element of peace.

When she'd resolved to return on foot to Les Grenadiers (for at least she wouldn't have to confront its proprietors until dinner), and at last addressed herself to the problem of where she was and in which direction she should go, she found the sterility had been transformed.

She was among palm-trees, their fronds quite still and not torn, their trunks straight; but she had the sense that she was in the open. For as far as she could see there was prairie. The palm-trees were frequent yet not hugger-mugger and all around them she saw pale green grasses. It was a simple landscape, palm-trees and grass; but birds enjoyed it, that was clear; and though the air should have been close and the sun was without doubt warm, she considered it refreshing.

It was also worrying.

She started to walk. She knew she had to keep the sun on her right cheek. The sun had barely left its zenith. It was of no use.

She was reminded of the pallid grass that grew in the woods in early summer at Quarr.

She bore hither and thither on animal tracks until her wits were confounded. Yet she held an obstinate course. She thought wheels had crushed her path only hours before and that the marks led her, a countrywoman, to her destination.

The view didn't change. The breeze off the sea didn't penetrate. Sometimes the palm-trees were in twos and threes. Sometimes they lay supine and dead. Dorothy rested on them. Often bushy fronds grew from a youthful bole. Once she passed a patch of sown wheat. She saw nobody.

Then in an eerie manner a large beady eye in a dark head with a beak was fixed on her. Its owner had frozen.

Dorothy caught her breath. She too was immobile. Between the palm-trees a trifle farther away were stalking what appeared to be very large birds. The one which had spotted her was staring at her hard.

Because the boles with bushy fronds were thick, a bird would be lost to sight; to emerge in pieces, beak, head, back and wings, leg. This was the queerest spectacle.

The dark head had altered its position by infinitesimal twitches. In the pool of the eye Dorothy saw comprehension. There was a cry and the flap of a grand wing, a general staring; alarm; and they hurried to get aloft; in all, Dorothy reckoned, nineteen or twenty; and dressing ranks in a skein; calling harshly. They were cranes.

Dorothy, who had felt weary, plodded on in better heart.

56 Lost

She saw no end to the prairie. She couldn't see out or where she might be; or what else lurked behind the furling boles, the palm-trees in groves of four and five big enough to hide an elephant.

She thought she heard herself sob. For wasn't that the pocket handkerchief of sown wheat? And wasn't the sun, which should have heated, when she tilted her hat, her cheek, now on her neck! Dorothy wished cranes would again stalk from cover. She perceived what impetuous unwisdom had led her to bolt, a trait she would have condemned in Esmond or Griselda.

She must have paused to take breath, got up and retraced her own route; how absurd.

Then her path in reverse came to a place where three other faint tracks met it. These she hadn't crossed before; but she did so.

Both the balls of her feet and her heels were sore: each time she put her foot down they reminded her.

Her thirst was considerable, and, used to quite a lot to eat, she would have liked a bite to stay her.

She wasn't afraid.

Her thoughts had revolved around the Boissy abode. She would have to elect to lay her head down in a den of vice and try to sleep the night. She and Stokes ... if there was no French or Turkish lady in Kerkennah (she'd met none socially or otherwise) upon whom she could throw herself? ... she and Stokes must journey to Sfax and, unaccompanied, to an hotel!

Might not immediate shelter be the more essential? Was she to see Les Grenadiers that night at all? Or not until her corpse was picked up in a fortnight or two, when Boissy and Ernestine sat their next guest on the black donkey Bachnine to be borne off to Sidi Fankral.

Previous acquaintance with deep gloom suggested to her that her spirit would lighten.

Her behaviour, therefore, was inexplicable to her when she opened her eyes to gape, through the wisps of hair that had fallen out of her hat, at the blind outer walls of two houses. Since she'd had no inkling of them, or that she'd been about to emerge from her jungle, she was rooted with shock.

Beyond the houses was dusty bare ground, fig-trees; perhaps an entire village.

Instead of making a bid for help, she had to dare herself to breathe; convinced that the rasp of the air between her tongue and palate was audible.

She was assaulted by voices, the cheerful voices of people.

These swelled to a hubbub. Some man was enjoying an argument. Dorothy felt shy; and then, in a strange way, fearful. She had intruded upon a scene in which she had no place.

As though caught eavesdropping she crept away. When a dog barked, she walked swiftly in the deep sand of the track. When a man spoke, quite closely behind her, she dived off it.

Soon she perceived that in order to be brave you had first to be afraid. Dorothy examined her actions and recognized the correctness of them. She had acted by instinct. Her instinct had served her well; why, she didn't know. It would take her to Les Grenadiers, which was patently in the opposite direction. She was also glad to have been prevented from wearying herself, to have been sent about turn.

A mere quarter of an hour later, she knew her hopes depended on such assistance. She sank down to consider the matter.

57 Dishevelled

The paucity of the shade, this puzzling shade of so many narrow trees, roused her to fresh effort.

When you are sensible, and are forced to see that you have not been sensible, you wonder how you can trust yourself. Her heart thumped against her ribs; and drummed in her ears. Quite absurd of it, since she had rested.

Dorothy couldn't find the lane with the sand that billowed over her feet. The sun was lower in the sky. She adjusted her hat-pin so the hat was tilted to protect her face. More strands of hair cascaded out of it. Her skin was burnished, she thought.

She walked steadily, in circles.

When she felt a slight breeze reach her in the prairie, she pursued it in renewed faith. She was relieved to stumble upon the sea.

She lowered herself to remove her boots and rub her toes. She sat like that, with stockinged feet, for many, many minutes; staring at a horizon that was empty of boats, and at a shore devoid of clues. She licked her lips.

This island was not wide: where Les Grenadiers was situated, one could cross it in an hour. It was *long*. The thought took hold of her that she was farther still from the house; not between house and Sidi Fankral.

It was a bedraggled Dorothy who set off beside a sinking sun to follow the beach. The sea was riddled with jagged rocks: it glowered at her with the colour of blood. The flicker of wind had dropped. She noticed how determined the sun was to go down. Her own veins rallied and she positively strode.

She had sun and sea on her shoulder and duly suffered grief: to cut a corner in the shape of (she assumed) a promontory, she'd struggled over tumbled cliff, wounded that it could be as lofty as it was. When she'd stumbled for the fifth time she didn't pick herself up for half an hour. The terrain was impossible.

Nightfall brought her back to the prairie.

58 Boissy

Gaston Boissy had congratulated himself: without Khalifa it would have been a nightmare.

Once it had dawned on them that Dorothée had been gone too many minutes, Ernestine (lest it was delicate) had been dispatched to investigate and the alarm raised. They buckled to with a will. She couldn't have got far. They searched on foot.

Ernestine's calling reverberated around the palm-trees. Boissy took to his horse.

In quite a short time he believed it was safe to eliminate Sidi Fankral and the peninsula. Kamel and Mansour had brought the fish and their consternation was plain. But Ernestine considered a wait was appropriate before servants were enrolled in pursuit. Boissy crossed the grey waste of the sebkra and thought he'd spotted her footprints. He'd ridden slowly. He dismounted and led his horse. He tracked her confidently for a while and then with misgiving. It seemed she'd perched on a fallen trunk. She appeared not to have trodden away from the trunk and couldn't have flown. He wondered . . . Had he deluded himself?

El Khalifa wove through the palms of the prairie. How he'd missed her Boissy couldn't imagine: he returned to Ernestine.

Now Kamel must keep the black donkey Bachnine; whilst Mansour should go with Madame, Hanane and the cart, towards home. An offering of food (to be stolen by dogs), water and a rug to remain lest the English madame seek here for them.

Boissy hesitated over the cart . . . no, she couldn't be supine.

In a gesture eloquent of perturbation, Mansour unwrapped and wrapped the fish.

When Ernestine had mounted her donkey, Boissy went to Ramlah, made circumscribed enquiries and then pursued every lane until most possibilities were exhausted.

Kamel was to go from the beach and wander, or sit on Bachnine to do so, whither he believed best. Boissy himself made for Les Grenadiers. If she were not there a hue and cry would be unavoidable. He told himself, This is ridiculous.

59 Stokes pitches in

The sun had dyed the sea crimson before Cynthia Stokes was cognizant. She had made full use of an afternoon of leisure. Her inclination was to laugh. But she set out to reassure Madame Boissy that her mistress was in sound health and able to walk back to The Grenadiers, no matter how!

"Stokes," said Madame Boissy, "Madame Lupus has been rather unwell."

"No doctor," said Cynthia, "discovered much amiss beyond her being plagued by her nerves. Moods. And," she added conscientiously, "her tummy upsets. Four or five of them."

Ernestine, who caught the gist of "nerves" though not of "tummy upsets", threw up her hands.

"Without water since mid-morning!" cried Madame Boissy.

Stokes, though, was less unsympathetic than might have been thought. Asked what Mrs Lupus was likely to do in the circumstances, Stokes said, "Manage."

She wondered aloud, "Whatever made her run off!" Madame Boissy shook her head and her eyes clouded. Stokes sallied out to meet her lady, who was odds on to be in a bad humour. The air was liquid, thought Cynthia, and the earliest stars had begun to render themselves visible. Intrigued, she was buoyed by a sort of secret thrill.

Soon, mystified, she came back.

60 Night

Dorothy had a dim memory of joking with herself. She recollected with horror her fancy that she might not see Les Grenadiers before night.

It was lunatic. Surely Boissy would have looked for her!

Her mouth was swollen and parched, for this day of winter had been quite warm. Her limbs ached. She grew solemn and, she thought, childish. Had she been in the Punjab or Ceylon, she thought, her mind would by now have been adrift. Her mind was not adrift. Her predicament, on the contrary, was that she'd retained clarity. Bodily exhaustion was, it seemed, attended by horridly fresh cogitation.

If she were to lie by a path, Boissy might find her. In that case, why hadn't he found her already? Were she to crawl away to the seclusion of a palm-bole she could well be missed.

Would he not shout?

The light went.

Pigeons had clattered in to roost between the stubs of the fronds. A chill descended and dogs started to bark. Dogs on guard in groves and gardens, she judged, since the sound was stationary. Shadows flitted in the prairie: the slightest stir made her jump. Dorothy was used to being out of doors at night. But not, she thought, all night. It shocked her to her very soul. However, that notion wasn't uppermost. There must be snakes in the palm-trees, and animals that roamed, wild animals! For the first time, she was glad Kerkennah was cut off from the mainland and possessed a modest fauna.

She clasped her knees in her arms. She would stay upright; and alert.

Soon, she started to suffer.

It was noisy; whereas the day had been full of silence.

An annoying bird swooped constantly about and from its throat came an ear-splitting wail.

She was past wishing to identify it.

The ground struck her as hard. She felt peculiar. She was, indeed, terrified; yet so physically in extremis that she could ignore this. Daring greatly, she tugged a decayed palm frond over her. It showered her with dust.

61 Weeping

For the first time in her life she failed to wonder at the magnitude of the firmament. The sky was soft and black, there was no moon yet, and stars pricked out all over it, filling it with ever more light. Dorothy turned her face to the ground.

Her ears were alerted to the breath of the wild and the cries of four-legged creatures, the grunting of snouts and tiny rustles in the grass, that pale green grass which had reminded her of the grass of early summer in the woods at Quarr.

Unknown insects throbbed out of all reason.

What would George have made of it? By dying, he had ultimately brought her into such peril. She whispered out loud, "My dearest!" She choked and inadvertently snuffed up such an insect into her nostrils. She heard a moan. It was she herself who had moaned.

People like her didn't moan.

He didn't come to her.

The air was cold.

When George had expired like that in the night, he'd remained with her: his beloved tones, the scent of him, his tread. His laughter.

Transfixed, she listened to snarling, a snarling between two or more beasts that was reminiscent of the high-pitched falsetto of foxes. Were there jackals? She sat up. She attempted to stand: her feet, caked by weeping blisters, wouldn't bear her. She crawled; and after a moment crawled back.

She had the uncanny feeling that the wild creatures had arrived to peer at her.

She knew that her best defence was defiance.

Her head drooped.

Oblivious, she dreamt of the children. They were hand in hand. As if for a photograph they faced her, unnaturally rigid. Esmond, Griselda, Ida in the middle, Roland, Bevis . . . They were too distant for her to perceive that tears had dried on their cheeks. She recognized that mossy bank; the ashen gorse; tendrils of honeysuckle in silver birch. The photograph moved. Ida had opened her mouth. What is it! asked their mother. Dorothy noticed they were in some kind of distress. Her own, impassioned torment leapt; though her feet were bogged. Who are you, Roland whispered. Your mother, she replied. Mother has gone away, she heard Roland mutter. She found herself awake; as though hit by a bolt from heaven.

It gave her the courage to endure.

Towards dawn, birds began to flutter. How she'd missed the Quarr chorus!

Half dead, frozen in her bones, and certainly as stiff as a corpse, Dorothy spent hours without sleep. Yet she must have slept a sweeter sleep for she saw it was light and she'd heard voices.

The barking had ceased.

A small hand touched her.

She clenched her eyes.

She was in the throes of a nightmare, for the hand, which she'd taken to be the hand of a child, was replaced by a hot, goat-ish smell; and the treble bleat was revealed to be that of an animal.

"Madame," it said.

Her lids ungummed themselves.

A child squatted beside her. Farther off, another boy hovered on the point of flight. The brown, silky tresses of goats seemed to fan the first rays of the sun. The palm-fronds and the goat-hair made those flicker crazily.

With her cheek on the ground Dorothy murmured through her strange lips, "Bonjour."

The boy let out a great sigh.

"What are you doing?" he said.

A self-important ewe thrust to the fore.

Puzzled, Dorothy felt for a web, a ghost of which lay across her waist.

"Inti maridah, tu malade," said the boy.

"Madjnounah," stated the other.

"Tu pas folle," said the rescuer.

"No, not mad."

She was calm. She heard herself say, "Do you speak French?" She said, "Monsieur Boissy, do you know his house. Les Grenadiers?"

"Yes," he said.

"Please take me there!" said Dorothy.

His eyes were bright and full of curiosity.

"Tu seule, madame."

"I am," said Dorothy.

"Where chaussures."

She wriggled her toes. She traced an arc with her fingers.

The other boy's steps echoed faintly beneath her ear.

She was aware next that somebody was attempting to jam unfriendly leather onto a bloated foot.

"Ow," she said, "ow!"

Her hat was being used: it flapped over her face. Her face was bloated too, and scratched. On her head was a rook's nest; the hair-pins prodded into her scalp.

She managed a wobbly smile.

"Can you walk?" asked the child.

"I don't think so," she said.

"Walk chouayyah, then donkey, maybe cart.

"Walk a little!" he pleaded.

He was bare-headed and almost barefoot: a few scraps of leather dragged themselves about beneath his feet. He had on a loose, djellabiyyah-like shirt. Looped around his middle was his sling-shot, plaited from esparto (it was the web she'd sensed on her waist: he'd put it down on her).

His hands were none too pristine.

The other child had head-gear, a turban of towelling with yellow tassels; and in one of his hands he held tight to roasted grain, because he'd untied it from a corner of his costume some moments before they'd spotted her. The wrinkled cloth still stuck out polyp-fashion.

"Come, madame," the boy said.

"I cannot," she said.

"Stand."

She tried to hobble.

"I shall have to remove my boots." Her head swam.

He shook his head wonderingly.

He pointed to her feet, and walked his arms to and fro. He carried her boots.

"Is it far?" she said.

"Marche," he said.

Dorothy leant on his shoulder.

The flock tripped after them.

Utterly amazed, she glimpsed, through the palm-trees of

the prairie, dry-stone walls and almond blossom; the welcome green of olive-leaf!

The pastoral paradise, although it was only the fertile land, crashed upon her senses: she gasped.

"Not far," said the boy.

In her stained, torn garments she sank onto a large stone the size of a Roman milestone, missed it and collapsed. On the other side of the wall a bedouin woman all of a sudden stood up; and as suddenly shot away, stopping like a deer to look from a relative safety.

62 Her deliverer

"Wait," said the boy.

He hauled her into the shade of a limy, plastered shell of a cistern.

"You," sighed Dorothy, "are called what?"

"Daoud ben Mustapha," he said, and grinned.

"Daoud," she repeated, "ben Mustapha." She didn't vouchsafe her own name.

He spoke to the bedouin woman in signs: she was deaf. Dorothy scowled about in a reptilian sort of way.

The sheep and goats were grazing too near, plainly torn between hunger and nosiness. They agitated her. He threw a small stone at them. The ewes seemed affronted. A flood of Arabic was directed at the other child.

"Les Grenadiers?" she said.

She wobbled; and despised her weakness. Her swollen tongue protruded; it lolled over her cracked lip.

"Thirst," said Daoud.

"Very much so," she whispered, "yes."

He looked hopefully for a passing donkey. But he plucked fruit from the prickly pear. Daoud had chosen his place with a shrewd notion of her desperation.

"Knife!" he said.

She was doleful. "No," she said.

With infinite caution he worked to strip a fruit of its clusters of spines, keeping the tips of his fingers in between them; spines so fine they pierced human skin at the least touch.

Then he handed it to her. She didn't take it.

He started to peel the fruit. A violent red juice spurted and dripped between his feet onto the white stones. He again held it out; a knob of soft flesh. Gingerly she received it and inserted it into her mouth.

"Good!" he asked.

Her glove had been immediately soaked by this virulent red, and she knew her lips must also be stained. He began on the next fruit. "The rosy are the best," he said.

"You eat one, Daoud," she said hoarsely.

Daoud did eat one but her thirst was incorrigible and she ate seven.

"Enough," he said.

The sun was shining quite aslant. "I have the strength to go on walking," she said.

Daoud is my first true friend, she thought in the recesses of her dim, weary mind.

"Wait," he said.

The pungent sweetness of alyssum rose to her nostrils.

She closed her eyes.

63 Her return

Boissy at this moment was tearing his hair. He'd been up all night, and out for much of it; he'd scoured the land between Ramlah, the Sidi Fankral peninsula and Les Grenadiers; searched the ruins of the Byzantine fort and was by now far farther afield.

Dorothy had gone off again and Daoud grown anxious

when M'barek arrived to plough between his olive-trees. It was work that made a strong mule struggle; for stones rucked in the soil, a yield with no cease.

"Cet homme M'barek," observed Daoud.

She gurgled.

After an animated confabulation, M'barek hoisted the lady, who was protesting vaguely, onto his cart.

Daoud climbed in with her. Her guide wouldn't leave her; not yet. He grinned broadly. The other child was rebellious. Daoud cast several more missiles in the direction of the troop.

M'barek, in a loose turban of yellow-gold, trudged by his mule, speaking to the latter: presently, when the going was less rough, he swung himself onto the corner where the crude shaft met the body. His legs dangled.

A whitish dog with a curly tail trotted in front.

Dorothy's form went bump-bump-bump on coarse, tilted palm-boards.

"Où ton mari!" Daoud said.

She didn't hear him.

Once he stroked her forehead: she was aware of this.

The sun warmed her.

She had dreams still more vivid, still more disturbing. She held red gobs of flesh in her ungloved hand, she stuffed them between her lips; her whole knuckle entered her mouth and she groaned; her knuckle twisted; she tugged it and it fell out with a plop.

Somebody had said, "Mon dieu, Gaston is out searching for you and with urgency!"

"I'm so sorry," Dorothy attempted to say; in a polite voice.

"You will go to bed. Soon you will feel better."

"Daoud," whispered Dorothy. "Where is Daoud?"

"Not money," Daoud said to the French madame in tones of revulsion.

"They won't take money. They are proud."

"Say . . . say I wish him to return to your house."

"I think you should not talk."

"Daoud," murmured Dorothy. "Tu es fier!"

"She's delirious," said somebody.

Daoud had gone.

64 Recovery

Stokes had fussed admirably over her, washed her and spooned liquid into her mouth; and soothed olive oil (the sweet-oil with which George had anointed the injuries of hounds) into her hands and feet.

The invalid slept and stirred again. Boissy stood with a hand on the pillow. "When will the doctor come?" she mumbled.

"We have no doctor," said Ernestine. "Kerkennah has no doctor."

Dorothy thought, Noll brought me to islands that have no doctor.

"I always wished to be a colonial wife," she said.

Ernestine said, "There is a local person."

"I can tell you his remedy," said Boissy. "He would break the skin . . . make cuts on your forehead and rub harissa into them."

After a long silence, Dorothy said, "What is harissa!"

"Hot spice," said Ernestine. "Red pimento."

"I shall not have that," said Dorothy. She added, "Daoud's fruits were red. The child saved me."

She dropped into a fever.

She recollected the bloody oozing fruits and felt them in her ungloved palm and against the roof of her mouth. The words "bull's testicles" came to mind, although she'd never seen butchered testicles in her life. She recollected the sweetness of the fruits and how they'd retrieved that life by quenching a desperate thirst.

She was in no doubt they were responsible; for hadn't she positively gorged on them.

Then her dreams of the daybreak, when she'd been comatose in the cart, came back to her. It was the dream of the night that illuminated her entire being.

She cried out, "*I must go home!*"

65 Cynthia Stokes

"You missed the bechi lamouni," Boissy was to say in the agitated days that followed, "a highly special fish, how could you miss the bechi lamouni!" Boissy was so concerned and Ernestine displayed such patent innocence.

Yet it was beyond bearing to remain until Oliver fetched her. She panted to be at Quarr.

Soon she wasn't so sure about them. There were times when Gaston would regard her whimsically. She believed he must be penitent, and that he'd felt the lapse.

It was immaterial.

To Stokes, Dorothy said: "I am going home, Stokes. If we don't see Mr Oliver shortly, you and I will travel to Sfax alone and to England. Won't that be pleasant!"

Cynthia chose the moment to say she wished to leave Mrs Lupus's service.

"What *do* you mean!" quavered Dorothy.

She gazed at Stokes.

Stokes was to be "wed".

"Oh, very well," said Dorothy, who felt weak. "Rather sudden. However, we'll talk about it when we are at the Grange again."

"No, marm," said Stokes.

"Who is the lucky fellow!" croaked Dorothy, as though she hadn't heard, which indeed she had not.

"Who is your intended?"

"He is a local man," said Stokes.

"From Plash," Dorothy said, "or Lackham perhaps?"

"Not a mite away."

"You mustn't be provoking, Stokes. I'm not strong. On the estate?"

"In Ouled Kacem."

"What!" said Dorothy.

"He has a shop in Ouled Kacem."

"Where is that?"

She knew already.

"But a two-mile from The Grenadiers."

Stokes pronounced this like guardsmen, although she was well aware it was not. She couldn't account for it to herself, this obstinacy; for she had no lust to bait Mrs Lupus.

"You fancy," said Mrs Lupus, "you will be able to make your way back to Kerkennah."

"I shall remain, marm," said Cynthia. "So to speak, when you depart."

Dorothy widened her eyes. It occurred to her that she'd never properly looked at Stokes.

"Don't be absurd," she said. "You cannot do that."

Stokes held her ground.

"You will accompany me (and perhaps Mr Oliver) to Quarr. Then we may consider." Dorothy roused herself to effort.

"You should reflect wisely," said Dorothy.

Stokes folded her hands over her middle.

"My dear woman," whispered Dorothy, "are you besotted!"

"I expect so," said Cynthia.

Dorothy detected no note of insolence. Stokes quite glowed; woodenly, but glowed.

"No no," said Dorothy, "this won't do. You shall not make a step which I am aware you will regret. I shall save you from it. Besides ... I have need of you." (It is *imperative*, wailed some inner Dorothy.)

"Thank you, marm," said Stokes, "I stay."

To her own ears Dorothy sounded chagrined. "You've been walking out?"

"Yes, marm."

Profound hush. Working herself up, thought Stokes.

"You've observed ... well, the circumstances in which you would live ... The man's family?"

Stokes nodded.

"Well," said Dorothy, "will you become a Mohammedan! Unless ... have I misunderstood ... can he be a Frenchman, by any chance?"

Cynthia said, "The fellows are permitted to marry Christians, it's only the women-folk who are forbid to."

"I fear I'm not up to this conversation. I never suspected that you, Stokes, would entertain me with such a . . . farrago."

"I don't wish to annoy you, marm," said Cynthia, seething. "I dare say you're still bilious."

"My consideration is wholly for you. Has he . . . you know, other wives?"

"No," said Stokes. "It's the Ottomans who chiefly have that habit, I understand.

"And what harm," maintained Cynthia Stokes stoutly, "if they do?"

Mrs Lupus's breath seemed to hiss between her lips. "Ughah," she uttered; and there was an impatient gesture.

"You haven't understood. I have urgent plans and they are not to be thwarted. It can't be helped," said Dorothy. "I have first claim on you. As soon as I am fit I shall travel, and you will, to Sfax. On the subject of this man, we may or may not be able to consult Mr Oliver," said Dorothy. "I might have a word with Monsieur Boissy."

"I'll not brook any botheration."

"Stokes!" wailed Dorothy. "Well, really!"

"I'm ever so blissful, marm."

"And I," said Dorothy, "am adamant."

"I shall not be allocating my principles."

"You mean 'abrogating'," said Dorothy.

Cynthia said to herself, Not any more than I do to work for you. A darn sight less.

"It's been an honour to work for you, marm."

"What age is he and what does he do? I act," Dorothy said, "in loco parentis. Before we go, I shall have to make his acquaintance . . ." (she sighed) ". . . I suppose. Once we are at Quarr, you will be at liberty. You'd better make the most of your last week."

"You will find him most personable," said Stokes, "I am sure."

"Good God, I can't allow you to be so foolish."

"I'll not accompany you to Sfax, marm, let alone Quarr."

"Run away now," replied Dorothy. She pressed her cheek into the chair-cushion.

"You may engage another," offered Cynthia.

66 Nothing happened to you

"Was I feverish for days?" asked Dorothy.

"Days," Boissy assured her.

"How we've prayed for the brother-in-law!" said Ernestine. Oliver was there in their midst, bursting with the strange places to which he'd travelled. But nobody was engrossed enough to listen.

Dorothy, to his surprise, fell on him.

She had to go home, she said, straightaway. She didn't wish to linger.

She'd been lost and had nearly expired.

"Dorothée wasn't," said Ernestine theatrically, "*found until morning!*"

"She is indomitable," said Boissy.

When the story was poured out, Oliver said: "Nothing *happened* to you."

Dorothy in the old days would have denounced him as horrid. Instead, she managed to say with some dignity, "Don't scoff. I must go to Quarr, do take me!"

"That's rather exasperating of you," he drawled. "Don't you want to sail to Malta? Nothing happened to you," he reiterated. "*Did* it?"

"I don't know," she spluttered.

"Formidable," said Boissy, with his lurking guilt; "tout à fait."

She said, "Dogs barked all night."

"Absurd," said Oliver to Boissy, "that she could get herself lost in so small a corner. She is a countrywoman."

"One is puzzled by the prairie," said Boissy. "It's a labyrinth."

They considered her a poor creature. They hadn't bothered to hide it from her, she thought. She pretended not to notice, and to take Boissy's compliments with grace.

Oliver could grapple with the quandary over Stokes.

Stokes said, "It's wizard you brought me, Mr Oliver."

"Do you understand," said Oliver gravely, "he may have built his own house and keep a shop, but . . ."

Dorothy interjected, "Couldn't you do better for yourself in England, what happened to your nice petty officer!"

". . . Kerkennah will not be rich. A living will always have to be begged from the soil. Water will never spout forth. The natives will never prosper, and not have riches to squander on provisions in his shop. You will be far from familiar comforts, and many different customs do tend to prevail."

"The sun must be so fierce in the summer," remarked Dorothy. "I had quite assumed, Stokes, you would complain of sleeping in a cubby-hole in Monsieur Boissy's courtyard!"

"I know when I'm suited," said Cynthia Stokes.

Dorothy snorted.

"You mustn't spoil her fun, Dolly," said Oliver.

Dorothy thought they were as bad as each other.

"How could you egg her on!" she said when they were in private. "How could you be so *irresponsible*!"

"You are such a spoiler," said Oliver.

She was stung to the quick.

Boissy said, "Slaheddine dropped in on me, that's the nub of it."

"You didn't have to introduce Cynthia, did you, to him," said Oliver, "so that she was slain!" Boissy rocked with inward laughter.

They make a joke of it, thought Dorothy. It is I who am to be deprived of her.

She regretted her own intemperance. Yet, she told herself, it had been Stokes's *fault*. The woman had frustrated the plan to depart, had taken her mistress aback. Well for Stokes that Oliver had put in an appearance!

"Ha!" said Noll.

"I don't wish to be hard on you," she said to Stokes.

"Don't mention it, marm," said Stokes.

Dorothy thought she would instruct Oliver to bestow on Stokes ten pounds in francs.

"Do stop talking about it," she quavered to Noll, "now."

(She was craven: she was to omit to pay a visit in Ouled

Kacem; despite a cordial invitation. Stokes was left behind like a layer of petticoat, affronted.)

Dorothy had been obliged to shrug off several irritations, since the boy hadn't come; and didn't.

"Send him a message!" she said.

Boissy had already ridden Barb Khalifa to Sidi Bouraoui to locate Daoud and beg him to visit the English lady; but he forbore to tell Dorothy of this subterfuge.

67 Daoud

"The boy may not come," Boissy had warned Dorothy.

Dorothy was at last triumphant.

She felt she could be intimate with Daoud in a way inconceivable with her hosts or Oliver Lupus. So her first words (no sooner Oliver had shaken his hand, conversed kindly in Arabic, and she could be by herself with him) were: "Daoud, I have to go to my home . . . my children are in need of me, tu sais."

She judged him to be younger than Esmond.

"Was that your brother," she enquired, "with you?"

"Chum," he said.

"Do you have brothers?" she asked.

"Yes," he said, with a happy smile.

"Sisters too?"

"Yes."

It was on the tip of her tongue to ask how many when he said, "He your husband?"

"My husband," she said, "is not with me. Monsieur is my husband's brother."

Daoud repeated his old question, "Où ton mari!"

"I am a widow," she said.

The child was still picking spines out of his fingers, she noticed.

Ernestine carried an elongated glass of grenadine out to the terrace.

Ernestine, being in Dorothy's opinion a practical, natural female, too natural, had fetched also a pair of tweezers. His palms were freshly marked by juice.

He produced a little bag, a screw of fig-leaf. Inside it nestled five rosy ones.

He took the tweezers from Madame Boissy and prodded gently against the base of a cluster of spines, no doubt overlooked. The fluff carried on the air and fell at his feet.

"Attention!" said Madame Boissy.

She took a step back. Dorothy recoiled.

Dorothy had been longing for more of those crimson gobs, even at the expense of delirium. She had gone so far as to search for a prickly pear with its figs ripe. The bigger, uglier, yellow fruit was more common. There were many prickly pear, not many which were bearing. But she held herself somehow aloof.

What she was used to doing with children was taking them for walks. She herself, after all, was keen to be stronger. The soles of her feet hadn't quite healed.

The idea that he might already have walked a long way never entered her head.

They might even get as far as the sea.

It was a grand day, in the enchanted sunshine of Kerkennah. "Yes, the sun always in Kerkennah," said Daoud. "Clouds over Sfax, blue sky for Kerkennah." The air, that same air which had blown away the spines of the prickly pear, was light. The fig-trees were showing more green.

Daoud's presence beside her attracted cheery waves.

She had unbent enough to acknowledge these with warmth.

They would go in a north-westerly direction; pass through the mimosa.

The water hung limpid and smooth in the bed of the sea. Dorothy was not unappreciative of its beauty; although it was a very stark beauty. She sat on the ground, her legs tucked to one side; and Daoud cross-legged beside her. He looked up at her, grinning.

"I have nougat and loukoum for you," she said, "that I shall give you when we are at the house of Monsieur Boissy once again."

"Merci," he said.

"Monsieur Boissy will call in on your father and measure you for new sandals."

"Merci," he said.

"I shall write to you. Letters."

"Not read," he said.

"You can't read or write!"

"Incha'llah I learn."

"But you *speak* French, and not too wretchedly!

"Monsieur Boissy, when I am gone, will endeavour to see you are not in need."

He didn't quite understand, so his tongue slipped across his lower lip, to and fro, to and fro, and retreated.

"Why you alone in the prairie!" he said.

They'd proposed an outing to Sidi Fankral and, "We never got there!" That was a pity.

Sidi Fankral was "normal", said Daoud. "Venerated man, in paradise some while."

She'd been detached from her party, Monsieur and Madame, the donkeys and mule-cart. (Her brother-in-law, Daoud should understand, had at the time left for Douiret and the "Grand Sud".)

"I was lost and decided to head for Les Grenadiers," said Dorothy.

"Alone, lost, all night!"

"That is so," she said, and laughed.

"Prairie dangerous," he said.

"Dangerous?" she exclaimed. "I am an English lady. How could it be dangerous!"

"You not safe alone," he said. "Wild dogs. Maybe bite you."

Wild dogs ran out and attacked the passing wheels.

"Comme les chiens partout!" said Dorothy. "Dogs can't resist the revolving of wheels."

He didn't admire her sang-froid.

He eyed her.

"How you lost?" he said.

"I was embarrassed and wished to escape from Monsieur and Madame ... You are too young," said Dorothy.

"No," he said.

"What do you mean, 'no'," she said. "You don't know what I'm tempted to tell you." She was sure he wasn't following her French.

"When Latin people, grown-ups, are marooned on an island, without much to divert them, their spirits become infected, I dare say," observed Dorothy.

His smile was one of total incomprehension.

"They tried to ... I thought they wanted to touch me."

She sounded so melancholy.

He put his arm around her and hugged her.

She couldn't misunderstand what ensued. He was making improper advances.

"How old are you?" she asked.

"Fifteen," he said.

"Fifteen," she repeated, dazed. "Heavens."

She wasn't offended.

She said, "Tu es trop petit, you are a little boy."

"No," he said, proudly.

To her surprise she stretched out and stroked his cheek with the back of a finger.

She was shaken because she knew she was soppy about him; and she'd wanted to hold him to her.

Dorothy didn't fail. Her duty was as transparent as the sea.

Perhaps she'd had a glimmer as to why Stokes was set to adopt a disastrous course.

She'd tapped Daoud's cheek; yet at the same time, although distracted, had a most haunting ache.

She'd found herself studying him, the bloom on his skin and his dark hair, his nose straight, she thought, from a Phoenician coin. Ever afterwards she would hear him speak to her in his confident treble.

68 Dearest children

At long last I say goodbye to the shores of Africa and am eager to shake each of you by the hand, for with what fortitude you have borne the loss of your mother – how she wishes she'd never gone away! Tomorrow we are to put Tunis behind us, she wrote on a view of the medina. *Close to our journey's end!*

"You're frightfully pensive," said Noll.

She disregarded him and bent over her writing-case.

She tore her picture postcard in half. There should be no diminution of the surprise.

After the railway engine had steamed into Holtworthy Halt, Dorothy was driven through the countryside, late in March, with a palpitating heart and a tremulous smile. What might be amiss at Quarr she was unable to tell. In the dream the children had summoned her back.

"Why the fidgets?" said Noll, unaware. "Soon we'll be there."

Only her own absence? she pondered.

Ida would be taller and slender; Griselda less gauche; Bevis away at school. Guy would toddle (no infant in arms) to clasp her skirts and his wee paws would have to be prised open to release her. She saw a household in uproar and the cavorting of dogs. She'd have been unnatural not to have pictured it already. Yet what else?

Grieving she thought, George is for certain with us in spirit.

Had he been with her or had he remained at home? She couldn't fathom that. She could revel in the scent of pine and heath; the swelling of bud on the trees; the beeches, the silver birch, the horse chestnut, the roadside elm; the oaks were still bleak. Hazel catkins hung quite fuzzy, the pussy she adored was blown; yet there were primroses along the banks of the ditch and the gorse was breaking out its golden blaze.

Unsuspicious, she pricked her ears: on the breeze, from far away, down, maybe, by the decoy, was borne the sound of a hunting-horn; or more of a warble.

"Stop the motor!" she said.

IV QUARR WOUNDED

69 Spillikins

In those Easter holidays that succeeded the loss of her master, Mop attached herself to Esmond. She was still the smiling dog she'd always been. A great melancholy hung over Quarr. It was a bitter spring. The point-to-point races hadn't been cancelled. In other respects some terrible changes were to occur.

Mop was confident in her understanding of the world and in her ability to deal with it. Not so, thought Esmond, the rest of us.

Mop sat beside Esmond and Gerald on the bank while they fished; or she flushed out and retrieved for them. The boys enjoyed – if that was the right word – some rough shooting; often while Dorothy, *rigid* from the funeral, was still pecking at the brown bread and butter that came with her early-morning tea.

Gerald Chieveley was a kind boy. He was four years older than Esmond. He would have blushed at the notion that it was beneath his dignity or that it spelt tedium to spend his holidays at the Grange with his Lupus cousins; and now he accepted Esmond's silences and laughter with unembarrassed simplicity.

It had transpired that Donkey Lorimer was a Trustee; of Papa's friends, one who was famously dense! Mr Lorimer was staying.

Mr Lorimer liked to clap his hand to Esmond's shoulder and amble about the place. Esmond's expression was a treat. Donkey's grey matter went unchallenged: in the old days he'd smirked when tormented.

He'd brought two of his offspring. The Lupus children

("Grieving children," said Nursie) were dragooned at intervals into entertaining them. Neither small Lorimer was a scream.

Uncle Noll had rushed home.

Uncle Oliver was an old hand at the fabulous. He would tell not a soul he was due. He dispatched ahead exotic presents and possessions in crates. They'd arrive at Holtworthy, whereupon a message would inform the Grange. Once, a dog-box with air-holes and a perforated-zinc window had delivered dearest Lalla; Lalla, swifter than all the dogs and so hardy, with her wispy, silken coat, she'd managed not to shiver in the English winter.

Oliver had come silently, too late; and sad.

He and Rupert were heard shouting at each other. There was perpetual hoo-ha.

Gervase Sturt went away spluttering.

The estate was entailed onto Esmond and most of the money. This was more than a question of primogeniture. Money was needed to run everything, so of course to the person who inherited the land had to go the means to do that.

Although *people* were provided for, and Dorothy would never have to worry her head, there had devolved a crisis for the Quarr Hunt.

Esmond was helpless and his Trustees were bound by their responsibility to him.

Well over two thousand a year, for four days a week, was what it had cost George, who had hunted the country at his own expense; well over.

Dorothy's prime purpose was to rid the Kennels of hounds. So long as they remained, she was reminded of that night when her husband had perished. The least sound of them was intolerable. She had to struggle not to clap her hands over her ears; and to prevent a spasm from surfacing in her features.

It was not in her gift, precisely; but she'd seen to it that the hounds were offered to the Hunt Committee (a Hunt Committee formed in haste, of recent date), on condition that they leave the Kennels at Quarr; leave for ever. (Of course she hadn't dreamt that this offer would have to be rejected.)

Kennels, stable-yard and dwellings "to stand empty".

It was useless to stare at her. Her mourning forbade all remonstrance, thought Rupert.

What happened thereafter was, she said, of small concern. She would prefer it if the present Saturday country around Quarr were to be seldom hunted. Should she be in earshot of the affliction of hound music, the wound would be beyond contemplation.

She was understood?

"You need say no more!" said unctuous Donkey Lorimer.

"George worshipped his hounds," said Cecily to Agnes.

"Rupert's pocket not deep enough," whispered Archie.

Dorothy, by denying use of the Kennels, had made it more ticklish. Sturt, Sawbridge-Walter and R. Lupus might otherwise have continued for another season; so as to have held off any ultimate decision.

The Quarr went back to 1769. The Hunt's fate was a matter both personal and historical.

Oliver had been the brother most devoted, after George, to hounds in their father's day. "Uncle Noll has spread his cloak wider," Archie mumbled to Griselda; "he doesn't *want* to afford it."

No one in the family did, or could. A relief, thought Dorothy.

Gypsies had filled the lane from ditch to ditch to view the Master to "the sod". Jem lolloped at Bevis's heels like a large dog. In age they were separated by a gap greater than that which existed between Esmond and Gerald; but neither was at all aware of it.

With no George there, somebody saw fit to frown on Gypsy Jem and signify that he shouldn't follow Bevis into the house. Yet Jem was not light-fingered. The stricture left Bevis burning, and he made more use of the service stairs. All the children were pained.

Their relations had been rendered odd.

When asked questions, Dorothy stared blindly into their faces; whilst Archie would melt away, Rupert claim ignorance and Lydie resort to a melodious titter.

Parcels of woodland had attracted the notice of another sort of heavy hand. The ground had dried up. Half-fallen timber was hauled away to the saw-pit to be logs for the hearth. Not content to stop at that, Runner Ramsey must have ordered the felling of mature trees.

It hadn't been George's practice to let the birds be disturbed at their nests.

Papa had been a great preserver.

The woodpeckers, who had bored or enlarged a number of raw holes, had been forced to start afresh, and the blackbirds, feeding a first brood, were disturbed in the undergrowth. The red squirrels lost their dreys. The jays, nuthatches, tree-creepers and goldcrests felt chivvied; the long-tailed tits didn't flitter through the tree-tops. The romance abandoned what had always been known, through its Scotch pines, as the Fir Wood.

It was a revelation to Ida, hostile to new orthodoxy, that George had been "rather laissez-faire".

The children were to learn by experience to champion Papa's every notion.

Ida caught Major Ramsey and broached with him this business of the slaughter in the Fir Wood.

The agent burbled, "My dear Ida, your father had set it in train."

The children didn't any longer have the sense that the world was being unpicked in a game of spillikins; or that a line of four shocked faces could call a halt.

With the Lorimers vanished *On Duty*, Griselda's third-most favourite book.

Bevis lay on the tiger skin and curled an arm round the tiger's head. This was deemed vexatious; he would be *stumbled* over. No one ever, ever, put a foot, let alone a shoe, on the Bengal tiger, lest their feet slide from under them, the tiger's underside was clothed in red baize! Bevis was little and the tiger had been gigantic; and hardly any of Bee stuck out.

The tiger's mask was set in a rather ghastly grin.

Quietly, for the tiger's ear alone, Bevis sighed.

70 A good home

It was Gerald's misfortune that his summer term began two days later than Esmond's, since he was there when the old lady found out about Little John.

In black from head to foot, Dorothy was driven to the Rectory and the door was opened to her at five and twenty past eleven. Gerald, told to accompany her, to his great discomfort, was to sit in the carriage or stroll to and fro.

"I don't need to mention that you keep away from the windows," said his aunt.

Parson Cornforth, innocent as ever, had shambled out to greet her. "My dear Mrs Lupus," he said. He took her hand. His trembled because he was moved.

Dorothy, for her part, was unaware that she'd been wrapped in a dreadful majesty. She accepted a glass of sherry.

She enquired after his daughters Mrs Beynon and Mrs Gibson; and his granddaughter Morwenna.

"I believe," she said as soon as she decently could, "my naughty creatures have imposed upon you."

"Not a jot," said Cornforth.

"Oh?" said Dorothy.

Cornforth quailed.

He pulled himself together. Hope glimmered.

"Dear Mrs Lupus," he said, "for how many years have we been acquainted? The good Lord does ... ah ... guide you through your sorrow ..."

"I don't speak of sorrow," said Dorothy. "I speak of mortification."

Cornforth recognized his Golgotha.

Guilt and defiance mingled in his eyes.

"Esmond's pony," she said, "has paid a prolonged visit to the Rectory stables. I can't imagine why! I shall ask Slade to see that he is fetched."

"The chap does adore his pony," said Cornforth. "Didn't we all at that age adore our ponies!"

"Yes, yes," said Dorothy impatiently.

"I dare say," she said, "Esmond has been . . . mooning about the premises."

She said it as though it were distasteful.

Mrs Lupus sat poker straight. Cornforth recollected that day when Ida had perched on his book-room steps, her habit falling to the floor; and the little girl, Griselda, had sat on his knee. He saw their rosy cheeks, faces as rosy as George's when small. He remembered how Ida had twisted him round her finger.

"Children far from a nuisance," said Cornforth. "Indeed, they bring charm to an old man. And a boy who has lost his father . . ." He thought he'd said enough. He was afraid it might not penetrate.

He wondered glumly quite how Mrs Lupus had known.

To Gerald, Dorothy vouchsafed not a word.

"She took Gerald to make him feel cut up," said Griselda.

Poor Cornforth had himself been put to the blush, in no uncertain way. He could only be thankful Dorothy's delicacy had persuaded her to say no worse.

Little John had a night in his own stall; Corbin took him by train to Fawernbridge to the fortnightly horse sales. "*Barbaric*. Your *duty*," had pleaded Ida, white in the face, "is to sell him, if . . . if sell him you must, to a kind and suitable owner. How *can* you punish Esmond! Aunt Lydie and Uncle Rupert, were *they* not at fault?"

Dorothy's nostrils were pinched.

"Esmond will be *wretched*. How could you be so unkind!"

"Don't speak to your mother in that fashion," said Dorothy. "Consider how you have aided Esmond's cause! *Your* conduct has been close to deceitful."

71 They feel defeated

Cravenly, in Esmond's absence, the announcement was sent to the *Chronicle* of the sale of the hunt horses; as well as saddles, bridles, harness, surcingles, blankets, bandages, boots, assorted cruppers, bits, martingales, buckets, racks, bins, pillar-reins and headstalls.

Ida's heart went very cold.

There were further scenes; with Dorothy, Uncle Rupert, Uncle Oliver. In the course of these the protagonists said too much.

One cry haunted Ida's outbursts.

"You were *there*," she would storm, "you were *there*, Ma, you *heard*, you *know* what Papa said to me!"

Dorothy shook her head (infinitesimally); her embarrassment at such a tantrum plain.

"They can't sell Dorcas, can't they turn her out for the summer and then see?" said Griselda. "They could get The Duchess in foal."

George's horses at the Grange were going too. His slapping hunters and the decent sorts.

Griselda said, "But you can't sell Corsican, he's carried Papa for five seasons and never a day unsound! You can't sell Carrickfern!"

"Why don't I ride Pasha?" said Ida.

When there was silence, Griselda said uneasily, "Papa did say Grenadier was mine, and Old Haunts was Ida's birthday present."

Rupert said, "Never fear!"

Dorothy observed that Ida wasn't grown up yet.

"All this seething and anguishing," said Dorothy, "I do wish you'd stop! I do dislike it."

"Our hounds," said Ida.

But four couple had already been drafted. They'd been carted to the station and from Holtworthy gone in the guard's van, with several changes, to Shropshire.

"Our hounds are to be dispersed," quavered Griselda.

"You mustn't!" said Bevis.

"Now, Bee," said Rupert.

Under his breath, Bevis tried twice.

Rupert, jolly Uncle Rupert, whipped on him and said, "Be very careful." And, seconds later, "That looks like dumb insolence."

Bevis had never understood what dumb insolence was.

"You silly children!" said Dorothy. "Do you imagine we feel no distress?"

Bevis and Griselda went and hung around Frank Fontley.

Fontley was still in the hopes of the dog pack's going as one. Same as the Brocklesby purchase made in 1896 by Mr Merthyr Guest.

Bevis was gnawn by anxiety.

"They lines go back a two-hundred-year," said Fontley, his face a mask.

"Mabbe the older ladies will be let to be pensioned."

"I'll keep Argot," said Bevis.

"You can't," said Griselda, "can you!"

The enormity of it started to defeat them.

Ida wrote to Esmond.

"But what to my matrons and whelps?" Fontley said.

Esmond's reply at least gave them a job to do. Instead of wild ideas of pricking the feet of the most highly loved horses, for that plan could go awry, they were to throw themselves into securing the best possible homes. Could the girls oversee the bidding? He thought not: they should employ a man to cap the bids from the dealers, Ida would need a fund in case of accident. And ... *PS. You did the max. you were able, on behalf my John.*

"He's loony."

"No," said Ida in a queer voice, "he isn't."

"What kind of man? Slade, do you think."

"Not a groom," said Ida.

"Or not one of ours," she added.

"If the beastly auction is to be held at the Kennels is there any reason why we shouldn't go!"

It seemed to Inkpen, in timid sympathy, that days of cudgelling their brains and nights of wet pillows had worn them down.

"These hollow eyes won't do," she said to them.

Bevis gripped her hand, though his mood was scathing.

" 'Why this, why that'!" had said Rupert. "It's of no use."
"You drive me distracted," had said Ma. "Your mother has enough to bear."
Archie said to Griselda, "They did look at two days a week. Fontley and one whip."
"Did they?" said Griselda.
"According to m'brother," said Archie.
Beer had already seen how the wind blew and was to cast off his red coat for a yellow, to go as first whipper-in to the Berkeley. Rita and Sid had been told to get from under Mrs Beer's feet, and the baby stationed by the greengage-tree. Boxes queened it over Mrs B.'s floor.
In the end, it was too much for them. The weather was kind to the sale. The day dawned delicate, warm-smelling.
The auctioneer was Mr Blanchard of Yeatman & Blanchard of Fawernbridge. There was a mill of folk from far and wide. A ring had been made in the big yard and forms rigged for seats two tiers high. A great number of fellows stood and craned where the horses were to be led in, while others stalked up and down the trestle tables upon which the many lots of saddlery were laid. These were to be sold in the afternoon. Interested purchasers could ask for particular horses to be taken from the stalls and trotted out; and there was much consideration of teeth, feeling of legs and picking up of feet.
There was much vivid curiosity on the faces.
The hunt horses were well known; yet not every man's ideal buy. They'd done a lot of work, maybe; and had their mouths spoiled being rid by a chap, maybe, with bad hands. The Master's quality hunters were different, and several gentlemen were present or had sent a head groom to secure an old favourite.
The first lot had been the terrier man's pony, Diana. Mrs Lupus had decided to have her withdrawn, with the view that

she might be useful in the stables at the Grange. Before the day was done, Mrs Lupus had changed her mind and had sent down that Diana should be put in.

Mrs Lupus didn't make a look-in; not in any circumstances would she have. It was as well nobody had told her the children hadn't kept a suitable distance.

Gus Hutchins brought his charges into the ring himself, not so proud that he would delegate that job to a hand.

All were warranted sound in wind and limb, bar two.

Farmer Dyce made room for Miss Ida and Miss Griselda; sought to protect them from the squeeze. Even had folk not been so intent, they'd have held their gaze from the Lupus gals; for there wasn't a soul that knew what didn't compassion them. Bevis and Gypsy Jem had wormed their way through the assembled gaiters at the entrance and stuck disembodied heads through the front-most legs.

No further female was present.

Griselda saw the three mares Dorcas, The Duchess and Bryony sold; then the covert hack Pewter; and couldn't bear it. "You can't depart on your own," whispered Ida.

The dealer from Folly Ash was to the fore. Ida was certain he'd have confrères.

The Hippogriff came in next. With his ugly head he set up a laugh. He was known, however, to go all day. His hard mouth didn't put off Farmer Rood, whose horses had to carry seventeen stone, and The Hippogriff went to him.

Marauder – "A pleasanter horse don't exist, to ride home after a day with hounds!" cried the auctioneer – fetched only twenty-nine guineas.

Sturgess the Lackham fishmonger acquired, of a mind to grow grand, Dorinda, the big roan Colin liked; for forty-three. Some loud-check-attired, bandy-legged tradesman got – "honest in his work though not safe over fences" – the one-eyed heavyweight cob, Cyclops. This was awful.

"To draw a hearse," whispered Griselda.

"No, no," said Ida.

The brown, Lascar, they thought, looked sad: however, he found a home with Sir Benet Synn.

The Tartar, heavy in foal to the travelling stallion, Columba, went to Wes Brown; despite her not having been covered this time by Mr Sturt's horse Martial.

For the un-cut two-year-old colt Cranford, out of Sable, property of Mrs Lupus, the bidding went higher.

More young stock from the Grange paddocks found good prices, dancing and jigging.

Horses did best on limestone. Everybody knew there was no limestone at Quarr. The sandstone had been exhausted in medieval times; and neither the flint and grey sand nor the gravel and clay were prime for breeding, although the Master had, a twelve- and a fourteen-year ago, laid the land-drains anew.

Slade looked on impassive, with folded arms.

The hunt horse Dryasdust, a seven-year-old, pure grey, was bought up for the Cattistock.

Rupert arrived late. Since he mustn't make a sign, and to force his way to them was a fool's errand, he could but glare. His nieces had no eyes for him.

A dismal stream of hunt horses, six more in all, Boney, Copper, Milky, handsome Arish Mell, Ranston and Done Dreaming, went under the hammer.

When the Master's Rajah was being led around the ring, hounds, quiet hitherto, began to mew.

Ida bent on the Coker head groom her most gimlet gaze. Wes Brown didn't stir a muscle.

"... carried the Master for two seasons," called Mr Blanchard, "honest and in manners perfect ... no blemishes ..."

Griselda's hands were wrung.

Bevis, on his knees, examining the rosy visages opposite, was rewarded by the sight of a familiar mannish figure. Miss Haunchley tapped several gents on the shoulder and thrust her rump into the few inches of plank that Mr Armour surrendered up to her. It was too much for Mr Rhodes. Armour had a tin leg. Rhodes gave Armour his own seat. Rhodes was distracted and let Rajah go to a stranger.

The black ex-charger, Agrippa, found two enthusiastic

bidders in Messrs Urnhurst and Manser. When Manser dropped out, shaking his head, a ferret-featured fellow entered. A chill crawled up Ida's spine and for a second or two she was close to swooning. She braced herself. But Agrippa, ears pricked, was knocked down to Urnhurst.

The Irish thoroughbred mare Strokestown (by Mick out of Boggydown) attracted the highest bidding so far: it was Mr Egmont from Rivers House over at Nyland who secured her.

The dealers had, thought Ida, kept their heads and been content to bide their time. That boded ill.

There was an unexpected entry into the bidding for the grey gelding, Siamese, in the shape of the frightful Mr Rodham. Blanchard was taking bids from all around the ring. These fell away. Griselda's lips were saying, oh no, oh no, please no. The auctioneer was looking, though, towards the back at what appeared to be a chin, so tilted that its possessor remained invisible. The hammer went bang. People glanced all round about them. "Name, sir," said Blanchard. They heard "Muscle" or could it have been "Musser". Blanchard's clerk noted it all the same.

Then it was Pasha's turn. "Darling old Pasha," said Ida. Their hearts leapt when the Rectory groom, Ben Hayter, raised a finger to his hat-brim. His face gave nothing away. "Buy him, oh buy him, *dear* Mr Cornforth," breathed Griselda, until Ida had to nudge her. And he did.

But Beauty . . . snaffle mouth . . . went to Ferret-face.

"You're not to cry," whispered Ida, "don't you dare." Griselda bit her bottom lip.

The showy chestnut gelding, Corinth, had taken the fancy of Captain Barge. Ida looked doubtful. "Close to home," said Blanchard cheerily. "And now then, gentlemen . . ."

The entire horse Noah II went to Farmer Maber. He too was fond of a grey. Maber wanted a piece of the Master.

Why, seeing as they at the Hall had a weakness for the progeny of their stallion, didn't Wes Brown go for the promising Modder River, inserted in the catalogue at this point to separate the hunters?

". . . fine middleweight," Blanchard was saying, already on

to Corsican, "... fifteen hands three inches, will carry a lady..."

At noon the selling of the saddlery began outside. The village was foregathered to watch the fun.

A steady hum from without accompanied the patter, "Lot number four, a highly desirable Sowter saddle, who gives me ... thank you sir ... seven guineas I am bid..."

The smart covert hack Absalom, who got one with no exertion at twelve miles an hour to a distant meet, went snapped up in a flurry.

Miss Haunchley had poked her neighbour and demanded he bid for Corsican for her. But she'd dropped out.

Corsican was gone to a stranger.

Blanchard broke for an early luncheon.

Uncle Rupert came and ordered the girls back to the house. He even took Ida by the elbow. She was furious. The ringside crowd wandered rather like shy children at a party, with glazed expressions; otherwise marked their catalogues, abstractedly. Ida directed a pleading look at the Coker head groom. Wes Brown touched his hat to her.

Bevis and Jem, who had filled their tummies with slices of raised pie at the refreshment tables, saw the remaining four hunt horses sold in the afternoon. The grey Sea Fever; chestnut Gascon, with his four white stockings; the bright bay mare Painted Lady, on whose near hock, everybody knew, was a bone spavin. The aged dapple-grey Prince.

Jem reckoned Painted Lady had been knocked down to the carrier from Lackham Magna. They'd be grim up at the Grange.

The brick cobbles already rang with the sound of the leading away of purchases.

Two nice three-quarterbred fillies; a mare and her excellent foal; a second brood mare covered (and got in foal, it was thought) by the teaser over at Mr Sawbridge-Walter's, old Coral Boy, as per the Master's wish. She'd been visiting and therefore brought back to Quarr.

Blanchard wiped his spectacles.

Such remarks went over Bevis's head, somewhat.

A more jovial mood took hold of the auction ring: its

composition had been altered. Gaps had been found by those there for entertainment. The fewer bidding, meanwhile, were swift of purpose.

Ida's heart would have been eased had she seen Wes Brown still to the fore.

The Master's favourite, Carrickfern, went to Coker. Brown had been sent to acquire chiefly him; and did so at a hundred and ninety guineas.

Bevis was very grubby.

The sale of Diana, unhogged mane combed with water down her neck, finished the horses. Not a single one had failed to make its reserve. Most would have gained their summer's rest.

73 Dear Master E.

When Bevis, Jem and Cedric Hopkins went to the farm to watch the slaughter of a pig, it looked there as though all was as of old. The boys hung by their tummies on the wall by the outhouses. Out of sight the horses went about their work or stood and ate their nosebags in a stolid fashion; the pair – Papa's conceit – of Percherons, Bess and Goggie; a half-way horse by the name of Maidie; and one crosspatch, the cob Milsom.

"How revolting you are, Bee," said Griselda by and by.

If all at the farm was serene, elsewhere it was a time of farewells. From the Quarr stables vanished three grooms; among them Corbin. Quick-As-Can-Be couldn't be thought to have shed a tear for her chauffeur but she would surely never be the same again. There had been no strict need to reduce the men: if there was not the work they would be happier in other employment.

At his house, Blue House, letters were collected from a mahogany hall table and on this venerated object here at school Esmond found one addressed in a careful copperplate. *Dear Master E.*, had written Titball.

Dear Master E.,

Hoping as how this finds you well as it leaves me in a sorry time. We never thought as how your Pa would go so soon, he would have wanted to see you grow up. It was a calamity and no one among the servants as unhappy as I. You do know how he dearly loved you. Do not doubt he looks down. Keep your head aloft, Esmond, you have bags of pluck. Your old Titball wishes to assure that though not at the Grange in his accustomed place he humbly does not forget you. And trusts he will see you some day, what a natter we shall have. As for me I am suited with Palmsbury-Bell Esquire and do my duty as best as poss. Some ache in my heart I wasn't meant to go from the Grange and miss you children sore. Remember me to your sisters and brother. Though you too big for me to presume to say it now, Be a good boy. I always think of our days at Quarr. Drop me a line please, if you have a minute. Trusting you are as ever brave, I remain,

Yours truly,

Chas. Titball

When Esmond next wrote to Ida, he put at the end: *I've had a letter from Titball, he wishes to be remembered to you.*

George had laid down that the children must see death; might see birth; procreation never. The children called it mating and so, for that matter, did Papa, except where fellow grown-ups were concerned. What he'd not armed them for was desolation and misery.

Ida raged at her own helplessness, at how she'd stood by and watched the horses sold, perhaps to less considerate homes, to less knowledgeable homes; to be treated, perhaps, to cruelties, or stupidity, or worked simply too hard.

Ida's remorse, over her having been so feeble, after her pretence that she'd nobble some person to hold off the dealers, to sift the strangers, oh that was enormous.

74 More than they can bear

The farewells were almost more than they could bear.

Some of the puppy-walkers didn't turn up, poor things, for the show; a puppy show held late and combined with a dreadful affair.

It went against the grain with them.

As swiftly as the familiar creatures disappeared, so did, very slowly, weird facts come out into the open.

The country itself was to be divided. The portion closest to Lord Maurward's he would add to his. The far larger part was to be taken over by two Joint-Masters, of which one was Mr Egmont of Rivers House, Nyland, in the former Monday country; the other, Brigadier Hesketh.

The most active of these gentlemen was Mr Egmont, his being in his prime. Hounds would be hunted by a huntsman; their hounds, that is.

It was disclosed that to Hesketh and Egmont too had been offered the gift of George Lupus's pack; and that they'd spurned it.

Dorothy Lupus had been driven behind the bays all the way over to Nyland. What had passed between her and Mr Egmont, whom she lumped among the ghastly, was a subject of conjecture.

"Interfering," went Archie whisper-whisper along paths in the shrubbery.

Neither the Quarr hounds nor Frank Fontley were wanted. While it was felt that Fontley would go on to become famous as huntsman to another pack, George's famed hounds were to be disposed of. Fontley appreciated these sentiments not a whit; although he wasn't one to let hisself get soured.

For the loyal puppy-walkers it was too much. Maybe there were reasons. But it was beyond some.

That, at any rate, was what was said to Miss Ida.

There were those that were loud in their agitation against such a turn. Their voices were not powerful. Even the puppy-walkers, farmers for the most part, couldn't have been so very loyal; not all of them. There were weasel words abroad.

Although Mrs Egmont and Gervase Sturt favoured George's light-coloured hounds, many the descendants of one bitch, the admired Eloquent '79, Mr Egmont didn't.

He planned, for a start, to acquire a draft with plenty of black and rich tan on them from the Grafton.

Egmont didn't think Belvoir Muffin had been brought to Quarr "soon enough".

George hadn't listened to advice, was "an obstinate fellow".

George had bred for speed, eh! He ought to have gone for stamina! George had "valued their *cry* too much" when he should have bred to the nose!

Captain Mercer said "balderdash" (and it was)!

If the Master's carrying of the horn could have been faulted it was in his "lifting of hounds too quickly". He had, on the contrary, bred for stamina rather than speed. That was why he'd developed that "bad habit", he'd lifted them to give the appearance of a fast run, whereas they should have "*worked* a scent"!

Those who considered the Belvoir blood had arrived in the nick of time (though Muffin was, ipso facto, quite untried) were confounded by others who stated no less than the truth, which was that Argot, Versus and Rasper had imparted consistent, sterling qualities (along with their conformation) to *their* progeny. Versus as a sire was an outcross, being himself from the Pytchley, a son of Picture '86, of the Lasher strain. The Pytchley dog-hounds were notably light-coloured. Versus was lemon and white.

Light-coloured hounds were supposed to have weak constitutions and uncertain tempers, as in horses.

Colin said, "They'm a-mutterin' behind Master's back, i'n um. An' er not hardly under."

As to whether her father had bred for speed *or* stamina . . . Ida said, "Hounds he hunted ran as even as any could wish for; a sheet would have covered them!

"Papa bred for *nose* and *cry*.

"For nose *and* cry!"

The talk, or echoes of it, had reached both the Tom Thumb and the Grange; to general bewilderment.

It wouldn't have been in Fontley's nature to have presented a glum face to the puppy-show-cum-sale-of-hounds.

It was by engraved card. There was no pandemonium, no thrusting crowd; simply a knowledgeable knot of gentlemen from the rest of England and one from the Welsh borders; and folk tended to drift off after the judging was over, with no appetite for any more.

First Prize out of the bitches of her year was won by the Rasper puppy Ravish; with Ebony second. The dog First Prize went to Sophist. Second to him was Topper sired by Trojan, whose own sire was Tulip; and *his* dam, according to Bevis, had been the blue and white hound Vagary. He dared not say however many of her great-great-grandsires you had to count back to the eighteenth century, but somewhere there was Valesman. "How on earth do you know that!" said Griselda. Bevis, it seemed, did know.

Ebony was Elflock's daughter, by Versus.*

The judge hailed from the Surrey Union.

Topper had been at walk at Lower Slaughter, and old Mr Holkham was cock-a-hoop; Sophist with Jacky Draycott's missus; so there was pleasure close to home. On the success of Ravish and Rustic, Farmer Box preened himself. By a horrid irony, Ebony had been on the other side of the country, with litter-sister Eldritch, in the Egmont stable-yard at Nyland.

The dispersal proved considerable. No offer had been lodged for the dog pack in entirety. George's two hairy Welsh hounds returned thataway. Rarity and Roguish and, Bevis believed, several other couple of bitches were to go to Devon. It wasn't as though he could recognize these strange bods. He thought he'd heard that Harebell and Hero were to go to France. To France? France! Almost certainly. And what of the pups born this last spring?

At least no Quarr hound was doomed to a bullet in the head. Old faithfuls, if already spoken for, would go into retirement on the estate.

* Quarr hounds were named for the sire, unless that sire was an outcross.

With such sparse information they had to be content. The judge, (together with some others thus honoured) had been fed cold mutton and boiled rice with jam in the dining-room by Uncle Noll and the silent Colonel.

No marquee and none of the customary speeches. A testimonial, by subscription, in the form of a silver tankard had been presented to the kennel-huntsman. A donation of twenty pounds to the Hunt Servants' Benefit Society was announced.

And Frank Fontley had been too sick (very near) to utter.

75 The Quarr broken up

With the pack gone, the Kennels deserted, Fontley went from his cottage to be huntsman somewhere in North Devon or Cornwall. Gus Hutchins might have come up to the Grange but he'd have had to have worked under Slade and he wasn't reckoning to do that. Colin went as second whipper-in to Mr Fernie's, which was a plum for him. Maurice was taken on at the Mill.

Brian had mended farmers' fences and was on for the Lupuses as under-gardener.

Those going touched their hats and shook hands shyly with Miss Ida, Miss Griselda and Master Bee.

For the children, the Sunday-morning visit to the stables had become a different sort of business. No one had to buck up lest not every animal receive his tit-bit and pats. None was heard to say, "That arched neck may be very pretty, sir, but you've eaten your ration." There was ample time to dawdle with all.

To welcome Esmond's half-term exeat the weeds had hurried to sow themselves in the unswept bricks of the Kennels yard and had straggled around its rails and the stables. Esmond stared and was dumbstruck. It was jolly unreal.

There the weeds were to flourish; silent and ghostly. Esmond felt to blame, for his not being older.

Outside the ticket-office, posted on the wall still, on the Holtworthy platform, there had been a tattered bill of sale in regard of the Quarr Hunt horses and others the property of the late Master; so that Esmond very nearly hadn't noticed the porter in his worn coat with cap waved in salute. The porter was a friend.

Their brother was gone again. Griselda devoured her book at night in a cloud of whirling dervishes, the moths and insects attracted through the open casement to the candle. The gas made in the gas-house by Poulter and fed up to the Grange didn't yet go upstairs.

In a July dusk, Ida watched fox-cubs dancing after moths; cubs from the earth in the furze of the Ladderback.

Nanny Sturt brought young Master Sturt and their baby to tea. Only Nurse and little Guy were in duty bound to be there, indeed Nurse had issued the invitation; but Griselda thought Nanny Sturt nice and infants intrigued her. Flo ferried tea into the garden. Presently Ida appeared with the goat-carriage and they had some merriment.

One particular traipse had led the children past the ground at the back of Hunt Cottages. A mound no longer bare had been attacked by a scavenger. Not, they thought, the spot to bury, say, the carcass of a ewe.

Clarence said, "Obliged to shoot some hounds, bin um. No gain fretting, they was better deaded yere at Quarr. Getting on, a-growing stiff, like."

"*Fontley* shot hounds!"

"Seemingly," said Clarence. "Can't be soppy, can us."

Bevis had been beaten in May by Rupert for baiting Mrs Styles at the farm.

Encouraging her onion setts to jump out of the ground was considered a puerile sort of prank. But Rupert could have had no means of being sure they hadn't jumped of their own accord; and, Ida observed, Mrs Styles had tied a new-born calf with a loop of twine in a filthy, dark shed and was beastly to the cob, small wonder Milsom was full of vices. Rupert said the sometimes crude – or ignorant – handling of horses existed the world over and that they might acquaint themselves with that fact without making it their affair. "Our farm," murmured Griselda. A soft heart made for poor judgement, he said. Was it now Uncle Rupert's business to beat Bee? they'd asked themselves; and such a novel grievance had been a cause for brooding.

76 The summer

The big chestnut in the lane at the Kennels was cut down; depriving the village of prize conkers. He was said to have become a danger, liable to drop a branch; no matter how well he bore. His innards when exposed were diseased.

The children with Inkpen took the tea-basket to the decoy, to the Folly Ash, to the river bank with David and the governess car, up into the valleys of the roof. Inkpen was game enough to climb a ladder. They took rugs and lolled about on the lead, surveying all that went on far below. No tomato sandwiches ever tasted better. No bottle of ginger pop was ever swilled into a more appreciative throat. The dogs sat at the foot of the ladder whence rose occasional puzzled yelps.

When they did go in the trap, Ma didn't go with them.

The old lady stayed indoors, swatting flies; swat, swat; swish, swish; bang bang; thump; and didn't bring her camera to capture baby Guy, now able to sit up, lifted onto the pony's back, his white skirts draped gorgeously around his plump wee legs.

There was plum cake almost whenever they asked for it.

There'd been the hay-making.

Esmond's thoughts at the start of the holidays appeared to be distant and dreamy. "It's the burden of his having inherited Quarr," Griselda confided to Archie.

"I expect," said Archie, "he . . . well, he isn't different from his sisters in his liking to shoot and fish, for you fish too,

Griselda ... his schooling, inexorable chasm, may take him away from you, classics and all that, he dwells in another region, somewhere you go to only through Christmas presents of illustrated myths and legends, isn't he a bit of a dab hand at his Latin and Greek!"

"Inkpen does the Romans in Britain," said Griselda.

"Yes, well ..."

But Esmond adored Quick-As-Can-Be, he always had, and was being industrious in discovering how to drive with short arms and legs; Gerald and he careered about in her; so had been forbidden passengers. Twice they'd run out of petrol and had to take David and the trap to buy supplies from the Lackham chemist.

All rode.

Ida jogged. Old Haunts had been gently summered; and out (before the flies were bad) for the months of May and June. At the usual time, she'd had him up. In the heat, the thought of a winter, dark and cold, without hunting to kindle the cockles of their hearts, was disagreeable.

The ice on the inside of window panes, smoking fires, perhaps a fancy-dress party at Coker, skating on the decoy pond, when there wouldn't have been any hunting anyway, and Ma would hold hands with Bee and a kitchen chair, stitching of lavender-bags and cutting out of bookmarks, twisting spills and dyeing pipe-cleaners for Christmas presents ... all was sketched in the wispiest pencil.

The cousins were descending on them for visits, but most were popular; Gerald of course, and Patience, Patrick and Barty Miers, Margie, Teddy; and then there were the two Lorimers again, twice. Uncle Rupert, who had grown quite horrid, and Aunt Lydie went north for the Glorious Twelfth; they were, it was gathered with some glee, to do a round of her Scotch relations.

Ma duly emerged from indoors and began to be seen on horseback with Uncle Oliver; she, mounted on her long-tailed hack Endymion, whilst he incongruously got Mother Goose to look a smarter cob than she had for several seasons.

Dorothy was nursing Guy; though she was impatient. She

positively longed to wean him and demanded that Nurse get him onto a bottle.

She'd had to convey to Oliver that she couldn't trot a great deal, without saying any such thing.

77 The philanderer

When it was Mop's time for being shut up at the stables with a bed of straw, on which she reclined, languidly remembering to lick herself, Bevis at least was a bit foggy as to why exactly.

Margie was a big girl, brought up in a mansion-block in Kensington High Street, and she was motherly. She had pigtails she could sit on.

"When my father was alive," confided Bevis, "a groom saw to Mop, but now she's our dog, or Esmond's, and I think I shall go and take her out to puddle."

Margie trotted after him, pleased to be occupied.

"And later," said Bevis, "would you care to ride, I might visit Bountiful and Blissful at Lower Slaughter."

Ida and Griselda had, unbeknownst to the elders, solicited homes for old foxhounds around the estate, from people with stables or good dry sheds. Hounds didn't make good pets really ("How do you account for Misty!" had said Griselda), and most people had been so doubtful it had proved indecent to press them; and there'd not been numbers of elderly hounds, two or three who'd had several litters, that was all, almost all. Mr Armour had taken in Peerless, and young Mrs Holkham, feeling her bones herself, had found a corner at Lower Slaughter for Bountiful and Blissful. Years ago they'd been there at walk.

Bevis said, "David is very quiet."

Margie didn't mind if there was indeed a very quiet pony. She'd ridden David before.

Clement Strange's Chips, who possessed an uncanny memory for bitches and had once hidden himself in a wagon and been carried all the way to Lackham Magna to call on a lady-friend, adept at whisking himself inside scullery doors and crouching beneath the table until the coast should be clear, had picked this moment to lurk in the back drive.

Chips had a gingery, wiry coat, a square jaw. He had, perhaps, some Airedale in him, because he was quite long in the leg. His gait was trim; he was dignified and he enjoyed pottering as much as he did his escorting of the bakery bicycle; and he was clever.

Bevis with Mop on the lead and Margie had strolled out of the yard; and Clarence alone noticed them go.

"You'm to look to she, Master Bee? Said, have um?" Clarence enquired. "They" being the older sisters, or "they" up at the house.

Bevis hadn't paid any attention. Gratified by the company of the big cousin, he was chattering. He also wanted to consider on which verge Mop would find the most interesting smells, and make sure she did her do. Bevis lost sight of a vital element of their walk. He let her off.

Before he could gather his wits, the mongrel Chips from the village had bounced out of the rhododendrons and Mop and Chips were making up to each other like billy-o. Mop twitched her behind and presented it to Chips in a coquettish fashion, her stumpy tail held, exaggeratedly it seemed, aside; whilst Bevis, poor Bevis, gazed at them dozily.

Then Chips had mounted Mop – Mop tried to snap – and was riding her. Margie's eyes were round and shocked.

"Oh dear," remarked Bevis.

Chips was quick but when he slid off Mop, who was panting, mouth open, he was forced to swivel his body. The two animals found themselves facing away from each other; tied.

Margie started to screech and was impelled to tear off to the yard for a pail of water and had lugged it back, close to hysterics, before Clarence bellowed. Margie hesitated. The odd couple shifted crab-wise and stood again. Margie emptied her bucket over them. The spaniel howled.

And still the dogs stood and the water which had sluiced them dripped from their bodies.

Clarence seemed angered.

He said, "That weren't kind. That there were crool. Come along of I, Missie."

Clarence took the lead from Bevis and clipped it on Mop's collar and held out the loop of it. Bevis stepped unsteadily towards them.

"Stop bi they," said Clarence. "A matter of a half-hour, mabbe, mabbe more. No telling.

"Now then, Miss Margie!" he said.

With that he marched her back and on towards the house, hoping devoutly as how he wouldn't get the blame. His place was taken by a grinning Foyle.

But Bevis had only twenty minutes to wait. With a slither and festooning wet stuff around their legs and a glimpse of brilliant red, Chips parted from Mop.

"You silly," said Griselda afterwards, "she is *on heat.*"

Bevis was abashed.

Their mother was extremely vexed.

78 September

Cubbing had started, but Ida and Griselda seemed indifferent.

Egmont, with his usurper pack, didn't meet within hacking distance of Quarr bar the once.

Esmond went out on his sister's Grenadier with Slade: the two of them came away at half past eight. Oliver couldn't, because of mourning: by custom he waited anyhow for November. Besides, Uncle Noll was stuffy and odd: it was how, Nurse said, sorrow had taken him, always.

They hadn't known him well.

In Griselda's bookcase *On Duty* made an appearance; mauled. Donkey Lorimer had been closeted with Oliver, Dorothy and Major Ramsey: as the Lorimers went, Donkey was heard to say, "That's settled then."

The children picked blackberries.

Esmond copied the most satisfactory of his summer's poems into a volume with a marbled hard cover. By the nineteenth of the month he would be back at Meavy.

Farmer Holkham, who, with his broader acres, kept no fewer than three teams of heavy horses, Clydesdale and Suffolk Punch, had lent a team of Suffolks and a man for the harvesting. With the sheaves trundled on the wain to the farm, the ricks made, and thatched, to attend the steam engine and thresher, the autumn ploughing too had begun; and Dorothy's Sable was turned out for the winter; to live out, finely bred or not, in the sheltered park with the broken-down steeplechaser, Darnley.

79 Still September

Far, far away, a foxhound, lost in an unfamiliar covert, found himself on his own. He loitered, a trifle conscious. A silence had fallen. A cock pheasant called, and a jay, as though undisturbed for some while.

Presently the hound emerged into undulating countryside. The wind blew, laced with drizzle, from the west.

He listened, sniffed the air. After a little reflection, he wandered down the hedgerow with that wind. It was stiff enough to stir the flaps of his ears. He put his nose to the ground from time to time. The upper body of a man poked from behind an oak-tree. The man's eyes were simple. The man whistled. It was a soft and guileless sort of whistle and the foxhound raised his head and stared. The man stared back. Soon he stuck out a hand and waggled his fingers. The hound took a cautious step. The man's mouth didn't open. The hound shied off at a bound.

He dropped into a more purposeful trot.

The hound became entangled in the outskirts of a hamlet. Here he attracted shouts; and a boy bareback on a shaggy pony cantered after him.

The drizzle turned to rain. Then the sky cleared.

The hound had covered miles before he drank from a pond and at twilight lay up in the lee of a hayrick. His stomach was hollow.

In the morning he stole chicken mash, sops of brown bread in a meat gravy with bran, barley and bacon rind, from some flustered Dorkings.

The day was more serious. He moved now without any thought. Instinct told him to avoid blandishments and missiles alike, he had grown wary. A female with a rolling-pin was proved to be ill-tempered, when he'd only been trying to snatch a cooked potato-skin afloat in the pig-swill.

By afternoon, his pads were sore.

Milkmaids still took their three-legged stools to Pansy and Clover and all in the meadow: these were the last days of summer. They were stripping out before trundling the churn to the dairy. They slopped for him a bowl (licked clean of cake) with frothy, warm goodness. He was grateful. They offered him no harm, and giggled when he went on his way.

80 Home-coming

Ida, with the melancholy nostalgia that wounded more than it healed, rode in October along the lane which passed Hunt Cottages and the Kennels. On an impulse she asked Old Haunts to open the gate. His hoofs went clop on the cobbles; over towards the mellow stable-yard arch.

He could hear ghosts.

As they rounded the corner, a puzzled face appeared in front of them, furrowed in wrinkles. The hound looked thin, yet held himself in a stout fashion. The stern waved hesitantly.

"Oh you darling," gasped Ida, "you darling." In a flash, her leg was over the crutch: she slid from the saddle, sank onto her knees by him and began to fondle him. His ribs were corrugated and his coat stared; his feet looked worn and the pads were tender.

"How far," she cried, "how far have you come!"

And, "Who are you?"

Ida wasn't able, infallibly, to tell the hounds apart; out of, say, sixty couple. Griselda had been doubtful over most. Esmond had, too; and Uncle Rupert. That was by no means extraordinary.

The hound, reassured, sat on his haunches and grinned.

"We need Bee," said Ida. "But what are we . . . what *are* we . . . to do with you!"

It was a ticklish question. She pondered. She was youthful enough to perceive that the grown-ups would feel constrained by absurd notions of propriety. They would seek to return him. Telegrams would be sent. The grown-ups would meddle.

"If I put you in here, will you be quiet, I wonder? For the minute, until we have a plan.

"You must be fed, old thing.

"You've got to stay, all on your own."

Her grey was standing, reins loose on his neck, ears pricked. The gate was to, behind him. She searched until she'd found a stall where straw hadn't been forked out, quite, from beneath the manger. She made it into a better bed. "Come," she said. The hound lay down, forelegs outstretched and head up.

The eye he watched her with was bright.

"Not a sound!" she told him. "Back truly soon."

She shut the door to the yard; saw the windows were fastened.

Would his own bench in the hound quarters have been a wiser choice? she asked herself. But he'd gone round the railings and taken measure of the lifelessness there.

She hustled Old Haunts to the Grange stables and gave him to Clarence. Griselda was easy. She'd had a book she couldn't put down. She was in the pinery. "Find me Bee," Ida whispered.

"Is he indoors!" said Griselda.

"Could you," said Ida, "go to the steam-house and gather up food?"

Griselda looked blank.

Ida said, "Flesh, biscuit! Or even cold porridge from the scullery."

"Who for?" said Griselda, her mind elsewhere.

Ida put her finger to her lips.

"Nobody about."

"You never know."

"Some of our dog-meat," repeated Ida. "Use your wits."

Knacker's meat was kept in the walk-in zinc safe on the steam-house's outside wall.

"If I'm asked," said Griselda primly, "for whom shall I say the food is?"

"Pretend," said Ida in alt, "some necessity!"

Griselda started to protest.

"Feign an air of mystery. Then they'll imagine you're playing. Say Bee wants it, you haven't a notion why."

"I *haven't* a notion why!" said Griselda.

"Collect a decent bowlful. Something . . . sustaining. The servants won't betray you." And Ida went to change out of her habit.

They met by the back entrance.

"Not barefoot, Bee darling, to cross the park," said Ida.

"How was I to divine I was to cross the park!" he said.

"And we may need you to fetch Jem, I haven't got it clear yet."

"Got what clear?" said Griselda, maddeningly.

Ida said, "Not by the ha-ha, no one must notice. Oh, I know . . . blackberry baskets!"

She sped them as fast as their legs could carry them. "I can't hear any sound," observed Ida, "can you!"

They hit her.

"We're going to the Kennels," stated Bee.

"We mustn't fail," muttered Ida. "We mustn't!"

"Calm down," said Griselda.

Still watchful, the foxhound lay where Ida had shut him. When the bolt grated back and the outer door swung wide, he stood; he greeted them; and he exhibited relief.

Griselda said, "I *see*. Oh I do see."

Ida said, "Dish out meat first, Grizel. Tip it from the cloth onto the floor."

While the hound gulped down these victuals, their little brother looked intently, for several months had gone by, and said, "It may be Homer."

Laughter burst from Ida; and was smothered. "What's funny!" protested Bevis. Ida said, "He couldn't be truer to his name, then."

"You're such a little boy," said Griselda, "and you're so serious."

"It's a name like that."

"Bee, it's imperative we hide him," said Ida.

"Like Homer with H?" inquired Griselda.

"No," said Bevis. "I know him, he's an R.

"Not Reaper. Reaper's older, has more of a dewlap, and other *tan* markings," he said, "altogether.

"I do know him," Bevis said.

"He can't remain at the Kennels alone. Somebody might hear him."

Bevis said, "Rumour!"

The hound shot him a glance.

And, "Of course I'm poz."

"We can't feed him this far away, not so very easily. I've thought about it hard and I believe we have to flourish him under the noses of everybody," finished Ida.

"Well . . ."

They had no quarrel with that.

"Well, what do the gypsies do when they want to hide a pony?"

"We haven't stolen him," said Griselda.

"Jem's people don't steal!" said Bevis hotly.

"We have," said Ida, "if we don't own up; if we don't tell. He must have been bought, for money. I don't suppose you can recollect who bought him, Bee?"

But Bevis could not.

By nightfall, Gypsy Jem had painted the noble hound jet, swearing it wouldn't lick off or be poisonous; and *dear* Mrs Slade, patently dubious, had been stampeded into fostering – "Well I never did, Miss Ida, no more than temporary, mind!"

– a nice black dog (a girt great creature, like to rampage terrible) queerly similar in conformation to Misty.

Slade had stared and then at Miss Ida with a wry grimace, saying, "You'll lose me my position!"; and it had hung in the balance.

"What are you up to, Miss," had said Slade, "if I may be so bold?"

Ida strolled down the path between their roses, and Slade followed her. "You'm over-impetuous," he said. "Throw your heart over without any horse under you. No pensioner, he yonder, if the dawg be what a body'd reckon."

"No," said Ida, "I dare say not."

"Small work d'make a rascal!"

"We'll consider the matter," said Ida, "tomorrow. We must go in for high tea, don't you see!"

Slade had reigned over the Grange stables for many a year: cajoled by the children he'd have shouldered the direst dilemma, kept his gob shut; and he knew he were daft. "You could fetch me rotten trouble, Miss," he said.

However, when all was said and done, Mrs Lupus wasn't that observant; and the uncles didn't come nigh the Slade dwelling, only the Master had done that. Who was to say what breed of dog it was!

"He'll spoil his nose by the fire," said Bevis.

"What does it matter now?" said Griselda.

"He'll sleep in the shed," quavered Mrs Slade.

"We may learn where he came from," said Ida, scrupulously; "and if so I trust we may settle it with our pocket money."

"Ida!" put in Bevis.

81 Stokes's constitution

Before Rumour, whose dam, according to Bevis, was that Vernal kicked so badly by Mr Bleadham's bay rig she had to be put down, and litter brother to Ruffler ... "Do you make it up, Bee?" ... and Rival, among last season's entry, Ruffler whom Papa drafted, yes before Rumour, or "Jet", could be discovered, Uncle Oliver (stuffy or not!) was to let the cat out of the bag.

Griselda had at that minute seated herself at the drawing-room piano. They'd marched in.

She rose hastily. "Continue!" said Dorothy.

"You don't need Stokes," said Oliver.

"How can you possibly know! Gentlemen don't understand these matters."

"She will be a nuisance."

"The woman is a godsend."

"You will say she's a pest."

"Continue!" reiterated Dorothy. "I hear you. How could she be a pest? You're absurd."

Griselda faltered on.

"She'll be bawling she doesn't like foreign parts."

"Servants have to go all over the place," said Dorothy.

"Getting an upset tummy."

"Then she may attend to me in a similar situation."

"Her constitution will be more temperamental than yours. Mark my words," said Oliver.

"I need her to pack. I have no notion how to pack."

"Of course not," said Oliver. "I dare say there are many jobs of which you have no notion."

"My hair, my hats ..."

"Can't you pin up your own hair?"

"If you're to be disagreeable, I shall remain at Quarr."

"Are you going away?" asked Grizel.

"It is not your affair," replied Dorothy.

"Rum," had said Cynthia Stokes to Mrs Cockerell, "though I myself, Mrs Cockerell, am cock-a-hoop. Him not an age underground. Proper scandalized you are I'm sure!"

Oliver was now prompted, once Griselda had "listened" to a conversation not intended for her benefit, to draw the children together and signify that he and Dorothy were to tour abroad.

For her health!

Bee paid no attention. Griselda's hand stole into Ida's.

Ida was livid. She was *incensed*, so much so that Dorothy chose to perceive a compliment.

"Does one visit Africa for one's health?" Ida enquired in such a scathing tone that Dorothy was amused.

"It won't be the tropics," pronounced Ma; in her eyes the sweet smile that George had loved. "Do control yourself!"

Uncle Noll would normally have been dragged to the school-room globe, had Bee jumping up and down on the crook of his arm and been bombarded.

Little was said. Grizel and Bee were dazed, unable to imagine how it might be.

Esmond would receive letters from both Ma and Uncle Oliver.

"I expect you're dying to learn ... *how long for*!"

Palpable lack of interest.

"When I have children," Ida remarked to Inkpen, "I shall *not* calmly go away for months on end!"

Miss Inkspindle said, "Won't you, dear?" Nurse had stroked Ida's cheek with her knuckle.

Ma had been getting ready for weeks before it had occurred to her to alarm the household; let alone inform her brood; for she had judged it of no particular consequence.

Merely, she had ceased to nurse the youngest, Guy.

At the sturdy age of nine months he had been amenable to a bottle.

With that ... farewell pecks on the cheek, "be good", "do as Inkpen and Nurse tell you", and a sublime disregard for appearance ... they were gone; Oliver with two camel-leather bags, the clothes he stood up in and a dressing-case; Dorothy with four trunks, camera paraphernalia, calf-skin dressing-case, two kid-covered hat-boxes and Stokes.

When Mrs Lupus had stepped into the carriage for the run to the train, she'd been glad that her children had restrained themselves. Any display or clamour she would have deemed indecorous.

A marvellous peace fell on the Grange.

82 The colour back in their cheeks

There was no one to say Mop's pups would have to be drowned. If Archie noticed a gay, black hound, chops exhibiting an amiable grin, trotting in front of Old Haunts and Grenadier at early-morning exercise, he let this circumstance pass.

A new moon had brought still air and a crisp sky.

That Rumour, a callow young 'un, not the type anybody might have expected to turn up at Quarr, should have found his way home! The children were infected by a queer optimism.

Nurse saw the colour was back in their cheeks.

Not a day went by but that they called at the Kennels. There, leaves had fluttered to the ground, and in flurries speckled the cobbles. But nobody came. Nor was a telegram enquiry received. They began to breathe more easily.

Then Ida hatched the grandest idea. What paltry fun those hunt terriers now had! And there was noble Pantagruel with no employment for his nose. Ma's dachshunds were idle! "The dachshunds?" exclaimed Griselda.

Would they be able to keep up? Even if surprising, they weren't used to running with horses.

"They're not entered to fox," said Bevis. "Neither is Pantagruel."

"It may be that we must start on foot," said Ida.

That was cried down.

Griselda said, "We ought to do it properly."

"Frank Fontley did go on foot with hounds," said Bevis.

"In the summer," said Griselda.

"They'll be terribly motley, that can't be avoided," said Ida. "Our legs might get tired keeping them together, there is that to be said."

Of foxhounds, Rumour and Misty; of bloodhounds, if Archie consented, Pantagruel; of dachshunds (long-haired), Gretel, Red Boy, Snuff and Mina. Perhaps Uncle Oliver's Lalla didn't quite count, in the desert she would have been a sight-hound. But she would be keen to be included. Of former hunt terriers, commandeered from Brian: Rags, Tiny and Dainty. They knew the job. There was black and tan Midge from the lodge. Mop and Rabbit mustn't be left out.

"Heavens," said Griselda. "Can you imagine!"

That made fourteen. "W. . .w. . .well!" said Bevis.

"It's no good being too precipitate," said Ida. "If we go mounted, I'll leave Old Haunts at home, have David."

"Suppose the nursery party wishes to drive out to watch?"

"We have to learn first how our pack will hunt."

"Who is to carry the horn?"

"Ida."

"She's a girl."

"We need Esmond."

"Bee darling, it's funny how knowledgeable you are but I don't believe you could take out seven couple and make them obey you, let alone hunt with them, and you can't crack a whip yet and I don't suppose you can get a note out of a horn."

"Rex Hoskins down the village has a cornet. Esmond is acquainted with a fellow who has learnt the trumpet since he was six."

"He must have exceptional lips," said Griselda.

"Can Ida? I mean, blow the horn."

"Miss Alma Lovell," said Ida, "who became Mrs Francis, carried the horn with the New Forest Deerhounds whenever her papa was absent; and that was twenty to thirty years ago. So it isn't so very peculiar. Not 'down the village', Bee dear. She had a wonderful, strong voice which rang through the glades and Mr Surtees had said she should be in the opera.

"Her father had one arm," she added. "If one is keen enough, one can triumph over most handicaps."

"What will people say!" said Griselda. "*Shouldn't* we wait for Esmond?"

"Does it matter what people say?"

"I suppose not."

"You ask Uncle Archie, Bee will go and be sweet to Mrs Foyle, I'll have a word with Brian. Don't let on too much, will you!"

"No," said Bee, with irritation.

"Shall we meet tomorrow at half past eight?" said Ida. "According to Porlock the weather will hold."

"Lessons," said Griselda, "I'll say to Inkpen we may be delayed. More so than usual."

"I imagine Inkpen's inured," said Ida.

Bevis presently shut himself in the library.

83 The Ladderback

Mrs Lupus had always accused Ida of being over-burdened with imagination. The event that now riveted everybody and caused the housemaids to go into fits was – all were to agree – a flawed work of genius.

Riding the pony, David, and astride, Ida "met" in front of the house. She had her sister on Grenadier, Bevis and Tanga, Gypsy Jem on foot; loitering at a distance, Brian, also on foot.

Pantagruel had had to be told to go with them. After that, Archie had been observed to go indoors. But, unable to resist, and obtaining rare amusement, he passed straight through, slipped from the side and prepared to train field-glasses on them from afar.

The faithful bloodhound, his doubts now assuaged, stood like a stock whilst the smaller animals, or the terriers among them, sniffing at his legs, milled around. He lifted his head and gazed at Ida in his sombre way. Ida was experiencing a little difficulty in making them understand they were congregated for a purpose.

Dorothy's dachshunds had been scolded so often for getting too close to horses' heels, and repulsed, that they would join in only to hesitate and hang back. Thongs, with lashes on the end, however harmless, they regarded with disapprobation. Red Boy beat a dignified retreat, and had to be fetched.

Walking David slowly, Ida moved off into the park.

The most youthful dachshund abased herself. Ida called: Snuff squirmed. Bevis had to dismount and made the mistake of trying to pick her up. For one thing she was unwieldy.

He brought an ignoble piece of string from his pocket and tried then to lead her. Snuff wouldn't be led by a boy with a rein over his arm and a pony. It seemed she was a lost cause. He loosed her. She consented, and paddled after them.

Rumour and the hunt terriers were past friends. Grizzled Misty, pretty blind, tottered on with a will behind the spaniel, whose eyes she'd use. She had to be addressed in hand signals, vigorous and large: she was deaf. Rabbit was behaving with decorum, and his face was intent.

The dachshunds, their minds made up, streamed after him. Their natures were sunny and they never seemed to recollect the painful piercing of their ears. Lalla, who would run with a galloping horse, kept level with Ida, if rather apart. Midge brought up the rear, like a dog who didn't quite belong.

The whips had to be rather careful not to threaten the perilous cohesion of this pack. Ida was forced to encourage constantly the lesser hounds.

It wasn't that the dachshunds weren't sporting. They possessed very good noses and their indiarubber spines were invaluable to them. They were no lap-dogs: they were loath to be mauled. They'd always been liable to go off, they'd give each other a look and race away, deaf to entreaty; and not come back for hours; were sometimes found miles from home working the Holkham hedgerows, still absorbed; or they'd lose you on a walk or, worse, when you'd taken a picnic-hamper out in the trap.

Grenadier had chosen to be a handful.

Ida went towards the Ladderback. Archie stopped to fill a pipe from his pouch.

The sun shone through a mist.

The knoll, with its furze clumps, brimbles, elder and briers, ascended alone from open ground; steep to the east, with two hollow dips in the "seat" of the western slope. Her voice would carry through the whole of it and she and her whippers-in would have a commanding view, one of them from below, she and the other from within. Moreover, it wasn't far.

Hounds, Ida reckoned, wouldn't be able to miss the high scent of fox: thus they'd grasp, those who were vague, what they were supposed to be after.

Might there not be a glimpse of that curious yellow cub? She'd known him since the previous May; also his rangy brother, and a sister with black-tinged ears.

Midge was a woeful laggard. Bevis had to speak in his tender voice to her: she became embarrassed.

Archie hid himself in the big old hedge a quarter of a mile away. Brian, out in the open, jiggled on one foot.

Jem, meanwhile, was an asset. For commands, the dachshunds looked to a person lower to the ground than Ida could be. They poured in with Rumour, Mop, the hunt terriers who so loved to run with the pack.

"Loo in, loo in!" called Ida, in mimicry of Papa.

The wind was slight in a pale sky.

Mop flushed out a bunny and Misty pitched head first into prickles. The dachshunds, in ecstatic tongue, and Mop, with her short bursts of carolling, Rabbit and Midge went away. Their tones mingled, rose and fell, rose and fell. The foxhound and the bloodhound had left off at a sharp word from the huntsman. It was a mercy the bunny wasn't far from the burrow. Game Misty had forsaken Mop and latched on to Rumour. Misty couldn't go anywhere without somebody ahead.

Neither dachshunds nor Mop returned.

The hunt terriers knew the earth and wasted no time in breathing terror to the inhabitants. They didn't go in without being told. Ida had no intention of losing a terrier underground; of having to let Brian bring his spade.

The noble fellow, Pantagruel, who would stick to any and only one scent if he but knew to which he'd been laid, boots, buck, or a waft in the air, without being hunting mad, was now aware that his master was upwind somewhere behind and he kept stopping to gaze over his shoulder.

Misty began to feel her age. She lay down.

Lalla hoped for deer or a hare: she was infectiously keen, though baffled by the English sport.

Ida dismounted, and attempted to gather her pack: she shouted at them. Her lips when she tried to put them to the horn seemed to have gone numb.

When Bee and Grizel had brought everyone back and, hidden from Archie, all four children were up in the dell, Rumour began to speak to a line.

Scent was confusing.

Midge chose the moment to snarl at the bull terrier, but the unwisdom of this passed without retort. Rumour was mute again. Lalla, out of curiosity, and Pantagruel, at Ida's bidding, went to him. Rumour was intelligent, he knew his work in whatever company.

Fogged though her eyes might be, Misty had been roused. Somehow Rumour's voice had penetrated! Though she remained at her ease, the old throat had swollen; to die away.

The dachshunds didn't admire the renewed presence of so many equine legs and tended to duck and flinch.

Midge set up a howl, but she'd suffered no harm.

Pantagruel sat on his haunches.

Rumour had been feathering a line. Ida had judged it time to leave the earth and show hounds how to hark to him when he now spoke more strongly. Pantagruel did then go to him again; and Rags, Dainty, Tiny too. Misty, dazed, staggered after the bloodhound: once he'd made up his mind, he covered the ground at a pace too swift for her.

The dachshunds, while Rumour ran steadily down the slope, maddeningly chose to stick their noses down another hole: Brock had cleaned out his bed. From Brock's abode, they elected to whisk through the bracken to their hearts' desire.

Still Mop half expected somebody to produce a gun.

Ida didn't blow "gone away". She collected Rabbit and, finally, Lalla.

Midge, with a funny look at her, set off home.

Rumour knew he wasn't hunting a running fox: Ida seemed to want him to hold to that line.

The deep notes of Pantagruel and Rumour were a thrill. If only those naughty dachshunds, whose voices echoed round the Ladderback, had been with them!

Rabbit bowled along, a keen if mystified expression on his face.

On the flat, a hare jumped up. To Lalla this was much better and she chased after Puss.

Griselda's attempt to whip her off was infelicitous.

For Gypsy Jem it was more than a body could bear. He yearned for Puss for "Mum" he said, "for to jug". For some seconds his threadbare foot-gear held him while he swayed. Then he was off after Lalla.

Bevis, amid protest, had to be dispatched to fetch the errants from the bracken.

Ida and Griselda passed through the gate into the post-and-rails enclosure.

Darnley and Sable had come bumbling up, and there was squealing; which was awkward and unnerved the bull terrier. Grenadier snorted and breathed fire; he tossed his head (in a well-bred fashion). To him, hunting was an exquisite pleasure; and this paltry.

Misty was done. Brian had legged it around the knoll. He coupled her, quaintly, to Midge before she could blunder into worse or expire.

Mop had chased after Jem and Lalla.

She was whistled and came. The proceedings had seemed to her like a romp. Rabbit, meanwhile, had detected Mrs Styles' marmalade tom balanced in some elder branches. An unattractive beast with his bull head and seldom-retracted claws, he couldn't be denied his courage. His perch was not substantial, but he knew himself safe. He settled for a long, unsympathetic glare at an old foe. Rabbit bayed him, springing in his muscled way to send the elder into the paroxysms of a leaf.

It was never thought politic to let Rabbit kill Monster; and the huntsman herself had to dismount, to seize her own animal, drag him away.

Rumour lost the scent. He cast around vaguely, lifting his head to look for the children. Rags, Tiny and Dainty looked to him for inspiration. Pantagruel, still downwind of his master, thought he'd done enough and, gloomy as ever, went home, which meant to a spot in a bramble-clad ditch from where tobacco smoke spiralled into the air.

84 His gun dog Mop

"The meet" had been a triumph. "Going to covert" had been accomplished not too badly. "Drawing the gorse" – well, Ida had aimed at education of the new entry. The run had been chaotic. The final print was blank.

Ida knew she'd been a fool.

Misty was ancient. She was to toddle back to honourable retirement.

There was a preponderance of terriers. Midge was considered unsuitable; as was Ida's own Rabbit. Lalla had her brain measured by Bevis. He pronounced it too shallow. They believed the dachsies, despite their music, to be an encumbrance. Mop had managed without any true offence; but would she ever do more than lollop companionably, and, poor girl, she was in whelp.

Mop hadn't earned dismissal.

"Pantagruel must," said Griselda, "be courted." All agreed.

Rags, Dainty and Tiny were useful sorts, and had shown themselves to harbour no misconceptions.

Rumour had been quite sagacious.

His black was beginning to rub off.

"Ultimately," said Ida, "ultimately, we have to say to ourselves, are we able to hunt with half a couple and a bloodhound, and three terriers?"

"Pantagruel hunts a human hare."

"We won't follow a *drag*, surely!" said Griselda. "That's a horrible notion. Even with red herrings."

Ida said, "A carted deer, what about that?"

The others blinked.

"There's a Master of Staghounds, who keeps a tame hind at the hunt kennels, in the West Country somewhere: she's taken to the meet in a pony-cart and enlarged, gives them wonderful runs, and is home by tea-time; and always on the friendliest terms, hounds and she, for they are housed together."

"Not sporting, exactly," said Griselda.

"Twenty minutes' grace, by law."

"Papa would have frowned on it."

Bevis said, "Quarr hasn't got a pet hind."

He added, "Bountiful and Blissful aren't very far away."

Ida went on, "And Lovell, when deer in the Forest were few, was known to take the stag home, rest him, feed him; and let him go free on his lawn!"

Grizel said, "We have to do it unmounted first. You did lay down, Ida, that we weren't to be impetuous."

"Bountiful and Blissful must be as decrepit as Misty," said Ida.

"No," said Bevis. "Misty is fourteen or fifteen. We pensioned her four years ago, I should think. Or more."

"I wonder," said Ida.

"It wasn't kind, don't y'know, to bring her out, Ida," quoth little brother.

"How *astonished* Esmond will be!" said Griselda.

Ida had already dashed off a letter. In a day or two a stern reply was to forbid the corrupting of "my gun dog" Mop.

85 Esmond

Those that championed the old Master's memory, his skilful ways in the field, were many; yet the fickle would go on waggling their tongues.

A foul mood was abroad.

Esmond was at Quarr for his half-term exeat when the smith, irked mightily, and being plain garrulous, could 'a bit his own out. "Be folk all over! No call to speak ill of the dead, be what I d'say to they!" he said.

Some late swallows came through and stopped for an hour on their journey south.

Esmond was dreamy and remote; like the swallows, no longer so chatty; and didn't appear to want to be in on it. He puzzled them. He listened to his sisters when they retold the story of "our first meet". He heard how Ida had "of course" persevered; and how Rumour had charmed the morose bloodhound; how they'd begun to work together; and harkened to Ida's voice. He heard, with a grin, how there'd been calamities; and hostility from certain quarters. How they hadn't yet *found* a fox; and how the horn had dropped out of Ida's jacket. They'd gone to Papa's dressing-room to examine his hunting-coats and discovered even his hair-brushes laid out and razor stropped! He heard what a brick Brian had been; how Uncle Archie's beard had shivered with what must have been mirth; how Jem became a broken reed whenever game for the gypsy pot hove into view. He uttered no more reproaches about Mop, now a size, and the accident over Chips.

They'd quite expected Esmond to say, "*I'll* be Master and *I'll* hunt hounds." Their faces fell.

He didn't even come to watch.

That had made Ida uneasy.

Then Esmond went back to Meavy as quietly as he'd returned home.

Ida said, "He needs an animal to ride. Grenadier goes well for him, but Grenadier is yours. Mother Goose, too strong for a boy, takes much too much of a hold, wears his arms out. David, such a slug."

"I dare say," said Griselda, "you're proposing now to buy him a pony. Really, Ida!"

"Shouldn't he be around to try it?" said Bevis.

86 Gilbie Cox

Gilbie Cox had a wonderful way with horses; but his yard wasn't truly edifying. This was a paradox.

There was his knacker's trade: a reek of blood (even if there were no sight a girl would rather not have seen) always hung over the stream and its bridge that carried the lane; and the cobbles "round the back" were slippery and pale.

Round the back he slaughtered. In the front yard were the animals he aimed to sell on.

Out in his fields were one or the other, being got fatter or sounder or biding. In the rear, cattle skins and big black paunches dangled from hooks, and lurid skeins of condemned meat; hoofs protruded from tubs, and innards lay sorted in heaps. More noisome, giant coppers would be a-bubble-bubble above the fire. The stench from them was horrid; and their froth. From Gilbie Cox's sheds the moos and moans of ailing or perhaps injured livestock (pure imagination! for Mort and Josh acted swift in dispatch) had been swollen since the demise of the Quarr.

Ida had gone to Uncle Archie and said, "Esmond has had no pony of his own since the stupid race, is that still just?"

Inkpen had said, "Ida dear, you forget you're but fifteen! You won't wish to grow up a managing female, I feel sure!"

The upshot was that Uncle Archie had told Slade to go up to thirty-five guineas, which was handsome; and Miss Ida, Miss Griselda and Master Bee drove to Folly Ash to cast an eye over what the dealer had.

Gilbie Cox had stabling for twenty-six. Besides himself, four of his brothers and an army of offspring were attached to the establishment. Gilbert had made his life in horses; Mort was a rougher fellow, more on the bovine side of it. It was a mystery: how Gilbie Cox would run a yard in which tots with coated, runny noses careered about in the dung, in the guts, in rent garments whilst Gilbie dressed himself tidily, in breeches and leather gaiters; how he could be gentle enough to soothe almost any animal, so daft he'd graze a breakdown on in last hopes of recovery; how he could deal as he did with a hard heart and too shrewd a head; and stand smiling shyly, touching his cap, while, as now, a dog ran on three legs in the yard with a sizeable bite taken from the skin of its flank, which was a bloody mess.

George had never sold to Gilbie Cox: he hadn't scorned to buy.

For the children there was the pleasant sensation in the performance of rescue.

Papa, however, might not have driven his children in a governess car to Folly Ash, he'd have summoned Gilbie Cox to the Grange.

They had to visit each poor beast.

There were the half-dozen green 'uns directly from Ireland; and a Connemara mare, eight Irish donkeys and four draught geldings from the same shipment. The brother who had a wife from County Longford, Biddy, had been over: that was Josh.

Then there were the hunters; ugly brutes, many of them; with crude, hog manes, long teeth and legs that brought pursed lips to your face when you felt them: they'd carry some devilish soul for a season or two. A brown mare showed the scabs of mud fever and was, Gilbie Cox said, in the isolation hospital.

Cox had two or three smart cobs, ride-and-drive; several halter-broken three-year-olds; a "pair" of carriage-horses, ill-matched; some New Forest ponies on the common; a pathetic Exmoor mare, aged and thin, her mane bedraggled, whose sweet eye and mealy muzzle caused the children a wrench; a Dartmoor foal; and a Lundy pony. There were two that were better bred.

How hateful that reek must be, thought Ida.

Slade said to Gilbie Cox they wanted to see trotted up those last two; also the Connemara and the dun Lundy pony, though she was smaller than what they were after, and pretty narrow.

Gilbie Cox was frank with them and, jerking his chin, said, "You won't be after *him*."

Indeed, when Ida said, "Well, old fellow," and went to look

at his teeth, the showier gelding had put his ears right back and pinched his nostrils and backed away from her.

"No vices, Mr Cox!" said Griselda.

The dun, the Connemara and the other little horse with quality were trotted up; their legs, their tendons, felt minutely; their pasterns and feet. Slade ran his hand over their backs and quarters and down the tail; passed it in front of the eye. The native breeds had kept their undocked tails. The dun was sent away.

They saw the Connemara saddled and bridled. Slade made them a signal he was keen on her.

She was only a four-year-old, with no doubt much to learn. But she moved straight; and, "Manners and temperament satisfactory," said Gilbie Cox.

Griselda was to try her. The party set off to the field, crossing the slaughter-yard. It was queer, none of the horses the dealer had betrayed any fear of it.

Ida whispered, "Will Esmond want a grey?"

"Whyever not, Miss Ida?" said Slade.

Ida said, "I have an inkling he might not."

Slade said, "Hmm," ruminantly.

The mare had been measured to be 13.3 hands. Even lacking Griselda's longer limbs – or limb, side-saddle – Esmond got Grenadier, who was hot, to go well for him. All the more sense to find him an animal he could grow into.

Once Griselda had tried her, and then galloped so Slade and Ida could bend their heads to the pony's chest to listen for the heart and she was believed to be sound in wind, all turned their attention to the other.

He was trace-clipped. Acquired at auction in the next county not a week previous, and come by train, he was thought to have been in the ownership of a fresh-widowed lady.

Some boy's pride and joy.

He'd been held by a skinny, little Cox; and had stood as quiet as anything, ears pricked, with kind eyes that had followed the Connemara round the seven-acre field. Once mounted he gave an exuberant buck but soon settled and it was to be observed that his paces were the more extravagant.

"A smart fellow," said Slade, with a knowing look; for he'd had his eye out and had been here not four days earlier.

"Too smart?" asked Bevis, who had been overawed, and trusted he wouldn't be invited to ride a strange horse.

"Not if he proves honest," said Ida; "and not to have been ill-treated; and jumps."

Grizel put him at a log of fallen timber.

A price was agreed at thirty guineas, to be settled, if all was acceptable, on the same date in January.

In this way they had a dark brown, seven-year-old gelding on trial for two months, brought to Quarr that day, with the oddly nursery name of Winkie; which they thought Esmond wouldn't change, seeing as how a swap of name, said Slade, did mean bad luck.

87 'Ware riot

The gypsies had vanished, and Jem with them; but Bevis knew comings and goings had to pass unquestioned.

Winkie was ridden by nobody, it wasn't to be dreamt of. The new gelding was exercised by the grooms or themselves; led out, that is; and long-reined over small jumps by Ida, who loped or galloped behind as well as her legs could carry her and scrambled over the hurdles and never a job at his mouth. She'd learnt this art from Slade. There was too much mud and soft ground to the pasture but the heathland and its sand were prime for winter schooling. She went in shoes, coarse knee-length socks, breeches, Fair Isle woollie.

Griselda ached for the Christmas holidays and her brother.

Her brain dragged its feet, dawdling over her poem: she couldn't drum the lines in, no matter how well she liked them. It was a favourite and chosen by herself. Her eyes would keep turning to the window panes, to a dark afternoon and the rooks, which had appeared in a black stream silhouetted as were the trees of the park and the woods that fringed the land below. The sky in half-light had conjured them from translucent gloom. You could hear them, you could see the foremost; but when you followed the swirl, back and back, you saw that the rooks were flying out of a sky, pearly and profound, in which there were no rooks, none at all. And then they were there, beating towards you, drawn out in fives and tens; amid such a din; caw-cawing on their way to bed.

Ida had taken the pack, Rumour, Pantagruel, Rags, Dainty and Tiny, to draw the scrub near the park's west wall.

The bloodhound never quite forgot his master, half his mind was not on his duty; he would stop and gaze over his shoulder, the furrows of his brow deepen.

Ida on foot had Griselda and Bevis to whip in.

The terriers had begun to cock their heads and fix her beadily as if to say, poor sport, poor sport.

It was the portion of park wall which gave onto the kitchen garden and the pippins, russets, "Quarrentines", codlins and "Brambleys" of Orchard House (let on a seven-year lease to Captain Barge).

Ida had thrust through the withy and alder. She could see Reynard had a regular run down across here from the gorse on the rise. She'd been nursing a horrible suspicion that she didn't possess the old Master's science. Then they did find. But they weren't in full cry; and they weren't running.

There were what sounded like gurgles in Rumour's throat. She heard one of the terriers go snap, snap; and there was a growl, the noise of affray.

Bevis screeched, "'Ware riot!"

In a few strides Ida was with them. For a split second, in that instant, from a whorl of brown grass, she saw the spit of a cat. It had repelled them: now it fell under a joint assault. Ida didn't even bawl at them, by instinct she dived in and drove them aside. Tiny wouldn't surrender her hold on a hind leg and Ida brought her crop down on her, until she backed off with a sour expression.

Rumour was chagrined by his error: anyone could have observed that.

Ida knelt.

The cat wasn't dead, it had made a last effort to crawl away. The head it tried to hold up lolled and drooped. It collapsed. It had been a large Persian with long white fur. The fur was sopping with drool. Tiny had bitten through her leg. The ribs and belly were hollow, dented, as though they'd been clamped. Slowly, very slowly, it closed its eyes.

"I suppose it's that Mrs Barge's," Grizel said.

"Yes," said Ida. "I recognize it."

Gently she gathered the cat up, pushing her hands beneath it. It wasn't dead. The terriers hopped about expectantly. "Take them home," had said Ida. She hadn't even rated her hounds.

Bearing a torn and sodden body in her arms like a breakfast-tray up the sweep to the front door of Orchard House, Ida had suddenly felt too young.

Griselda with a bad chest had been put to bed with a mustard plaster, two sets of bed-socks and her bed-jacket, strings tied, and a stone; with nought better to do than lie stiffly beneath the mask presented to her by the Master after the eight-mile point between Lackham Spinney by Lackham Parva and Eastover Ditch. On the wall beside that were mounted her brush, from the time she'd been blooded, and a pad from the last season. Also precious was a water-colour of the famous 1876 black fox, all black but for a few white hairs at the tip of the brush, hers since she'd been told to pick her memento from George's possessions; and the hoof on her bedside table, which had belonged to darling Truffle, given to her by Papa to comfort her and to carry her through her dreams.

Today, she mumbled the stubborn words:

"Whenever the moon and stars are set,
　　Whenever the wind is high,
All night long in the dark and wet,
　　A man goes riding by.
Late in the night when the fires are out
Why does he gallop and gallop about?

"Whenever the trees are crying aloud,
　　And ships are tossed at sea,

By on the highway, low and loud,
By at the gallop goes he.
By at the gallop he goes, and then
By he comes back at the gallop again."

She sighed. "'Windy Nights'," she recited out loud, "by Robert Louis Stevenson. Whenever the moon . . . "

There, pencilled beside it, in a more childish – a *babyish* – hand was "Grizel". So too was "Esmond". Through the volume, with its tattered plates, "Ida" could be discerned, "Bee", more of "Esmond"; and "Roland". In one place, "Mother".

"Fancy! Miss Griselda," had said Flo, "you had he learnt afore!"

"I was little then," said Griselda.

The old life was oddly distant.

They would encounter Pasha, who fed from a Rectory manger, with Sawyer in the lanes; but not Corinth.

88 Furmety

When they were feeling rather hopeless (although there'd been a hoarfrost and there arrived a flush of additions to their picture-postcard collection) a message came up from the Rectory to bid them ride over to luncheon. Quintus Cornforth wished to put some red beef into them.

The proprieties (Miss Inkspindle) neatly circumvented therefore, the children, with Clarence, eager for his certain helping of dinner in the kitchen, duly set out for Plash.

In their tidiest brown habits and felt hats, the girls, with Bevis, in hacking-jacket and corduroy cap, rode, since they were bidden to luncheon, up to the front door. They would surely visit Pasha in the company of their host.

Old Mr Cornforth ran out to squeeze their hands and make them feel at once at ease.

They were peckish and Bevis, at least, was glad not to have to perch too long in the drawing-room whilst Mr Cornforth drank a glass of madeira.

"Tuck in!" the latter cried, when he'd carved and said grace.

"Rumours," he said at one point, "*rumours* have reached me that you people may be in spirits again. Sawyer brings tales of your doings from the Tom Thumb, don't you see?"

They looked a trifle conscious.

"That's the ticket," he went on. "When you're not so very happy, the dear Lord does turn your thoughts in another direction. He's decent like that, what!" They gazed at him, Bevis with his fork half-way to his mouth.

"I've heard Mrs Barge has kicked up. Called on the Colonel, has she!"

Ida said, "She may have left her card. Porlock hasn't mentioned it. Uncle Archie will have hidden. He always does."

"Poor dear fellow," said Cornforth.

He chewed in silence.

"Well, you owned up, Ida," he said.

"Are we being scolded?" asked Griselda.

"If I were you," he said, and straightaway took a mouthful of roast potato, so they had to wait until he'd finished it, "if you'll listen to advice from a crock . . ."

"No, no!" they all cried, as he'd expected them to, indulging himself.

". . . I should simply walk out with your pack along the tracks in the park until they and you are one; and not try, then, to hunt more than one day in the week."

He beamed at their surprise.

"Think I didn't know!" he said. "I may be able to provide you with an aid. But that's a secret until we've had pudding."

For young who had endured the boiled rice and jam of the Grange almost day in and day out for years, plum duff rolled from the cloth, with hot mincemeat sauce *and* whipped cream, was (he knew) a treat. To Cornforth's taste the Lupus roast meats and the Lupus birds high enough to have dropped off their necks made up for a want of sillabub; yet he'd kept a memory of childhood!

Ideas hurried through their heads, though, not all of those quite acceptable.

Ida had visions of a human aid. An aid, what had he meant by an aid? She foresaw hindrance, or embarrassment; akin to that upon Lorimer's ordering at Advent, the ass, of a Yule Log from the estate, when they never had a Yule Log and didn't want Quarr tradition to be altered, no, not a jot. Ida had grown hot under the collar.

"So! We'll visit the horses," said Cornforth, wiping his mouth.

Their silence made his lips twist.

There were carrots and apples in quarters for Pasha; and for the long-tailed mare; for the black mare; for the aged cob that went in the Rectory trap, and for the new five-year-old, Xanthus, a bright chestnut, acquired to take his work.

When every animal had been patted and Xanthus's points had been admired, when Ida had whispered to George's grey, Cornforth rubbed his hands.

"Now here," he said at last, pulling open the top of a stable door, "we have Furmety."

He still stood in the way. They craned round him. He was drawing the bolt of the bottom half.

Out of the dim interior rose the head of a foxhound, expression enquiring, and then the body; and Parson Cornforth spoke sweetly to her and she stepped out through the door to them.

"She'd been injured, d'you see," he said, "feel the bone here, Ida, it hasn't mended as it should, she won't ever be what she once was, Hesketh and Egmont were all for destroying her, and I said, I said to them, I know a small pack where she could be a godsend, didn't say where, or whom, or what, none of their affair, she's young, got some life in her yet, they'd got her apparently in a draft from the Duke, then she'd met a gin; and they hummed and hah-ed, or Egmont did, so I said, I'll give you ten and six for her. Could have cost many a merry guinea! Pedigree in my pocket. Good bloodlines there."

He patted it.

Furmety was a strong, aristocratic-looking hound, with a

fine head and generous eyes, excellent feet, plenty of bone; and attractively marked.

"Pity it had to be a lady. On occasion a nuisance to you. I heard you had a dog-hound."

A stealthy finger (Grizel) poked Bevis.

"Rumour," said Ida, "came back."

"If you'd like her," the Rector said simply, "she's yours."

He stroked his white beard.

"You'll have to lead her home. One of you must walk. On foot."

Ida said, "Because of our habits . . ."

It had to be Bee.

89 The boys on their own

He still couldn't crack a whip; but he could blow "gone away", with cheeks sucked in; *and* a big tooth not down. He didn't have enough lung for the death.

Bevis had been looking through books in the library, books about hunting, and hound-breeding, and at all their plates; and reviewing his memories of Papa, at first to comfort himself, rolling them over like mown hay, so he should never forget; and then because in recalling such glimpses of his father, on and on, he saw what at the time he hadn't seen.

When cub-hunting, Papa had gone out at daybreak for purposes to which eleven o'clock was ill-suited, to pick up the line of a cub on the tranquil journey to the earth after a night's forage. That had been no whim, no hoary tradition.

Often, Papa was very small; at a great distance, or only heard. Yet Bevis and Papa both knew that in the winter a fox lay up in hoops of dry bracken, if possible on a jut of land level with or higher than the earth, well away from it yet within earshot. Bevis knew that foxes would leave the nursery earth to air over the winter, and that a fox might not use his earth at all but live in the open. He knew that a fox would cross fields from his lair into another ground by a regular route; and how a grown dog-fox might travel far, be weeks abroad.

Bevis knew that Papa, when he drew, took thought to the wind, so his cleverest quarry didn't slip out no sooner hounds entered; and that he hunted his coverts well throughout the season, so foxes broke and didn't ring them.

It was Bevis who'd put himself in charge of Rumour's dinner or, as he'd say, pudding; and, by and by, Furmety's; for it was he who could state that Quarr hounds were fed porridge cooked from oatmeal *more than a twelvemonth old*, into which modest pieces of boiled flesh, usually horse, were stirred; and cabbages four days a week in summer. Too much meat diminished power of scent, as did a dirty bench. Bevis shook up their bed-straw daily, and changed it every five. A while since, Rumour had come from Mrs Slade's to be kennelled at the stables.

("Bless my soul, Slade," averred Mrs Slade, "if they childer baint a-courting trouble! Whatever will their ma go an' say!")

Bevis squatted by Rumour and Furmety for hours.

They might curl up and go to sleep. Then they would dream. He reckoned he could follow their dreams as he followed a remembered Papa. Their legs and pads might work: they were trotting. Their skin might twitch and their noses dilate; their eyelids flickered: drawing covert. They might whimper and give throttled tongue: they'd found. Their legs and bodies were galvanized, thrilling to some scent or sight. Then the dream would leave them. They might sigh, or snuffle, bury their noses; and they slept quietly again.

The weather was mild for the time of year: no more than a morning frost, red skies at night, firmer going. There was unlikely to be snow for Christmas. Inkpen and the girls were to be driven by Clarence, a clod with engines, in the motor to Fawernbridge.

Tanga was saddled for Bevis; Winkie, whom he hadn't been able to take his eyes off for the two days he'd been home, for Esmond; and Mother Goose for Gerald.

Mop's puppies, born in the third week of November, had opened their eyes whilst Esmond was still incarcerated, had learnt to lap and at three weeks mumble shredded raw meat; and it was Ida who'd started keeping an eye out for homes; if hardpad, which had swept through the Hunt Kennels almost every year, spared them.

Bevis was bent on hound exercise.

To his deep, if slightly suspicious, gratification, the big boys said they'd follow, and *see how he did*.

Even the picking up of Gypsy Jem (Jem was back) by prior arrangement, didn't mar the genial mood.

Gypsy Jem had got a moth-eaten felt saddle, made for a much smaller pony and a tot, and rigged it on the skewbald by means of an old roller and a large crupper. He had no stirrups. He did not look trim.

Bevis, with whom the hunt terriers weren't popular and who wouldn't have attempted to part Pantagruel from Uncle Archie, was rather cheery: he rode ahead, his one couple in close order, along the narrow lane; followed up by Jem. Gerald and Esmond went side by side, chatting about pheasant and duck.

Bevis met the Bedlingtons from the Mill: the yapped insults Rumour and Furmety treated with disdain.

There was the ring of hoof-beats over Slepe way; and they trotted smartly by a wagon and horses. Arthur Morder, for he – "Our lodge-keeper's wife's fancy-man," Esmond told Gerald – it was, hooked his chin to them, and the oily curl that dangled onto his forehead bobbed about in merry fashion.

"Changes his smock as need be," observed Esmond; "he used to help out for the shepherd."

"Are you to show us some sport, Bee?" called Gerald.

"Oh I say!" said Esmond.

Bevis reined in, and twisted in the saddle. Jem's lizard gaze went from one to the other.

"I dare say I might," Bevis said, "if that's what you fellows would like."

This was greeted by head-wagging and benevolent grins.

"But we've been getting Furmety fit. She mustn't try her leg too much, Ida don't want it to start aching."

Bevis cast his eye around the countryside.

Ida keeps to the park, he almost said. He bit his lip.

"He's a solemn little beggar," murmured Esmond, in what would have been an odiously superior tone had Bevis heard it, "one never knows with him."

Bevis felt his jacket.

"Didn't come out with my horn," he said. "D'you reckon, Esmond, that Porlock would find it for Jem if we were to send him off for it?"

"Well, well," said Gerald, "look what I've brought. You'd left it in your bed! Lulu put it on your chimney-piece."

Lulu, or Lucy, was Gerald's favourite housemaid.

"Lead on, Master Huntsman," said Esmond.

Bevis's chest swelled.

As in "pretending", which he must have given up years ago, Gerald said, "Jem can whip in for you, and we'll be your field."

90 Lead on, Master Huntsman

Bevis took his cap off, shook it and set the brow straight above his eyebrows. He gathered up his reins, sounded the tiniest peep of the horn; and hounds, who'd been lolling and milling, raised their heads.

Between Holkham's ten-acre and the lonely thatched cottages of Maggots Row, there was a ground that fell away in a combe, with brimble and bracken on the slopes topped to the north-east by a blackthorn spinney. Usually there were goats tethered and quite often adventurous fowls would scratch the grass bare. A warren had undermined the farther end. But Tanga, like the Irish horses, never put a foot in holes.

Esmond was dispatched to the lee.

Going in to draw towards the warren, riding with the slope half-way from the bottom, Bevis calmly let his hounds work.

They tumbled in and out of the dead bracken. He tried for the sweet note George would sound to tell hounds where he was and to encourage them.

Then Esmond was standing in his stirrups, waving his cap.

Bevis could see Esmond well.

Esmond, believing his brother hadn't noticed, cupped hands to mouth and gave a bone-shivering holloa.

Still Bevis waited: for hounds to hark to it or, better, to hit off the line for themselves; which they very soon did. In the blackthorn, Rumour spoke; and was on; and they went up and through and out of the spinney in tremendous fettle.

When Bevis and Gerald saw the red coat streak in the sunlight straight across the meadow, their excitement was unbounded.

Winkie fairly danced, yet the field was meticulous in reining in behind the huntsman. The fox was already at the far side, outstripping hounds; who ran strongly, Furmety showing no sign of weakness.

The indulgent grins had been swept from the faces of the big boys and absolute delight reigned.

Indeed their sole solecism was in crying Bevis on as though at a Rugby football match.

Their fox had veered to the rise into Dyce land. They saw him stop and look round; and slip on now in no great hurry.

Then he must have been turned, for hounds circled towards the village. The church tower, with bare flag-pole, poked out of the dip. Perhaps even at that minute Parson Cornforth had stumped in at the west door.

Gerald had opened the first gate.

At the next, they popped over rickety rails and ditch. Jem, pitched out of the saddle, clung to Rosie's neck for all he was worth.

In a nook somewhere at Lower Slaughter, Bountiful and Blissful cocked their ears.

Up at the Dyce farm, Roy tore into the paddock to fling a saddle on his bay pony, Cherokee, mud and all; and to kick him lickety-split along the crest of the track, to hit them off from Middle Barn fork.

Some Holkham sheep bunched hastily away; and, once fled from it, whisked round to confront the rumpus.

Still their gentleman had made as though for Plash. The hound music, eerie and wonderful, with only Rumour and Furmety, brought folk into their orchards and vegetable patches, arms akimbo; broad smiles to their lips. The butcher stood at the door of his back premises in his stripy apron; whilst Hubert shot from the front on the black bicycle.

There was a brief check. The huntsman rode up and gazed at them. They cast, heads down; and teetered on the bank, scenting the air.

A quarter of a mile before the village, Reynard had gone over the lane to Quarr; not, it appeared, swimming the Brook, but zigzag to paddle through the ford.

Hounds had plunged in and so over-run the line, couldn't pick it up; they came back; and after ridding themselves of great sprays they puzzled it out; and spoke again.

Bevis splattered on. In a remote part of his head he heard the plonk-plonk-plonk when Tanga's hoofs hit the shallows, a noise from which another Bee might have taken a degree of pleasure.

The newest Mrs Blackmore in her pinny and to the elbow in flour was bouncing up and down; and the jack donkey wound his tether close on the stake.

Billy Strange held the hunting-gate for them: Bevis, Gerald, Esmond, Roy; Hubert and bicycle; pursued by a hard-breathing horde of urchins.

In the tray of Hubert's bicycle bounded a parcel of sausages with a scribble on it in blue pencil.

When hounds somehow lost their quarry in the boggy fallow by Spindleberry Bottom, and looked to him for guidance, the huntsman, hitherto capable, now instead of casting closer to the Lovat Dell slid from his pony, put his arms round their necks and hugged them.

His cheeks were very pink.

Ida did remark, "Had you forgotten what the Rector's advice was!" Nobody could be vexed with him. His triumph was sweet.

91 The first subscriber

Quick-As-Can-Be wouldn't go; but there was wild-fowling in January. Gerald was dragged away to visit his Chieveley relations before he returned to Rugby.

Only Ida could hope to manage the pack entire; of, that was, Rumour, Furmety, Pantagruel, Dainty, Rags and Tiny. Yet after a tussle with her worst self even Ida saw that Bevis, who had some sort of a gift, had wrought wonders. A huntsman liable to fall off, drop his horn, lose a stirrup, let a branch tweak his bowler off (Nurse had ordained that he wear a hat with a crown), and who mustn't be over-faced and was therefore grateful for the tactful opening of gates, and who, no matter how much he worshipped his hounds, nursed secret doubts about their going so far as to kill Reynard, was perfectly comic. Ida, though, decided that it behoved her to see what little bro. could do. It had not been a fluke. Since *she* had decided, that was that. She dared any soul to mock.

Ida put aside dreams of taking Red Boy from his fellows and of running him with the pack.

The whipper-in must have a decent saddle, she said. He must be better turned out. Rosie's feathers might be trimmed and her mane pulled. Ida was a stickler for neatness.

No sooner said than the whipper-in was absent.

That prime scenting morning, hounds, hunted by Bevis, found the vixen in the big covert, Quarr Wood, and ran her, through Styles's cabbage, to the Ladderback; where she saved her brush, going to ground.

Griselda whipped in for Bevis; whilst Ida had elected to ride the grey, and side-saddle, so looking more the thing.

There was a last, magical day before Esmond went back to Meavy on the fourteenth, when Bevis or, to be correct, Ida met at Loose Lane Gate, and Bevis drew a blank in Bluebell Copse and went on to Brimblebed. A fox had slipped out quickly for the Pie Wood three miles away. Though they lost him there, a glorious run, a point of some magnitude, was enjoyed by one and all.

Esmond had proudly handed Ida his cap-money; and Roy had produced the silver threepenny bit from Ma Dyce's pudding. Hubert had a farthing, Ceddie Hopkins and Ginger Foyle an ha'penny between them. The keeper's son Lip had got a mulish grey donkey: he'd come armed with two humbugs.

It would have been beneath Ida to have glanced at these to see whether they were wrapped or likely to be sticky. She would fit herself out with a bag-purse.

Barty Miers had blushed and whispered that his Cousin Archie was a certitude in the imminent future.

A Coker contingent had arrived in the shape of Kit Brown on the Shetland, Idle, who in temperament had much in common with the Hanham donkey, if better paces; and a nursery one in the person of Flo, pushing Master Guy in the perambulator.

It was plain that word had got about.

So it was that the Master found herself pacing to and fro, buttoned and scarfed against the chill, on the terrace, between a lame Colonel and their old champion, Parson Cornforth.

With their whiskers and flowing beards, these two appeared to belong to an earlier day; yet few devoted so much sympathetic thought to the young Lupuses.

"Child," said Uncle Archie, "is it possible you have forgotten some niceties? Should have made sure farmers acquiescent! Don't suppose it's entered your head, eh? And they might expect you to kill a leash of foxes."

"Roy Dyce . . ." said Ida.

"Roy Dyce ain't his father," said old Cornforth.

"That was remiss of me," said Ida. "I'll visit the Holkhams and Farmer Dyce forthwith.

"Thank you for reminding me," she added; so that Quintus Cornforth twiddled on his boots and put a paw out to pinch her chin.

"Strictly speaking, the country, even Quarr itself, isn't yours to hunt," remarked Archie. "Egmont does come this way."

"Not often," said Ida.

"Nevertheless," said Archie.

"Rum how he neglects this side of the country," said Parson Cornforth, "I've said it many times."

"I'll write to him," said Ida, "and ask if he will surrender it to us."

The grizzled beard to her left waggled while the jaws beneath it chewed this over.

"By Jupiter, he shall," said the Colonel, "surrender!"

"However," said Ida, "I contemplate our acquiring more hounds."

"Ah," said Cornforth, "you do, do you."

"We come to the nub of it," said Uncle Archie.

"It's in their blood," observed Cornforth to Archie.

"Bee has amazed us," said Archie, "but . . ."

"He'll be sent away to follow Esmond at Meavy, I don't doubt, when your mother is once again at home," said Cornforth.

"Ought to have gone," said Uncle Archie in a voice so far from the Colonel-ish that Ida and the Rector had to hide smiles.

"One day, possibly this May or June, ready for next season, we might lay our hands on a retired huntsman. He will have been forced to leave his tied cottage and be glad to bring body and soul to Quarr. One of the Hunt Cottages stands empty."

"He will, will he!" said Archie.

"Indeed yes," said Ida. "And we shall have a draft of hounds. Furmety and Rumour will be the foundation of a very fine line."

Furmety had won all their hearts. If her past wound hurt her she didn't say so.

"Meanwhile," said the Master firmly, "our present huntsman, who has inherited Papa's horn, since I have tried constantly and not achieved such success, for we must admit he understands that which I do not . . . at least, not quite . . ."

"Well said!" uttered Archie.

"Bee needs another two couple until the end of this season. It's no use saying 'what about Bountiful and Blissful?'."

"Hum, hum," said Cornforth.

"A foxhound is a fellow who can grow obstreperous," he said quite sternly (echoing Slade), "without enough occupation.

And Miss Inkspindle, I don't doubt, is in despair over your lessons."

"The woman has demonstrated inordinate lenience," said Uncle Archie, "I fear."

"Fiddle," said Ida, "she believes us to be quite promising. M'sister is not at all lazy."

"I see," said Parson Cornforth. "And Bevis, I gather, squanders his brains?"

"What wisdom in that, Ida?" continued Uncle Archie. "Hounds you'd be sent in January could be less than desirable; those to whose names there'd be cause for discontent, crimes even."

"You and I, Lupus," said Cornforth, "are conspirators in this mischief, don't y'know."

"Am no friend to mischief," said Archie.

Nobody would credit it! thought Cornforth to himself.

"Is it not somewhat far-fetched to imagine Bevis could exert his authority," said Archie, "over three couple, let alone teaching the strangers the country and his ways? And what is the saying he won't, you won't, tire of it all?"

"Don't you see," said Ida, "we must retrieve some of our own; and *their* music. Our dear Quarr hounds.

"They should sleep on proper benches," she added, "I'll set Poulter to work."

The draft of two foxhounds was agreed upon: Quarr hounds if made available to them; for preference, bitches. "What I do see," said Parson Cornforth, "is that you require some subscribers. Will you permit me to be the first?"

Ida would have flown; but she kept her feet, where they were always to remain, on the ground.

92 The floods are out

"I might help you there," mumbled Uncle Archie later. "If you like, I could dig out the sales records."

It was colder and the sky threatened snow.

Dick Hanham stumped off to the village to have words with the poacher, Toady Trenchard; and Quick-As-Can-Be's valves went to be ground by Drake at the smithy.

These dark, moon-less evenings, when the light was gone by half past four, Bevis would trip by the beam of a hurricane-lamp to the "Kennels", Sable's old box, to see to hounds, last thing, as Frank Fontley had, and say good night.

He rubbed sweet-oil into Furmety's scars lest the skin callus.

Once he heard the scream of a rabbit.

Ida and Griselda pored over kennel records. The skeleton of the sale revealed that quite *gross* sums had been paid for certain lots. These staggered them. One hundred and seventy guineas for three couple? But the precise identities in each lot were not made: such was balm! Unless Uncle Archie had other papers? The upshot was a letter from Miss Lupus to the Master of the West Somerset; very polite, fairly insistent. This gentleman, with whom they were unacquainted, had bought four couple. Porlock found himself setting a postage stamp to a similar letter to a Captain Heber; who, it was thought, hunted a small private pack over a corner of the Chase and surrounding.

Rumour's secret was preserved.

The soft snow had fallen for two days. They went out into this hush and fed sops to the birds.

They exercised, circumspectly, with greased heel and frog.

Slade said, "Frost-nails . . ."

It was not to lie. On the third day, it thawed rapidly and on top of that came heavy rain. The Friggle began to spill its banks. Swans, black-headed gulls in winter plumage and a huge flock of pewits stood sentry in meadows and pastures. In no time the floods were out.

The huntsman gazed at the sheets of water around Plash with a mixture of dismay and delight.

Through them, shattering the reflections, though at the ford the current spun over his axles and splashes leapt at the shafts, in an old-fashioned phaeton behind a pair of startling black horses drove a jolly Captain Heber. The manes and tails, which he kept long and unplaited, were full of Cavalier curls; and, Ida observed, globs of mud. One on the back seat, one in the well, rather chilly, there reclined a sentimental couple of foxhounds. "Forgive me," he said, "Miss Lupus, for turning up without warning. I've brought you what you sought of me. If ever you don't have a need for them any more I trust you'll let us have them; and, no, I'll not take a guinea."

In this fashion Sappho and Flapper regained Quarr.

"They're yours," he said. "Good show!" he said. He looked not very much older than Gerald. "Won't be any trouble to get to settle."

He wouldn't even stay to tea.

"There are crumpets to toast," said Griselda.

"Great jumping panjandrum!" he said. "But I'm putting up at Coker and my lamps under such grey cloud make your floods look perfectly ghastly, I don't doubt."

Through these also came a telegram, reply paid: ONLY CAN OFFER YOU HOUND SNOWMAID STOP GRATIS.

There were gasps of consternation.

Why! How could he part with Snowmaid!

"Ours not to reason why," said Griselda.

"For heaven's sake, Grizel," said Ida.

She said to Archie, "I have to accept."

"Now see here . . ." said Archie.

"Uncle Archie," said Ida, "it's *Snowmaid*!"

"Does that mean much to you?"

"Yes," said Ida.

Ida remembered how Papa, before he died, had said, "Ask Esmond from me to take care of m'brother Archie, for always!"

"Snowmaid was one of the last," she said, "to come upstairs. We know her well."

"Ah," he said.

"Bee would tell you that for her breeding alone she is irresistible! Her dam was Tireless, who could trace her line back to Eloquent. Tireless had the most wonderful cry, which Snowmaid has inherited; she was true to her name and once got out her fox from the belfry! She was lost on the railway.

The sire was Shimmer, whom you will yourself, Bee says, recall! Papa considered Shimmer to be an Adonis among hounds!"

"Humm!" he said. "What are you going to call yourselves? When soldiers volunteer to storm an impregnable rampart, they form what is known as a 'forlorn hope'."

"Is that us?" said Ida, humbly.

Snowmaid was put on the train.

93 Hold hard

They hadn't forgotten; not Quarr, not each other. And Snowmaid had fawned upon Bevis.

They were never to discover why she'd been so easily let go.

Their music had been swelled. They now appointed an earth-stopper, the gamekeeper's son Lip, mostly for next autumn; since Griselda was frightened of venturing out at two in the morning, even with pony and terrier (out of humanity you didn't stop any creature in), and though she might have been prodded to visit the lairs to put to at first light Ida deemed it ineligible, saying she couldn't countenance it. Also there were the whelps to consider. Brian's lore (either Brian or Hanham had stopped for Master in the Coker and home coverts of the Saturday country) had proved hard to impart.

There was a Treasurer.

Well-wishers, too; they'd taken, that is to say, subscriptions: from Miss Haunchley, Doctor Mahon and, though he'd not have dreamt of turning out, Gervase Sturt; Mrs Rupert; Mr Rhodes, old Mr Holkham, Farmer Holkham, Farmer Dyce; and from tradesmen in the village, Clement Strange the foremost. Fallen stock fetched up and the carcasses had to be dealt with in the steam-house (where sheep's heads in the wool were boiled for the household dogs), after Slade had declined to contaminate his yard; and that reduced the need for Cox's gory cart to call.

Cecily descended on the Grange, with Lupin and Agnes. She thought it behoved her to show Dorothy's brood some degree of compassion, left as they had been with no female relation in residence. Her visits had punctuated her year and there were drawbacks in her remaining at home during these intervals she would have spent at Quarr.

They appeared in need not of compassion but of "a hand on the rein". "Dearest Ida," she said, "what will your mother say! Should you not 'hold your horses'!"

Ida chose to cast a deaf ear. Ida said cryptically, "We were left to our own devices." And, "Ma won't be back for months yet, months. They're not expected until June! Why don't you speak to Uncle Archie? He knows all about it."

"Your uncle runs away from me," said Cecily.

"Shall I ask him not to?"

"Ida!" wailed Cecily. "Hunting! So many hounds! The whole establishment wrapped round your finger!"

Ida grinned, for it seemed a compliment.

"Hounds," said Cecily, "were *banished* from Quarr! Your mother may be so grieved! How can you blithely bring them back; and ... from what I hear ... *hunt* ... um, after a fashion!"

Ida winced.

"Presenting your mother with a fait accompli has *never* proved fruitful," ventured Cecily (who was rather fonder of Ida than she was of Dorothy).

"She sends us picture postcards," said Ida. "Lots of them."

"Well," said Cecily at a loss, "one does!"

"Precisely," said Ida. "I don't suppose Ma spares us another thought."

"She *must*!" exclaimed Cecily (mendaciously).

"Isn't this a futile discussion?" said Ida.

"Forgive me, dear," said Cecily, "Is this not very *treacherous* ground? You are *children*."

"Yes," said Ida.

"*Children* feel consequences."

"You go and find Uncle Archie," said Ida kindly. "Or Nurse. Or Miss Inkspindle. Or Porlock."

"They are servants," quavered Cecily, who was the weaker willed.

"Uncle Rupert, then, or Aunt Lydie."

"They are irresponsible," said Cecily.

"I can't help you, then," said Ida in a grand manner. "Besides, it's not really the same, y'know: we *children* ..." (she smiled!) "... are not the old Quarr, how could we be!"

"Donkey Lorimer," said Cecily.

"Don't you dare!" said Ida.

"Please don't be uncivil to me," said Cecily.

Ida patted Cousin Cecily's shoulder. "Papa would have been so proud," she said.

Cecily threw up her hands.

"What is Esmond's part in this?"

Cecily glimpsed the first look of vulnerability in Ida's face. How like Dorothy she'd be, one day!

Cecily confided to Agnes that they were all "hopeless!": as Ida had predicted, nobody had perceived the least harm.

Archie bolted from Cecily. But Ida had gone to Archie and said, "Why did you call us 'the Forlorn Hope'?"

Uncle Archie stopped and, with reluctance, brought his gaze to bear on her.

"Youthful huntsman. The two and a half couple," he said. "Many hurdles. Lessons!"

"Oh, is *that* it!" said Ida, pleased.

94 A lawn meet at Quarr

Towards the end of the season, on a morning late in March, a Saturday, at eleven o'clock, hounds met at the Grange, right in front of the house, on the carriage-sweep and the lawn.

It was a proper occasion.

Pinkie carried out trays of glasses in which the cherry brandy slopped in the spring-like light.

Bevis gripped the buckle of his reins. He knew he mustn't go into the big covert and not be seen for half the day; that he had to go away on the first fox or risk getting on to a vixen; for, were he to do so, he would have to whip off. The rein lay loose on Tanga's neck; and Bee on Tanga stood calmly in the midst, much in George's manner.

The whipper-in kept hounds bunched.

The huntsman was neat in breeches and glossy new leggings, sturdy coat of a brown-green weave. His black jockey cap Inkpen had been obliged to get made for him: there was none in a boy's size to be purchased. The Master set store in a suitable appearance; nothing flashy.

Parson Cornforth, similarly gaitered, with sandwiches and a flask slung in a satchel, looked ready to stride for miles.

There was Uncle Archie, on his gammy leg, in the azaleas; pulling at his beard and somehow all of a twitter. And, poor chap, he'd been so much improved!

Miss Haunchley had driven over in her trap; attended by a terrier, Ripper, who bulged with muscle.

A lad from Coker Hall had jogged over on a nervy, excitable animal; to "gie un a what to think to": he hung well away.

Slade had got the mistress's gelding, the hack Endymion, sound and fit; for you never could tell, mabbe his lady 'ud fancy a day with them. Slade had had to blister the shoulder, soon after mis'ess had left. He'd a mind to come out for a time.

Nurse stood on the steps, with Mop and Muddle (s. Chips, d. Mop) and Rabbit. The dachshunds smiled on the world.

Mrs Cockerell hovered behind Porlock.

Inkpen meant to follow, for she was stoutly shod and wielded an ash-plant. She also had charge of Flo, who led the pony, David. The basket for infants had two pannier pieces. Ida had said it was for a larger child, and that Guy couldn't sit sideways, strapped in or not. Therefore he rode in a makeshift square basket, tilting and tipping; as if on an elephant.

Guy crowed loudly.

The whipper-in caught herself thinking, for no reason, of Papa: the story of Pasha and The Duchess, when they'd leapt the Friggle Brook by Lackham Parva, across the widest, swirliest water, say twenty-five foot of it, where its bed was trappy from big holes; though done, after a hard gallop.

If hounds took a leap, though to be wet, you leapt. If hounds slithered straight into water to swim, you had to ford it or swim your horse.

Miss Morwenna, on Merrily, kept in reach of Nurse.

Still at some distance, a Dartmoor pony kicked along by a tot on a leading-rein beside a mother in a droopy-brimmed hat hastened shyly to join them.

The head groom's missus, with Misty on a string, ventured into view.

The rest of the field consisted of Roy Dyce, Ceddie Hopkins, the butcher's apprentice Hubert; and Lip Hanham on the unhandy donkey. Keen as keen. No Gypsy Jem.

No Esmond yet, or Gerald. Before the last days, in April, Esmond would certainly be home.

The huntsman had been able to account for a brace of foxes; during February and March. This wasn't all joy; since the reward was seen to sit heavy in the bellies of the two and a half couple.

"Remember, Bee," had said Parson Cornforth, "they must always first give up to you each and every fox they kill, so long as you are up with them; for one day you'll wish to present the mask or brush and it *never* does to let hounds grow unruly. Only then may they break him up."

The cusps and needles of the Macedonian pine, beyond the azaleas, stirred in little puffs of breeze. In the air, a smell of warmth and loam carried to the Master's nostrils. The biting wind had gone. It was positively balmy.

We may mount Bee more grandly, she thought.

"Do you proud," said Cornforth now. "Picture of health and happiness! I shall ride my nag with you next season, mark if I don't!"

The great Quarr Wood summoned him. Bevis moved off across the park first, to the decoy: Reynard was of a fancy to loiter in the bog myrtle to snatch mallard.

In the stable-yard, Clarence rushed his work with the notion of making after them.

The children's "Fir Wood" was a blank. With a sweet note (he hoped) of the horn, the huntsman trotted on; and was disappointed at the pond too.

He became sure as dash it he'd find in the mightier covert. He wouldn't potter all his short day if he could help it.

The cherry brandy, instead of firing his heart, had rather gone to his head: it wasn't unpleasant.

Huntsman, hounds and whip went in by Grampy's Oak (Grampy Lupus at Bevis's age had been immortalized beneath it with a fistful of pheasant feathers and a goat, by a miniaturist).

The trees were very quiet. He felt almost cowed by them. Griselda had hived off from him.

His papa, said Slade, had spared his horn; and, when he did blow it, Slade said, hounds had fair *flown* to him.

Calling, encouraging, Bevis steadied. He mustn't draw over his fox.

Miss Haunchley and the Rector had followed him in; with Ripper on the lead; they stopped every so often and strained intently.

Once Bevis saw Furmety's tan muzzle. He listened to them: a whimper, tiny cracks of the undergrowth.

He walked his pony on and into a broad, mossy ride. Arrested, Tanga stood with ears forward; head drawn high. Bevis was transfixed, for there, but a few yards ahead, Rumour, alone, confronted a very large dog-fox. There was silence.

Don't know you, do I, Bevis thought.

The two fell on each other, rearing on hind legs and tumbling over and over; with an unearthly lack of noise. Open-mouthed, shocked, the huntsman knew an agony of fear for his hound. The fox was not going to run. Rumour got him by the nose, shook and shook him. No pack arrived. The mask was let go, but the fox staggered: Rumour was at his throat, his neck. The huntsman was stuck in his saddle. Then the noble Rumour had dispatched the fox. Bevis moistened his lips. He mustered his breath to sound the death.

Champing and fidgeting in the sunlight outside the covert, the field pricked up and a quiver ran through one and all.

Ida thought, O happy day!

They came pelting to the horn: Sappho, Flapper, Snowmaid, Furmety.

V THEIR MOTHER

95 Lurk

The Grange, breathing in the mid-afternoon sun, appeared much as it always did when approached from the park. A sash window, which might well have been open, was shut; although some of the leaded casements in the old wing were ajar. Upon the top steps, the dachshunds were sitting up. Ears cocked, every so often they shifted weight, expectantly, on their forepaws.

Griselda was at a loss.

Their field had jogged with them towards kennels before saying "good night". Roy Dyce, Morwenna Beynon, Ceddie Hopkins and Lip Hanham. The under-groom from Coker had broken off earlier, and Slade with Endymion; as well as Hubert, encumbered with a bag in which trotters, chitterlings and a pig's pluck had been awaiting delivery. Inkpen, Flo and Guy were long gone; the last two off to nursery dinner. Of the foot-followers, Miss Haunchley and Parson Cornforth had kept in touch and were now strolling contentedly, well behind. Uncle Archie had evaporated.

Yet something ... Her eyes bored into the front of the house. Its panes reflected back the rays of the sun. In that black glitter Griselda caught a movement.

Grizel gulped. She had no notion why.

The huntsman's shoulders betrayed unconcern.

She twisted in the saddle. The Master's eyes met her own and read them. "What is it?" said Ida.

Grizel said, "I dare say ..."

The Master shook her head in patient mystification.

Griselda stared at the drawing-room windows. The sun had

gone in. She looked back. The sun was behind a cloud. When she resumed her examination of the glass she saw, on its feet, a form that was that of their mother.

Ma, who must have been gazing at her children . . . at their companions . . . It couldn't be!

"Lurk!" said the whip.

"Lurk!"

"Grizel?" called the Master. "What's the matter!"

"Don't you *see*," said Griselda.

"It's Ma," Ida said slowly.

"What?" said Bee.

"Yes," said Ida.

The shock, with everybody flushed and only a trifle, deliciously, weary in the saddle, didn't quite register.

Ida drew a breath.

"You go on," she said.

What else could they do? Ida had her leg over and was slipping to the ground. Grizel took her reins. "Go on away from the ha-ha, away from the grass, away from this immediate view. Preferably with Roy Dyce, Ceddie Hopkins, Hubert and Lip too!"

Morwenna Beynon (she'd enjoyed her day after all) hesitated, uncertain of the social niceties ("It's Ma!" had cried Ida Lupus in a glad voice).

Ida plucked up the skirt of her habit and, crop in hand, somehow managing to tug off her gloves, ran; ran to the terrace and up into the house.

96 The dear surprise

It has gone awry! thought Dorothy.

She had time to wash her face, remove her crumpled garments, hear accounts of the doings of her children from Porlock and Nurse. Not even the youngest was there. She grew less entertained; more, bemused. Disappointment had been replaced by chagrin. Oliver irked her: he kept roaring with laughter.

Presently she could embrace little Guy (she also extended two fingers to Miss Inkspindle).

"Porlock, where's m'brother?" had enquired Oliver. "The old fellow not around?"

Ominous, thought Porlock to himself, that Pinkie's not to be dispatched to call the children in.

The party waited; consumed a late luncheon; and waited.

By and by, across the park, a pageant came. Assorted young, mounted on a variety of animals, with five foxhounds. One or two grown-ups, indistinguishable; perhaps a terrier to heel.

Dorothy had discovered enough to be in no doubt: these were no cavaliers or roundheads, no Light Brigade, no dervishes; no pony was an elephant with a howdah; no child in a solar topee.

Hounds with their sterns gay trotted close to Tanga. One raised her head then and beamed adoringly at Bevis.

There wasn't a soul in hunting scarlet yet the very drabness made Dorothy fancy she saw a ghost. Not a human ghost: the spectre of a scene, with all its incongruity, she'd trusted she'd never witness at Quarr again. Thank Heaven, no one was unwell (and their sore need of her was not likely to make itself apparent on the spot!).

So that, to Ida, Dorothy's first words were, "I do wish Griselda wouldn't ride astride!"

"She can't whip in properly, side-saddle," replied Ida; and bit her lip.

Ma stared at her with an expression torn between the wounded and the vexed.

Stag at bay, thought Oliver.

"I'm sorry to observe," said Dorothy, "that Bevis is not at school. Nor is he, am I to gather, in quarantine?

"You may go and change out of those clothes!" she said with a funny sort of glimmer.

Grizel and Bee had parted at the kennels (the stable-yard).

Grizel marched herself straight to the slaughter. No more fell on her head than a nod, only half frosty.

Bee lingered, since he had work to do. He'd feel for thorns or rips in their hound-ish skin. He had to see to the pudding, even if he was to break off and go up and greet Ma before he fed. Still in a dream, so that Dorothy could find it in her to laugh, he trailed in: Bee was just the same!

Towards four o'clock, Archie limped by way of the shrubbery to the side door . . . "I believe, Dolly, you should countenance," he went whisper-whisper, "th. . .their . . . this . . ." He too was observant. Well, it had been *he* who'd ordered the motor and, cravenly, told the servants not to ruin the meet! A quagmire of honour there!

Peace must have abandoned Quarr, he thought. With what reprehensible cowardice he'd followed hounds. And those innocents!

He slunk to his den, not keen to brave her; or them.

97 Bee's gift

It was Ida who told Ma how Rumour had walked home; and how they hadn't been able to trace his new owner in the sale records. How after many attempts (Ma didn't appear to mind the killing of the Barge cat) and the coming of Furmety (a veil over her provenance), Bee, rather than the Master herself, had triumphed, and had won the admiration of the bigger boys, Gerald and Esmond. How (for Ida wanted to believe Ma couldn't fail to sympathize) Esmond had been bought a pony, Winkie. The acquisition of Papa's beloved Snowmaid; and of Sappho and Flapper. How they now had a proper pack, with which Bevis showed pretty good sport. How Bee had a gift, a rare gift: everybody said it was so.

"I'm so sorry," said Ida, "we weren't here. If we'd had any idea . . . !"

"It must be in your blood," said Dorothy.

Swift to seize on this, Ida said, "Shall Bee take you round kennels? Will you see Winkie?"

"From whom did you beg his price?" asked Dorothy. "You'd be wise not to dissemble."

"I took it upon myself," said Ida, "to . . . um . . . organize it."

Dorothy smiled. "I dare say you've missed me," she said. "Uncle Archie, if he it was, has provided you with diversion.

"Well, I'm pleased you've 'told' me!" said Ma.

For several days, they feared (not privy to Dorothy's mood) it was touch and go.

Bee was gratified to show off his hounds, their benches, the hospitable-ness of the stables. Ma learnt their names and how to recognize them. She was gracious to Slade. "Isn't that my Sable's box you've given over to them?" she asked. Whilst that went on, Bevis decided to spare her the complexities that related, every now and then, to having one dog-hound amongst four bitches; and how attentive licking on the part of a lady (or ladies) meant separation for either Rumour or those on heat.

It didn't occur to him that Ma might have understood this.

Instead, Winkie was approved. She said he must be a nice ride for Esmond despite "a somewhat straight shoulder".

Griselda swallowed and managed a tactful silence.

"Would you have a look at the pudding-house?" asked Bevis.

These were the first hurdles. The going got stickier.

They'd had subscriptions. From actual grown-ups, who had stated the intention to continue to subscribe next season. Some had promised to come out.

Ma didn't ask who these grown-ups were.

There was a Hunt Treasurer.

Ma didn't say "who is this Hunt Treasurer".

She wasn't at all used to being told of their doings in such a friendly fashion. She thought Ida in particular much improved.

Once the contents of the trunk stuffed with tasselled red fezzes, burnooses, fine cloth for turbans in lots of colours, leather slippers, beads, scented rocks and stones, glittery powder to throw on the fire and make terrific smells, scorpions in collectors' boxes and many more exotic toys had been fully assimilated, Uncle Noll had gone up to town; taking Lalla, so it was to be presumed he had an onward destination.

What passed between Ma and Uncle Archie they alone knew.

"If you mumble," had said Dorothy, "I can't make out what you're saying. I must be stupid or deaf!"

98 Esmond

Primed, she mused, to feel further astonishment, it was a docile mother that shook hands with Esmond and said how do you do.

"Your train arrived on the dot?" she enquired.

"Isn't this intriguing!" said Ma soon. "Be frank with me, is your new horse all you'd hoped?"

He brushed his hair from his forehead.

"Yes, thank you," he stammered.

"I might join in," said Ma.

"Join in?" said Esmond.

"Wouldn't that be fun?"

"Oh?" he said. (Uncomprehending! she thought.)

"I'm about to speak to Slade. You've no notion of how diligently I've been hacking in the park. To re-accustom my muscles!"

"Your muscles?" he said.

"There is no indecency in 'muscles'. One may mention them."

He regarded her woodenly: she was utter doom.

"Dense boy!" she said, in high gig.

"May I cut along, Ma?" he said.

"Esmond!" she protested. "I do realize it's tremendous for

you to be at Quarr but is it beyond you to sustain a brief conversation with me?"

She noted that what Griselda called his "burden" had begun to weigh. "Such ages . . . !" she remarked.

"Mm," he said.

This wasn't the Esmond who'd shed tears in the pinery. He was taller, and in his demeanour a reserve that baffled her.

"Do you not join in?"

"I tread circumspectly, Ma," he said (in the strangulated way he would address her!).

"Quaint of you!" she said.

"It's their affair. I don't butt in."

"Well!" exclaimed Dorothy. "You take a stern view! I, my dear, am not at all one to butt in."

Esmond sighed. "You've been abroad a while."

"What has that to say to anything?"

She scrutinized his face. He was so like George!

Esmond fiddled.

"Don't fiddle!"

With an effort, "I wait to be asked," said Esmond.

She laughed.

"Prim and proper?" she said.

The bitter pessimist in Esmond had always anticipated that some day, *dash* it, there'd be grief. Triumph was a bolter, and had been bound to elude Ida, Grizel and Bevis! And Ma was Grief Personified. His nerve had got a lot stronger. He stared quite kindly at her; recognizing her for what she was, a female with an inability to rule the merest passion.

Where she was not herself the cause of grief, she'd snipe and be acid. She was vile like that. She was out of control.

He couldn't bear it.

"Splendid you're back, Ma!" he said, to be civil.

Dorothy listened: he'd torn off, with a whistle to Mop and a word to a person in the hall. Dorothy followed. She'd left him in the dark. "Ask Slade to come up to the house," she said merrily to Porlock, "would you? I shall 'ride to hounds'!"

Porlock glowed. "In honour of Master Esmond's return,

they are to meet tomorrow, on a Thursday, ma'am," he replied, "at the Griffin Gate, I believe . . . ?"

99 An inglorious day

When Slade had figged out the bay gelding (no double bridle: the vulcanite Pelham bit in which Endymion went for Mrs Lupus), it could not truly have penetrated (had surmised Porlock) that the mistress was to do him proud.

The weather was not so balmy.

Beside the relics of Quarr's grandeur, two stone griffins atop pillars, Mrs Lupus looked about her critically.

Lip Hanham on his donkey gawped up at her with a mix of doubt and awe. Roy Dyce was cheery; and a toothy, speculative smirk flickered in his features.

"Explain to me," called Dorothy in a musical voice, "tell me once more, Bee, which of our hounds is that?"

The huntsman raised his cap courteously and said, "Sappho, Ma."

"Is that the best name you could think of?" remarked Ma in an aside to Ida.

"Sappho was bred at Quarr," said Ida. "Papa and Fontley named her."

But Endymion had decided to fidget, sidling and snorting.

"You *don't* take exception to a donk!" said Ma, with gay humour. She patted him. "Silly billy," she said.

She brought him up to Old Haunts again. "That's a light-coloured hound," she said. "I suppose you admire her markings?"

"It's Snowmaid," said Ida.

"Ah, Snowmaid."

"Papa adored her."

"You know that, do you!"

Ida smiled. She tapped her nose absently with her crop.

"Don't do that," murmured Dorothy.

Dorothy continued to take an interest. Roy Dyce and Lip Hanham had tucked themselves into the lane. Dorothy manoeuvred (Endymion was not to gain the upper hand) until she could speak. "Is she your very own donkey?" she said. "And that," she said to Roy, "is a nice sort!"

Lip was petrified but Roy Dyce, with some social standing in the neighbourhood, nodded.

"All are well at Upper Slaughter?" enquired Mrs Lupus.

Esmond began to squirm.

The huntsman could hear the solid trudge-trudge-trudge of a genial supporter who would have raced through his church jobs to be there to see them move off.

The Master took out her watch. It was a quarter past.

Of the Treasurer there was no sign.

It hadn't occurred to the stranger (Ma) that a cap might be taken.

The steps ceased with an abrupt grate, their owner thunderstruck to behold Endymion.

When confronted by Esmond – oh so politely – the stranger only said, "It's common to jingle your coins, Esmond."

His eyebrows rose.

"D'you know, I quite assumed that we should be in the park!" protested Ma, when Bevis took hounds to covert; and, at a jolting trot, "I shall stick to your grey," she said to Ida. "You may be my pilot."

This animal's manners! Dorothy thought.

The huntsman swept past Maggots Cottages, where he'd found so memorably once, without a glance.

"Bevis!" called his mother.

"Don't," said Ida.

"Why?" said Dorothy. Then, because she was quick-witted, "Oh I see, it's 'not done'. I'll remember that."

Ida said, "He's going to Slepe Wood."

"Why didn't you say so before!" said Dorothy.

Whilst still outside Slepe Wood, Dorothy noticed Cornforth.

His granddaughter, with a respectful Ceddie Hopkins behind, came up with them then; both having started out, for different reasons, late. Derrick, under-groom at the Rectory, hung back: he would stop in the lane.

Little Miss Beynon, with aplomb, rode up to greet Mrs Lupus. Morwenna was assured vis-à-vis grown-ups.

"'Morning, m'm," whispered Ceddie.

Knotted black clouds were scudding out of the west. Tender leaves, part-unfurled, streamed and bobbed in the breeze.

"Are we to get wet?" Dorothy said.

"Listen!" said Ida.

"What is wrong with the park?" asked Dorothy.

Mrs Lupus's get-up consisted of a dark blue habit, black bowler, copious face powder and a veil. Morwenna judged it to be excessively dressy; she couldn't help but think Ida did too. "Are we not chilled by this wind?" said Mrs Lupus.

Dorothy's ears omitted to convey to her the information (a high "loo, loo!") that appeared to entrance her companions. She stifled a yawn. The huntsman's voice was borne away.

But Ida was alert: Esmond, hitherto a slight figure in the distance, had vanished.

Under Dorothy's gaze, a sandy fox quietly left covert not a hundred yards from her. Dorothy snatched at Endymion's mouth and he gave a plunge. She pointed. "I saw the fox!" she said. "What do we do now?"

Ida shook her head.

Ma said, "Don't you have to holloa?"

The music was diminishing in the distance.

"They're making a mistake!" said Dorothy.

"Buck up, Ma!" said the Master.

Ida led the field and they skirted the wood; with hounds gone out towards Bliss. A brisk gallop was enjoyed, although Mrs Lupus was faced by a powerful ditch and couldn't, as was plain, put her heart over.

When she could draw breath she said, "I do wish this horse wouldn't take hold!"

And she said, "Slade is too inclined to be remiss! How could he send him out so fresh!"

Her expression was a fixed and rather discomfited one.

She cried cheerfully (though vexed), "I must have him in a more severe curb!"

She was hardly in the first flight; gates had been opened for her. Nobody could see how it was that at the first check Endymion careered (poor Endymion didn't have a hard mouth) into the midst of hounds; causing the huntsman to screech.

"Don't screech," said Ma. "I'm having my arms pulled out."

"'Ware hounds!" piped a voice behind her, a voice that subsided in embarrassment.

Since Bee's reproach had *seared* Ida, to the soul, the latter offered an exchange of horses. A tree-stump allowed the proposal to be implemented.

"Do hold the field up, Ida, whenever necessary!" cried a plaintive Bee. "I don't half wish you didn't hamper me!"

"Of what is the child complaining?" enquired Ma.

Esmond put his gloved hand across his mouth and nostrils. He breathed hard. He muttered, "O Lord!"

Ida got the lathered Endymion (whose business it wasn't to carry anybody 'cross country) to go more kindly. Dorothy had never ridden Old Haunts, but he was a gent. He didn't find Mrs Lupus's hands sympathetic: he tried his best. Ida refused to suffer. There wasn't a single anxious glance. Yet Morwenna, Ceddie, Roy, even little Lip, they all knew what this had cost her.

Hounds had hunted on slowly. Their fox went to ground below Berry Haze. Whereupon Mrs Lupus said, "I'm ready to go home."

Ida said, "Yes, do!"

"I might be your pilot, Mrs Lupus, on another occasion," stated Morwenna. "Ida is preoccupied with other . . . I mean, she has to be."

"You haven't been fit. You don't have to stay out, Ma!" said Ida. "And you'd like your Endymion."

"It's a wonder what Quarr air can do to one!" said Dorothy in a gentle tone that brooked no dissent. "Nevertheless, I think . . ."

Dorothy looked about her at "the little band".

The light was harsh and wintry – and the blackthorn thick in flower. Ma's pallid face seemed to say, I have honoured you with my presence. I have elected to join in, to be one of you. Naturally, we abandon our "fun" together!

Ida stared.

"Don't frown at me, Ida," said Ma. "It doesn't become you."

"I suppose, uh, it *is* getting on," the Master said.

Ida had crumbled, it was rather dreadful.

It occurred to Griselda that Ida had pleaded to all for ... oh, for patience.

Thus they did no more.

Ordinarily, no one would have minded: when Bee had an entire blank day, even, there could be pure delight.

100 To crown it

The whip lingered to tidy up a gap. It was easier to attend to it there and then. It was a labour of a few minutes. She dragged a larch spar from a denser stretch and hooked it up; to stop cattle. She carried a loop of twine: it duly proved itself handy.

She mounted and devilry got into her. They weren't far off. She could pick out a line. Grenadier, who (less prone to hot up) so relished his work and being asked to whip in, could certainly hop over a few fences more.

One of these was a thorn hedge; quite stiff, because it was high in body, a tyrant that had been laid this February; yet quite inviting. Grenadier got his knees behind a strand of wire, a strand that a less bold rider might have spotted, and somersaulted.

A proper purler.

She lay there with the tender sensibilities of a person that knows herself to have been rolled on (perhaps); and is winded; alone under an empty sky.

Ought to fall better, thought Grizel, gamely; aware of (in

this order) crushed ribs, a numbed shoulder, a bad throb above her left wrist, a ripped glove, a kicked face.

Grenadier, trembling slightly, was on his feet. He shook himself.

"Old fellow," said Griselda, "it wasn't your fault! Have we lamed you?" He lowered his head for her to get his reins, awkwardly, over it. He was walking sound. His legs were unmarked, though they might be sore later. He and she had both acquired the tiniest more mud. She slackened his girths and fumbled, in a daze, to tighten them again. With a bit of a grin for her predicament, she scrambled on (not easy); and (yes, he was sound in all paces) caught up.

Esmond glanced under his brows; and didn't say a word.

Dorothy was telling Morwenna, who was an intelligent child, some of her adventures in Africa.

Grizel had ploughed on ahead of Ma. All might have been well had not Lip, on foot, been hauling his donkey towards them. His eyes grew round. His arrested manner got Ma's attention. "Why are you so muddied, Griselda?" she said.

Her daughter had a fearful throb in her arm and a gashed cheek but twisted in the saddle and smiled.

The effect of this smile wasn't what she'd hoped.

Grizel's hair and hat were dishevelled. One glove had been in a cow-pat. With her other hand she managed Grenadier. Unable to collect both reins properly, she'd loosened the curb, riding him on the snaffle. Her crop was tucked under her thigh. She bore all the appearance of a person who has taken a toss.

"What is the matter with you?" said Ma.

Everybody halted.

"Don't fuss," Grizel said numbly.

"What a mess!" said the Master. "Hurt yourself? Never mind, Ma! It isn't as though it's a collar-bone. I don't suppose for a minute it's a cause for alarm."

"Wire," Grizel said.

"*Wire*? That's *our land*!" exclaimed the Master over-loudly. "And no red flag either? What can have *possessed* Jacky Draycott!"

Griselda was grateful that Ma didn't start gobbling.

Dorothy was indeed far too spent; what with the fresh air and exercise.

"Wire! Can you imagine! No flag!" The Master rattled on in this vein.

The most loyal of their foot-followers had melted away.

"Quite merry," was the pronouncement. "Of course Bevis will discover that the day comes when the hounds run off after a deer or a hare, or kill a pet dog; or, in general, riot!" said the stranger.

It was Nurse who bathed the kick, leaching the dirt out with lint, the dried blood; and suspected a broken arm that Dr Mahon should be summoned to splint.

"I'm afraid we didn't catch our fox," Dorothy told Nurse.

101 Perplexity

She was tempted to confide in Nurse. But she held back.

Dorothy had indulged the "Hunt" with her presence out of her good nature, yet absently. There'd been moments, it dawned on her, at which she'd been made to feel embarrassed; but it was the kind of embarrassment in oneself that had to be treated with disdain. She laughed at this. Closely bound up with the dream that had changed the course of everything had been a small figure of sturdy aspect (though physically slender), who had slaked her thirst, who had laid his sling-shot across her waist, who had not run away as he might have, who had been responsible: Daoud. She could still hear his voice. She could recall his skin. His rather firm touch.

She'd had so many shocks.

These thoughts, utterly unimportant, remained uppermost. It was as though all this to-do (with children and hounds) was happening at Quarr and their mother wasn't able to give it heed.

Why had she not enjoyed Daoud's company for a second afternoon, a third? Because the conviction, so vivid, that had followed the dream had obliged her to make haste to depart. She'd had to act in that swift, resolute fashion; in order first to coerce Stokes and then to overcome resistance in Oliver. She didn't blame herself for the subsequent regret. Mothers knew what to put first.

Or was it that he, *he* hadn't visited her afterwards when there'd been a hiatus? He was bashful. Daoud wasn't remotely bashful. His gesture she might even have judged *gross*! At the time the little afternoon with him had been no more than a passing episode; of the kind of which one shouldn't make too much. So what explained her present state of mind! Ever since she'd been back at home, she'd felt odd.

102 A friend to licence

Ma hadn't been put off, though her day had been inauspicious.

Esmond said in tones of revulsion, to Gerald, "She is positively keen." Esmond and Bee had wanted to show Gerald some good sport. Ida had announced a meet at the Tom Thumb. Then Ma refused to be seen there. She said it was "unsuitable".

"It's traditional," said Ida.

"Your grandfather met at the covert-side. What is wrong with the Grange? Or some feature in the park?"

"Our country goes beyond the park," said Grizel.

"I dare say I could ask the Sturts," said Ma, "whether you might use Coker."

"We can ask for ourselves," said Ida, "if we wish it, although it's civil to write a line or two to Mr Egmont first. We do hunt into his country with his consent.

"Gervase Sturt," said Ida, "is a subscriber."

"Gervase Sturt let us have ten guineas," said Griselda. "And *that* was at the tail of the season."

"How preposterous!" exclaimed Dorothy. She concealed

the warmth of that response by saying, "I shall become a subscriber."

Ida said, "You may."

"Oh, do I have to be acceptable!" said Ma, in high humour.

"Yes," said Esmond baldly. "You do. Everybody does."

"I remember," said Dorothy. "D'you know, this all brings back Papa to me."

"Would you rather we met right in Plash?" said Ida.

"Plash is a lovely meet," said Griselda.

"And have the whole village to stare at us?"

"What we should do, y'know," said Esmond, "and it's a shame we have so few horses in the stables . . . I suggest, Ida," he said, "that Slade be persuaded to accompany m'mother. You'd like that, Ma. Is Ida to lend you her precious grey?"

"I am not so selfish," said Dorothy. They all stared at her.

They met at the cross road, half a mile from Plash. With a respectful head groom (clever in handling the difficult) behind her, with Gerald, who was a big boy, and in addition the under-groom from Coker, Simmy, with the young gelding, Mrs Lupus was less conspicuous. Among the children was, she thought, a Strange, and a Brown (with a Shetland) and also a Holkham; and old Mr Holkham was there, with his pretty pony and trap.

The day was magically still, every sound carried miles. It was not a great success, though.

She demanded the huntsman's attention when he was drawing Spindleberry Bottom; whistled to Furmety with no business to; and thrust ahead of the Master.

One instance, as she tucked herself into a gateway, tried Slade's tact. "We dursn't trample the line, m'm," he was obliged to say. Bevis came to lay hounds on, and again she was a perfect hindrance.

"I expect I have much to learn," she remarked to Ida.

Then she was left behind.

Also the gypsies were in their lane near the old Kennels.

Whilst Grizel neck-reined Grenadier happily she was no use as a whip: Jem, in her daughter's stead, had not awoken any glad feelings in Dorothy. Slade had mounted him on David, he'd been turned out quite tidily, in cast-off breeches, box-cloth gaiters and jacket: it had caused her, to the contrary, to eye him with disfavour.

"If Grizel is hors concours as your whipper-in, with an arm in a sling, why is riding side-saddle precluded?" had asked Dorothy.

Very soon (although it was customary to hunt on into the fourth week of April) the Master said the season had ended.

"*Next* season, Mr Cornforth and Aunt Lydie will be hunting with us," said Bee to his elder brother, "and that may help."

"How!" said Esmond.

"Who's to say, when Aunt Lydie comes out with us," observed Esmond to Gerald, "Ma won't send Winkie to auction? She doesn't as a rule play the same nasty trick on a fellow twice, but ... I think ... Do you like your parents?

"I don't like m'mother," Esmond said.

The one almighty hurdle was got over.

Bevis said, "I don't think I can be sent to Meavy this summer term."

"Why not?" asked Dorothy.

"I am needed."

"Somebody else shall feed the hounds."

"You don't understand!"

"I am a friend to licence," said Dorothy.

"Please, oh please!" said Bevis.

"Wait! If I allow you to remain for now, will you go without a murmur in September? Otherwise we must manage altogether minus the little huntsman."

"Better I stay."

"Accept the bargain," said Dorothy, "for it's rare and marvellous." But Bevis didn't laugh. "Word of honour," she said.

A lagging voice said, "I see."

Somehow she was reminded of Daoud.

Ida had anticipated this matter of school. It was her *secret* idea that Mr Cornforth should prepare Bevis for his Common Entrance.

In Ida's head (to the back of it) was that bigger pack, a pack not yet of twelve or fourteen couple, but six, seven.

Eventually, she might (she'd thought) hunt hounds herself, whilst Bee would do so in the holidays. They would employ hunt servants, in the end. Egmont would yield the whole of the old Quarr Saturday country, at the least. That had been leaping ahead. Ida was practical. Unless they kept down the foxes, the farmers wouldn't be so acquiescent, the likes of Poacher Toady would be slinking back to dig out the fox they'd run to ground.

She'd long ago spoken (guardedly) to Ma. Dorothy had been compliant: Bevis might start at Meavy in September.

Why? wondered Ida, with some foreboding.

103 The eager subscriber

On the subject of fences, Dorothy was full of enterprise. She sent for Jacky Draycott. She didn't reproach him over Griselda's wire. She hadn't given it a thought. Her orders were that, over the summer, every hedge should have a gap from which all the elements of hedge were to be grubbed; and into which was to be built an arc of spread rails. Mrs Lupus had designed the whole so as to make it impenetrable to stock. It was ingenious. Mrs Lupus permitted herself to feel quite pleased with the envisaged result ("Never seen what hereabouts," said Draycott). Any bank was to submit to another sort of treatment. Its ditches were to be diverted ("Diverted, m'm?" asked Draycott) or piped. Its top was to be flattened and smoothed. If the bank had to be defended, that rail should be stout, of a modest height and set close. Did he have the men? She assumed so. If not, Brian could be spared.

Mrs Lupus said, "We don't want broken necks, do we!"

Jacky was fair flabbergasted.

"And Major Ramsey will ensure that similar is done on the tenanted farms. Our men will know just how."

The first Ida had wind of it was from Brian. "Heard tell of thik ther contraption, have 'ee!" said Brian.

She went cold.

Many deep breaths later she said, "Look, Ma, I expect it's an intelligent sort of notion . . ."

Dorothy smoothed her sleeves.

"But it won't do, you know. Nobody wants to court special jumping places; and all identical! It would *revolt* us. Besides, from what I gather . . . of course, we'd get over *any* fence . . . you've only got to drop a leg between the bars to have a nasty fall and injure your horse too!"

Griselda said bitterly, "You want the whole county *to sneer at us*."

This tussle raged over three days, until Uncle Rupert came and hooted. Rupert and Lydie roared until tears ran down their cheeks. Ma surrendered.

Taking back her orders wasn't easy.

In the final week of the holidays, Dorothy said, "Have you forgotten to hold your point-to-point races?"

Esmond gulped.

Gerald said hurriedly, "Lots to amuse us already, Aunt Dolly."

Ida said at last, "You don't recollect Esmond's race with Quick-As-Can-Be? We didn't dare."

Ma looked most extraordinarily puzzled.

She'd adopted a custom of accompanying Bevis to the steam-house. She liked to watch him. He was so serious. It was so comic to see how these large foxhounds obeyed him, fawned on him. This continued until she noticed her garments smelt of cooked flesh.

Ma suggested he put wild garlic into the pudding. She constantly drew on her fund of wisdom. Ma had imported dachshunds; had bred from them for ages. "Are we to have whelps from your Snowmaid," she asked, "in memory of Papa? And hasn't that other one, Furmety, got a suspect leg?"

Ida and Bevis weren't deficient in schemes. These, with her there, did tend to fall into disarray.

It was Ida's aim that the huntsman should have a thirteen two. Tanga was clever, and could get over the ground; yet she was old. Bee wasn't the boldest of riders, and he'd had some scares when keeping up with his hounds. "A bigger animal, when he discovers he can manage it, might paradoxically help his nerve," she said. What did Slade think?

So Slade said to Mrs Lupus, he hoped as how he wasn't previous, he'd heard of a quiet, nine-year-old mare that had carried a lady for two seasons and would suit his own.

He was granted permission to nose about the country.

"Then young Master Bee, a-growing out of Tanga, m'm, what of he?"

Bee was to ride Winkie, Esmond had said, when he himself was away. The nobility of this was kept from Ma.

Mrs Lupus graciously accepted that a new pony for Bevis might be contemplated.

"If we could but add *several* horses," said Ida to Slade, "to the stables on the sly!"

The most immediate need, in May or by early June, of the Hunt – "the Quarr, Miss Lupus's" – was to acquire a draft. Ida rode over to Coker to consult Gervase Sturt. Old Lady Sturt patted her hand: old Lady Sturt approved of Ida.

The Master consequently wrote a letter to Mr Sturt's acquaintance – and theirs – Captain Heber.

Before his reply could be anticipated, Ma announced that they were to be ready for the tailor from Fawernbridge.

Griselda's mouth fell open. "What for?" she said.

"I," said Ma, "did say I'd be a subscriber. Don't you remember? I thought I'd subscribe in kind. You shall be in canary."

"Yellow?" said Griselda. "Have we been invited to a party?"

"A canary, long-skirted hunting-coat for Bee and I suppose . . ." (long-suffering sigh) ". . . Jem. As well as for you, if one of my daughters must ride astride. For Ida, and for you ordinarily . . ."

"What!" said Griselda.

"You'll look charming!"

"In what?"

"In canary."

"Not yellow *riding-habits*! Oh, Ma!" wailed Griselda.

"Yellow is a good riding colour. Breeches can be almost yellow."

"Buff," said Griselda. "Fawn."

"String gloves are yellow."

"Gloves are gloves," said Griselda.

"A valuable hour or two in the library has unearthed some splendid information," said Dorothy. "Were you aware that Mr Drax clad his hunt servants in plush coats of canary, their blue collars bound in gold lace? On either side of the collar was a gold fox with silver brush. They wore red waistcoats, white breeches, black velvet caps and white gloves . . ."

"We'd die!" said Griselda.

"The members were in scarlet," said Ma, "but the Master, Mr Drax himself, had a sky-blue coat, cream-coloured waistcoat embroidered in gold and a top-hat . . . Your hunt collar could be russet, I fancy. Scrimgeour may sew a russet collar on my jackets. Russet is pretty with my dark blue.

"Some day you might hand your whip's coat down to Bevis," she added.

It was not a lark, no, to roast her children.

"What about their boots?" said Griselda. "White tops?"

"Tell Ida to make herself presentable," said Ma. "And Nurse must be with you when Scrimgeour measures you."

Griselda particularly loathed being measured for riding clothes ("the inside leg").

Ida tried to contain herself. "I know somebody is in yellow, is it the Berkeley? When *was* this, Drax was in the olden days!"

"Well, it was from eighteen thirty-three to 'fifty-three," confided Grizel.

A frightful snort issued from Ida. "Yellow habits," she choked out, "she simply cannot."

"We can be in maroon if we prefer," said Griselda.

"Don't," said Ida, "don't!"

"Ma," said Ida, "you don't quite understand! We have a scratch sort of pack, and very small; we're only children!"

"It would be such fun," said Ma.

"It would be dreadfully," said Ida, "vulgar."

Dorothy was stung.

"We should be tidy," said Ida. "W... we're as neat as pins.
"That's why Mrs Slade shortened the coat for Jem and took in those breeches. And modest," said Ida. "But no more."
"Was Mr Drax vulgar?" demanded Ma.
"I expect he was eccentric," said Ida.
"Think of all the regiments of the Empire!" said Ma.
"We aren't soldiers," said Ida. "You *can't* wish us to be ridiculed. If . . . simply suppose . . . we were to go out with Mr Egmont's, would you permit us to be from top to toe in *yellow*?"
The force of this struck home.
"I'm disappointed that you adopt such a view," said Dorothy. "The man may take his measurements. We shall discuss it by and by."
It was not to be mentioned again.

104 Poignant memory

Dorothy thought, with dignity, that she would never observe the English pastoral of Quarr with quite the same eyes again. North Africa had put paid to it. At puzzling moments, she would be regarding the park and a different, inky horizon would spread palm-fronds over a shallow, crimson sea, palm-trees insinuated themselves between the oaks and the old turf frizzled under a fiercer sun.

Daoud, though a child, was a stranger who had fed her, when Boissy was hunting high and low for her, the red fruit of a prickly pear. He had pinched her and she'd had a disturbing sensation. She had melted towards a boy who had thought he wasn't too young. He had hugged her. He had pinched her, here. She hadn't been unduly startled. Daoud hadn't offended her. She thought she'd hesitated before she'd laughed him away. She hadn't laughed. She'd been so sad. But . . . quite indecent! Her duty had been as transparent as the sea. Before, that is, it was flooded with crimson.

Dorothy accused herself of mawkishness.

It was curious that the most intimate touch was the touch of breath; more intimate than the perception (unavoidable) that he was indeed not too young. It seemed probable to her that she'd never be "touched" again. Should she attempt, then, to return to Kerkennah, in order to be breathed upon? She could discover how Stokes had got on!

With Daoud, she'd had a sensation so brief, so tantalizing now and irretrievable, that parting with it had proved to be, and was still, the most ghastly wrench. And, although convinced that restraint was a thing for which one lived to be thankful, she did at times wonder whether a lifetime of that didn't border on the lunatic.

How much more of a pity that George had had to go and die!

105 Progress

Archie Lupus would never turn up to church, so it was a time since Cornforth had set eyes on the fellow.

"Been lying low?" enquired Cornforth.

"No, no," said Archie. "Have you?"

"I?" said Cornforth.

They chuckled.

Cornforth had skulked in at the side door. He said with dignity that he would go in to Mrs Lupus via Porlock and the front; but in the meanwhile the two of them might toddle in the sunshine.

For big creatures they were all three – Quintus Cornforth, Archie on his gammy leg and Pantagruel – adept at vanishing into the shrubbery.

"I'd say young Bee looks what he is, a sturdy boy, among his hounds," said Archie. "Wouldn't you?"

"I've heard about the canary, if that's what you mean," said Cornforth.

"Uncomfy sort of notion," said Archie.

"Ha!" said Cornforth.

"Progress, though."

"D'you say so? You do, do you!"

Pantagruel's jowls drooped and his gloom-filled lower lids grew heavy.

"Ida means to acquire a draft."

"I fear so," said Archie.

"Think they'll manage, eh!"

"I'd say two couple," said Archie. "Ida has started to correspond with that fellow Heber. Hopes to go right over to the Chase. I don't see how, myself."

"Have the sense not to embark on young hounds, have they?"

"I devoutly trust that is so."

"Stands to reason he ain't parting with unentered hounds that have been out at walk."

"Heber," said Archie, "was mighty taken with Ida."

They stroked their beards.

"Yes," said Cornforth. "Yes."

While Archie hauled his lame leg along at Cornforth's elbow and Pantagruel padded at their heels, Bevis and Jem set off, with Rumour, Furmety, Snowmaid, Flapper and Sappho, to investigate what Jem had stated to be ghosties at the old Kennels.

Fellows from the builder in Lackham Parva were pulling the place all about.

When run to earth, Jacky Draycott said it weren't to do with him, ask Mrs Lupus.

"It was to have been a surprise," said Ma.

"What was?" said Ida.

"The hounds may return," said Dorothy.

"Well . . ." said Ida. "I'm not sure. Bee is rather little to be going back and forth across the park umpteen times a day."

"I quite thought you'd be delighted! You made enough fuss . . . a great to-do when . . ."

"I know," said Ida hurriedly. "But Slade hasn't signified resentment, has he?"

"We're all aware of how long-suffering the stables can be

on your account," said Ma. "And of how you presume upon that!"

There was a ruffled silence.

"Mr Egmont has told me of a very knowledgeable sort of man, retired from, I believe, some hunt in the shires."

"Retired what?" said Ida, bewildered.

"Huntsman," said Ma calmly, "I feel sure. He will be journeying over to see me, on Wednesday."

"To see *you*?" said Ida.

Dorothy flushed. "You may accompany me, Ida."

"Did you drive all the way over to Nyland, then?" asked Ida.

"I did," said Ma; with the air of a person who has put herself out.

Ida was speechless.

She said at last, "What is his name?"

Ma said, "Maud Gulliver. He is a strong batsman (although perhaps past it!). Mr Egmont thought that would recommend him to Gerald and Esmond."

"What else," said Ida faintly, "did Egmont tell you! Which hunt in the shires?"

Ma shrugged. "One of them," she said. "You'll soon discover. I presume he has suitable encomiums."

Ida said, "What is it that he's to do at Quarr?"

"Carry the horn," said Ma gently. "Naturally! Make himself useful in the management of our beloved hounds! What did you imagine!"

106 A voice from the past

Despair and hope fought such a battle in Ida. She told Gervase Sturt, "It may be that it's our best chance, although it has arrived too precipitately. Bee does have to go to Meavy. This may be a good man. The Treasurer has never heard of him."

Ida was well aware of Mr Sturt's liaison with gorgeous Mrs Egmont. If he was uninformed now, he would rapidly acquaint himself with the facts. "I'm thankful you're so approachable," said Ida; and Gervase Sturt laughed.

She was still feeling a trifle cheered when Mrs Cockerell caught her by the baize door and whispered that she . . . that all the children were to come out the back where they'd be 'stonished. "We got Master Bee," said Mrs Cockerell.

There in the servants' hall, with a large piece of a chocolate Victoria sandwich on the table in front of him, was Bee. A thin, elegant figure rose to its feet.

"Hallo, Miss Ida. Hallo, Miss Griselda. Keeping well, I trust?"

It was Titball.

Griselda ran to hug him tight.

"You'll sit down and have some tea," said Mrs Cockerell.

There was much rejoicing. The children, Mrs Cockerell, Titball, Pinkie . . . and, "Won't you join us, Mr Porlock . . ."

"Esmond will be so sad to have missed you," said Ida.

"Is Master E. as merry as ever?" said Titball.

For some reason . . . perhaps it was that Griselda said, "We're none of us quite so merry," whereupon Mrs Cockerell said, "Oh duckie!" . . . a small tear rolled down Titball's face to his chin, wobbled and dropped into his cake. Ida was smiling and crying. There they all were, with chocolate filling on their lips, stirring their tea hard . . . except Bee who was stoic and Mr Porlock with a crisp white handkerchief to his mouth . . . saying "one day you shall come back to Quarr, when Esmond's grown up", "it isn't the same without you", "terrible your Papa had to go and die" and the like.

107 A brooding melancholy

Without George, she was quite lonely, although one didn't admit that.

After George had died, so much had been tidied away. His hair brushes might still be laid out in his dressing-room, but Dorothy was a widow. She didn't, to put it indelicately, lie on their bed for him. She had been obliged, almost overnight, to become a gal again; a gal who, nevertheless, had nursed Guy and would at a future date shrivel into a travesty of womanhood. And though she'd taken to heart George's early strictures on her "moving" and all that kind of thing, she had enjoyed the consequences of being married, she'd truly adored her husband and missed what they did. It was not unlike riding: she was aware that her pleasure in horses was not of the order of theirs (all the others), but in her own way she took *inordinate* pleasure from riding; and, perceiving that George's passionate nature might attain an elation beyond that which she herself was able to feel, she had entertained whole-heartedly all that which, now she was a widow, she no longer had! And just as she had once stared with awe at her own reflection "afterwards" and put her hand up to her flushed cheek and smiling eyes, she now saw that a light had receded from her very gaze, as though those eyes, Dorothy's, had mislaid the experience of her ever having been married to George.

108 Maud Gulliver

Mr Maud Gulliver was shown into the business-room. Ida had imagined that, had she wished to engage hunt servants, she would herself have done the talking.

Ma had placed her in a corner, from where she could observe.

It was the day when news was to reach London of the Boer surrender; the War had dragged to an end.

Ida's first sight of Gulliver put her off him. He was dressed in a suit of murky serge with a moleskin waistcoat. He'd trodden up the drive with a brown bowler on his grizzled head and leather gloves on horny hands. His whiskers were trimmed. He was the picture of an old-fashioned, bow-legged countryman. Yet . . . yet he had pale eyes that blinked a lot and a blue-veined nose.

Ma perused his "characters", and laid them on the bureau. She failed to ask any of the right questions. She enquired about his family and pronounced 1 Hunt Cottages to be thoroughly dry and cosy.

Ida didn't care how many sons he'd had or whether they were in the merchant navy or had "wed" the daughter of the Duke of Buccleugh's gamekeeper ("I wanted to ascertain whether or not he was a fit person," said Dorothy afterwards, "to be loose with *my* daughters, you silly!"). Ida needed to learn his views on hunting, on kennel management; sustenance, injuries and colic; on breeding, on the preservation of fox and covert; on terriers and earths; on sweetness with farmers . . .

Maud Gulliver had gone as a wee chap to the South and West Wilts; and on as second whipper-in to Tom Firr, notable huntsman of the Quorn who had himself whipped in for the even more celebrated John Press when with the Cambridgeshire, John Press consequently to go to the Blackmore Vale when Mr Digby was Master. From the Quorn he'd garn after one season, he said, to the Puckeridge, esteemed by all and sundry.

"I can perceive that," said Dorothy.

In his worthy sojourn north of London he'd grown an instinct to head torrards Sarum, so when there'd been an opening . . . through a broken neck, he'd understood . . . up on the Mendips he'd stepped in. "A wild type of terrain and some passionate gentlemen over thataway," he said.

"Indeed," said Dorothy.

Maud Gulliver would be honoured to instil much of the accumulated science resident in his brain-box into the folk at Quarr, indisputably into the young rip-and-riots that he was positive the lady's children were. That was in the way of being a witticism, o'course.

Ida squirmed.

"I consider them sporting myself," said Dorothy, "but I believe they're quite sensible!

"I can offer you a cottage, as described to you; bacon and milk; hunt livery; as well as forty pounds a year."

"I rate meself above an agricultural wage, m'm."

Ma's voice overrode his: "Faggots, potatoes, beer money, coal! Your work shall not be great.

"Miss Ida will take you to acquaint yourself with our hounds, who at present are kennelled at the Grange stables. You may start as soon as is practicable."

Ida said, "Mr Gulliver, where did you hunt hounds?"

Maud Gulliver shook with mirth.

They stared at him.

"Many a day!" he replied.

Ma smiled feebly.

Ida said, "Where were you huntsman, Mr Gulliver?"

Ma said, "Mr Egmont has vouched for you, and that will do."

Ida said, "Ma!"

Dorothy said swiftly, "I notice that you have acted as first whipper-in on occasion. I feel you are just the individual for our little affair. Mr Egmont will have mentioned to you that he is to surrender my husband's old Saturday country."

Ida gasped.

"We intend to enlarge the pack. You will be responsible for laying hands on the right hounds. You are a sound judge of a foxhound?"

Ida began to tremble.

He is sure to have the most dreadful hands, she thought, and he'll ruin all the horses.

"I don't think . . ." she said.

"Go along," Ma said, "with your Mr Gulliver."

Ida's brain seethed all the way to the stables. She didn't attend much to the story embarked upon by this monstrous imposition of a person. It was a horsy yarn: Maud Gulliver hated gypsies, it seemed, tinkers and Irish nags . . . these, he said, were dishonest.

"One of our whips is a gypsy," said Ida, absently. And

Maud Gulliver slapped his bandy thighs until she wondered if he was about to fall over.

Grizel had hidden, Bevis curled up on a bench with his head on Furmety's shoulder. He looked up at Ida. She saw he had utter faith. Then he noticed that she was frantic.

Maud Gulliver patted Bee on his crown; and pulled Flapper's ears so hard she yelped.

"I likes to round the years," said Maud Gulliver.

"I expect you do," said the Master. "But Papa, who was Master here . . . you will be aware of that . . . Papa did not."

"Ah," said Gulliver. "A gen'leman, weren't he!

"I abominates light-coloured hounds," he said, "and light-coloured hosses. I dessay that there . . . were a mistake."

"This fellow, Rumour," said the Master, "should have enough dark on him for you."

Bevis was looking more and more mulish.

"Ida," he said defiantly aloud, "hounds don't take to him."

Maud Gulliver bristled, "Ho, my tiddler . . . !"

"Not so tiddly," said Ida.

The morning's post had brought the reply from Captain Heber. He recognized the pull of Quarr and felt certain their father's Eskimo and Ringlet would be delighted to find themselves at home. He thought he might presume on the special bond between the Chase pack and theirs and beg not a price but the pick of the first litter, whenever that should be. On the other matter, he had a couple of ladies, entered last season, by his fine hound B.V. Cornet '94, ex his own Mischief '96, herself by the Brocklesby Tracer. Plenty of bone and stamina, splendid cry. Possibly full sisters weren't what was desired? Yet these had been at walk together and were friends of Ringlet's. He ventured to suppose they'd run "covered by the same sheet as yours". He wondered whether they'd all care to poddle over on Tuesday of next week: they were warmly invited to luncheon and for the afternoon and (!) expected to stay to tea. Mr Sturt would bring them, unless their Hunt Treasurer could face the drive, in which event he, Heber, would be "quadruply" thrilled.

"Come away, Mr Gulliver," said Ida now. "Come away."

109 The Treasurer

They crept into his den in their night-clothes, Ida, Grizel and Bee. Archie wasn't afraid any longer of so many at once in this sanctum of his. He could have supported Esmond, Gerald on top; even that previous bugbear, Gypsy Jem.

He hadn't stopped his whispering. Esmond thought he never would.

His wound would never heal. It remained disgusting. He'd be one day more lame, one day less.

Ida was pale. He managed to look at her with his once-piercing gaze.

"Ida had wanted to cross-question him," stated Griselda, "and then when she did have the chance she didn't!"

"He ought to be an excellent man," said Ida. "The trouble is, I suspect he is not."

"You yourself contemplated the selfsame circumstance," said Archie, "back in March, I recollect?"

"Perhaps Ida took against him from the start," said Griselda, "but she believes not."

Archie glared at Ida. "I see," he said. Her smile was tragic.

"Uncle Archie, we'd rather give up," she said. "Bevis agrees. I shall beg Captain Heber to take in our hounds."

"Do you, Bee?" asked Archie.

They agonized for Bee. He nodded.

Bee wasn't the solemn little boy he'd been when Rumour had come home to Quarr: he was altogether older. "I do," he said.

"We can't carry on in this fashion," said Ida.

"No," said Archie. "It's fortuitous," he said, "the next season's subscriptions have been . . . so far not in . . ."

He watched while the last glimmer of hope died.

"Good night, then," said Ida.

Archie and Pantagruel padded up and down in the moonlight of the terrace. A hush lay over the Grange. If the foxes of the woods and furze were out about their business, they didn't betray themselves. If the weasel and the stoat were hunting, no ghastly shriek came to tell him where they might be.

He pictured Cornforth asleep. The old boy had nodded off by his lamp, no doubt: worn out after a powerful day. "You and I, Cornforth," whispered Archie, "have at heart the interests of courageous children, therefore . . ." He straightened his shoulders rather pathetically and began to shake.

110 Mrs Egmont's message

Gervase Sturt had been swift. He'd got a message (Coker had the telephone, on a line from Lackham, but he eschewed it, and telephone hadn't reached Nyland) to Rivers House. Her answer was as prompt. Considerate, she'd told Simmy to eat his midday dinner there, a twenty-three-mile off. Mr Sturt had let it bide till breakfast.

From Gervase Sturt's beautiful, sloping hand, Ida read:

> Mrs Egmont says that her husband in good faith drew to your Mother's notice this man Gulliver.
>
> Mrs Egmont is of the opinion that Egmont, who is your sincere well-wisher, believes Gulliver to be as honest a fellow as one would care to employ.
>
> It seems Egmont didn't suppose your Mother would take him up on what was a purely idle remark!

"What does that mean?" asked Griselda. "He thinks you're grown-up, Ida, if he calls Egmont 'Egmont' to you and not 'Mr'."

"Yes," said Ida, in a dull tone.

"Or can it be that his feelings towards Mrs Egmont's husband prevailed?"

"It is too bad," said Ida. "She makes the entire countryside hoot, poor Ma."

111 The Colonel

The soldier's habit of sleep had deserted him. He woke in a state of wretched exhaustion. The Quarr dawn chorus assaulted his ears. An especially poignant song of a thrush seemed to be altogether too close. On my chimney, he thought (he was in the low, old wing). The birds all sounded very cheerful. Out of doors it was still, and the scent of early summer would begin to fill the air with the sun. Archie moaned.

Once he'd waited for his water, he put some things on. He dressed with detached care; in (despite half-pay of £300 a year and a private income) his darned and battered shooting-jacket over a threadbare shirt and wing collar, waistcoat, baggy drill breeches, wool stockings and boots.

He picked up his hair-brushes and pommelled his head.

He was an honorary bloodhound; for it was accepted that one bloodhound wouldn't live happily without another. He went to let out Pantagruel. The hours from then until it was time for breakfast and after breakfast until ten-o'clock-ish were hollow ones.

He knew where Dorothy would be at ten: in the morning-room, since Mrs Cockerell came to have settled any matters that pressed (cold pork and potatoes).

His gloom had plumbed the depths. His back was always straight: today he felt he must be bung full of pig-lead.

"Hm," he said.

"We don't have the money for a man at present," he blurted out. "D'you see, I hold the purse-strings."

"I don't see," said Dorothy. "If you refer to Gulliver, I shall pay his wage."

"That's not how it's done," said Archie. "Haven't you grasped that I am Hunt Treasurer?"

"I had not," said Dorothy, and laughed.

"Dolly," said the Colonel, "it isn't a game of pretence."

"No, it's priceless," said Dorothy. "Why else do you imagine there are plans afoot for a bigger pack?"

"Your plans," he said.

She stared at him. "Won't you sit down? The room is too small for a man who wishes to stamp up and down."

He put his hands behind his back and ignored her.

"Oh, very well," she said, as though humouring an invalid.

"I never could understand," said Archie, "how you could drive away from Quarr that which George loved so much . . . which we all loved, all except you. You weren't wholly to blame, yet you might have made possible more . . . you failed . . . forgive me . . ."

"Stop!" said Dorothy.

"And then on your return . . . I understood it even less . . . you embraced the . . . um . . . nature of what the children, bless them, had pursued, indeed; but to such a degree that they've been tried beyond bearing!"

"You sound very stern," observed Dorothy lightly.

"Listen to me!" shouted Archie.

"Your enthusiasm has run away with you . . ."

"Nonsense," said Dorothy.

"You might have looked on with the sort of delight others have. But no, you must have a finger in every pie. You can't let Bevis alone. You want to 'counsel him'. Over the most absurd matters, your 'least clumsy way to wield a knife', or 'the correct position of the tongue in order to whistle'. The benefit of your science, in respect of dachshunds, has to illuminate his every error. That boy, with his absolutely uncanny authority over his hounds! You dictate to the Master. You force upon them this Gulliver . . ."

"They'll be gratified," said Dorothy, "to find how valuable he is."

"They are distraught!" said Archie.

"Oh, pooh," said Dorothy.

"I'm amazed, Dolly, you didn't seek to acquire a bagged fox for them."

"I didn't think of it," said Dorothy.

"If you'd been one of my junior officers . . ."

"I perceive," she said, "that you have become a doting uncle. I hadn't realized. No doubt Cornforth has been burbling around Quarr, egging them on."

"And Gervase Sturt," said Archie. "Old Sir Hereward and Lady Sturt . . . egging, I mean. Not to mention Mahon, Miss Haunchley . . ."

"That trout!" said Dorothy.

". . . Rhodes. Barge of Orchard House."

"They killed his wife's cat!"

"Even so."

"Gracious!" said Dorothy.

"Also both Holkhams and Strange and some solid fellows. Rupert and Lydie."

"Ida has been distinctly underhand," said Dorothy, "to accept the guineas of half the countryside! Without a word to me. They used to be so frank and honourable!"

"Do you wish to be Treasurer?" asked Archie. "I fear there may no longer be a Hunt."

He had a singular and forbidding expression on his face. She wasn't a coward. "I knew," she said quite softly, "that my children longed for me to be with them once more."

"So Oliver told me," he said.

The wind was taken out of her sails.

"No, he can't have," said Dorothy.

Archie stroked his beard.

"You have tormented them so much they are defeated. You, Dolly, have made your children cry a halt . . ."

"Don't be absurd," said Dorothy.

". . . to the one, *darling* enterprise that brought solace after George's death."

Dorothy flinched. Two tiny spots of colour rose over her cheek-bones. Her fingers crept to touch her mourning-ring.

"Ida is at this minute writing to ask a chap who is a good friend to them to take their hounds."

"What 'chap'?" asked Dorothy.

"A friend of Sturt's, a Captain Heber. He hunts over the Chase."

"How improper!" exclaimed Dorothy.

"For Heaven's sake!" exploded Archie.

After an uncomfortable silence, Dorothy, thinking of Daoud, said: "What is it you wish me to sanction?"

She did what she always did when her throat burned and she'd been stung. Orders went to the stables for Endymion to be brought up. Mrs Lupus would enjoy a solitary hack.

By the time she'd calmed down, she and Endymion were inside Quarr Wood. It was a lovely day. The leaves were in that heart-breaking flush of their best green. Deep in the covert, a woodcock called. The sun dappled the mossy floor of glades; the bluebells had wilted; a roe-deer doe in mottled coat slipped across the ride.

A gentle canter found her by Grampy's Oak.

Once she'd been to visit those faithful horses, her mare Sable and George's aged Darnley, she approached the house. She saw a small party of children, followed by Mop and Rabbit (Mop and Rabbit ranged ahead). They were trudging away from her. Ida, Griselda and Bevis. Dorothy thought of how Archie had said, "Far more sensible to let Bevis have some licence now than be thumped at Meavy." Was Esmond bullied at Meavy? It hadn't occurred to her. Why should he be? She was, she thought, genuinely *puzzled.*

They walked with their heads down. They didn't so much as glance over their shoulders.

Dorothy, inexorable, overtook them.

She slid from the saddle (the condescension!); held up the skirt of her habit, on the cloth of which were sticky little bits from the pines and dusty pollen, and hooked her arm through the reins. She and Endymion kept pace with them.

In their paws were grasses and tan, clenched fronds. The royal fern. "Botany with Inkpen?" she asked.

They nodded.

"Where did you find the osmunda?" she enquired.

"Down near the pond," said Griselda.

"Ah," said Dorothy. Mop had been in the water.

"Shall I say to Gulliver that he isn't to come to Quarr after all? Since it was I who promised he might?"

"Yes," said Ida at last.

Endymion trod delicately, at this stroll. He pressed his whiskery muzzle into Griselda's neck, and breathed.

"Uncle Archie seems to think that Bee could miss Meavy for a while now (I don't know what the school will say!), if need be until his final year before Winchester, and go to the Rector next September for lessons. I myself have caused you, Bevis, to be behind in your Greek and Latin."

Ida said, "He'd like that."

Griselda patted Endymion; rather awkwardly.

After a shattering second or two, Bevis allowed himself a small skip.

"Is it settled?" said Dorothy. "Brian can be spared from the garden. I don't know whether you'd want to call on him?"

Dorothy examined every stone of the front of the Grange.

"Suppose," said Ida, "Bee were to make him stand very still ... could you take a photograph ... of Rumour?"

Ma could be charming when she chose to be.

113 A new leaf

The contrite and the huffy (still) combined in Dorothy to lead her to send them without her over to luncheon in the Chase. Gervase Sturt undertook to drive them and Ida could be trusted to make sure their faces were washed properly of the dust from the road ...

Of this wonderful day Mother garnered but an inkling.

I will behave, she thought (in her chagrin). I shall rein myself in! That idea amused her.

Bevis was to kennel the dog-hounds now adjacent to the ladies: Rumour and Eskimo kept each other company; Ringlet, Mimic and Mellow joined Furmety, Sappho, Flapper and Snowmaid. Slade grinned ruefully at the forfeit of a second box; and at hounds out to wander his yard, two couple turn and turn about, eternally bothersome.

What had been feasible for Slade once was perceived to try him: Ida saw that hounds must have a yard of their own with fresh air, the afternoon sun, protection from the westerly. Yet they were far better off at the Grange, where they could be interested by all that went on and not merely closer to Bevis but also to Brian, Clarence and Ginger; all of whom, of necessity, had a benevolent eye to them.

So new quarters were to be constructed out of a former saddle-room; and, though the estate carpenter and Poulter might labour at no cost to the Hunt, Uncle Archie had gone, with Ida and Bevis, to the smithy to ask to Drake to work some attractive railings. Uncle Archie had disgorged eighteen guineas for Mimic and Mellow.

It was whilst Bee was engaged in winning their confidence, helped by Ringlet who remembered him, that his mother came upon him unexpectedly.

The boy had collapsed in a romantic pose at the foot of his pet tree, the copper-beech within a stone's-throw of Porlock's cottage – not somewhere, as a rule, she went.

His shoulders were pressed against the grey bark, and his legs stuck out before him. His hat seemed to be pulled down; but he must have been able to see, because she could hear his voice. Ringlet had flopped, and was so flat that only a languid stern and her breath rose and fell. Mimic's forelegs were stretched out in front of her and, with head cocked, she was staring fixedly at Bee. Mellow was still on her feet. Both of these were evidently anxious to please: in the depths of their eyes was, perhaps, a degree of mystification. Bee's crop and couple lay beside him. "Hallo!" said Ma.

"Hallo," said Bee, cautiously.

"Have they begun to feel that Quarr is their home?" asked Dorothy.

"Not yet," said Bevis. "Mellow hopes Captain Heber will fetch her soon."

"D'you think so? Poor Mellow!"

"Mimic knows she was put into my hands," said Bee. "They both do."

"My store of knowledge," said Ma, "doesn't extend to foxhounds exactly, but . . . do animals not amaze you!"

Bevis suddenly realized he should have shot to his feet at her first appearance.

"Oh," said Ma, "please don't get up. May I sit with you?"

"On the ground?" said Bee.

"Why not? I sit on the ground for outdoor tea."

"On a rug," said Bee. He took off his hat and wedged it between his knees.

"Do you couple them still when you take them farther afield?"

"To be on the safe side," said Bee. "Mimic and Mellow. I can trust Ringlet. All the hounds bred at Quarr have settled at once."

Bee made an observation. "They like you!" he said.

"Yes," said Dorothy, with unwonted modesty.

"Were the photographs all you'd hoped?" she asked, as once she had enquired of Esmond about Winkie. "We can try again."

Bee made a noise in his throat.

"What?" said Ma.

"Most glad of them," said Bee. "Ida too. And Grizel."

She smiled.

"Tell me, Bee . . ." she said.

"You'll get damp," he said.

"Oh, never mind! I'm not so old I'm ripe for rheumatics."

He sucked his cheeks in, nonplussed.

"I wonder if you remember the day I came out with your pack," said Dorothy, "and you screeched at me."

"Screech?" said Bee. "I don't think I screech."

"When Endymion carried me closer than I'd wished to go. What did I do wrong?"

Bee reached out for Mimic and crumpled her ears.

"Captain Heber don't round ears either," remarked Bee.

"Papa and he would have got on well, then," said Dorothy.

"And I don't believe I shall."

"I'd like to learn," she said.

"You might have injured a hound," said Bee mildly. "Thrusting like that."

"And why was Ida hampering you?"

"She ought to have held you up. I was to cast. All those

horses' hoofs! The fewer hoofs to confuse the scent the better. If you bring the smell of horse to the line of the fox, you make it harder for hounds. That is all they have: scent. I myself can't, y'know, follow it."

"No," said Ma. "I guessed that."

"A deer will leave a slot, I can track deer: a fox goes so light he rarely reveals the foil. Not to a man. D'you see?"

"Thank you," said Ma. "Is that all?" she asked.

"It's enough," said Bee. "A body doesn't want to make herself unpopular in the hunting-field."

She smiled.

"I dare say the huntsman is entitled to screech," she said.

"Papa did. Not screech . . . well, he would roar at folk."

"I can imagine!" she said.

"So it's invisible. See?" Bee said.

She pinned her lips together.

"There and not there. It goes like this . . ." (he waved his arm) ". . . mysterious. To hunt hounds I have to understand it well, to be of help. Hours and hours, after it. I wish I had a nose.

"I shouldn't half like to have! And then, weather brings good scenting days and poor. And a tired fox may drag his brush; or a clever fox be ingenious.

"There *are* huntsmen who," said Bee, "stand on the spot where hounds have checked and, to cast, send hounds out in a circle round themselves and horse."

"That seems logical?" said Ma.

"Papa," said Bevis, "would often cast upwind, loop-shaped.

"If near a hedgerow, especially one with a ditch, he would direct hounds forward or back on each side of it – I dare say the modern chaps do *do* that! Of course, left to themselves, our hounds have a solid notion. The fox pits his wits against them. The huntsman, however, may hatch an inspired thought, y'know."

"And when is scent good?" she asked.

"When the earth is warmer than the air," he said slowly. "When the earth isn't frozen and there's a snap in the air."

It was on the tip of her tongue to say, how poetic. She managed to contain herself.

"I'll try not to screech at you," Bee said, "next season!"

114 Plangent echoes

Dorothy had sat on the ground with Daoud; and had a fond memory of it. Instinct had caused her to brush him away. The puzzle was that he was child enough to be smaller than Esmond. His lashes were as lustrous as Bee's; and Bee's, she believed, would be less so with age. Daoud's voice was a light treble. His air of authority ("Marche," he'd said to her) had been far from assumed. It was, it seemed, natural to him. She had visions of his telling his mother or his sisters what to do. Yet with no self-importance. This sense she'd had of divining a little of the essence of a stranger, whose custom, habit of life and way of thought was remote, had made her brain quite swim. It was more plangent, in its claim on her memory, than the other disturbance of her emotions.

She saw the homely face of her younger son in the shadow of the tree. (Neither of *them* ever pawed her: they shrank politely, she was thankful to say!) There was no bloom on that cheek, only a sprinkling of freckles. Bevis hadn't inherited the delicate features that were Esmond's. She came down to earth.

"I'll leave you to it," she said. "It does strike damp, after all."

"I did say so," said Bevis.

115 Bee loses Snowmaid

Slade took advantage of Esmond's half-term exeat to discover his opinion on a likely purchase; but Bee had yet to come upon his heart's desire, in the way of a new pony.

He'd want a grey, please.

Bee's hands were now extraordinarily full. People no longer fancied that "the novelty" would wear off. Ida saw to the supply of flesh; the oatmeal (over a twelvemonth old) was housed with Slade's feed-stuffs.

The odd man, Poulter, had made a trolley for the traipse between steam-house and stables. The jostle in the steam-house had begun to be intolerable; so a proper place, in which to cook and cool the flesh and to boil the meal before it was put into the hay-boxes, closer to the hound-yard (not so close that Slade would look upon it with disfavour), was imperative. Ida visited the old Quarr Kennels to observe how hounds and hunt stables had dealt in harmony.

Bevis had to be very responsible.

At a rather public juncture, on Esmond's last day and when Uncle Rupert and Aunt Lydie were staying up at the house, Bee, accompanied by Gypsy Jem, led the pack out for summer exercise.

They went mounted. They took, at a walk or jog, the lower drive; Loose Lane towards Slepe; the lanes behind Higher Slaughter; and on to cut across Coker (an early riser, Sir Hereward waved cheerily); making for home slap through Quarr Wood.

They didn't even chatter much.

They were as watchful as ever. It was still quite fresh; there was a radiance in the air, and the singing of birds. They ambled.

When they got in . . . no Snowmaid.

Bee was perplexed. He stared out across the park. She would be up at any minute. He was ashamed, true, that he hadn't known she'd left them.

Jem might have *counted* the four and a half couple.

Bee often exchanged glances with Snowmaid, or spoke to her. Furmety was the one that trotted at his stirrup: his papa's Snowmaid was a dear friend. On their own, Bevis and Jem went back for her.

Hounds were supposed to be obedient and keep with you but it was no great occurrence for dogs to be lost, Ma's dachsies went off regularly.

Snowmaid would turn up apologetic. Bee wasn't alarmed. Jem had said he'd seen her through the wall!

A fruitless rush-through of the wood . . . and Bevis had

gone rather cold. The pit of his stomach was hollow. Breath seemed hard to acquire; and his previous belief in himself had been pricked by misery.

On their second appearance at the stables, Clarence with a prong and a barrow of muck bellowed, "Baint along a ye, then?"

They shook their heads, somehow believing Clar could conceal her safe return to tease them.

Bevis reckoned they had to summon the others.

Inkpen was rattled by the interruption, Ida sanguine. For the moment, Esmond was nowhere to be found.

"Is Winkie in? We'll wait half an hour," said Ida. "Perhaps Esmond wouldn't object to going back on your track, and Jem can show him exactly what you did."

"Jem saw Snowmaid into Quarr," said Bee.

They all looked at Jem: a flush spread up his face.

"It isn't that we disbelieve you! She might have dashed after you the way you'd come!"

"She's not daft!" said Bee.

Snowmaid could carry a line on the road when no other would own to it. Yet the element of doubt had stuck. Jem was so stout . . . but could he not have felt impelled, on the spur of the moment, to say he'd seen her at the hunting-gate?

"Word of honour?" asked Grizel. Ida frowned at her.

"Ah," said Jem unhappily.

"I disremember when I bin mistook," he said.

Half an hour passed and there was no Esmond. Grenadier and Griselda went with Jem instead. Ida, Bevis and Clarence set off on foot, with Furmety to help; as well as Mop and Rabbit. "We should have collected Pantagruel," said Ida.

A bloodhound was a gloomy thought: they were, bar Clarence, made despondent.

The sun was at his zenith, and then the time must have got to one o'clock. At the Grange they were to have luncheon; without children.

It was a big covert. Bevis felt weary.

They called and whistled and sent the spaniel – "Snowmaid, seek Snowmaid!" – through the undergrowth. They listened. Bevis sounded his horn, again and again. Snowmaid always answered to the horn. They listened for any mew of distress. There was only the whirring and clatter of cock pheasant (hens with clutches were presumed to have sat tight, divested of scent). They separated, and came together again. Ida said, "She's home by now! Clarence is missing his dinner and has jobs to do.

"We shall have to tell Uncle Archie."

Esmond was cantering to meet them and Bee was gladdened. Snowmaid's back!

But no, Esmond had hurried to join the search, once he'd discovered what was up from Ginger Foyle.

Straining to hear among the trees, Bee had been conscious that he'd gone out blithely first thing; and was a changed man.

116 Dorothy's Waterloo

She exclaimed, "Oh, how naughty of Snowmaid!" A number of disagreeable comments rose to her lips; and some (regrettably, thought Ida) were propelled through them, with heat. "I could have predicted this!" There were strictures on the capacity of a boy to cope with hounds. It was as though the pent-up tumult of the past sixteen months had suddenly torn up and was racing at her shoulder. She had reverted to form.

Must Ma gobble? thought Ida. It was so inappropriate.

"Another thing . . ." Dorothy began.

Esmond was pretty cool.

"Oh, shush!" Esmond said. And, "Not now, Ma!"

Griselda gasped.

Dorothy put her fingers up to her cheek. The rims of her lids reddened and her gaze swelled with indignation. Had he been brought up to be *rude*? She was staggered.

She seethed.

Ungallant of him. Perilous. So "Mother" is to be reduced to a juvenile state! I? she thought at last.

Esmond insisted. "Shush! You're not *helping*."

She swallowed rather like an ostrich. There was a perfectly ghastly silence.

"Why did you go through the covert, Bee!" grumbled Uncle Archie. (They rate him *trustworthy*, him! Dorothy complained to herself.) Uncle Archie had been queer these ten days from his nerves and was a spent force: his contretemps with the widow had told.

They had his permission to take Pantagruel to the ride and press a handful of Snowmaid's bed-straw to his muzzle.

But Bee often went through the covert. He kept them together. It was the directest way back. (Parson Cornforth was to be more forthright, recommending a third pair of eyes.)

Ida said, "This is uncharacteristic of Snowmaid in the extreme."

Everybody knew – oh, Ma didn't – that Snowmaid was as constant as she was sagacious. And it would be very odd for a lady to wander.

Had there been some *reason* for her having been parted with so easily by her sale purchaser?

Esmond said, "I'll find Hanham."

Ma regarded him measuringly and interjected, "That seems a sensible notion."

It was Ida to whom Esmond spoke: "He won't keep it from me, if he's set a gin."

My child *dismisses* me, and my opinion, thought Dorothy.

"Don't look so outraged, keepers are tempted to do what they shouldn't. Sorely!" said Esmond. "Is he aware you go through at this time of year? How often do we walk the dogs to that gate? He has his nesting birds to consider. Why else do we employ him! How many pheasant did you disturb, Bee?"

"None," said Bee. "Do they not sit out in hay? A cock got up, one cock! Wasn't that so, Jem!"

Jem swished his closed lips to and fro across the teeth within.

Nobody met his eyes when Ma ventured to open her mouth and say, "I wonder whether or not you might visit the Coker gamekeeper."

She assumed it must relieve Esmond to whistle some plaint

or other ... *Orphée*. So peculiar when the matter under discussion was important! What *manners* ... !

"I had Snowmaid when I entered Quarr," said Bee.

Esmond had stuck his hands in his pockets. She disapproved!

Orpheus? The case wasn't that bad. She shot Esmond a timid, private smile.

He looked away.

She'd contrive to be unaware.

"What a pity Rupert and Lydie have chosen today to drive over to Nyland," observed Dorothy to Archie.

"Better to entertain the impossible, Bee," said Ida.

Jem swallowed. Griselda noticed he'd tried to speak. "Whisper," she said quietly, tugging his arm. "Thik Toady," he said.

"Toady Trenchard," said Grizel out loud.

"Certainly," intoned Ma. "Trenchard's van."

It was the vision not of a lifeless body but of Snowmaid with a leg in a gin that stoked their anxiety. She was unlikely to have got her head in a wire snare; which was a fate that perpetually awaited a dachshund.

"Should you not take Furmety back," said Ida kindly to Bee.

"I have to push on at my pudding," said Bee, in a dull sort of voice.

By late afternoon, with no sign of Snowmaid, Hanham (irked fair by the commotion to his birds) had sworn to Master Esmond that he'd set no trap; young Lip had joined the search with Syl at his heel; Griselda and Ida had found Trenchard's van deserted (they'd pinned a note to it) and ridden right to the keeper's cottage at Coker, all of five miles, where Mrs Burgess had shaken her head and vowed that she'd tell Burgess as how a hound was lost but that she doubted he held with gins. Ma, much to the surprise of her children, had got out all the men that could be spared and whose tea this minute stood on the hob.

Esmond had the prospect next morning of a painful return to Meavy, with a business unresolved at Quarr. The day had begun to seem long. The hounds had sensed the unease. They did often make a noise: this, though, was so singular!

The singing Dorothy had hoped never, ever, to hear again carried on the air. It caused her to shiver involuntarily.

117 A Tartar expires

In her skull revolved a number of dismal recollections. She'd been peeved with Stokes on the subject of gloves! How the woman could have mislaid three . . . it was *still* beyond her! One did not mislay three. Wrapped in black tissue in pairs as Bevis might couple hounds. She, Dorothy, had flown at Stokes; and had not thought the worse of herself for it. A petty victory. But Dorothy had been glad, in the end, to dispense with Stokes.

Gloves were of consequence.

When George had died, mourning had not been adequate to dull the pain. She'd been consumed with sorrow for *him*, on his behalf, that he should die and at his age. In the past she'd puzzled over people's selfishness: she, in contrast, had been so sorry for George, taken in the full vigour. Of late, she'd "felt" his death more than she had at the time. These days she traced her pity to its root: herself. It was uncomfortable. ("Never again" his beloved face, his laughter, the touch of his breath.)

Recent moments had seen her stuff all the fingers of a gloved hand into her mouth and gnaw upon them. (That horrid, island dream, with a fist in her mouth, and the plop when she dragged it out.) Dorothy supposed, if now she could be so bereft, she was wonderfully selfish. The extinction of George had expended a Dorothy she recognized yet considered a stranger. It was at the memory of *this* stranger that Dorothy (Dorothy!) was forced to blink away a mist! The stranger that had continued to believe she was of the quick and not of the dead; who had thrilled (no, unjust!) to the lascivious attentions of a child; a mistress who – and she almost rejoiced – had been unhinged enough ... stupid enough ... to have been fierce with Stokes; a Dorothy Lupus for whom Dorothy Lupus had retained a secret admiration.

A mother who had come down hard on Esmond. But Esmond, she acknowledged, was lost to her.

Daoud ...! Bevis ...! she thought. Esmond.

She could look back and mourn for her own person. One had a moral duty to make light of this tragic view. It and Mrs Lupus had to be thrust bodily, almost, beneath the waves. That was how one managed to drown kittens or rats.

118 Bevis

When all had fallen into bed exhausted, to recoup their energies, the last, Ida, at ten to ten, their mother saw that it was to be a light night and decided to sally out once more; whimsical or not. Rupert and Lydie were in the billiard-room. Always, there was the undergrowth you hadn't penetrated, the clearing you'd missed; the hollow overlooked.

No matter the protestations, a trap seemed the most likely; for who knew what trespasser might be about! The thought of one of George's favourites, a bright tan and white lady, in agony, trying to gnaw her own leg off, now galvanized Dorothy.

The children couldn't go out at this hour but she could. She dressed for it and collected a stick.

But wouldn't Snowmaid have uttered some sort of noise? If she'd sprung a gin would she not have howled ... and she couldn't have been far from Bevis? Shrieked, even.

Dorothy made brisk work of the park, scuffing the dew; and the odd slug. A rank, bruised smell of new ensilage drifted on the air. Quartering that air were phalanxes of swifts.

Of course she gravitated to the oak with the four centuries' girth; she would; and she leant against its iron guard. When

George was alive, how they'd stroll (often and often) to the old fellow, in rays of a sinking sun! With this thought she felt impelled to press on.

Transfixed, Shepherd Grace's dog Flake had spotted the passer-by. Dorothy's lips curled at the scrutiny. Grace had folded the flock within a square of wattle off to the west and was making tidy. Dorothy noted that ahead of her, oblivious to this, deer had emerged to browse; where the briers, full with roses, spilled from the covert's edge.

Their silhouette was distinct: so far they were not the weird, dainty wraiths of the real gloom.

Bobbing their scuts, they were gone.

When she'd got all the way across and she looked back, it was plain that the light had, on the whole, altered. She saw that the old turf glimmered and danced palely. It rose, hovering behind her; beyond it, in the distance, was home. The mass of the dark wood close at hand, a pallid but full-ish moon and a sky of wispy cloud, with as yet few stars, completed a photographic picture.

Flittermice swooped jerkily over her head: she was too aged to hear them. The gnats had stopped biting: the mosquitoes were in earnest. The last, sweet bird-song of twilight had subsided. Only a nightingale sang in a thicket of hawthorn.

It was improvident to have come without a lantern.

She'd had the intention of walking up to fifty yards from the main ride; to and fro, to the left, until she'd reached the gate; where she might go into the lane and glance about; then to and fro, at the other side of the ride, all the way back.

When she went on she was brought up short by Brock in the grass, wending along his own path through purple orchids: he gave her a hard stare.

She entered the wood with a sigh.

It appeared unfamiliar. The branches of the big trees, heavy with black leaf, bore down from above menacingly; and her steps made a deafening shush-shush-shush under them. The adolescent bracken, with its hooked tips, was monstrous. When she halted she was listening to scuffles and scamperings.

Her eyes grew more accustomed.

A stoat ran across. She had other company: the little owl is out to dement me, thought Dorothy. And a low, juddery call reached her from what she judged was the vicinity of Grampy's Oak: a nightjar.

She couldn't resist sticking her finger into several foxgloves; and obtaining reassurance from that.

A dog barked: no, it was a roe-buck. His body thumped the undergrowth. She gaped.

For a while, pigeon after pigeon had left the roost in alarm. They were doing so no longer: asleep.

She trod quietly. In the derelict region below Quarr Wood's great stand of beeches (and confused by brimbles, ivy and fallen ash) she almost managed to make, as though blind, an idiotic circle. But she saved herself the humiliation.

Sometimes she called, "Snowmaid!" The screech owl caused her to jump. There was one particular glade that, by its unearthly beauty, ravished her. Its silver birches were festooned with honeysuckle; and a larch-tree stood sentinel. She breathed in the scent of the night. She could smell the ground; the decaying leaf and the dry. She clasped at a bracken frond, and slipped on; poking with her stick. When she brushed through twangy branches she raised an arm to shield her front.

At other times she banged with the end of her stick to warn the adders of her approach, should any be coiled in the heather.

It occurred to her that, however wretched this was about the hound, she did admit to a feeling of thrill in being out; whether the moon went behind cloud or not. The moon had waxed lemony.

Yet what folly if she were to discover a hound injured and alive: Snowmaid would have to wait whilst she, Mrs Lupus, summoned somebody!

Here, in a goaded state of mind, she'd cantered Endymion a fortnight earlier.

The floor of the wood would keep jumping to startle the foot she was in the process of setting down. After she'd stumbled on for quite another half-hour, she discerned with relief that the trees were thinner. She burst into the ride.

Her feet went softly over the velvet of the moss.

She made out . . . made out Bevis astride the hunting-gate in the moonlight. The dark forms of, she thought, Rumour and Eskimo lay below him, ears cocked, their heads turned towards her, alert, the white in their coats luminous.

"Ma?" murmured Bevis.

"Hallo, you!" she heard herself saying for the second time in a matter of weeks. "Are you not afraid of the night?"

"I thought you were the man."

"What man!"

He didn't reply.

"Your mother will deal with any man," she said. "Can a poacher be abroad?"

"No," he said. His voice was very desolate.

"You didn't want to run away?

"Did you encounter a man?" she pursued.

"Y'know, I've found her."

His mother stared about.

"I'll show you," he said, and scrambled down.

"Is Jem with you?"

Bee said, "I swear she wasn't there before.

"Will you follow me?" he said politely.

"What do you mean?" she asked in response to his previous remark.

"We covered every inch."

The hounds, Rumour and Eskimo, turned their brown eyes up, showing the whites.

What solemn faces! Dorothy thought.

Beyond the park, she knew the lane to be lush with cow-parsley, Queen Anne's lace, vetches and honeysuckle and masses of pink campion: within, there was an expanse of water-logged ground, rushes and rust-coloured trickles, lovely in a different fashion, over which the ragged robin, a little behind the campion, unfurled its painful tatters; and the presence of bog myrtle.

Twenty yards in from the wall, Bevis pointed to a shape rolled in sacking; of which he tweaked up a corner.

"She must have been put there after we'd gone," he said. "I don't reckon that this was where it happened."

"I can't see properly," said Ma.

He fumbled to prime his lamp.

There was a hiss when he struck a vesta on the sole of his shoe. The wick flared; was mended and burned blue.

It was a hideous sight. The gin had caught Snowmaid's nose. Her jaws were broken and her chops were mangled. Her eyes were full of terror. Her forepaws and hind-claws were torn; and caked in blood. The poor girl had struggled. The tip of her muzzle hung right off.

"Could you help me drag her to a nicer place?" said Bee. "I'll bring Brian for her tomorrow. I don't suppose we can carry her home between us, do you? What will Ida say!"

Dorothy turned in the dark and smiled rather sadly at the hounds. They stood with lowered heads, their flanks sunken.

She wondered quite how Snowmaid had died; but she didn't mention that to the child.

The countryside was suddenly unfriendly.

"I don't like the sacking," he said. "He wrapped her in it. D'you suppose he'd set a . . . a *gross* gin in Quarr Wood and came to check it after we, Jem and I, had gone by? Why didn't Pantagruel tell us where she'd bled?"

"I'm sorry I'm not strong enough to carry her home," said Ma.

"No," said Bee again.

"Such traps are perfectly savage," she said.

"It wouldn't have been the gypsies," he said.

They dragged Snowmaid into the wood and left her to the protection of a holly. "Foxes, *leave*!" said Bee.

"Shall we go round?" Ma asked.

"This is shorter," said Bevis.

"I don't mind," said Ma, "I thought you might have preferred the lane."

The screech owl glided over them.

"Not really," he said.

So Bevis, Rumour and Eskimo plodded beside Ma down the long ride; collecting moths. She held out her hand and Bee took it.

119 The last of Snowmaid

Breakfast was muted. There was Esmond to be got off. Rupert and Lydie would convey him to the Halt and bustle on to Enmoor. "Is Bevis still asleep?" asked Ma.

"Hound exercise, I *think*!" said Ida.

Dorothy dawdled until the uncles and aunt had risen from the table and the door had shut on them. Then she said, "Do you wish to bury her near all the other dogs, with the family dogs? Or can there be a special place for hounds of which I'm unaware?"

"Papa didn't permit sentiment," said Ida, "to overwhelm him, but I see no harm. Do you, Grizel?"

"Ask Bee," said Griselda.

"These things will happen!" said Ma, quite gently for her.

They smiled quaveringly.

Presently Bee and Brian took David and the trap ("Hop up, son," said Brian, who fair compassioned the huntsman) to Quarr Wood and brought Snowmaid to Kennels. They abandoned her in the shade: Ida and Griselda discovered her there.

Brian and Bee trudged with picks and shovels out into the park; scattering grasshoppers in wild arcs.

The spot was some ten minutes' walk from the gardens; and secluded, because so rarely disturbed.

They put their backs into the digging. The pit had to be deep enough; otherwise any remains would be unearthed. It meant going down into the gravel. That was a labour.

Snowmaid was to be buried a little apart from the Lupus dogs – some of which had been alive in the eighteenth century – and parrots, cats, the nursery rabbits. Almost as if to say, there will be other hounds; there are certain to be!

It was a glorious summer's day. Ida carried out for Brian a tankard of cider from the barrel in the cellars. Normally the children loved cider barrels; the twisting of the wooden tap;

and raising of the spigot to persuade the liquid to flow.

Brian let Bee have a drink of his.

Bee felt woozy, straightaway.

When they were ready, Brian went and brought Snowmaid in his wheelbarrow. Ida and Griselda had gone to find Ma.

Forehead speckled by sunshine through the straw of his hat, Bee sprawled.

When Ma came, Bee asked: "Where is Jem?" But it had been more than Jem could bear: he'd made off.

With a studied lack of ceremony, Brian and Bee removed the hateful sacking and lugged Snowmaid to the hole. She had been a trifle got at by a fox. Her chest was torn, too; some inner organ attacked. They dropped her in and put her legs tidy. They shovelled in a layer of soft until she was covered; and filled up with the gravel and dirt. Brian had kept a roll of turf.

Bee brushed his hands, and Ida squinted towards the greenery. In the glare a fellow was heard knocking out a pipe on a boot: Uncle Archie.

The mound would have to settle and her name be chiselled into a more permanent memorial. From his pocket, Bevis drew his funny old fossils.

"What are those, Bee?" said Ida in her natural voice.

Everybody gazed down.

"I called in at the churchyard," said Bevis.

"Is Papa giving them to Snowmaid?" asked Griselda. "His sea-horse and thunderstone?"

Dorothy didn't laugh. She had half expected to hear that clamour which – it was quite apparent to her – she desired more, oddly, than she dreaded. She felt its absence. In vain, for at the Kennels this was a dozy afternoon and no hound sung.

Quarr hounds, season 1900–01

lady pack

Amah
Amity
Amulet
Araby
Arctic
Ardent
Artemis
Artless
Asphodel
Astral
Attica
Aura
Blissful
Bountiful
Bunty
Burnish
Dauntless
Decorous
Dido
Diligent
Domino
Dulcet
Echo
Elegy
Elfin
Elflock
Epic
Faithful
Fearless
Flagrant
Flinty
Follow
Frenzy
Harebell
Harmony
Hebe
Helix
Hero
Honey
Hurry
Madcap
Madrigal
Mazy
Melody
Modesty
Moonmaid
Peerless
Precious
Radiant
Rakish
Rapture
Rarity
Ravage
Relic

Rhapsody
Ringlet
Rocket
Roguish
Romany
Ruthless
Sanguine
Sappho
Silken
Sippet
Siren
Snowmaid
Terror
Tireless
Topaz
Tragic
Trophy
Tumult
Velvet
Vivid
Wakeful
Whimsy
Wily
Wistful

dog pack

Adamant
Amorous
Arcady
Argot
Arrant
Bellman
Blazon
Bowman
Dagger
Dasher
Dragoman
Ensign
Eskimo
Harpist
Homer
Hostile
Muffin
Paris
Prancer
Prosper
Prussian
Rasper
Reaper
Rigorous
Rival
Roister
Royalist
Rufus
Rumour
Sapper
Satirist
Sirius
Talisman
Trojan
Vandal
Vanquisher
Versus
Vigilant